Sammy Blue Eyes

Frank Beill

Stairwell Books

Published by Stairwell Books
161 Lowther Street
York, YO31 7LZ

www.stairwellbooks.co.uk
@stairwellbooks

Sammy Blue Eyes © 2019 Frank Beill and Stairwell Books
All rights reserved. No part of this publication may be reproduced, stored in or introduced into a retrieval system, or transmitted, in any form, or by any means (electronic, mechanical, photocopying, recording, e-book or otherwise) without the prior written permission of the author.

The moral rights of the author have been asserted.

ISBN: 978-1-939269-92-8
Layout design: Alan Gillott
Edited by Rose Drew

For Jessica and Annabel. My story continues.

Part One

Chapter 1

1886: Hull, Yorkshire

Six cold stone steps took me up to the dark oak doors. If she dragged me through them, there would be no escape. That was all my ten-year-old self could see when Grandmother was hauling me toward the orphanage that was going to be my new home. Even if it had been a baker's shop filled with free cream cakes I would have resisted. The building was enormous compared to our squat terraced house in one of Hull's back streets. Until that moment the only large buildings I'd ever been close to were churches and education board schools. This place turned out to be like both and worse.

This institution was still new when I first made its acquaintance. So large it filled the whole of the land between two streets. It needed to be big because it provided home for over a hundred children and staff. The castellation (that's a word I was to learn much later) on top of the outer walls hid the grey slate roof. It gave the place the appearance of a medieval fortress. Later in my childish daydreams I imagined archers taking up position, hiding in the battlements ready to repulse a besieging army. Such flights of fancy were far from my mind that first day. My only expectation back then was to be thrown into a dark dungeon surrounded by scurrying rats and never to be able to leave.

'They'll take good care of you, Sammy.' Grandmother's bony fingers gripped my hand, jagged fingernails clawing into my skinny wrist. I wanted to believe there was a tear in her eye, but she was ridding herself of me: her brown grandson. I was an embarrassment to her in a town where every other person's face was white.

Snotty tears rubbed into her thick woollen skirt as I tugged at the folds, trying desperately to hold her back. On reflection I don't know why I wanted to stay with her. Perhaps it was the security of the familiar. Much of my time in the orphanage would be grim but the place did contain those few precious souls who showed me genuine affection during my childhood. Grudging indifference was the best I'd ever received from Grandmother.

'Is Mary coming with me?' I looked up into a face as grey as the threadbare knitted shawl wrapped around it. She looked so old; old and tired, although she couldn't have been more than fifty years of age, probably less but to a young child she was ancient.

'Not today... she'll come when she's a big lass. When she's ready.'

Sharp finger ends dug deeper into my wrist to haul me up to the door. She wasn't going to tolerate any nonsense from me. She never did.

'Don't wanna go, Grandma!' I tried digging my heels into the ground but there was no grip on the well-scrubbed stone flags. My feet were pinched in tight buckled shoes. They fitted me - near enough - when mother bought them second hand from the tat-man's handcart, but a year had passed since then. Shoes were only ever worn *for best*, on Sundays. The rest of the week I ran barefoot on the cobbles, like all the other children in our street.

'They'll look after you, lad.'

She gave me another sharp yank, almost pulling my arm from its socket. My feet didn't touch a single step. Her free hand strained to push open a heavy door. The other remained occupied with restraining my vain struggles. The door creaked open and another jerk threw me into the frightening darkness of a carbolic scrubbed lobby. Whenever I meet this antiseptic smell I'm back at this moment.

She stooped to squint through a small window high above me in the sidewall. Her shawl slipped down exposing patches of bare aged scalp that lank wisps of grey hair couldn't hide. She tapped on the glass.

'I've brought me grandson, mister. He's expected.' She spoke loudly to get the attention of someone inside, but I couldn't see anything except the shaft of thin light coming through the narrow window. A pane of glass slid open.

'What is his name?' Did the brusqueness of the man's reply indicate offence at this intrusion by an old ragged woman and her mewling child?

'Sammy, sir.' Grandmother deferred to someone she believed to be of a higher status. 'Sammy Smyle, sir. He's expected.'

'Do you mean Samuel?' I could hear a sneer in his words.

I stretched up on my toes, trying to look over the sill of the window while the adults talked. I saw the scalp of a man inside the room. He was looking downwards trying to find something behind the glass, just out of my sight before raising his head. All I could see was a pale face with round-framed spectacles perched on the end of its nose.

Was he an enormous owl?

'Aye, sir.' She never called me *'Samuel.'* No one had ever called me *'Samuel.'*

'Yes, we are expecting him... and Smyle is spelled with a 'Y'? Is that correct?' The man gave the impression of being even more insulted by the possibility of my name having an unusual spelling.

'Yes, sir with a 'Y'.' She probably didn't know what the letter 'Y' was. An 'X' was the only symbol she knew. The only mark she ever needed to scratch onto a document.

'Have you brought his things?' The man looked up from his papers and down towards me for the first time. He was Mr Mason or 'Old Stoney' as we called him, behind his back, of course. Officially he was known to everyone as the Master.

'Aye. I have, sir.' Grandmother grabbed the small brown paper parcel from my free hand and held it up to the window. It contained my whole world - all except the patched clothes I stood up in and a crumpled paperback book squashed into the torn pocket of my oversized woollen jacket. (I would *grow into it, too* or so Mother had said.) I was determined to keep a tight hold of my book: my only real possession; the only thing that really mattered. Father gave it to me.

'There are formalities to be taken care of.' The sneer remained in his voice, I was certain. 'I'll get one of the boys to look after Samuel.' He turned and disappeared from my sight.

I began crying again. It brought a swift retort.

'Stop snivelling! I told you before!' Grandmother raised her hand; ready to let me feel her bony knuckles. It wouldn't have been the first time.

Before her hand could fall on my head, the inside door of the gloomy vestibule opened allowing faint light to enter from the next room. Mr Mason reappeared in the doorway accompanied by a gangly, red-haired boy nearly as tall as himself. The Master became more than just a disembodied face in a window. A white wing collar strangled a wrinkled neck that emerged from a lean body trapped inside a suit of undertaker black, but it was the boy's clothes that really took my attention: a long blue jacket, with waistcoat to match, over a white shirt and blue corduroy trousers. Never before had I seen a boy dressed so smartly. His boots were so black and shiny I daren't look at the toecaps for fear of being blinded.

Mr Mason scrutinized me with the hard stare of a carpenter sizing up a hunk of wood, trying to decide what possible useful end product could be fashioned from such poor material.

After an examination lasting what felt like an eternity he said, 'This is George.' The boy took a half pace forward.

'Take him to Mrs Grainger and get him a slice of bread and dripping and a mug of tea. He looks as though he could do with feeding up.'

Without a word the boy gripped my elbow to lead me through the inner door and into the heart of the building. From one world into another.

'You be a good lad, Sammy!' Grandmother called after me. She pulled up the shawl to cover her head again. 'Don't give nobody no cheek!' These were the last words she ever said to me. I never saw her again.

***

George led me into a huge stone flagged hall where a wide stone staircase climbed so high above me it must have reached up into the clouds. The only light in the hall limped through a stained-glass window half way up the stairs.

'Is this a church?' My voice echoed around the room. I paused to stare upwards. 'Does God live up there?'

'Don't be daft!' George grasped my wrist and tugged me towards a door at the far end of the hall. 'There's only dormitories up there.'

'What's dormitories?' I asked. This was the first of many new words I had to learn. Many of them the hard way.

George shook his head in disbelief and continued dragging his unwilling burden to the door. His look conveyed amazement at my ignorance of a word I learned he himself had heard less than a year before. I remained intrigued, pondering the existence of strange creatures called *dormitories* lurking upstairs. I kept looking behind and upwards anticipating the appearance of one of these beings at the top of the staircase ready to swoop downwards.

My guide pulled the door open and yanked me outside. Dazed by the sudden bright sunlight I stumbled down more stone steps. When my eyes adjusted I was amazed to see a yard full of boys, all dressed in suits identical to his.

'It's playtime,' George said but I could guess this for myself, although playtime here looked more exciting than the rough and tumble I was used to in the yard of Runcorn Street Board School. Boys played with real cricket bats and proper balls, not lengths of rough stick and cobbles tied around with rags. Mind, they still used wickets chalked on red brick walls. Other boys chased around on the stone flags, playing tag.

I dawdled a moment wanting to take in the amazing sights. George gave me another sharp tug, but he didn't need to pull so hard now. Something else was even more interesting. The yeasty, mouth-watering aroma of freshly baked bread wafted down the yard and George was leading me in the direction of its source. Heads turned to look at me, eyes staring. My brown face was as much a novelty to them as everything here was to me.

At the end of the yard a short flight of stone steps led to yet another solid looking door. A half-open sash window beside the door was the origin of the magical enticement flowing into the yard. It was far more delicious than the aroma of Grandmother's feeble efforts whenever she baked stodgy loaves. The experience was made perfect by the rich smell of meat simmering in a pot. These delights were accompanied by the loud clattering of metal pans being shuffled around on a hot stove. Above this noise I could hear the high-pitched sounds of young girls chattering and laughing.

George mounted the steps. At last, he had let go of me. I was not going to wander away from the kitchen's magnetic smell. He knocked on the door and waited.

When the door opened a large woman with beetroot cheeks appeared. George received a stern glance before she turned her head to regard my ragged countenance.

'The Master sent us,' George stammered apologetically, distracting the woman's attention.

'Is this the new lad?' Before he could answer, her serious gaze turned back on me. 'And what's your name, young man?'

'Sammy,' I mumbled with eyes cast down towards my aching feet.

'Speak up! Can't abide mumblers.'

'It's Samuel.' George came to my assistance.

'Let the bai'n speak for himself, George Smith!'

I tried to take a closer look at her, although most of her large frame lay hidden inside a dark dress stretching all the way down to her ankles. A spotless starched apron covered the dress from her neck to where I guessed her knees must have been. Hands white with flour were at the ends of bare pink forearms that looked like hams. More flecks of white dotted both her red cheeks and a small amount of dark hair peeping out from beneath a white cap. Though her voice seemed fierce, I thought there was kindness in her eyes; or perhaps later experience clouds my memory.

'Sam... Samuel Smyle!' I found my voice recalling what the Master had called me. I didn't want George, my new friend: my only friend here to get into trouble for trying to help me.

'That's better.' The fierce expression broke into a sudden smile. Hers was the first smile I'd seen since entering the building. 'And I suppose the Master has sent him to get some't to eat.' She turned to George again.

'And a mug of tea,' he added.

'We'll see what we can do.' She nodded and looked back at me. 'Do you like beef drippin', child? Spread thick with brown jelly on a fresh white crust?'

The sight of my tongue licking my lips was all answer she needed before disappearing back behind a closed door.

'That's Mrs Grainger. Mrs G everyone calls her,' George confided. 'Not a bad sort. Bark's worse 'an her bite. As long as you stay on the right side of her. Won't tolerate no nonsense, though. Thick drippin' if you're a good lad... Thick ear if you're not!'

George gave a wink and smiled for the first time, exposing gaps where missing milk teeth were making way for their adult replacements. This was the first time I'd looked closely at his face, having so far seen only the back of his head as he hauled me along. Freckles covered a pale face while above it a shock of flaming, short-cropped hair still managed to stick out at every angle possible.

The door opened again but this time a girl in a white pinafore appeared. Her hair was as red as George's, but was forced under a white cloth cap like Mrs G's. Her skin was pale too, although not afflicted with the same mass of freckles as George's, just a sprinkle across the bridge of her nose. She was the prettiest girl I'd ever seen, although this meant little back then to a ten-year-old.

'Mrs G thought you'd want some't as well, George.' She turned back inside the doorway to produce a tin tray on which sat two steaming mugs of tea and a plate with the biggest crusts of bread in the world; both lathered with brown-flecked dripping.

'I put three spoons of sugar in each mug.' The girl stepped down onto the top step. 'I know that's how many you like, George. Mrs G said that the new lad looks as though he needs some goodness putting inside him.'

'Thanks, Sal.' George grabbed a mug and one of the crusts, which he devoured as though he'd not eaten all day.

'And who is this little mite?' Large blue eyes fell on me for the first time. 'Lord, I've never seen a boy as brown as you afore. You must've been standing too near the oven when your mam was baking bread!'

'Ain't got no mam!' I grabbed the other crust fearing George might take this one too. 'Not no more.'

'Nor have we. George and me. He's me brother.' Sal still held the tray, on which now stood only a steaming mug. 'No father neither. Like most here.'

'Got a father,' I spluttered through a full mouth, letting crumbs roll down my chin. I'd never tasted such good dripping before. Sal must have sprinkled some salt on it; it made the beef fat taste even better. 'He'll come and get me when he gets back.'

'That's what a lot in here say,' George muttered before washing down a mouthful of bread with a gulp of hot tea. 'But they never come and take 'em away.'

'Drink your tea afore it gets cold!' She pushed the tray in my direction. I picked up the mug and took a sip. Strong and sweet just like the ones Mam made for Dad when he came home from sea. He always let me steal a sip, pretending to cuff me around the ear for my cheek.

'You've bin crying.' Sal took a close look at me. She put the tray down on the stair and lifted the corner of her white apron to dab my eye corners. She tried to wipe the stains from my cheeks. 'I think you'd better take him to a tap and get him washed proper, our George.'

'Aye.' His words came through a final mouthful of bread. 'Mind it's bath night, tonight.'

'Get his face washed!' she ordered. 'Don't want t'others starin' at him!'

But they were going to stare at me anyway. Washing wouldn't make much difference to what the others would see.

***

'Let's have a look at you, boy.' Old Stoney stared down at me through wire spectacles perched on the end of his nose.

We were alone in the office on the other side of the little window. I was still the block of rough wood and his look told me he continued to ponder a possible end product or even if there could be one. I tried standing tall, but I was small for my age. It would be a long time before I shot up in height and it would be under warmer skies, far away from the grey of my native town.

'Pick up the slate and a piece of chalk from my desk.'

I remembered Grandmother's departing order and did as I was told.

'Rest on the chair over there and write your name on the slate.' He nodded in the direction of a wooden one in the corner.

I followed his orders, not only to obey Grandmother, but because it was my nature to try to please my elders. She always saw the worst in me: the child of a marriage of which she disapproved. Mixed marriages between English and Scots or even the Irish she could just about accept but her beautiful blonde daughter marrying an Indian seaman was beyond toleration. Mind father never saw India in his life. He was brought up in a Methodist mission in Cape Town, but his face was still brown. Grandmother never saw beyond that.

I knelt in front of the chair, bare knees chafing on the rough wooden floor and placed the slate on the seat. The shrill squeal of the chalk scraping on the dry slate set my teeth on edge. I licked the end of the rough chalk and tried again. The letter 'S' was followed by 'A' and 'M' but after scrawling those two letters I paused. What should come next? I shaped to add another 'M' but remembered what the Master asked Grandmother and I tried to write the name that would gain his approval.

Mr Mason looked over my shoulder. 'Hmm,' he muttered under his breath. 'I can see that we have much work to do with you, Master Smyle.' He picked up the slate and pointed at my shaky scrawl. 'Samuel is spelled with an E - not an A! It is S – A – M – U – E – L!'

He picked up a duster from the top of the polished desk and rubbed out the offending letter A. He inserted the required letter and held the slate close to my face to show me his correction.

'Wipe the slate clean and write the alphabet for me.' The tone of his voice suggested he anticipated my failure in executing even this simple task properly.

He passed the slate and cloth back to me. I tried hard with the letters, but writing was not my strong suit back then. My mind raced over what might be his next command. It would have to be numbers. I could count up to one hundred. Well, just about.

Would he ask me to count backwards from one hundred? Mam could do that. She did it one day while stirring a big pan of stew on the kitchen fire. A beam of satisfaction crossed her face when she finished the recitation. Memory of this happy event made another tear well up inside me. I gave a sniff and held it back. I had to be strong.

'Do you know your times tables, boy?' he said glancing at my scrawled attempt at the alphabet.

'Yes, sir.' It was lie, although I had managed to learn some things on the days when I attended the Runcorn Street board school. I was safe up to my six times table but anything after that would be no more than guesswork.

'Recite the five times table.' He sat behind his desk now.

I stood to attention my shoes still pinching my feet. I began the chant, which I'd learned in unison with fifty other boys in my class. 'One times five is five, two times five is ten...' and on and on until I reached twelve times five.

'Enough, child.' The Master leant back in his seat. 'Let's try you now with a bigger number.'

With a heart sinking into my feet my eyes dropped to examine the floor. I begged the boards to open up and swallow me, aching feet first. Mercifully a knock at the office door drew the Master's attention away from me.

'Come in!' he shouted.

The door opened and Mrs Grainger entered, now with hands clean and forearms glowing pink. Every sign of flour was gone. I prayed for her to have come to lead me away from this purgatory to more food.

'Beggin' your pardon, sir.' She looked across the room in my direction and smiled. I tried to stand as erect as a guardsman. 'Mr Silver is here with a delivery. He says he can stay to measure up the new boy.'

'Ah, good.' He nodded to her before turning back to me. 'We shall continue with this at another time, Samuel. Go with Mrs Grainger and get your uniform requirements sorted out.' He nodded again and turned his attention away from me and toward a pile of dusty ledgers perched on the desktop.

My rescuing angel crooked a forefinger indicating to me to follow her, but I needed no beckoning and marched behind her like an obedient grenadier. My squashed feet didn't mind stepping out the room, into the hall and up the stairs to the place where the dormitories lurked. Never before had I climbed a flight of stairs so wide or as high as these. How different these stone steps were from the narrow wooden ones in the two up, two down terraced house I used to call home. A house I never saw again.

At the top of the stairs Mrs G turned and gave me a warm, maternal smile. This was the first time I could remember receiving such a look since Mam died. One that never came from Grandmother. For a moment it made me forget about the ominous presence of the dormitories on this floor.

'The sooner we get you into some proper clothes the better, you little mite.' She took a firm hold of my hand. Though her hands were rough from years of hard work her touch was gentle. I didn't resist being led along the corridor; it was far too long and wide to be called a landing like the tiny one we had at home. I may not have felt happy but with her I felt safe. No wild ravenous dormitory dare confront Mrs G, of that I felt certain.

We went through yet another large door. Did this one lead outside again? I didn't know doors inside a building could be as big and heavy as the ones in the orphanage. We entered a room larger than in any house I'd ever seen. Circled around the centre of the room stood twenty or more stools while along the walls were benches piled with clothes. My fear returned. Were the dormitories hiding in among these clothes like the giant rats that ran around the back streets of Hull, awaiting their opportunity to jump out onto me?

'This is called the Sewin' Room.' Mrs G waved a hand around the cavernous chamber. 'This is where the girls learn to use a needle and thread.'

At the far end stood a man who, at first, I took to be no taller than myself. On closer examination I realised my mistake. His body was almost bent double. Most of his face lay hidden behind a mass of crinkly steel grey beard and long ringlets that hung down from inside a black satin skullcap. All I could see of his face was a large angular nose and dark eyes, which I could feel reaching into my soul. He was ancient; I swear I'd never seen anyone as old as him before. Not even Grandmother. Fear of this strange creature overcame me. Was he a *dormitory*?

'This is Master Samuel Smyle, Mr Silver.' My guardian let go of my hand.

'Samuel. That is a good name! A very good name. A prophet's name, no less.' The voice was deep and guttural with an accent as thick as tar. He shuffled awkwardly towards me with one hand resting behind on his hip. 'Ve vill need to make a special suit for this Samuel. Are you a prince from the Indies?'

I took half a pace back in fear of this hobgoblin but when he said 'prince' he made me think of Mam. She called me 'her little prince' when she held me in her arms and rocked me gently off to sleep.

'But such blue eyes. Never have I seen such blue eyes in so dark a face.' The old man nodded with his whole body. He pulled a tape measure from its hiding place around his neck.

'I vill make you a suit fit for a prince. No fit for a king!' He gave a chesty laugh and inched closer to me.

'Do not be afraid of old Moshe,' he half whispered. He struggled to take the tape in both hands and measure me from shoulder to wrist. 'I too am a stranger in this land although I have been here for a hundred years!' I felt his laughter rattle in his chest.

'You've been here as long as I can remember!' Mrs G laughed too.

'I have made suits for generations of gentlemen in Hull and now I make one for a prince!' His arms went around my chest to lasso me with the tape. The skullcap burrowed into my stomach and he took the measure of my thin waist. His hair brushed across my face and I caught the strong smell of tobacco. It wasn't like the friendly aroma of father's clay pipe; more a pungent, old man smell. He mumbled the measurements to himself in a strange language I'd never heard before.

'Stand on a stool. Let me measure your legs. I cannot be reaching down there at my age.' He chuckled to himself.

I climbed onto the nearest stool but it had legs of uneven length which made it rock uncertainly. I waited nervously for the tailor to take more measurements.

'That is it! His suit vill be ready in three days.' He nodded in agreement with himself and ambled towards the door.

'Good day, Mrs Grainger. Good day, your highness.' While one hand continued to grip his hip, the free one rose in a rotating backhanded wave before he disappeared through the open door.

'Now young man, we'd better be finding you some proper clothes to be goin' on with while Mr Silver is makin' your new suit.'

Mrs G eyed me up and down as I continued to wobble on the stool. 'Let's see what we've got for you. We've not had many your size though.' She pondered a moment. 'Get yourself down an' take those old things off. You're makin' the place look untidy!'

***

'Cor, who's that hiding in there?' George said, taken aback by my new appearance but after a brief pause the twinkle came back into his eyes and he laughed. He always found it easy to break into fits of giggling.

'It's me... Sammy!' My protests came from inside the smallest blue jacket available in the Sewing Room, but it still hung down close to the knees of corduroy trousers in need of rolling up at the bottom by several inches.

'Don't you be laughing, our George!' Sal shook a fist at her brother. 'You'll be having the poor mite in tears again.'

'Are you old enough to be here?' George looked closely at me.

'I'm ten! Soon be eleven.' I tried to stand tall, but my efforts felt dwarfed by my temporary suit.

'When'll you be eleven?' My ginger haired inquisitor remained unconvinced.

'Don't know, but it's soon... Grandma said so.' It was to be some time later that I discovered my actual date of birth from Mr Mason.

'Well, I'm eleven already!' George took a deep breath and held himself upright.

'But you're big for your age!' Sal angrily thrust her hands on her hips and glared at her twin. 'All us Smiths are! What's left of us.' Sadness filled her words.

'S'pose so.' George gave way to his sister, which I soon discovered he always tended to do. When he knew what was good for him.

'Let's go and get some tea.' Sal demonstrated her seniority over her brother, which I discovered later, was the whole of thirty minutes.

She grabbed my hand to lead me out of the yard and into another enormous room. This one was even bigger than the Sewing Room. Wooden tables stretched its full length with equally long benches beneath them. More uniformed children sat inside waiting to say obligatory grace before daring to eat while others queued at a long table by the side of the room where Mrs G and two of the older girls doled out bread and hot milk.

All heads turned towards us. Was it because I was new? Was it because of my clownish appearance in my outsize suit? I wanted to believe this was the reason, but knew this wasn't the half of it.

A few of the girls – they sat separately from the boys – giggled while some boys glared in my direction.

'Don't let them be bothering you!' Sal said loudly, so the whole room could hear. 'Some of them here ain't got half a brain between 'em!'

'Here he is!' Mrs G distracted my attention. She smiled at me before turning to her assistants. 'An extra thick slice of bread and butter for Samuel. We need to build him up a bit.'

Chapter 2

'Master Smyle! Boys take off all their clothes when they have a bath!' A thick Scots accent boomed in my ear. It belonged to Mr Rodgers, the man who was to become the bane of my life in the orphanage. 'Jolly Rodgers' we children called him, but the origin of this nickname came from the pirate flag, not from his sense of humour… that is, indeed if he even possessed one. I never saw any evidence of it. Inflicting pain on children was the only thing that seemed to suggest any hint of satisfaction on his face.

The room fell silent. All eyes focused on this first of many confrontations with my tormentor. I was doomed to lose all of them. Naked boys sat in pot bathtubs slowly miming rubbing soap onto pale bodies, not daring to stop for an instant out of fear of the all-seeing eyes of our tormentor. Other boys paused momentarily from their task of carrying pails of steaming water to the tubs from the fireplace at the far end of the bathroom. Everyone wanted to see the outcome although all knew how it would end. At some time, each one present had fallen victim to the wrath of Jolly Rodgers. Maybe this debasement experience was an essential rite of initiation into the world of the orphanage.

'But Grandma gave me a good scrub down last night.' I tried pleading with him but it did me no good. Rodgers only saw begging as a sign of weakness.

'Be that as it may, Master Smyle! Wednesday night is bath night here and you will clean yourself all over… whether you think you need it or not!' Booming words echoed off the bare brick walls and paved stone floor.

Merely removing my jacket and rolling up shirtsleeves above my elbows did not satisfy him. A huge hand flicked in my direction and I felt a stinging sensation in my left ear. It wouldn't be the last time I felt the force of his perpetual ire.

'And you always call the masters here *sir* and the ladies *ma'am*. Understand, boy?'

'Yes, sir.' I understood. I learned quickly, especially with a beating on offer as encouragement.

Bare hairy arms were folded firmly across his black waistcoat. His glowering dark eyes burned right through me like hot pokers. He wasn't tall, but he was broad, very broad. He didn't look like a schoolmaster. More like one of the draymen who drove carts laden with barrels of beer or bags of coal along the town's streets. His ruddy complexion suggested he was a man who belonged out of doors rather than in a classroom. Quickly I came to wish him out of my life.

I removed more clothing until I was bare to the waist.

'He's brown all over!' a voice muttered from inside one of the white pot tubs further down the room. Immersion in steaming hot water turned ivory naked flesh pink. Bath night was a communal male activity in the orphanage. I'd never seen other boys naked before except for the ones I'd seen swimming in the town's docks. The orphanage boys had never seen anything like me before.

My shoes and the rest of my clothes came off. Slowly I edged barefoot across the cold stone floor towards an empty tub.

'Pick up a piece of soap, Smyle! Move, boy!'

The words spurred me into action, anticipating a sudden repeat of Rodgers' ill temper. I grabbed a hard lump of pink soap from the pile on the bathhouse shelf. My big toe went into the water to test the temperature. It was hot; too hot.

'Get in, boy!'

I stepped into the tub fearing another stinging ear. The scalding hot water made me dance a painful jig. While my feet boiled the rest of me shivered with fear. I was afraid to sit down but I was more terrified of what Rodgers might do if I didn't obey his command. Not quite between the devil and the deep blue sea but it felt near enough. The devil won this round and I forced my bare bottom into what felt like a boiling witch's cauldron.

A noise echoing from elsewhere in the bare room drew my tormentor's attention away from me.

I cringed, sitting up to my waist in the hot water. Rising steam vapour disguised my tears. Gradually, I became acclimatised and tried rubbing the hard lump of dry soap onto my body, not knowing what was supposed to happen. I'd never been in a bathtub before. As a small child mother bathed me in the wooden bucket that served all the family's water needs. This was how I'd seen Grandmother bathe Mary too. I'd grown too big for the bucket and made do with standing beside it to be scrubbed down by her. I continued running the soap up and down my body because I could see the other boys doing it. Once I realised it helped to wet the lump in the hot water, it became easier.

'It don't come off!' Muttering echoed from further down the line of tubs as my skin refused to change colour.

'Silence, boys!' my tormentor ranted again. His eyes burned into me. 'Give your head a good scrub as well! We don't want any of your slum nits here! Carbolic will sort them out.'

I wanted to scream out 'I don't have no nits!' but thought better of it and obediently rubbed the soap into my hair. Tonight's humiliation was only the first of many defeats I was to suffer at the hands of Jolly Rodgers.

***

The carbolic smell of well-scrubbed boys was everywhere. I carried my new day clothes wrapped in a bundle up to the dormitory, all the while trying to avoid tripping over the hem of my handed-down starched nightshirt. Despite a couple of quick tucks sewn into the bottom, it still trailed on the floor. Mrs G promised that when the girls came in to do their sewing another one would have its hem taken up properly. Then I would have my regulation supply of nightwear; but such things were new to me. I'd never worn a nightshirt before, always sleeping in my day shirt if nights were cold and most of them felt very cold after mother died.

Sal had contradicted George's teasing by explaining that a dormitory was the place where we went to bed and not some monstrous carnivorous creature that lived at altitude. Sal put me right on many things. She and Mrs G fulfilled the role of mother during my time in the home. Sal and her twin were chalk and cheese and the best friends I was ever to know in Hull.

The flickering oil lamp at the top of the stairs cast long ominous shadows all around me. I would have been frightened but for the sound of laughing children's voices coming from further along the upstairs corridor.

I was told to go to the Nelson Dormitory. They were all named after famous mariners. I pushed open the heavy door. The babble inside stopped instantly and all heads turned to look at the 'Wee Willie Winkie' figure coming through the door.

A friendly voice broke the silence. It called to me from the end of the row of beds to my left.

'Sammy! Get down here!' The voice belonged to George, like the rest of us dressed in a stiff white nightshirt. He perched on the edge of the last bed in the row with his back towards the tall outside window.

His smiling face made me feel welcome and I marched down the aisle between the two rows of double beds. The other boys sat on their beds watching me by the flickering light of oil lamps. My face burned. I could feel every eye on me.

Something slipped from inside my bundle. It was my book: the only reminder of my former life. I shoved it back into my clothes. This was the one thing I would never let go.

'You're sharing with me.' George patted the mattress alongside him. 'Hope you don't snore!'

'Don't think so.' I hoped he didn't either. Grandmother's deep grating snore could wake the dead; especially if she took a nip from the bottle she kept by her bed. A *nightcap* she called it. I always tried to get to sleep before she began to rasp the night away.

'Not slept with nobody for a long time. Not since Mam died.' I always shared her bed when father went back to sea. That is until Mary arrived. Often as not all three of us slept together. All I needed to say was that I was frightened, and she'd let me squeeze in beside them.

'We all share here.' George nodded. 'Put your things on the chair. We'll sort out a chest in morning. It'll be lights out soon. Get in and let's get the bed warm.' He swung his long legs under the sheets.

I did as he bade, first hiding my book in my nightshirt's surplus folds and then under my pillow. I tried to snuggle but the rough sheets felt cold on my bare legs. The bed head held a brass plate with the engraved legend 'F.A.BARRETT, MAKER, BIRMINGHAM.' Later, I discovered other copies of this nameplate on every bed head, which made me think that Mr Barrett must be an industrious man making all these beds on his own.

The pillows were made of flocks with every bed covered by a blue counterpane underneath which was a blanket. When we came to make the beds, I discovered stamped in large capital letters on every blanket was 'U.S.A.' Originally, these blankets were made for the United States Army in their Civil War but not delivered for reasons I never learned. Anyway, this helped me to dream of my book's hero out on the American frontier. I came to think of this discovery as some sort of lucky omen. Well, I tried to persuade myself this was true. Luck seemed to be in short supply.

'Did you have this bed all to yourself afore I came?' I tried to isolate myself on the far edge but before George replied, he turned over to my side of the bed.

Something icy cold touched my leg. I recoiled to the edge of the mattress.

'Your feet's freezing!' I almost jumped out of the bed and back onto the bare wooden floor.

'Sorry! S'pose I'd better keep me socks on.' George's voice was remorseful. I could hear others in the room laughing. He pulled the offending appendages back to his side of the bed. 'Used to share with Daniel Sargeant but he left to go to sea three weeks ago. Well, he was fourteen and ready to leave.'

'Is that when we leave here?' I still had no idea what lay ahead of me or for how long. Grandmother told me nothing. She probably didn't know anything. Probably didn't care. She was rid of me and that was all that mattered to her.

'Yes, that's when we finish our schooling and are ready to go to work.' George nodded in agreement with himself.

I wanted to ask so many questions, but all conversation came to an abrupt end. Boys near the door leapt from their beds and went down onto their knees. They knew what came next; they recognised the familiar heavy footsteps outside. All the others in the room followed suit.

'Time for prayers.' George scurried out of our bed and onto the floor. 'Get down here! Quick!'

I did as I was bid and adopted the same posture of supplication as everyone else, scuffing bare knees on the rough floorboards. My eyes closed, and I pretended to pray.

The door swung open followed by the plodding sound of heavy boots on bare floorboards. It was Mr Rodgers doing his nightly rounds to make sure everything was 'shipshape and in order,' as he liked to say.

My prayers became real and I pleaded for the teacher not to come anywhere near me. There was lots of praying in the Hull Sailors' Children's Home. Lots of organised public prayer because this was a Christian establishment. Lots of private prayers, mainly because of the way Christianity was practised on us.

'Good. Turn out the lamps, boys.'

No one complained, knowing better than to question his orders.

'No talking! Get to sleep.'

We all scampered back into our beds. Every lamp was extinguished, and the door slammed shut. Moonlight shining through the window beside our bed broke into the darkness.

'We can still talk as long as we're quiet,' George whispered.

'Do we all have to go to sea when we leave here?' I tried to be quiet.

'Not all of us. The girls don't!' George giggled.

'Shurrup, Smiffy!' An angry loud whisper came from the next bed. 'You'll have Jolly Rodgers back!'

George buried his face into his pillow and tried to control himself. After a few moments he whispered again. 'Most of the lads do... but some get jobs on land. Get themselves apprenticed. Somewhere where they can live in.'

'Oh!' I didn't want to show my ignorance. What was an apprentice? I didn't know.

It wasn't long past eight o'clock, but I'd been through a lot and although exhausted I felt too tired to sleep. My mind raced over the events of the day. Despite being among other boys and sharing a bed with George, I remained surrounded by strangers. I missed my mother more on that night than at any time since she died. I missed Mary, even though all she ever seemed to do was cry. I missed my father, although I'd only ever seen him for a few days every year. I even missed my grandmother but not for any sensible reason.

Tears rolled down my cheeks. I felt alone and wretched. I turned my head away from George and tried to sink my face deep into the rough pillow to prevent him from seeing me cry, although he wouldn't have been able to see my tears in the darkness.

My bed mate interrupted my self-pity.

'Sammy, are you a nigger?'

'What's one of them?' My head turned towards him.

'Dunno, but some of the other lads said you was one.'

I shrugged and rolled back again. Over the next two years I heard this word many times, mainly whispered behind my back. I hated it. One thing I have learned in life is that racial bigots usually confirm their ignorance by not even having the ability to use the correct insults. Fortunately, on that first night my ignorance protected me from feeling any worse.

***

My first morning in the orphanage was also the first in my new school and the source of more surprises. Unfortunately, few were pleasant.

The most agreeable event was the appointment of George as my permanent guardian by Mr Mason. This meant he was made responsible for keeping me clean and tidy, not to mention under control too. George led me into a classroom that looked very much like the one at my old school. The schoolmaster's high-legged wooden desk dominated the front of the room while on the wall behind it a blackboard ran the room's full width. In the top left-hand corner someone had written the day's date beautifully in neat and curling script. A skill I was only ever able to envy. Rows of desks with black cast iron legs bolted onto the wooden floor rose in tiers from the front to the rear of the room. On each level four double-desks obediently faced the front and the teacher. I hoped we wouldn't be sitting in the back row. It looked so high I thought I'd become dizzy.

'What are girls doing here?' I whispered to George. The first surprise was the presence of girls in the classroom. Runcorn Street Board School maintained the strict segregation of boys and girls.

'We have all our lessons together.' George nodded knowingly. 'Except for when we do exercises in the yard…. and arithmetic, of course. Girls don't need to do that. They learn cooking and sewing instead.'

He led me up the side of the classroom, next to the panelled windows that stretched the full height of the room. A further surprise came when I counted the desks and worked out the room couldn't hold more than forty pupils. A change from lessons where there were often more than fifty boys in the class.

'That's our desk.' George pointed to one on the third tier. 'I used to share it with Sal, but she's moved to sit with Annie Phelps.'

I looked across the room to see Sal sitting with another girl on the far side. Sal smiled at us or was it only at me? George usually got a sisterly scowl. As I remember back then I don't think of Sal smiling usually. George was the one with the almost permanent smile while she was always the serious one, mothering both her brother and myself. Looking back, I realise her firm expression hid a pretty face but it wasn't something that ever came into consideration during my time in the orphanage. She was just Sal.

Mr Rodgers entered like a dark avenging angel dressed in a flowing black academic gown. Everything fell silent. I was sure that even the birds on the window ledges stopped tweeting out of terror. All class members stood to attention displaying what was supposed to be respect for our schoolmaster. Abject fear would have been a better description. He mounted the bare wooden dais on which stood his desk. This ended any thoughts of relaxation until our playtime, which always felt an eternity away.

'Good morning, class,' he said but I feared there would be nothing *good* about it.

'Good morning, sir,' everyone chanted in unison, waiting for his nod before daring to sit down again.

He called the class register, using only surnames unless, like George and Sal, more than one scholar shared the same one. Every pupil dutifully answered 'Yes, sir' loudly and clearly. I learned a mumbled reply would bring an instant reproach, if not worse. Without saying anything further he announced: 'Assembly!'

Everyone stood and followed him out of the room to the place where only a short while ago we enjoyed - if *enjoyed* were the correct word – bowls of a hot, salty stodge masquerading as porridge, washed down with hot, sweet tea. Mrs G said this was how Mr Rodgers decreed porridge should be. Other classes followed us into the room. These groups were made up of the orphanage's older inmates. Neat lines of young people stood waiting but the room lacked any sense of eagerness in its anticipation. Resignation would be a better description of our feelings. This ordeal was something to get over and done with as quickly as possible as far as we children were concerned.

The Master entered followed by Mrs Mason, a woman of indeterminate age hidden within the masses of a long, dark dress. We were never able to fathom the cause of her great volume. Was it the size of her body or a great number of undergarments? She shuffled to the seat before a mahogany upright piano in the corner of the room.

Now commenced my first experience of the daily ordeal known as *morning assembly*. While the orphanage was supposed to be a Christian institution, to me its main purpose was instilling within us the fear rather than the love of God. The thin paper volume tucked safely inside my jacket held more importance for me than any religious text. Mr Mason was a solemn gentleman until he spoke the word of the Lord. I never understood how so much sound could come from such a slight body. His eyes glowed with holy fervour. I didn't know if he was acquainted with the way to Heaven, but he really knew the road to Hell because he described it to us in no uncertain terms and told us we were all doomed to follow it, if we did not mend our ways.

We began with a prayer declaimed rather than spoken by the Master. A hymn followed. 'Fight the Good Fight,' I think it was that first day. This was always a favourite. It made us open up our mouths and lungs. First Mrs Mason struck up the opening bars of the tune and then after a brief pause we children lunged into the words, always a syllable behind our elders. Another short prayer came from the Master, followed by everyone chanting in unison the Lord's Prayer. I mumbled the words, not yet knowing them by heart. Two years later I could recite them in my sleep. I repeated them, at least, once a day every day and twice on Sundays. Finally, shrill young voices gave vent to 'He Who Would Valiant Be,' trying to drown out Jolly Rodgers' harsh baritone and the Master's booming flat bass.

At this point the Master decided he'd put us in the right frame of mind to commence our day of learning. He left our class to the mercy of Jolly Rodgers and the rigours of English grammar. It felt strange to be drilled - and drilled we were - through this subject by a man whose first language I assumed to be Scottish.

Our teacher's predator eyes roamed the classroom searching for the next victim to pounce upon. He forced individual class members to stand up and recite verbs. Today fortune smiled on me and I managed to evade his fiery gaze. *'Beginner's Luck'* suggested a less fortunate George at our playtime but my good fortune would soon run out.

***

'You are innumerate, Smyle!' Jolly Rodgers snarled, eyes aflame. The nine times table defeated me. He cornered me like a ravenous jungle carnivore about to bury sharp teeth into its next meal. I bit my lip; I was not going to cry. The ground obstinately refused to open up and swallow me. The only blessing was that the girls wouldn't see my latest humiliation. They were safely upstairs doing their sewing lesson with Mrs G.

'I suppose that's only to be expected from the likes of you!' he sneered, and turned away. The short bamboo cane that doubled as both a pointer and his instrument of punishment swished through the air to indicate the next victim. 'Tell him, Jackson.'

An unkempt boy with one half of his shirt collar tucked inside his jacket and the other sticking out arose unsteadily to perform like a trained dog. As he stood his dangling jacket sleeve caught the slate on his desktop. It clattered to the floor and the boy stooped to pick it up.

'Leave it boy! You're a fool, Jackson. A clumsy fool! What are you, boy?'

'A clumsy fool, sir.' Jackson straightened himself but I could see him quivering, expecting to feel a slicing blow from our tormentor's cane.

'Louder! I cannot hear you, boy!' Rodgers screamed, eyes bulging. I was sure they would pop out of his head.

'A clumsy fool, sir!' Jackson shouted.

I could see both the tears in the boy's eyes and the demented half smile crossing our teacher's face.

Some in the class giggled but I only felt anger.

'Don't encourage him!' Our inquisitor was not amused, but then again he never was. So much for Rodgers being *jolly*. The cane thwacked on his desk. His face turned an even darker shade of puce and large blue veins rippled across his temples. 'Recite, boy. Start with one times nine is nine.'

Thomas Jackson stood to attention, screwing up his eyes in preparation to commence his recital. Clumsy and untidy he may have been, but he knew all his multiplication tables. He could go far beyond the normal twelve times twelve that is the limit for any normal human boy. I discovered this arithmetical wizard could do all this and multiply as well as doing the dividing of impossible numbers in his head, but Mr Rodgers could not see beyond the boy's gauche manner. He delighted in ridiculing him on every possible occasion unless he could direct his ire towards his new *little brown friend*.

Now the teacher chose the eleven times table to inflict on his next victim. Stanley Vicars was his selection. An audible sigh of relief came from the other boys when Stan's name was called out. He'd spared the rest of us, if only for a moment. Stan occupied a half empty desk. His usual class partner was sick and confined to bed. He stood up and the hinged heavy wooden seat clunked upwards into the metal supports of the backrest. This provided another source of nervous merriment in the room. The gangly boy chanted the multiples but once he got to eleven times eleven, he was in trouble.

'No, Master Vicars! Eleven elevens are not one hundred and twenty-two! Hold out your hand!' With a single bound Rodgers leapt from the dais toward his quarry on the front row. It was all done in one continuous motion culminating in the cane hacking into the boy's palm.

'What are eleven elevens, boy?' He breathed the words into the child's ashen face.

Stan's arm was back down by his side with fingers clenched into his palm, trying to relieve the pain.

'Eleven elevens is one hundred and thirty-three, sir.'

'Other hand!' He demanded the boy's submission to punishment. I swear I could see glee in Rodgers' eyes. The cane thwacked into flesh again. The second hand clenched and I could see tears well up in Stan's eyes.

'Right! Who knows what eleven times eleven is?'

No one responded to the request, not even those who knew the answer. Bodies tried to sink down into the tight spaces between desktops and backrests. No one dared to take the chance. Even the correct answer might result in a stroke of the cane. The teacher's manic eyes scoured the classroom. I prayed they wouldn't focus on me.

'Master Scrivens. What are eleven times eleven?'

This next luckless target held the mistaken belief that safety lay by hiding in the sanctuary of the classroom's back row but there was no hiding place from Jolly Rodgers. James Scrivens stood up nervously. His red cheeks were heavily pock marked. Its hue took on an even darker shade now than even that of our teacher's visage.

'Eleven times eleven is one hundred and twenty one, sir.' His eyes closed and he waited for the inevitable painful response. I could tell he was praying silently.

'That is correct, Scrivens!' With another single bound Rodgers returned to his desk to give the class a manic glare. On arrival he gave the desktop a whack with his cane. What had the desk done to deserve this? Was it only meant to act as a reminder to us?

They'll look after you, lad. Grandmother's words rang in my ears. I resolved I would learn all my tables off by heart. I was not going to give Rodgers any reason to punish me, but he didn't always need a reason.

Chapter 3

Maybe I'm making my new life sound intolerable - especially when Jolly Rodgers was around - but the Hull Sailors' Children's Orphanage was not a prison. There were some good times too, but these came usually after the end of the school day and after our domestic duties in the home were completed to the satisfaction of those in authority. In the main we were required to keep both the buildings and ourselves spotless. Then and only then were we at liberty for what remained of the day until it was time for our evening meal and each week there was always one afternoon of freedom. This was the time when we went off on our adventures.

It was on my first free afternoon that George and Sal took me to what became my favourite place in the whole of Hull: Pearson's Park people called it. Our regular walk took us past a railway station which everyone still called 'Cemetery Gates,' even though the railway company had long ago renamed it *Botanic*. The original name came about because the station was facing the entrance to the Hull General Cemetery, a reminder that was not going to disappear. We always kept to the station side of the road, well away from the forbidding graveyard. After turning right here we walked along the side of a newly fabricated wide road. This highway had also undergone a renaming to become *Princes Avenue*, but inevitably locals used older alternatives. The name we children used was 'Prinny Bank' – short for Princes Bank Avenue. People like to cling on to the familiar when everything around them seems to be changing quickly. Maybe this explained the importance of the book my father gave me. Something precious to hang on to.

Open fields stretched off into the west beyond this new road. Further along the road clusters of new houses were sprouting up.

These were big houses, being built for important Hull people who wanted to be away from the town's smoke and grime. A few were already occupied but most remained under construction with builders shouting and hammering away as they worked on them.

'Mrs G says these big houses will need servants. She reckons I'll be able to go into service in one of them. She'll put in a word for me.' Sal's eyes glowed at the prospect. 'Be much better than one of them old houses in town. I've heard they've got rats and mice.'

Pearson's Park was only a ten minute walk from the orphanage. Its towering iron gates were daunting to a small boy. The metal arch carried the motto *Providentia Fido*. George said the words had to have something to do with dogs. Neither Sal nor I were able to contradict him. It was years later that I discovered it meant 'In providence I trust' and it was the Latin motto of the Mr Pearson after whom the park was named but I learned later that he went bankrupt, so I guess his trust in providence must have been misplaced.

Walking through these gates was an entry into a new world. I'd never seen so much grass before or such an open expanse of land without any sign of fences or buildings. Everything seemed to shimmer in the sunshine. Then again, the sun always shone on our days here. Well, that's how I remember them.

'It's like the Wild West!' I was about to burst with excitement. 'Is this the prairie?'

'No, it's the park!' George looked at me as though I was stupid. 'What's the Wild West, anyway?'

'It's in America. It's where there are red Indians and buffaloes and wide open spaces... as far as the eye can see!' I was quoting from what I had read.

'That sounds like poetry.' Sal sighed, gazing wistfully across swathes of neat grass towards the bandstand in the centre of the park. For just a moment her serious face slipped away but soon her composure was regained.

'Let's find somewhere to sit before the butter on this bread melts onto me pinny.' Whenever we went on our expeditions Sal always managed to bring some food from the kitchen. Mrs G always turned a blind eye.

The cool shade of a willow tree provided us with a place to sit; we could stretch out our legs across an old blanket borrowed from the

Sewing Room. Like our bed blankets it carried the legend U.S.A. In my mind then that made it perfect for the occasion.

'How do you know about this Wild West place, then?' George's teeth were poised ready to dig into a huge white bread and butter doorstep.

'Me Dad told me all about it. He's been there! To America. That's where he'll be now!' I nodded vigorously. I wanted to believe it. 'His ship sank off the coast of America, so he'll have swum ashore. Good swimmer, my Dad.' I didn't know this to be a fact, but it had to be true, didn't it?

George was about to interrupt but Sal caught his arm.

'He gave me this book.' I pulled my most treasured possession - my only possession - from inside my jacket. It was the only thing I had left that didn't belong to the Hull Sailors' Children's Orphanage. 'It tells you all about it.'

'Let's have a look.' Sal placed a slice of buttered bread carefully on the apron stretched out in front of her. She held out a hand to take my treasure.

I didn't want to let go, but it was Sal asking me and she was my friend. She wouldn't laugh at me, even if she thought I was silly. I knew I could trust her.

'Buffalo Bill – King of the Border Men,' she read the title out loud.

'Buffalo Bill,' George repeated. 'What's he then? Half man, half buffalo... like them half men, half horses?' He began to chortle.

'No!' I shouted back indignantly.

'There's a picture of him... on front.' Sal held up the book to let George see the engraved sketch on the dog-eared front page. The figure of a bearded man with blond locks flowing from beneath a pale Stetson hat dominated the cover. In his hand he brandished a colt revolver ready for action.

'He's very brave! Rode for the Pony Express. Drove a stagecoach. Was an army scout. Shot buffaloes. That's how he got his name. Does all sorts of things... in the Wild West!'

'Well.' For a second George looked dumbfounded by my outburst. 'What's the Pony Express?'

I had so many things to tell my friends. For once here was a subject where I possessed all the knowledge – or so I liked to believe.

***

Summer was the easiest time of year in my new home. Evenings remained light until late so George and I could play in the yard until dusk. Every evening ended the same way, with a visit to the kitchen door to say goodnight to Sal. She helped Mrs G with the washing up and getting the bread mixture ready for baking in the huge oven the next morning. Unfailingly hidden beneath her apron would be something pleasant, usually slices of bread and jam. There was a goodnight kiss on the cheek for George and it soon became her custom to give one to me too. It made me both happy and sad, reminding me how much I missed my mother's kiss before going to sleep.

The first Monday of every month was the happiest time in the home for most of our fellow inmates but the worst of times for the Smith twins and me. It was visiting day when friends and family could come into the home between six o'clock and eight in the evening. We took ourselves as far away as possible from this, not wanting to hear the happy chattering nor to see the cakes, pies and sweets the visitors brought in. At first, I hoped to receive a visit from Grandmother with Mary. She might have been running around by then but eventually I gave up any hope of ever seeing a present of a currant cake or a packet of butterscotch arrive for me.

Mrs G supervised these meetings and she quickly noticed if anyone failed to receive visitors. Somehow magically on these evenings a plate laden with thick slices of bread and a jar of her homemade rhubarb jam always waited for us on the table just inside the kitchen door.

Winter was a difficult time for all of us. Lots of time spent looking through the window on wet and windy days, sometimes gazing out on a world white with snow. If the weather allowed, Jolly Rodgers would organise a Sunday walk (not a voluntary activity and after church, of course) for the boys: through the Botanic railway level crossing, beyond the cemetery and out into the fields. He called it a hike but it felt more like a forced march. We would walk two abreast and he would set the tempo with 'left, left... left, right, left' and woe betides the straggler who could not keep up the pace.

In my imagination we were the United States cavalry in our blue suit jackets, the same colour as the soldiers' uniforms. We were in search of untamed savages but the wildest people we ever saw was a family of gypsies sitting around their campfire. George got a sore ear for tarrying to admire the gypsy horses; he loved horses.

On our return I told Sal about seeing a Sioux encampment and how the warriors must have taken part in the massacre of General Custer's Seventh Cavalry. George confirmed my fantasy, but she said she didn't believe us and that boys didn't have any sense.

***

Then there was Snelgrave or "Smelly" as most of us called him. Edward Snelgrave wasn't an orphan; his father was very much alive and a sea captain, but his mother was dead or so he said. Some said she had run away with another man. He came into the home several months after me. Smelly never let anyone forget he was of a higher social status compared to everyone else in the home or so he believed and told every other child. He never allowed me to forget that I was several steps down the social ladder, if indeed he thought I even justified a place on it.

'My grandfather used to take shiploads of your lot across to the West Indies!' he snarled the first time he set eyes on me. 'Bloody savages! Only fit for cutting sugar cane and picking cotton!' He looked at me in the way you would at something nasty you had trodden on in the street.

'My father's Indian!' I was not going to tolerate his insults.

'All you bloody niggers are the same!' He used the one word I'd learned to hate more than any other. His thin lips curled, disgust written over an acne-pitted face.

'I'm not a nigger!' Months of irritation welled up inside me; months of sniggered remarks, usually only half overheard when I walked past small groups of boys. Here was someone who dared say it to my face: a focus for my pent-up anger. I screamed like a banshee and leapt at him, even though he stood head and shoulders taller than I. Surprise gave me the advantage. I knocked him to the ground and began to pummel him with my fists.

From out of nowhere a crowd of boys gathered and stood around us in the yard, stamping their feet and making animal noises to urge on the one-sided fight. I would have given Smelly a real thrashing but for the intervention of Jolly Rodgers.

'Get off him, you little animal!' Automatically the teacher took the side of my youthful tormentor. His Scots accent always became more pronounced whenever he was angry.

'He called me a nigger, sir!'

'So?' The disdain in Jolly Rodgers' expression told me he saw no misdemeanour in Snelgrave's insult. He grabbed me by the scruff of the neck and landed heavy clouts on either side of my head. 'We do not tolerate such behaviour here. Go inside and stand by my classroom door.'

Snelgrave pulled himself up and disappeared into the crowded yard. Stinging ears couldn't prevent me from hearing him sniggering behind my back. Four strokes of the cane but I would have done it again.

Smelly made sure he never confronted or even came near me on his own again.

***

'He's nowt but a bully!' George rammed his fist into his left hand. He was angry with himself for leaving me alone in the yard in order to make one of his regular playtime visits to Sal in the kitchen. 'I've a good mind to…'

'Hold yer horses!' Sal interrupted his flow. 'You'll finish up getting strokes of Jolly Rodgers' cane, an' all! Bullies like Smelly always get away with it.'

'Rodgers said I was the bully! Called me a little black animal. Said this place was too good for the likes of me!' I felt thoroughly sorry for myself. I couldn't stop a tear rolling down my cheek leaving a clear channel through the accumulated grime of the day.

'Too good for the likes of him, more like!' I'd never seen Sal so angry. A black buckled shoe stamped on the playground flagstone. She was always the moderating influence but at times a sudden burst of temper matched the flame in her hair.

Thereafter one or both of the Smith twins made it their duty to be with me at all times. I'm not sure which one of them frightened Snelgrave most but I knew I'd never want to be the object of Sal's anger, much as I loved her.

The best thing the Master ever did was to put George Smith in charge of me. How the twins put up with Sammy Smyle and his Wild West fantasising I'll never know but I am eternally grateful they did.

The days passed into weeks and weeks into months. Gradually I gave up any hope of seeing Grandmother - although, in retrospect, I don't think *hope* is the right word. It would have been nice to see little Mary growing up though. I never gave up hope of father turning up and taking me away, far away to somewhere warm and welcoming, somewhere where I wasn't different.

****

Following the schoolyard incident with Smelly, Jolly Rodgers introduced me to a new 'treat.'

'Pick up that bucket and shovel, boy!' he commanded. 'Get out into the street and fill up the bucket with what the horses leave behind!'

I knew he was enjoying this. The evil glint in his eyes looked extra bright. There was to be no playtime for me after my other official tasks had been completed.

'And don't think of stopping until you have filled the bucket up to the top three times! See that heap at the bottom of the garden?' He grabbed my head and pointed it towards the rear wall of the orphanage. 'I want to see that taller than you by Saturday night!'

George was standing a few yards away.

'Smith! Don't you dare think of helping this brat or I will find something for you!' The teacher's rage was in full flow.

My friend had the sense to disappear quickly.

So began my acquaintance with what came out of equine intestines. My only consolation was that future crops of the rhubarb that went into Mrs G's pies and jam were better than they had ever been before. She praised my contribution in achieving this at every opportunity, much to the chagrin of Jolly Rodgers.

Chapter 4

Hull: April 1888
Two years passed and the orphanage's routine had come to rule my life; that is until one dinnertime –that's how we always referred to our midday mealtime. It was Tuesday and Tuesdays meant Mrs G's special meat stew with huge doorsteps of crusty fresh bread to dip into it. It always contained large chunks of potato, carrot and turnip and lots of meat – though we never knew what kind. I think it depended on what the butcher Mr Wilkinson had not managed to sell to his other customers.

For once we were late in joining the dining room queue thanks to one of Jolly Rodgers' foul humours during our arithmetic lesson. As usual the girls had escaped from this torture to spend time under Mrs Mason's supervision in the sewing room. Sal was in the dining room already: ladling hot stew into mugs held out by eager children anticipating the best meal of the week. When she saw the two of us, her normal staid demeanour changed completely. She glanced quickly towards Mrs G and then at us. I'd never seen her so agitated before. This was not our Sal. She gestured for us to come closer but we knew breaking ranks would bring swift retribution. Jolly Rodgers had followed into the dining room and stood so close behind us we could feel his hot breath coursing down our necks.

I glanced at George to seek his opinion.

'One of her moods!' he shrugged. We kept our place in the slow-moving line knowing what would befall us if we even dared to look like breaking ranks.

She continued gesticulating for us to come to her. This wasn't our Sal; she never got overexcited; angry sometimes, yes, but never overexcited - this was our role in life. Mrs G's stew was always sufficient cause for excitement in George and me, but it didn't explain Sal's unexpected display. She was always the calming influence. 'Pouring oil on troubled waters' she said but I knew it was an expression she had learned from Mrs G. There were some people in the home who I would have liked to pour boiling oil onto.

'He's coming!' she shouted. Sal never raised her voice in the dining room or anywhere come to that - unless she was arguing with her brother, of course. Usually a withering look achieved the desired result from George - and me.

But who was coming? We were still well down the plodding queue, not even halfway to being served and still unable to hear what it was she wanted to tell us.

'Selina Smith!' Mrs G turned to Sal and fixed her with an admonishing frown. 'What's come over you lass?'

'He's coming, Mrs G! I mean Buffalo Bill! I mean Mrs Grainger… Ma'am.' Sal could hardly contain herself.

I'd never seen Sal go into such a tizzy before, but I'm sure I heard her say the magic words: 'Buffalo Bill'. I was always the one who brought up this name in conversation, usually to groans from anyone within earshot.

'Be that as it may, lass… we've got all these dinners to serve!' Mrs G's stern expression remained, and Sal went back to doling hot stew into the large tin mugs held out by bemused children. They were more anxious to eat than hear what Sal had to say.

I wanted to get nearer to Sal. I needed to find out more. She'd said 'Buffalo Bill.' I was sure she did. The boy in front of me got a shove in the back. The queue had to move faster. Unfortunately, it was Edward Snelgrave.

He turned and leered at me. 'Stop your shovin', Sambo!'

A sharp elbow jabbed into my ribs and I stumbled backwards into George, gasping for breath.

'Pack it in, Smelly!' George tried swinging a punch in my tormentor's direction, but fortunately for both of them air was all he made contact with. His target kept well out of reach.

In a brief stroke of luck Jolly Rodgers had moved away from us to supervise children at the dining tables but sudden the commotion in the queue attracted his attention. He headed in our direction like the *Cutty Sark* in full sail.

'What's going on?' Sharp eyes burned into the tail end of the queue where we remained.

'Nothing, sir. I tripped over my shoelace, sir.' I bent down, pretending to retie my boot.

Oh, how I wanted Snelgrave to feel Jolly Rodgers' wrath, but telling the truth was more likely to result in George and probably me too being on the receiving end of summary punishment. For once Snelgrave showed wisdom and remained quiet or was it that he was more interested in getting his portion of stew?

I rubbed sore ribs to ease away the pain. The line continued shuffling along. George and I picked up mugs from the table end. We drew nearer to Mrs G and Sal and the delicious smell of the hot meaty stew bubbling in the huge black pan on the grate in the fireplace close behind them.

Snelgrave thrust his mug in Sal's direction to demand his share. Most of his portion missed the jerking mug. Steaming liquid splashed over his hand. He yelled out in pain and dropped the mug which clattered on the tile floor.

'Serves you right, Master Snelgrave!' Mrs G showed him no pity. 'I hope that teaches you some manners! Go stick your hand in cold water.' I don't know how much she saw, but she would have taken Sal's side no matter what happened, especially if it concerned Edward Snelgrave. She alone among the adults in the orphanage had the measure of him.

Jolly Rodgers' cuff to Snelgrave's ear on his way out of the dining room made my painful ribs feel much better.

At last, it was our turn. I held out my mug, but Sal's attention remained distracted from her task.

'Careful, Sal,' I begged her with a smile, not wanting a repetition of Snelgrave's "accident." I suppose it could have been one.

'He's coming... Buffalo Bill... He's coming to Hull!' She concentrated on the meeting of my mug with the contents of the ladle. Her aim was better this time and I didn't lose any of my delicious, steaming dinner.

'When?' I asked. Magically the ache in my ribs disappeared completely.

'Who said?' George demanded evidence.

'It was in the newspaper. Eastern Morning News.' She nodded vigorously. George held out his mug but blobs of stew fell on the table. 'John Morgan, the butcher's boy, told me this morning… when he brought the meat.'

'He'll tell you owt, he will!' George shook his head. 'He's always telling you tales. I think he's sweet on you.'

'When's he coming?' I interrupted the bickering before Sal became agitated again. This news was too important for things to be allowed to descend into another one of the twins' squabbles.

'He said that Buffalo Bill and his Wild West Show are going to arrive on the fourth of May and…'

Her words were cut short.

'Selina Smith! There's hungry children here who need their dinners!' Mrs G shook her head angrily. She couldn't possibly understand the importance of Sal's news for me. No adult could, not even her. 'And they wants it afore it gets cold!'

'See you later.' Sal went back to her work and we picked up chunks of bread from the huge red earthenware bowl on the end of the serving table.

A dozen or more children sat at our table, waiting to say grace but my thoughts were not on either God or even food.

'Don't you want that?' The prayer had been said and George had almost reached the end of his portion. Mine remained hardly touched. I was oblivious of time… Reality… Everything.

He startled me back into the real world. I dug in my spoon and lifted a large chunk of meat. It hovered halfway between the mug and my mouth. I lapsed into another daydream.

'If you don't want that, I can find a home for it.' George soaked up the last of his stew with a thick slab of crust, scraping it around the bottom of his mug.

The meat went into my mouth and I chewed dreamily.

'Anyone for seconds?' Mrs G's voice called from somewhere in the distance, somewhere across the swaying grass of the wide prairie beyond a herd of grazing bison.

George shot out of his seat, faster than a greyhound to beat the horde of thirty or so other boys who all wanted more of the feast of the week. Seconds were usual at dinnertime, especially when it was stew day. Normally I ran neck and neck with George to be first for any extras, but today I rode the open range, alongside a tall man clad in buckskin with golden hair flowing in the breeze.

***

'That's less than two weeks' time!' My excitement echoed off the playground walls.

Sal had joined us after finishing her work in the kitchen.

'There's going to be a parade through the streets of Hull.' Sal added more colour to her information. 'Cowboys. Red Indians. Buffaloes. Everything.'

'And the Sultan of Turkey an' all… riding on an elephant!' George remained unconvinced of there being truth in the butcher boy's story. I pulled an angry face in his direction.

'Why would Buffalo Bill come to Hull? Don't make no sense!' George was adamant. I was forced to admit the same conclusion to myself, although I did not want to believe it. There was no sensible answer to his question. The two things did not go together.

'He is! George Smith! And that's all there is to it!' A stiff finger prodded into George's chest. Sal could be even more adamant than him. What people say about red hair and a fiery temperament going together was true in the case of the Smith twins, especially when they argued with each other.

'We'll have to ask somebody else!' I interrupted this latest confrontation. This matter was more important than a petty squabble. 'Somebody who'll know the truth. Somebody sensible who reads a newspaper!'

'That's right!' Sal's lips pursed angrily. 'Then we'll see who's telling the truth, George Smith!'

'Does Mrs G read the newspaper?' I asked. Hopefully my best adult friend - my only adult friend - would be the one to resolve the argument.

'She only reads it after the Master and Jolly have finished with it, just afore she uses it to start the kitchen fire.' Sal shrugged. 'Don't usually come into the kitchen for a week or more.'

I gasped. 'A week! Can't wait a week!'

'It'll have to be the Master or Jolly Rodgers then.' George nodded firmly.

'There's got to be somebody else.'

I really didn't fancy approaching either of George's suggestions. Both Sal and George shook their heads. There were no alternatives available to me. We had no money to buy newspapers.

***

'Please, sir.' My stomach tied itself in knots. 'Please, sir.'

'What, boy?' Mr Rodgers snapped back, offended by an unwarranted interruption to his suppertime supervision. When he saw the source of the nuisance, offence turned to anger.

'Spit it out, boy!'

'Please, sir. Have you read the newspaper, sir?' I knew I was making a terrible mistake, but desperation to know the truth overcame any common sense I might have had.

'Yes, I have… but why should the likes of you want to know anything of newspapers?' he demanded loudly. He wanted everyone in the room to be fully aware he was exercising his authority.

Silence ruled as all eyes focussed upon my tormenter and me.

'Please, sir. Is Buffalo Bill coming to Hull?' My voice quavered, and corduroy-clad knees knocked together.

'What in creation is a buffalo bill, boy? Ducks have bills… not buffaloes!'

This tirade encouraged giggles from certain factions in the room, especially Edward Snelgrave and his cronies.

A large hairy hand grabbed the top of my head and twisted it around forcefully until I faced back towards the end of the queue of children waiting to collect their supper. Painfully the rest of my body followed. He released his grip but the sharp sting of a hard clout across the back of my head ensued swiftly.

'Get back in the queue and don't waste my time, you little pickaninny!' The heavy Scottish accent became a harsh staccato reflecting his anger.

I darted quickly out of reach of further blows and joined the others. Snelgrave sniggered loudly. I knew the word 'pickaninny' was being added to his vocabulary of insults. It would await his use at a time when it would cause me the maximum of hurt and aggravation.

Anger added to my frustration. I needed to know the truth. It not only concerned the visit of the bravest man in the world, my hero. There would be others with him from America and, at least, one of them must know of my father's whereabouts. Surely America couldn't be such a big place, could it?

***

The next day brought further misery but it did not come from my continuing frustration in not knowing the truth about the Wild West Show's visit to Hull. Worse was to come.

I stood alone in the playground, wracking my brain. Who could tell me if the butcher boy's story was really true? George said he needed to have a word with Sal, but I think he was still hungry – he was always hungry - and went to get something to tide him over until dinnertime. My mind strayed away from the moment. Lapses in concentration were just as dangerous in the orphanage yard as they were for a lone scout in the depths of the wildest Red Indian country.

Unseen hands grabbed both my arms from behind and dragged me backwards across the yard floor. The heels of my boots clipped on the edge of each flagstone, before my assailants spun me around and dropped me in a bundle on the hard floor. My hands scraped on the rough pavers attempting to arrest my fall.

'Pickaninny! Pickaninny!'

A gang of leering boys surrounded me; all chanting and stamping on the yard floor. One ugly face stood out from the crowd: Snelgrave. Once again bigotry showed its ignorance. They couldn't even use the correct insult and repeated the word used by Jolly Rodgers. I knew it would come back to haunt me.

I struggled to sit up. Tears streamed down my cheeks. Sore palms went up to my mouth to ease their pain. I could taste the dry dirt on them. I anticipated more pain and insults.

A body fell across my legs.

It was Snelgrave's but he wasn't trying to jump on me. Behind his flattened body stood George, red hair aflame and fists ready to take on all comers.

'Who's next?' my saviour demanded.

Outnumbered though he was, no one dared take on an angry George Smith - not even the oldest boys in the orphanage.

'Come on! Who's next?'

Fire blazed in his eyes. They scoured the surrounding mob for would-be heroes, but the cowardly gang faded away into the crowded playground. Snelgrave followed, slinking away on all fours like a wounded animal.

I felt hurt, but it was neither my sore palms nor my bruised knees that really pained me. What hurt most was that I remained an outsider to the majority of the orphanage children despite having lived with them for nearly two years. I always would be.

George breathed heavily. He held out a hand to pull me up.

'Got a hankie?' The tone of his voice remained harsh; it always took him time to calm down. I nodded and stuck a hand into my jacket pocket.

'There's stains on yer cheeks. Don't let 'em see yer crying.'

I wiped my face and brushed the dirt from my trouser knees. George put a hand into his jacket pocket and pulled out the result of his visit to Sal: a fluffy, squashed slice of bread and butter.

'Want a bit?' He offered it to me.

I shook my head. I was in no mood to eat.

'What's going on?' an adult voice enquired from behind us. A voice I didn't recognise.

We turned to see a thin young man in a dark suit. His shoulders were so wide the jacket hung as though still strung on a coat hanger. Thick round spectacles hid his eyes. It was Mr Jason, a new teacher who had joined the orphanage only a week earlier. He taught the class with the youngest children in it.

'Nothing, sir!' we replied in unison. The law of the playground forbade us from revealing the truth of what happened to adults, especially teachers.

I grasped the moment. 'Please, sir. Do you read the *Eastern Morning News*, sir?'

'I'm afraid not. Why do you ask?' He smiled. He didn't jump down my throat, the usual adult reaction, if I had the audacity to ask a question.

Don't speak unless spoken to.

I paused for a moment, but I was desperate. I needed to know.

'I've been told it's in the paper that Buffalo Bill and his Wild West Show are coming to Hull, sir. Is it true, sir?'

'I'm sorry but I don't know... but I've heard from people who have seen the show in Manchester that it is a truly remarkable spectacle.' There was unexpected kindness in this adult's voice.

It existed; Buffalo Bill's show really existed. This fact alone excited me but what if it wasn't really coming to Hull? I still felt frustrated. My chin dropped onto my chest.

The door to the schoolrooms opened and one of the older girls emerged ringing a hand bell to tell us playtime was over and to return to our lessons.

'Off to your classroom, boys,' Mr Jason ordered but not in the harsh, *no questions* way of Jolly Rodgers and the other adults. It sounded more like advice. In an instant I wished he was our teacher. Many times over the following years I have reflected and wondered whether the decisions I was about to make would have been different if all the adults in authority in the home had shared Mr Jason's kind nature.

'I will see if I can find out something about Buffalo Bill.' His words almost stopped me in my tracks. Apart from Mrs G, he was the first adult to show me a friendly gesture in my whole time in the orphanage and for a long time before then.

'Thank you, sir,' George and I mumbled in unison. For the first time in two years I really meant *thank you*, apart from when I said it to the twins and Mrs G, of course. She was different.

***

The answer to my question came much sooner than expected and from an unexpected source. Before suppertime the orphanage had a surprise visitor.

Mr John Thorne had provided most of the money to set up the Hull Sailors' Children's Orphanage. He was a shipbroker, although I didn't have any clue as to what a shipbroker might be or what one did. Needless to say he made a lot of his money out of the prosperous trade of the port of Hull and much of the town's prosperity came at the expense of lives lost at sea. *It was his Christian duty*, he said - and the Master repeated this endlessly in our assemblies – *to help provide for the widows and orphans of those poor departed souls*. However, he was not like the Master: he practised his Christianity more in deeds than words.

Mr Thorne's visits were never announced well in advance. Maybe he wanted to keep the Master and the staff on their toes by surprising them. He wanted to see that his money was being well spent. For we children these visits were always a pleasant occasion, because they were always accompanied by a large delivery of cakes from Borrill's the bakers.

'The children will not want their suppers, sir,' I overheard the Master's wife say to our benefactor. Apart from morning assemblies and girl's sewing lessons she seldom appeared among the children but Mr Thorne was visiting and it was important for her to be seen with us.

'Children will always find another corner to put their suppers,' he reproached with a twinkle in his eye. 'Ravenous beasts are children.'

Although the day had started badly, improvement had begun with meeting Mr Jason and now with the arrival of Mr Thorne, it neared perfection. Well, perfection for an almost twelve-year-old orphan, that is.

Mrs G and some of the older girls laid out the sweet delicacies on plates in the dining room. Wet tongues licked hungry lips. Manna from heaven waited to meet its inevitable fate. Everyone wanted to get nearer to these rare delights, but we waited our turn in an orderly fashion. To do otherwise might result in exclusion from the feast. The aroma of freshly baked cakes tantalised, and sugar twinkled invitingly on brown crusts. What might lie beneath these tempting pastry shells: apple, pear, raspberry?

Mr Thorne stood alongside the Master, who for once allowed himself to be present at an occasion where wolves devoured our quarry. Usually he never stayed around at our mealtimes. Occasionally the Master appeared to ensure grace had been said then he disappeared. Our benefactor's age was a mystery, for all adults looked ancient, but I estimate he must have been about fifty years old. Flowing dark mutton chops contained curly strands of grey but otherwise he was clean-shaven. He was what my grandmother would have described as a 'fine man', although others might have called him portly. His confident bearing and dress displayed the prosperity of his business.

Mrs G looked across the room towards our esteemed visitor for instruction. He continued smiling benignly in return.

'There's no need to say grace, children. I can see from your faces that you will be eternally grateful,' he announced.

The statement was made much to the chagrin of the Master who would have demanded, at least, two prayers and a hymn before allowing any of us to accept even a slice of bread and jam. George and I were eternally grateful the Master was normally absent at mealtimes.

Mr Thorne nodded towards Mrs G. Our surrogate mother took control of the feast.

'Take only one cake each. There may be enough for seconds when you have eaten the first one,' she ordered.

The trick, of course, was to be at the front of the queue, get your cake and eat it quickly before slipping back to the tail end - but you must do this before any calculation of possible seconds and who might deserve to partake. If one worked surreptitiously in this way, it was theoretically possible to get three cakes. It never worked for George and me because we were too noticeable, especially when Sal was involved in distributing food. As always, she stood at Mrs G's right hand helping to supervise children some of who were older than Sal herself.

As we tucked into the cakes – mine was sweet apple – our founder walked amongst us chaperoned by the Master. The other teachers were also present, but they kept a discrete distance, making sure good order was maintained. The rule when anyone visited – and especially Mr Thorne – was to keep silent unless spoken to but there was something I needed to discover. Our visitor must be a man who would know the answer. Someone of his importance must read the newspapers.

I edged towards Mr Thorne who continued his promenade around the room talking to happy children as he walked among them. Full mouths made replying difficult when he spoke to anyone but the looks of satisfaction seemed to be enough for him. George looked puzzled by my strange perambulations; his attention maintained its focus on the table and the remaining cakes. The time for Mrs G to call out 'seconds' drew nearer but we moved further and further away from the food. I understood his puzzlement.

Finally, we converged on Mr Thorne's route and for once in my life I was glad I stood out from the rest.

'And who might you be, young sir?' John Thorne appeared amused. Was it because of my brown face? There could be no other reason.

'This is Samuel Smyle.' The Master didn't give me the opportunity to reply for myself.

'Are you making good use of your time in this fine home, young man?' The self-satisfied smile told me he knew what my answer would be even before he asked the question.

I swallowed down the last morsel of cake.

'Very good use, sir.' I tried to reply dutifully but before he had chance to either ask another question or move on to another sycophantic respondent, I continued speaking without drawing breath. 'Is it true that Buffalo Bill and his Wild West Show are coming to Hull, sir?'

At first, he seemed taken aback by my question. Behind Mr Thorne's back I saw the Master scowling. I was pleased Jolly Rodgers stood across the room and well out of earshot.

Our visitor smiled.

'Yes, it is true and he is leaving Hull directly after the performance to return to America. He will be leaving on a fine ship, the *Persian Monarch* from Alexandra Dock. My company has been involved in making the arrangements for his departure.' The smile became a rather smug beam but it was what he said was all-important to me.

He turned to the Master and spoke quietly. 'I would like to say something to all the children.'

The Master nodded his agreement and clapped his hands loudly to get everyone's attention. Silence fell and munching went into slow motion.

'Mr Thorne has something to say to you all.' The Master's eyes scoured the room seeking any dissidents.

The thumbs of large hands plunged into the pockets of a mustard yellow waistcoat and John Thorne stuck out his prosperity. He adopted the pose of a giant canary with the long tails of his black coat hanging behind him like wings and tail feathers.

'This young tyke here has asked me about Colonel William Cody. You may have heard of him as Buffalo Bill.'

My body sank into my suit. Was my summary dismissal by Jolly Rodgers the previous evening nothing but a rehearsal for a total public humiliation now?

'Well, I am pleased to tell you that he is coming to Hull with his Wild West Show and, as is Colonel Cody's custom, thirty tickets have been set aside for scholars from this orphanage to attend his show!'

My heart leapt but then it sank. Only thirty of us could go to see the show. There was more than four times that number in the orphanage. How could I be certain to be included in that select band?

Chapter 5

Doomsday. That's what it felt like to me.

Time for morning assembly and once more the Master's voice resonated around the rafters in the hall. Funny how it was the Master's spoken voice that achieved this while his singing voice only managed a low rumble. The sound strained through a shirt collar inside a black frock coat. He looked in readiness to attend a funeral. This occasion was to prove more like this for me. All my hopes and dreams were to die with his words.

'Ten children will be selected by Mr Jason from his class and ten by Mr Childs and ten by Mr Rodgers.'

There was no chance of Jolly Rodgers selecting his 'little brown friend' for anything – except more strokes of his cane.

'That's us out of going then,' George muttered under his breath, echoing my thoughts.

'Got to go!' I hissed to myself, shaking my head and gazing at the floor, all the while holding back tears of anger and frustration.

Two grueling hours of arithmetic followed the assembly with Jolly Rodgers seemingly taking every opportunity to bait me. It felt he was doing it even more than usual. He tested my ability with long division several times, well aware that figure work was far from my strongest subject. I worked hard in all my studies knowing the penalties for poor performance but with figures I had a blind spot or maybe it was only because of the way the subject was taught to me. I would be become far more adept with using numbers in my later life. He must have known my desperation to perform well and please him, but we both knew I could never do that no matter how hard I tried. The cat was playing with the mouse: taunting me, wanting me to trip up in front of the class. Humiliation was his favourite form of torture. The use of physical violence only came into play when he lost patience - a commodity which he had in limited supply at the best of times.

'Got to go!' I repeated in the playground during our short playtime.

'Perhaps, Mrs G could put in a word for us with the Master.' George was clutching at straws and he knew it. I shook my head and slowly we kicked our heels around the yard.

Sunshine bounced off the flagstones, not a cloud in the sky; birds sang. Joining in with their joyous chorus was a whistling drayman driving past in the street on a cart laden with wooden barrels. For me it was the depths of darkest winter.

Mr Jason was on yard duty again, patrolling to keep a check that mayhem did not rule. He walked in our direction.

'Well, boys. You'll be looking forward to going to see Buffalo Bill.' He smiled at us.

'Don't think we'll be going', sir.' I didn't look up preferring to examine the scuffed toes of my boots. 'Unless you pick us to be in your ten pupils, sir.' Now it was my turn to clutch at straws.

'Won't Mr Rodgers be picking you?' He looked mystified by my apparent dejection.

'I don't think so, sir.' I shook my head and went back to appraising my toecaps.

'We're not exactly his favourites, sir.' George gave a shrug.

'That's a pity, boys.' His lips tightened, and the smile disappeared. A hand went into his jacket pocket and pulled out a folded sheet of newspaper.

'I thought that you might want to see this.' He held out the paper. 'The Master said he was finished with it.'

I accepted the offering with a mumbled 'thank you, sir.' I unfolded the newspaper but before I could say more to him raucous shouting at the other end of the yard returned Mr Jason's attention to his policing duties.

The crumpled sheet was a page from the *Eastern Morning News*. I stared at a large advertisement for 'Buffalo Bill's Wild West' and a tear blobbed onto the paper. A day ago, this information would have been the answer to all my prayers but now it felt more like coarse salt rubbing into a very sore wound.

'Steady on, Sammy.' George's arm went around my shoulder. 'It's not the end of the world.'

But it felt like the end of mine.

***

Nothing ever interfered with George's appetite. My inability to do little more than nibble at a dinnertime favourite, meat and potato pie was his gain. He tried to cheer me up but he fought a losing battle. Anyone else would have left me to my misery but he refused to give up. He needed reinforcements and, once again, we found ourselves sitting on the kitchen doorstep to await their arrival.

Sal joined us. I was squeezed between the Smith twins. Arms twined around my shoulders as though coming from a twin-headed ginger octopus.

'There's no consoling him, Sal.' A dispirited George sounded exhausted from his prior efforts.

'But there's got to be some't we can do!' Sal's attitude was always more positive than her brother's. 'Maybe we could buy tickets.'

'What with?' I muttered, speaking for the first time. The twins scoured the newsprint, which they held out in front of me, but I didn't want to look at it again. My eyes remained downcast.

'Costs a shilling to get in!' George pointed to the advertisement. 'Might as well be a hundred pounds!'

'Look there.' Now Sal's finger pointed at the page.

George peered at the spot on the printed sheet where he thought his sister's finger pointed. 'What? *Important Notice – Wanted Fifty Rullies.*' He read out the wording of an advertisement printed beside the one for the show inserted by a business in need of fifty horse-drawn carts.

'No, underneath that, you ninny!'

I looked up and saw what she meant. I read out the headline '*Buffalo Bill's Show – Wanted Fifty Lads To Sell Programmes*'.'

'That's it!' Sal said. 'Knew there'd have to be an answer. Get yerselves down there. Bet they let them lads in to see the show for nowt.'

'What? Twag off?' George said, seeming astounded by what his law-abiding sister appeared to be suggesting.

'I feel hungry.' My face broke into a smile for the first time since morning assembly.

***

Friday, the fourth of May 1888: the day of the grand arrival in Hull of Buffalo Bill's Wild West Show. It was a day for everyone in the home to be seen in public in the best possible light. The policy of the Hull Seaman's Children's Orphanage was that we children should attend as many public gatherings as possible; all dressed in our smartest Sunday best. The home depended entirely on the generosity of public donations. Being seen in public - well dressed and well behaved – to display to the prosperous of Hull their donations were being well spent in order to encourage them to give the home even more.

Everyone took an early breakfast to stoke up the energy for a four-mile march through the town centre and onward to the Alexandra Dock railway station. Here the local worthies would greet the showmen's arrival on special trains prior to a grand parade through Hull's streets. We orphanage children needed to arrive early to find a prominent position, so everyone would be aware of our presence. We would be on view just as much as Colonel William Cody's entourage.

'Look at them bai'ns!' People in the streets smiled, seeing us in our smart uniforms trooping in double file along the pavement. The girls were dressed in long, dark blue coats over matching frocks that came down to their ankles. Their hair was tucked tidily into tam o'shanter bonnets of the same colour. The orphanage wanted to obtain the good opinion of everybody in the town but more than this it needed their money.

The teachers placed themselves at strategic points along our ranks to make sure everyone kept up the pace in good order and allow no one to slip away. At our head was the Master wearing his bowler hat and carrying a rolled black umbrella. A red faced Jolly Rodgers strutted at the tail end with his chest stuck out like a proud cockerel presiding over his flock of hens.

For us 'United States cavalrymen' it wasn't a long journey. We were accustomed to such long expeditions after Jolly Rodgers' forays out into the countryside, but the smaller children were not built of such stern stuff. The procession of children had almost doubled in length by the time we reached our destination. I could hear muttered complaints behind us, usually followed by Jolly Rodgers' strident demands for silence. Many pairs of Sunday best shoes were still in need of breaking in. Marching on the lumpy dockside cobblestones at the end of our trek did nothing to soothe sore feet.

A single storey grey brick building could hardly be called a railway station. In no way could it compare with the mighty cathedral of Paragon Station in the town centre built by the disgraced *Railway King*, Mr George Hudson. Surely it had to be the biggest building in the world or so I thought back then.

In front of the station buildings were two empty rows of comfortable chairs anticipating the arrival of their occupants, but they were not meant for us. I ached to sit on one of them. As to how my weaker brethren felt, I could only guess. These seats were destined to rest the posteriors of local dignitaries after their arduous carriage journeys from either the Town Hall or offices in the High Street. They would be travelling the whole of a mile and would "need" the comfort of these seats. We children would have to continue standing for a good while longer. It was going to be some time yet before anything actually happened. Patience wore thin and sore feet became fidgety feet. One child felt the full force of Rodgers' wrath for daring to sit on the ground. A cold wind from the River Humber whistled around our legs. Even in the height of summer the people of Hull could depend on a sharp breeze coursing into the town's streets off the estuary and it wasn't going to be the height of summer for months yet.

People from the town gathered around us. A select few dressed smartly: beneath warm overcoats gentlemen wore dark suits and top hats and ladies wore colourful dresses Sal could only dream about. They wanted to be seen by those occupying the reserved seats, but more than that they wanted to be seen close to them.

The majority of the milling throng consisted of people like those with whom I'd shared my old back street life. Too many faces were etched permanently with sadness when today should have been a happy occasion. Women looked old beyond their years, wrapped up tight in dark knitted shawls with threadbare woollen skirts trailing along the floor. Waiting children, dirty-faced and without shoes or coats shivered in the cold, or from hunger. Probably both. I remembered being one of them. Few men from the labouring classes were present. Today was a working day and earning money to put bread on the family table was more important than taking time off to observe these wonders from a different world. The few men in attendance all looked identical in their flat caps and dirty mufflers with worn faces hidden from the world behind drooping moustaches or beards. Even the best dressed among the common people wore patched clothing. The clothes of the others looked more like ragged jigsaws with pieces missing.

I craned my neck to look into the crowd. Maybe there would be familiar faces. Would Grandmother and Mary be here? For all I knew they might no longer be in Hull or still be alive, for that matter. How was I to know? Who would bother to tell me?

'Look at them!' George distracted my attention from scanning the faces in the crowd, to the arriving dignitaries. 'Look as though they need carriages… the size of their bellies! Poor horses having to drag all that heavy weight around!'

Surely Buffalo Bill and his Wild West Show couldn't be far behind. I fixed my gaze on the station buildings and strained my ears to get the first sound of the loud hissing and rattling noises of a steam engine's arrival.

'Where are they?' My cold feet shuffled and stamped with impatience at the absence of my hero and his clan.

'They arrived last night.' Mr Jason's voice interrupted my agitation. 'Well, the first train did. The others arrived in the early hours of the morning. The Red Indians and cowboys are staying in the Emigrant Shed.'

The teacher's fund of knowledge amazed me.

'I spoke to one of the men from the station yard.' He nodded sagely. 'He said that Colonel Cody and some of the others stayed in hotels in town last night.'

Buffalo Bill had been in Hull for several hours and no one had told me. Before I could explode my attention was distracted once again.

'Here comes Colonel Cody now!' Mr Jason shouted, pointing away from the station and back in the direction of the town centre.

Snorting loudly, two coal black horses strutted over the cobbles pulling an open carriage in our direction. Hot breath steamed from their nostrils and out into the cold morning air like the release of condensation from an overheated locomotive. Well, this is how I remember it. Buffalo Bill stood up. He smiled and waved his yellow Stetson hat toward the crowd. Long fair locks flowed down onto the shoulders of a tan buckskin jacket. I couldn't see his face. His large hat blocked my view until his hand dropped to his waist and revealed handsome features that a golden goatee beard could only enhance and not disguise.

He was everything I imagined he would be... and more... and he was real.

'He's just like you said he was, Sammy!' Sal jumped up and down, almost as excited as myself.

'He is an' all!' George's bottom jaw hung down in disbelief.

The carriage drew to a halt alongside the dignitaries. In one bound my hero leapt to the ground, still waving his hat to the cheering crowd. The Mayor of Hull stepped forward. His black silk top hat offered no competition for a yellow Stetson. The polished gold chain of office strung across a frock coat gleamed in the sunlight. He shook hands with our famed visitor. Surely the most famous man in the world. At least, as famous as Queen Victoria. Other passengers may have alighted from the carriage before it disappeared back towards the town centre. I didn't notice. My eyes remained transfixed on one person.

Everything became a dream. William Cody floated on air. A cowboy in an enormous sombrero and hairy chaps led a horse to him. I swear the animal was so pure in colour it shone silver in the sunlight. In one easy movement the centre of my attention swung into the saddle to the accompaniment of the tumultuous applause of everyone around him and us.

'You all right?' George's hand grabbed my shoulder.

I turned and looked into his eyes. Sal's arm tugged around my waist. Momentarily, I returned to reality.

'Aye!' I shook my head in an attempt to clear it. Tears began to ebb in my eyes.

'Thought you was gonna faint,' Sal shouted above the loud noise of the crowd's cheers.

'He's real, Sal! He's real!' My words became a squeal and tears of joy blobbed from my eyes.

'Look over there!' George's shout caught our attention and our eyes followed his pointing finger. More mounted figures appeared from behind the station buildings. They'd been there all the time and we didn't know.

Hull could never have seen anything of such brilliance before. Cowboys in bright coloured shirts and bandannas led the way, waving hats or lassos to greet the crowd. Behind them came hairy brown animals, the like of which Hull had never seen before, snorting heavily as they lumbered across the cobbles escorted by more riders to keep them in order.

'They stink!' Sal pulled a handkerchief from her coat sleeve to cover her nose and mouth.

'They're buffaloes!' I wanted to show off my knowledge, although I discovered later they were actually bison but no one contradicted me. No one knew more than me. 'Ones that he ain't shot!'

The wind was knocked completely from my sails before I could expound further. Following behind the animals came the Native Americans. Buckskinned braves sat on horseback with their squaws and children trailing on foot after them. They looked proud and fierce, but this wasn't what caught my breath.

I looked at my hands then back at the figures in the parade. The Indians were not really red. They were brown. Just like me. We were all the same colour.

Then came another shock. At the front of the tribe rode their leader, mounted on a frisky brown and white Palomino pony. His fluttering headdress was a cascade of eagle feathers, flowing from his head down his back to the rump of his steed. Beneath this bonnet was a bronze face, streaked with black, white and yellow war paint.

I recognised the face. I was certain.

'It's me father!' I screamed but my words disappeared in the noisy tumult surrounding me. 'Father! Father!'

The leader on horseback couldn't hear me and continued looking straight ahead, aloof from everything and everyone around him.

'What's up?' George must have seen me shaking.

'It's him!' I continued screaming. 'Me father! Said he'd got to America! Didn't I?'

'That's Red Shirt.' Mr Jason interrupted my exclamations, although he couldn't have heard what I'd shouted. 'He's the chief of the Sioux tribe.'

'It's me father!' I yelled in his face.

He smiled until he saw I was serious.

'I don't think so, Sammy.' His firm hand fell on my shoulder. 'Maybe he only looks like him?'

I wanted to run out into the middle of the parade, but firm hands clasped my shoulders.

'Is there a problem, Mr Jason?' Jolly Rodgers' sharp accent cut through the noise like the blade of a cutlass.

'No, Mr Rodgers.' There was a smile in Mr Jason's voice. 'The children are just getting very excited.' His hands gripped my shoulders even more tightly and I bit my lip.

The tail end of the parade disappeared into the distance on its way to the Holderness Road football ground where the next day's show would take place. Barefoot urchins ran after the mounted figures. How I longed to be one of them again, but Mr Jason's firm hand kept a tight hold of my shoulder.

'It's me father, sir!' Tears streamed down my cheeks. 'He was shipwrecked in America. He's come back for me! I knew he would.'

The teacher smiled benignly but before he could reply, another voice chirped in.

'Tellin' one of yer stories again, black boy?' It was Snelgrave's sarcastic voice. 'Don't listen to him, sir. He's always tellin' tales.'

George lunged at the interrupter, but Mr Jason's free arm wrapped itself around his chest. Sal managed to grab one of her brother's arms, too.

'What's going on here?' Mr Rodgers could always be depended upon to be around whenever we were in trouble.

'Nothing, Mr Rodgers. Everyone's getting overexcited.'

'Time we were getting back to the home. Mrs Grainger will have one of her special stews waiting for us.' It was the Master's voice. 'Let us get back into our classes. Double file!'

'It *was* me father, sir.' I looked up plaintively towards Mr Jason. 'Look at me skin. It's the same colour, sir.' For the first time in my life I wanted someone to see I was different... but the same as someone else. Someone special.

'Everybody in line!' Jolly Rodgers demanded loudly and everyone obeyed dutifully.

Chapter 6

'Not seen nowt like it!' George sat perched on his favourite seat – the kitchen doorstep. 'Them horses was wonderful. Specially that one that Buffalo Bill was on. Better than them old nags in Hull.'

Our late dinner was over and most of my stew found its way inside George's stomach adding to his own double portion. I was too agitated to think about eating.

'But it was me father.' I stamped hard on the yard floor. I was too animated with frustration to sit down.

'When did you last see your father?' The ever-sensible Sal echoed the words inscribed beneath a painting hanging on the wall of the main hall. It showed a young prince under interrogation by his Roundhead captors. I felt as much a prisoner as the boy in the painting.

I joined George sitting on the step but paused before answering. I tried hard to remember when it was.

'Not sure.' I scrunched up my lips and thought even harder. 'It was before I came here.'

'Course it was, daft 'apeth!' George playfully swatted my head. 'You wouldn't be in here otherwise!'

'You've bin here nearly two years.' The ever-sensible Sal again.

'Suppose it could've been a year afore that.'

'So, it could be three years since you last saw him.' She nodded firmly. 'It's that long since I last saw me Mam before she died and there's times when I can't remember what her face was like. It's only when I dream that I can see it really clearly.'

Did Sal have dreams? The thought never crossed my mind but surely even her dreams must have been sensible. I still did not want to agree.

'I reckon that he's the first brown man you've ever seen since yer father went away.' Even George sounded logical for once. 'An' he won't really brown. He was red – a Red Indian!'

I knew what they said made sense, but I didn't want it to make sense. I remained certain as to the true identity of the leader of the Sioux in the parade.

***

There were lots of sleepy heads in the classroom that afternoon. The long trek down to Alexandra Dock and back again, not to mention the fresh River Humber air, all took their toll. We waited to be told who had been lucky enough to be selected to attend the show. I maintained my best behaviour, even though I knew there was really no point and when the end of the school day came I got the reward I expected.

At last, Jolly Rodgers announced his selection. He gloated in my direction; I swear he did. The class had waited all afternoon to hear his choice, but he left informing us until the last possible moment in the school day. It was deliberate. Just another way to torment us… and me, in particular.

'First Mary Hardcastle…'

Slowly, after announcing each one, he chalked each pupil's name on the blackboard. It made the process drag out even longer. Oh, how he must have enjoyed the torture he put us all through.

'Selina Smith.'

It pleased me to hear Sal's name being called out. If anyone deserved to go to the show, she did. The names continued to be called and chalked up, but none came as a surprise until the very last one.

'And finally, Master Snelgrave will be the tenth pupil in the group.' His words cut right through me with the force of a Sioux tomahawk.

Snelgrave had done nothing to deserve inclusion. Even if he didn't pick George or me, Snelgrave had to be the least deserving person in the whole orphanage, let alone in our class. His selection must have been intended to hurt me even more than simply excluding me, I was sure of it. Rodgers knew the boy to be my worst enemy and just how much Snelgrave loved to taunt me.

'The rest of you will report to Mrs Grainger tomorrow lunchtime. There are lots of cleaning jobs around the home that need to be done.'

He pulled his pocket watch from in his waistcoat and checked it. It was well past four o'clock. He must have known the time intuitively anyway. We all did.

'Class dismissed!'

The only pleasant surprise of the whole afternoon was that Jolly Rodgers didn't stay behind long enough to enjoy the sight of most of us trooping dejectedly from the room. Snelgrave made a point of smirking in our direction but from a safe distance.

***

'I'll ask Jolly if you can go instead of me.' Sal looked determined as we walked together into the yard.

'No, Sal!' I touched her arm. 'It'll do no good. He might stop you going… out of spite for daring to ask.'

'He's right,' George chimed in. 'We'll do what we decided to do an' go down there to sell programmes.'

I nodded in agreement.

'I'd better go an' help Mrs G with getting supper ready.' Sal left us in the yard to plot our escape the next morning.

***

Our early arrival for breakfast must have taken Mrs G by surprise. George and I were renowned for our tardiness in the mornings, especially at weekends. We were determined to have a good tuck in, not knowing when we would eat again.

'Better not eat too much,' I whispered to George, scoffing his second bowl of near solid porridge. 'We'll not be able to walk!'

I looked up from my half-eaten second helping and noticed Sal gesturing from behind the serving table. She wanted us to go to her.

'What's Sal up to?' George asked.

'You stay here, George. I'll go an' see what she wants.'

I walked across to her, bowl in hand and pretended to ask for another refill of soggy oats. She maintained the pretence by ladling tiny extra amounts into my bowl.

'You two'll be needing some't to eat later.' she whispered, conscious of Mrs G standing only a few feet away. 'Get round to the kitchen door. There's a little parcel inside wrapped in some newspaper. Some bread and a bit of cheese.'

My mouth opened but the index finger pressed across her closed lips stopped me expressing thanks.

'Get round there quick afore the cat gets it!'

I went back to our table with little more porridge in my bowl than before and hurriedly told George what she'd said. We gobbled up the last of our food, washing it down with sweet tea before sidling out of the room in the direction of the kitchen door.

George tucked the small parcel into his jacket and we scurried back to our dormitory. Being early for breakfast meant everyone else remained downstairs in the dining room. This left the dormitory empty for us to make our preparations.

I threw open the sea chest at the foot of our bed. Hidden inside were clothes "borrowed" from the sewing room the previous night. These were things new children brought with them but no longer required once they had been kitted out with their uniforms. We were the ones in need of them now. Our normal navy blue attire would make us too conspicuous. Fortunately, in the last two years I'd grown to a more normal size for my age and clothes to fit me were available. George proved more of a problem because he was big for his age and few new children were as old as us. He kept on his white shirt and blue corduroy trousers as there were no substitutes available in his size. A grey tweed jacket with patched elbows - two sizes too small - had to suffice as his disguise. I found a thick grey-flecked Shetland jumper and a pair of brown trousers.

The most dangerous part of our route was getting out of the orphanage building. It was the wrong time of day for children to be allowed outside. Anyone on the premises spotting us in our change of clothing would know immediately we were up to no good. I prayed everyone else still remained safely eating breakfast.

Going down the staircase to the bare entrance hall provided the most frightening part of our escape. If anyone saw us here, there was nowhere to hide, nothing to duck behind. Our luck held out until we reached the foot of the stairs. The outer door handle turned with a loud clunk. George grabbed me, and we fell backwards. The door to the under stairs cupboard wasn't closed properly and we tumbled into the darkness.

I scrambled clumsily onto my knees and gently pushed the door behind us until it almost closed. *Almost* because shutting it completely might have made a noise. It left a chink through which we could see who it was crossing the hall.

Through this narrow gap I could see Jolly Rodgers marching in the direction of the Master's study. How I prayed this would be the last time I'd ever see him. I'd find father with the Wild West Show and he'd take me away from the orphanage forever. The thought of never seeing George or Sal again didn't cross my mind.

My tormentor stopped for a moment and turned his head. He must know we were there. Had he noticed the open cupboard door? Sweat trickled down my neck and I held my breath. I imagined George's freckled face turning crimson in the darkness.

Jolly Rodgers turned his head again as though he'd thought about something he'd forgotten but then he continued walking in his original direction. The click of a door closing told us we could breathe again. In an instant we were back out into the hall and through the same outer door Jolly Rodgers had used to enter and through into the yard. The air outside felt fresh as it coursed into excited lungs.

We ran as fast as we could to the wooden gate leading to the freedom of the street. It was locked.

We could have tried to escape through the garden at the back of the orphanage, but I knew the gate there was usually locked. Our only other possible route took us back through the house and the chance of bumping into Jolly Rodgers. There was only one other choice.

'Over the wall!' George half whispered. 'I'll give you a leg up!' He knew I was useless at climbing.

His hands made a stirrup for my foot, nearly throwing me over the wall. I still dangled on the other side when he went past me dropping to the pavement.

'Come on!' He grabbed my legs and hauled me down to the ground. 'You'd be no good up in the rigging!' The rigging of a sailing ship was the last place I ever intended to be. The only ships sailing across the American west were called prairie schooners and they were the covered wagons of emigrants heading for a better life.

'What you two been doin'?' a voice croaked from behind us. 'Thievin'?'

The oldest man I'd ever seen in my life waved a knotty walking stick in our direction. He propped himself up with his other hand using the orphanage's brick wall for support. Shaggy white hair dangled from beneath a shapeless black cloth cap down over an unshaven face as white as chalk. His body was hidden inside a voluminous, dark patched overcoat that looked as old as the man himself.

'Stealin' from orphans! Should be ashamed of yerselves!'

The stick wafted closer to us but we didn't stop to explain and ran off in the direction of the Spring Bank road, leaving the old man wheezing accusations towards us.

'That was a shock!' I gasped. We turned the street corner and merged into the milling folk on the main road's crowded pavement.

'It'd have been more of a shock if we'd jumped over a second later!' George laughed. 'We'd a jumped on top of that old geezer!'

The town centre was the destination of the majority of people we walked along with. Although there were shops on Spring Bank, it was Saturday, the day the people of Hull went 'in town' to the open market to do their shopping. It was still early in the morning and most people would be at work until midday. Then the real invasion of the town centre would begin... once workers received their week's pay.

'D'you know the way to Holderness Road?' George asked. We darted in between pedestrians walking too slowly for us.

'Thought you did.' My head turned anxiously in his direction.

'Wish Sal was here. She'd know. All I know is it's on t'other side of town.'

This was all I knew too but as to exactly where Holderness Road was to be found – well, I was no more certain than George.

A brainwave. 'Trams must go there. Let's follow the tramlines!' I said.

'Aye!' My partner in crime could provide no better suggestion.

And follow the tramlines we did until we came to the Savile Street terminus of the horse drawn service from the Botanic railway station to the town centre.

'Now what do we do?' George scratched his head and looked across the road.

We stood at the junction of Savile Street with Dock Street. Across the street from where we stood we could see ships tied up to the quayside of Queen's Dock bobbing up and down in the water creating a gently swaying forest of masts.

'Well, I don't think we take a ship!' I gave him a playful shove. 'Better ask somebody.'

But we didn't need to. The answer to our puzzlement appeared in the shape of a horse drawn tram trundling up the street from the direction of Monument Bridge. On its front the words 'Holderness Road' were written on a board mounted between the upper and lower decks above the driver's head. The vehicle turned right from Savile Street into the next road and we trailed behind it.

'Look!' I gave my friend a nudge and pointed to the nameplate attached to the side of a pub on the corner of this next street: George Street. 'They've named a street after you!'

'Give over!' he replied not noticing the street we were walking into. His attention focused on two brown mares hauling the tramcar. 'When I'm working with horses I want it to be with ones like them the cowboys have. These horses look old an' sad.'

'You'd look sad pulling a tram round Hull all day!' I gave him another nudge, which made him stumble off the kerb edge and into the gutter.

We continued following the tramcar rolling along in the shadows cast by George Street's tall buildings. In turn this thoroughfare became Charlotte Street and the tram made its way towards the bridge crossing the river from which Hull took its name.

'What a stink!' George slapped his hand across his mouth and nose. I caught the strong sewer stench too and followed suit

We neared the North Bridge over the River Hull. The narrow river also served as the main sewer for the homes and industry clinging to its banks. I looked over the side of the bridge and noticed the absence of water. The tide was out. Keelboats and barges that fed the riverside oil mills and factories lay stranded like beached whales on slimy banks of brown mud, waiting for the incoming swell of dirty water from the Humber estuary to bring them back to life.

Crossing to the river's other bank made no difference to the foul smells. We followed the tramcar along a street called Witham. Here the reek of overcrowded humanity living in tight courts with overflowing outside privies mingled with the acrid fumes of oil mills and hot blacksmiths' shops.

'Glad we don't live round here.' George mumbled from behind a hand holding a grey handkerchief that had once been white.

'Let's get a move on.' I'd had enough of the stink. 'Let's follow the tracks. This tram's moving too slow.'

We gave up on caution and ran along the pavement ahead of the tram. Not many yards later we saw the words 'Holderness Road' written in white lettering on a row of black tiles half way up a house front. Gradually the stench subsided and a more palatable sooty smell from house chimneys filled the air. We'd moved into an area of newer terraced houses with less obvious signs of industry. In between groups of buildings were open fields. They waited to be built upon as the town sprawled out further into the surrounding countryside.

'It is on Holderness Road, ain't it?' George looked worried.

'Course it is!' I was less certain of the show's location than my words suggested but when we saw a crowd milling ahead of us our uncertainty disappeared. On the corner of Buckingham Street a rag tag army of boys filled the pavement, spilling out onto the main road. Passing cart drivers shouted at them to get out of the way.

'There's no point waiting, boys!' a brown suited man in a bowler hat shouted to the throng. 'We've got all the boys we need to sell programmes.' The accent was strange to my ears; it was one I'd never heard before.

Boys' heads dropped dejectedly but none slumped further than mine.

'Is that it?' George's face mirrored my disbelief.

'Can't give up now!' I was determined despite being engulfed in the centre of a youthful swarm drifting back in the direction of the town centre. 'Come on!' I urged, and we swam against the tide of unsuccessful would-be programme sellers.

The football ground lay a few yards back from the main road with its entrance squeezed in between houses and a chapel. Burly men stood in front of newly erected fences decorated with bright posters advertising the show. The men's task was to dissuade any obvious non-paying intruders like ourselves from trying to enter. I wanted to linger to look at the artwork, especially the depictions of my hero. We moved away quickly as one of the men moved in our direction.

'There's got to be another way in!' I wasn't going to be discouraged that easily.

Chapter 7

'So how are we gonna get in?' George kicked a loose stone across Holderness Road. It bounced three times before rattling into the gutter on the other side.

'We've got to circle the camp and look for a weakness in its defences. That's what Buffalo Bill would do.' I wasn't certain what my hero would actually do, but I thought my scheme had the right sound.

'Aye, but it's Buffalo Bill we're wanting to attack. Won't he have thought of that?' I sensed my ally might be developing cold feet.

I shrugged my shoulders. How I wished Sal was with us, if only to give her unusually pessimistic brother some encouragement.

'Come on! Let's find a way in.' I tried to sound authoritative.

The back ends of the houses in Buckingham Street ran alongside the football ground. Perhaps we could find a promising "weakness" from where to make our attack.

Everything in this street looked new. House bricks still wore a bright untarnished red. Mind, the houses were still packed as tightly together as those in Hull's older areas. The street was built in the same continuous terrace style as most of the town. Narrow dark courtyards ran off at right angles to the main street, each one made up of rows of houses standing face to face. In this way landlords could cram more houses onto a piece of land and more houses meant more income for them as long as their tenants could afford to pay the rents. If they couldn't make the payments unlucky families were out on the street with the little they owned.

White sheets that looked like flags of surrender flapped from washing lines strung between house fronts in the courts. Happy barefoot children playing chase games beneath the fluttering linen reminded me of someone I used to be.

'There's a school over there.' George pointed to a large building to our right. 'Maybe we can get in through the playground.'

The gothic style Board school dwarfed the surrounding houses. Thin perpendicular windows stretched almost up to its slate roof. It looked more like a church than a school. A red brick temple of learning? Well, maybe. The words *gothic* and *perpendicular* came from the Master. Once I overheard him conducting some benefactors around the orphanage and he used those words to describe our home.

'Don't fancy trying to get over them railings. Do you?' Now I was the one who sounded defeatist. The tall vertical metal spiked rails cemented into the top of the outer schoolyard walls were not an inviting proposition. Ordinary brick walls posed a big enough problem for me. 'Bet there's a big wall to get over at the back an' all.'

We continued our hunt down the street, trying to discover a tempting 'weakness' but all we saw were ordinary Hull people living their lives; the kind fate had denied to us. Screaming young children played a game of tag around us, spilling in and out of the street's courts like waves onto a beach. Little girls skipped along the flagstone pavement, careful to avoid tripping themselves up with their hairy skipping ropes. A ragged-trousered boy ran past, using a stick to bowl a bent metal hoop along the bumpy road.

Mothers shrieked even louder than their children. We heard 'Wait 'til your father gets home!' more than once. A returned father was something I hoped to meet as soon as we broke into the camp. Adult males were absent from the scene, apart from a second-hand clothes' hawker pushing his handcart over the street's wooden sets. He rang a hand bell and bawled out unintelligible words to announce both his presence in the street and a readiness to trade.

Both the courts to our right, Harold's Avenue and Drewton Terrace ended in high brick walls, which separated them from the football ground beyond. Dark muddy passageways at the rear of the courts' houses also reached the same forbidding brick and mortar conclusion. At the end of the street I learned one of life's simple lessons: if you reach an insurmountable obstacle then the best thing to do is to try to go around it. Buckingham Street's housing ended at a two-bar wooden fence separating the street from an open field. A sagging cart-horse tied to a stake in the ground chomped on what looked like mainly weeds. We managed to scramble through the fence's horizontal bars without difficulty.

A turn to the right took us along a path, really no more than a muddy groove worn into the clay soil by years of feet and hooves. It ran beside the high wall of the street's final building. A powerful ammonia reek of urine wafted from the other side of the yard wall. We both grimaced at this all too familiar smell. Its strength told us that animals, probably horses must be stabled in there. Once past we could breathe more freely. From our new vantage point we were able to look into the next field to see the football ground's shed covers at its rear in the distance. More importantly, we could see people, corralled animals and tents. The entire cast and crew of Buffalo Bill's Wild West Show were encamped there, waiting for when it was time to put on their show.

Chains of grey smoke drifted upwards from open campfires into the clear blue sky. Sitting around them were noisy show people drinking from steaming mugs and smoking cigarettes. The clattering noise of pots and plates came from inside large striped marquees. The tantalising aroma of frying bacon wafted in our direction. There is something special about this smell; it is guaranteed to give me an instant appetite. An age had passed since we crammed salty porridge into our bellies. I don't know which of our stomachs rumbled the loudest.

'Fancy that stuff Sal gave us?' I whispered, even though there was little chance of anyone hearing. The nearest members of the show squatted over a hundred yards away from us.

'Rather have some of that bacon!' George's words echoed my desire, but we made do with consuming squashed hunks of bread and cheese while we hid behind a thick bush considering our next move

'What do we do now?' George swallowed the last of his food, but the smell of frying bacon still tempted him more than the song of a siren. 'I'm still hungry.'

'We've got to get in and find me father. Get everything sorted out. Follow me.' I tried to sound assured, but this show of bravado was as much for my benefit as his. I brushed breadcrumbs from my 'borrowed' trousers and stood up.

We crept along the side of a high brick wall, the one that had appeared so impregnable from its other side back in Drewton Terrace.

The assembled performers were too busy to notice two small figures slipping into their campsite.

For once luck was on our side. We slipped into the section of the camp nearest to the wall, which was occupied by the Native Americans and their tethered ponies. This was where I wanted to be. This was where father must be. The tribesmen squatted around a crackling wood fire, speaking incomprehensibly. Most smoked cigarettes. Something never mentioned in my novel. They should have been smoking peace pipes.

I crept along the wall almost on all fours. I tried to look through the legs of the ponies, desperate to spot my father. A quick glance behind told me I was alone. George had disappeared.

What to do? I was torn. Continue my search alone or track back and find him?

I scrambled back and discovered my friend stroking one of the ponies and talking to it. This hypnotic state didn't last for long. Before I could get to him two braves covered in menacing full war paint leapt out of nowhere and grabbed him. George struggled and screamed with terror, trying to break free but his large captors proved even too strong for him. They dragged him off in the direction of their campfire.

Sidling carefully in between the ponies I tried to stay as close as possible to my friend but what could I do: a twelve year old boy against a whole Sioux war party? Where was Buffalo Bill? He would come to George's rescue. That was what he did and always in the nick of time.

All the other fierce looking warriors squatting around the fire took to their feet. They surrounded George, trying to get a closer look at their captive. One of the braves slipped his hand into George's red hair and ruffled it. He gave an admiring look and spoke to his companions before laughing loudly. He intended scalping George. Of this, I was certain. The red hair would make a fine trophy.

I leapt into the midst of the group and shoved away the would-be merciless barber. He was not going to take a ginger scalp today. The surprised brave leapt wildly in the air narrowly avoiding falling into the blazing campfire.

'Let him go you varmints!' This word appeared in my novel. Buffalo Bill always called his enemies 'varmints'. My fists rose like a boxer waiting for the start bell.

Surrounding us stood a band of fierce warriors in full war paint. Surely some of them must have taken part in the massacre of General Custer and the Seventh Cavalry but I was intent on defending my best friend even if it were to be our last stand. He'd protected me so many times before. All other thoughts were gone from my mind.

'What do we do now, Sammy?' George shook with fear, almost in tears. This time the threat was too much even for his bulldog courage.

Loud guffaws of laughter came from the assembled group of warriors as though in mocking reply before their final assault. I didn't know such fierce tribesmen could laugh. Were they only taunting us?

One member of the group stepped forward. Empty palms rose trying to show he intended us no harm. A broad smile beamed from beneath the war paint. His head turned quizzically to one side and he looked directly at me. 'You are not white man. Why you here?'

'I've come for me father.' My words made no sense to him and, at the time, they didn't make a whole lot of sense to me either.

'Father?' The warrior looked bemused.

Before he could ask further questions a tall figure in full war paint arrived amongst the group. A war bonnet of flowing eagle feathers made him look even taller.

'Father!' It was my turn to repeat the word. It was Red Shirt.

The chief spoke words that made no sense to me, but his manner told me he must have been questioning his braves about our intrusion because all the while he pointed at us.

I examined Red Shirt closely. Was he my father? Father looked so tall the last time I saw him, but I was much smaller then. I tried to see behind bright streaks of white, red and yellow grease desperate to recognise the face beneath.

'Is it yer father?' George whispered, squeezing closer to me.

'No,' I muttered, my head dropping to my chest. The red men could kill me now, if they wanted to. I didn't care anymore. All my hopes sank, right down to the depths of the Atlantic where my father's ship must have finished up.

The chief spoke to us in an unintelligible tongue. It only brought forth blank looks of incomprehension from us.

'Red Shirt want to know what band you from?' The warrior who spoke in broken English translated his leader's words while looking directly at me.

'Sailors' Orphanage!' George spoke on my behalf. Some of his courage had returned.

'No, you!' The warrior pressed a forefinger onto my forehead.

'Like he said... Sailors' Orphanage!' I realised my fists were still raised and I lowered them slightly. I posed no threat to anyone present.

The translator shook his head and muttered more strange words to Red Shirt who also shook his head and shrugged his shoulders.

'Not know *say-lass ore-fanage.*' The go-between turned back to face me. 'Why you here? You... like us!'

'Always thought I was,' I whispered to George before speaking up. 'I'm looking for me father.'

A lot more muttering and shaking of heads took place between the members of the war band.

'What's happening, Sammy?' George looked bewildered.

'Dunno.' I didn't understand the situation any better than he did.

Amidst all the strange gabbling I made out the words 'John Nelson.' Lots of nodding took place among the group and I heard the repeating of that name and also the words 'Cha-Sha-Cha-Opeoyeo.' Later I learned these words meant 'Red Willow Fill The Pipe,' which was the Lakota Sioux name given to this John Nelson. I learned later it had something to do with him smoking tobacco in a pipe.

One of the braves ran off in the direction of the food marquees. The others remained and continued to inspect us. Were young boys such a novelty for them? Surely not, I saw some of their sons during the grand parade.

'Are they cannibals?' George continued to tremble with fear. 'Looks like they're sizing us up for dinner!'

'No. They only eat buffalo meat.' I wanted to reassure my friend, although all I really knew about the Sioux tribe was what I'd read in my dime novel.

'We send for John Nelson. He speak our tongue.' The warrior with a few words of English spoke again.

We waited, hoping that standing back to back would give us extra protection. The tribesmen slowly circled us, just as I thought they would when attacking a wagon train of settlers on its way across the Great Plains. Well, this is what my novel said they always did. Occasionally, a warrior would prod one of us inquisitively. One snatched a strand of hair from George's head and rushed back into the group to display his strange booty. All the time Red Shirt remained in the background, watching with arms folded and aloof from his warriors' strange antics.

The tribesman who had rushed away returned with a white man. He had the bushiest brown beard I'd ever seen. It grew all the way up his face until it merged into a crumpled sombrero. Out of this thick bush stared a pair of doleful eyes separated by the bridge of a long, weather beaten, red nose. It all gave him the appearance of a sad old hound.

'What have we here?' The words drawled out in a much thicker and slower version of the strange accent we'd heard from the man on Holderness Road who announced that our services selling programmes would not be required.

Red Shirt turned and spoke to the newcomer. To my surprise the old hound seemed to understand what the head warrior said to him. To my greater amazement he replied in what at that time had the sound of the same weird heathen tongue.

'The chief wants to know what you young fellers is doin' here.' Several teeth were missing from the sad hound's mouth. The few remaining ones were stained deep brown from years of tobacco, chewed as well as smoked.

'He specially wants to know what a young injun is doing in this place.' Gnarled fingers struggled to escape from the ends of buckskin sleeves too long for his arms. They managed to break free and came to rest on his hips. He waited for our reply.

I coughed to clear my throat before going into my life story. Mercifully my life so far was a short one but I brought it up to date by telling them about my mistake, thinking Red Shirt was my father and how I was certain he must still be alive in America.

Periodically Nelson stopped me speaking and turned to the chief to translate instalments of my tale. Well, I guessed this was what he was doing. The chief nodded along with him until I heard the word 'orphanage' in among all the Sioux words. Red Shirt put out a hand to stop our interpreter in mid flow. He tried repeating the word back to him. I could see a look of incomprehension in his eyes as he said it.

'The chief ain't heard of no orphanages.' The American gave us a lopsided grin before attempting to explain the meaning of an orphanage to all the tribesmen. Their bewilderment didn't seem to be clarified in any way by Nelson's attempted explanation.

Again, the chief raised his right hand, palm forward to arrest the American in mid-sentence. Red Shirt's few staccato words and grim expression indicated even to me that he was not happy with what he was being told.

The interpreter turned back to us and gave another broken toothed grin. 'The chief reckons you boys have been put in a prison. That's the closest he understands to be an orphanage. He wants to know what you've done wrong to anger the great white queen.'

Nelson went back into conversation with Red Shirt and his band. It led to much shaking of heads and mumbling among the warriors.

'They ain't happy.' John Nelson stated what looked obvious, even to two naïve young boys. ''Cos a child has lost its folks don't mean it should be locked away. Well, not among Lakota Sioux anyhows. They'd join another family and be brung up as their young uns.'

Broken teeth appeared again, and he gave a chesty cough before laughing. 'And we calls 'em savages!'

There was heated conversation. Frequently, John Nelson gave his head a vigorous shake and broke into English. The exasperated words 'No, chief! You can't do that!' were heard more than once before being translated.

After a great deal of deliberation, the old American hound dog turned back to us. 'I reckons you boys could do with some vittles.'

We nodded in agreement. Sal's bread and cheese was long forgotten.

'How's about some bacon and beans… washed down with some real American coffee?'

He must have seen us licking our lips at his suggestion. He slipped in between the warriors and us. All the while he continued talking and gesticulating to our captors. 'Follow me, boys,' he said.

We offered no resistance to being led in the direction of the delicious warm smells wafting from the food marquees. We left Red Shirt and his men still deep in their deliberations. The tempting odour of sizzling pork meat completely overwhelmed us. Through the marquee entrance we could see long trestle tables and benches at which sat American and Mexican cowboys eating and talking together. I half expected to see a Wild West version of Mrs G. serving up food but to my surprise we were in an all-male domain. All thoughts of the orphanage and the Sioux warriors disappeared immediately and I was in a buffalo hunters' camp out on the trail.

'What was the chief asking?' George's senses remained firmly in Hull.

John Nelson hustled us towards moustachioed men in check shirts and white aprons ladling food from huge iron pans. These cooking pots were even larger than the ones used by Mrs G.

'Said he wants to speak to "Grand Mother England." That's what he calls your Queen Victoria. 'Bout settin' you lads free,' Nelson said to us before giving a nod to a man who looked to be in charge of this empire of wild western nourishment. The head victualler was as broad as he was tall, and he wore the loudest red and white check shirt I'd ever seen.

'Give these young uns a real cowboy meal.' Nelson half turned his head towards us. 'The chief met her royal majesty when we was down in London.'

Somehow, I didn't think he was telling us everything Red Shirt said to him, but the heavy thump of two blue enamel plates landing on the serving table distracted my attention. Mountains of steaming baked beans sat heaped on top of greasy rashers of bacon while enormous gleaming brown sausages stuck out from the mounds of food like naval cannon. On top of it all fried eggs perched like saucy French berets.

'Do you drink coffee, boys?' Nelson asked.

We nodded our assent to the question, although neither of us had ever tasted this beverage before. We weren't going to turn down the opportunity to sample the thing that all real western American men drank.

'Sit yourselves down, boys and eat up.'

I didn't notice John Nelson leaving us. We sat engrossed in observing the company in which we found ourselves; not to mention, of course, tucking into the mountains of food on our plates. Less than half my food was eaten and already my stomach felt the strain. I needed a respite, so I tried the coffee. I took a mouthful and immediately spit the hot liquid back into the enamel mug. I'd never tasted anything so foul before.

'Too much sugar?' George said, surprised by my action.

I shook my head, unable to speak. My mouth still tingled. Finally, I managed a single sound. 'Ugh!' These American men must be real men to drink this witch's brew.

Gingerly George took a sip from his mug. His reaction was the same as mine.

Further down the table unshaven faces beneath tipped back Stetsons and sombreros laughed at our sudden revulsion. How did they manage to drink hot coffee without any problem? I wasn't sure whether I envied or pitied them.

Our feast was interrupted by the arrival of the Sioux warrior who spoke a smattering of English.

'Come with me! Come now!' War paint could not hide a look of anxiety.

A heap of uneaten food remained on my plate and surprisingly even George had a substantial hill of beans left uneaten. It went against the grain to let food go to waste but we both admitted defeat in our battle with the sheer scale of Wild West cuisine. We lowered ourselves slowly from our bench seats and followed the warrior.

'What's up?' I asked.

The brave gave me a look of incomprehension.

'Why do you want us to come with you?' A less colloquial expression proved more understandable for him.

'Come. Red Shirt take care of you. Come!' He became more insistent and he led us out of the marquee, back in the direction of his campfire. A young female member now stood among them. She looked about our age.

Once we were back among the Sioux, they formed a circle around us again, but their posture told me this was a protective formation rather than one of attack. I would learn circles play an important part in Native American culture. It has ritual significance because it is the sacred circle that sustains life and ensures harmony.

The girl stood in the centre with Red Shirt.

'I am Laughing Waters.' She spoke English clearly, although with the same novel accent as the American men. Her appearance was striking. Her skin was a dark bronze but her delicate features were unlike those of the harsh faced warriors. Coal black hair in a long braid hung down her back to the waist of a tan buckskin dress.

'I have been to missionary school and speak the language of the American. Red Shirt wants me to give his words to you.'

'I thought that Mr Nelson...' She cut me short.

'Cha-Sha-Cha-Opeyeo told the chief that you must be returned to the orphanage. He said this is what the great white queen would want.' She nodded seriously. 'But Red Shirt has met the great white queen and says that she is wise. She has many children. She would not want to punish children because they have no family.'

George and I nodded in agreement and continued listening. Her words were melodic. George gave me a nudge with his elbow, which made me aware my mouth hung open. I shut it again quickly.

'Red Shirt says that you may join the great family of the Lakota and grow to become great warriors.' She interpreted his words with the chief nodding firmly behind her. 'You have shown great courage today.'

'Well!' Amazement reduced me to muttering. I came to seek my father but now I was offered not only a new family but also a whole tribe... and so was George.

'What do you think?' I turned to my friend. It was his turn to let his mouth hang wide open now, but it was open in disbelief.

'Dunno.' George went deep into thought, which for him was an unusual place to go.

The tribesmen eyed us with anticipation.

'It'd be a great adventure. Touring round with the show. In America!' I wanted desperately to win him over to the idea. 'No more Jolly Rodgers! We'd be free!' It all seemed so simple to me.

'What about Sal? Can't leave her.' His head dropped. The pull of what remained of his family was strong. 'We ain't even seen the show!'

My friend – my best friend in the whole world – was not persuaded. All I could foresee ahead of us were great adventures and an end to my torment. No more Rodgers, Snelgrave and all the others.

'Come on, George.' His reticence was making my decision difficult.

George turned and burst through the wall of startled braves to run back in the direction we'd used to enter the camp. I wanted to run after him – to bring him back – but I didn't want my new friends to think I was running away from them. I shouted after him to come back but the ginger head didn't turn. This was the last I saw of my best friend for many years.

'You will stay?' The girl's coal black eyes enquired more than her words.

'I will stay!' But at that moment I was far from certain I was making the right decision.

Chapter 8

The girl led me away from the braves to join the women and children who were camped around their own more domestic fires. Only warriors shared the glow of Red Shirt's campfire.

This was the start of a new life, but my feelings were not at all like the ones I remembered on that first day in the orphanage. It was just as much a step into the unknown, maybe even more so, but this situation differed in one major respect. It was my decision. For the first time in my life it wasn't someone else telling me what to do. If I'd known back then how big a change this was going to be maybe I'd have run off with George back to the home. Looking back, I'm glad I didn't chase after him, although I was to miss the Smith twins desperately for a long time afterwards.

Even before I saw the Sioux families I could smell them. The strong aroma reminded me of times in Grandmother's house when the breeze blew from the direction of the smoke houses in Hull where herrings were turned into kippers. On those days this heavy scent engulfed everything in our street and far beyond. It didn't take me long to become oblivious to my new companions' smell because it soon became mine too. Seeing the Sioux children playing took me back to my street urchin days when I ran around barefoot, but these children all wore moccasins. The women's simple clothes were made from animal skins, like all of the garments, but contrasted sharply with their men folk's peacock plumage used in the show. My first impression was how poor they all looked but, like so many first impressions, it was wrong. The poverty I thought I saw on that occasion was restricted to looking at material things. In spirit they were the richest people I would ever meet.

I learned the tribe's true name to be Lakota, and that they were a band, not a tribe. 'Lakota' means friends or allies while the word Sioux means little snake or enemy and was a name assigned to them by others, usually their enemies. I soon learned that Lakota was a far more accurate description of these most generous of people.

'You will be my brother.' The girl smiled for the first time, displaying brilliant white teeth. Her warmth made me feel more relaxed but then her demeanour became almost bashful. 'What is your name?' she added, prodding me with her forefinger.

I'd been invited to join her band, to become her brother, yet no one had bothered to ask my name. For the Lakota what happened to me now was simply a matter of course involving no fuss or formalities. I was a child with no family, someone who belonged to no one. All of this was normal for an orphan in their culture.

'Sammy... Sammy Smyle,' I replied.

'No! No! You must have a new name. A Lakota name.' She smiled the widest smile in the world and I knew at once how much I was going to enjoy my new sister's company. For a moment I wondered what had happened to Mary, my real sister. She was brown too, although not as dark as me as I recalled.

'But first you will need new clothes. John Nelson will come looking for you. If you change into Lakota clothes, you will be invisible. He will think you ran away with your friend.'

Once again, a new life meant a change of wardrobe. Would the Sioux have their own Moshe Silver on hand to provide my new clothes?

We stood in the midst of the families. Intrigued eyes carefully examined the new arrival. On some faces I saw suspicion. Here was a boy who looked as though he might be one of them, but he was dressed in English clothes, with blue eyes, and shorn of his mane of black hair.

My new sister made an announcement to the throng. I guessed it must have been Red Shirt's decision she gave them. Immediately, children and squaws surrounded me, all wanting an even closer look at their newfound relative.

'They all want to know why a native of the Great Plains is lost in England.' The sharp poking and prodding I got amused her. One of the children tried to nip a chunk from of my arm.

'Ger off!' I yelled. I'd felt in less danger when the warriors took me prisoner. Laughing Waters just giggled at my predicament.

A woman intervened and shooed the others away. Her manner and the deference shown to her by the others told me she must be a senior squaw. She looked like an older version of Laughing Waters but most of the women would look like Laughing Waters to me for some time to come, although none could be as pretty as my new sister.

'Are you my mother?' I asked.

The woman returned a look of incomprehension.

'Yes, she is your new mother, but she does not know it yet!' My sister still found the situation amusing.

I began to have second thoughts about my decision. Maybe Red Shirt believed I had the makings of a warrior, but I wasn't so sure. In my imagination I'd always been on the side of his sworn enemies anyway. I could still follow George back to the orphanage, if I really wanted to. It wasn't too late. The real world of Hull was only a matter of yards away.

Laughing Waters chattered with her mother and the others. They used words I wasn't going to understand for a long while, but my new mother's attention wasn't on her daughter as they conversed. She was smiling at me. No one had smiled at me in this way for a long time, not even Mrs G. It made me want to cry but I held back the tears. If I were to become a Lakota warrior I would have to start behaving like one.

'Our mother is called Yellow Flower.'

'Do I have a father... and brothers and sisters?' I wanted to know all about my new family.

'Our father is called Dog That Stands.' I felt disappointed not to be the son of Red Shirt himself. 'And you have two more sisters. Red Shirt thinks our family needs a son!'

The others sidled back to their places around blazing log fires. Laughing Waters continued speaking to *our* mother who in turn continued smiling at me. I felt embarrassed. I was unaccustomed to prolonged signs of affection. After receiving this information our mother went back into the crowd where she began shouting what appeared to be instructions to the others.

'Mother is getting some new clothes for you to wear.'

'Where from?'

The Lakota had no wagons or tents on the site and there was definitely no sign of a potential Mr Silver. I knew their temporary home in the Emigrant Shed lay miles away on the dockside.

My inquisitiveness made her laugh. 'Someone else is wearing them.'

'Someone else?' Should I feel appalled by what she said?

'Things do not belong to people. People are what belong. We belong to our land and we belong to each other.' Again, miles of perfect white teeth gleamed. 'You are with your people now. Our world is different from the white man's world.'

As someone who owned nothing in the world but an old dime novel, adapting to this new philosophy wasn't going to be difficult. In a matter of a few minutes my life had turned upside down. The colour of my skin had always singled me out as different but here it made me the same. Now I felt part of and no longer different from. I felt acceptance.

Yellow Flower returned with a bundle of garments, which she held out to me. She tried to say things to me. I took the clothes from her but shook my head to signify my lack of understanding.

'Mother wants you to get changed quickly.'

'Where?' I looked around but there was no obvious place to hide myself and get changed.

'You are thinking like a white man!' Her expression made it clear I was going to be a constant source of both bemusement and amusement. She grabbed my free hand and dragged me in the direction of the tethered ponies.

'Go there.' She pointed to the animals. 'The ponies will not care what you look like without your britches on!'

Swapping clothes among a shuffling herd of animals felt sillier than getting changed in the middle of the crowd of people. It would certainly have been more comfortable. The animals paid me no heed, pushing and shoving me with their rear ends. I pirouetted from one foot to the other trying to remove my pants and replace them with buckskin leggings.

Re-emerging from the herd I couldn't help but notice the smell of my new garb. It wasn't too dissimilar from that of the animals I'd just been among. I soon learned that access to laundry facilities was not a central concern of a travelling show. The orphanage's carbolic smell was left far behind.

'You look like one of us now!' It would be some time before I could look into a mirror and be able to verify Laughing Waters' statement. 'But you need to let your hair grow longer.'

She pulled free the red ribbon tying her tightly braided hair, and tied it around my head to disguise my offending lack of hair. She gave a warm smile and a nod that said *'That will do for now!'*

Eager hands grabbed my 'white man's' clothes from me. I didn't object. They weren't mine anyway. The garments disappeared into the crowd to be dispersed among the children. From time to time I saw familiar items, but worn by someone else.

Before I had time to wonder what would happen next, the general hubbub of the camp was interrupted by the sound in the distance of a band striking up a tune.

'The show will start soon.' My sister nodded vigorously.

'Can I see it?' My begging seemed to perplex her.

'See it? We are in the show!' Her words nearly knocked me over.

'There'll be people in the audience who'll know me.' Terror grabbed me and tied my stomach in knots. Would a manic Jolly Rodgers leap out from the crowd waving his cane and haul me back to where I really belonged?

'They only know Sammy Smyle... the orphan. You are Lakota now. That is all they will see!'

I lacked her confidence. Jolly Rodgers had all-seeing evil eyes.

***

Mercifully our contribution to the show was to come late in the performance. Laughing Waters led me to a private spot where we could see all the other acts taking place in the arena without getting in the way. It meant peeping through a gap in the continuous fence of wooden boards separating the performers from their excited audience. Our viewing place was close to the gate where the entertainers were to enter and leave the arena. Her running commentary described the show better than one of the programmes I'd intended selling only a few hours earlier but what was to really impress me on that day and afterwards was the massive effort behind the scenes to speed everyone in and out of the performance area. This was something even those in the most expensive seats could not see or appreciate. My real business education began here.

The most amazing sight of all was the audience. The number of people watching the show dwarfed even the masses I'd seen the day before waiting at the dock station. I'd never seen so many people in one place at one time and they'd all paid to be there - except for a small group of orphans, of course. My surprise wasn't confined to the sheer number of people. What made me stare open mouthed was to see all of them smiling, waiting in eager anticipation of their entertainment to come. Seeing so many Hull people looking happy at one time felt just as unexpected and unreal to me as seeing the Lakota braves laughing and smoking cigarettes.

The band fell silent and the crowd hushed to hear what I thought had to be the loudest voice in the world. It filled the entire amphitheatre. Laughing Waters told me this extraordinary man was Mr Frank Richmond and he was known as 'The Orator.' His task in the show was to keep the audience informed about what was happening. I craned my neck, trying to see the source of the loud words but my line of sight was obscured. How Jolly Rodgers and the Master, sitting somewhere out in the audience, must be envying this man's booming volume.

He announced that Mr Levy, the cornet player, would play 'The Star-Spangled Banner.' A rumble like thunder filled the auditorium as the crowd got to its feet to honour what they believed must be the national anthem of their American visitors. It wasn't until many years later that the United States Congress adopted it officially, thanks largely to one William Cody championing this tune in every performance of the show around the world.

When the music ended the Orator made the announcement everyone wanted to hear. 'Ladies and gentlemen, Buffalo Bill and Nate Salsbury proudly present America's National Entertainment... the one and only... genuine and authentic... unique and original... Wild West!'

The band struck up again. The full mounted company swept past us in a cloud of dust and a rainbow of colour erupted in the arena. I could only see part of what was happening. The riders galloped around and around, all the time whooping and screaming out what I thought were war cries. Never before had I seen such brilliant colours and I doubted whether anyone else in my grey hometown had either. There were Indian braves - my new people - in their war bonnets with faces smeared in brilliant multi-hued war paint... Mexicans in wide brimmed sombreros that offered the audience no shade from the brightness of their silk and velvet clothes... laughing cowgirls in jackets and hats in colours so vivid they shouted life to all who saw them... and the cowboys in large Stetsons and leather chaps with their double-fronted shirts wrapped in tinted sashes.

The crowd roared its appreciation. An unbelievable spectacle but the best... the very best was yet to come. The whole mounted cast wheeled around and around until a lone figure dressed in a tan buckskin suit and mounted on a shimmering white horse cantered into the centre of the stadium. This was the man everyone had come to see: the hero of my dreams.

I felt my eyes moisten and I quickly rubbed them with a rough buckskin sleeve.

The rest of the company stopped its circling and joined their leader to form a tight bunch at the centre of the arena. Without warning the whole entourage broke free to race at full speed towards a terrified audience.

The galloping horde stopped short as though a single brake was applied to each one simultaneously before they careered into what now looked like a very flimsy protecting fence surrounding the performance area. The crowd gasped. I exhaled with relief too. All hats, sombreros and war bonnets rose in salute before being waved at their patrons. The audience went wild with delight as a cloud of perspiration and heavy breathing rose into the cool night air above the arena.

The Wild West Show had begun.

A huge magic carpet transported the dour townsfolk of Hull on a journey, thousands of miles away, to the brilliance and warmth of an irresistible continent. Here in the north of England exciting stories would unfold before amazed eyes.

Every event in my real father's novel came to life in a tableau more spectacular and noisier than I could ever have imagined. Again, the arena flooded with vivid hues – mainly red and orange, this time – and the mounted horsemen of my new people took centre stage. Leading out the warriors was Red Shirt in his headdress of eagle feathers that shimmered in the arc lamps' bright yellow artificial light. His war bonnet became a flowing stream of living colour. Seconds later Buffalo Bill and his white stallion, Old Charlie, returned and joined them to an explosion of even greater rapturous applause.

How excited George would have been to see the performers' magnificent mounts in action. The next section of the show would have especially delighted him: horse races, featuring proud animals galloping up and down the arena. They snorted like angry dragons about to breathe fire. Nothing like the saggy backed workhorses plodding around the streets of Hull. These fiery animals would have been the real stars of the show for him. Although parted for only a few hours I missed him and Sal terribly. I wanted them to be with me, enjoying everything I was enjoying.

The horse races gave way to an exhibition of sharp shooting by a girl Laughing Waters called 'Young California' - and *young* she certainly looked. I guessed she couldn't be more than a couple of years older than me. She ran into the arena, the fringed leather trimmings on her buckskin jacket and skirt rippling in the bright light. For her first trick glass balls were thrown into the air only to be disintegrated in flight by her rapid rifle fire. She went on to perform many more extraordinary tricks with her gun. I discovered later Annie Oakley should have appeared in Hull too but there'd been a disagreement with Colonel Cody and she had left the show's British tour.

'This is called Cowboy Fun,' Laughing Waters said as the scene changed. Cowboys performed tricks at high speed and nearly all of them on horseback. Galloping horsemen hung down from their saddles with arms outstretched to pick up items from the ground. Wild horses were allowed to run free before being lassoed by cowboys. Then to the amazement of the audience the captors of the untamed animals jumped aboard these unruly mounts. Somehow the brave riders managed to stay aboard the bucking broncos making the ecstatic crowd cheer and applaud wildly.

The spectacle was mesmerising. I lost all track of time, forgetting I was to be part of the event too. Even the arrival of John Nelson at the reins of the Deadwood Stage couldn't bring me back to reality. A mounted band of fierce warriors whooped loudly, chasing in the dust of the stagecoach around the arena. Just when all seemed lost for the travellers a group of cowboys led by my hero came to the rescue. During this event I felt uncertainty as to where my true loyalties lay now. Did they remain with the man I'd worshipped for so long in my imagination or did they now rest with the Native Americans?

This part of the performance concluded, and I felt a tug on the fringes edging my buckskin sleeve. It was reality in the shape of Laughing Waters grabbing me. I was back in Hull again and somewhere out there in the audience sat a real villain: Jolly Rodgers. Had I been missed yet? Would he be looking for me?

'Us soon. Come!'

She led me back to join the squaws and children who were waiting to enter the arena.

After a display of bareback racing by some of the younger braves, the Orator announced there would be an exhibition entitled the 'Life Customs of the Indians.' It would be as much an education for me as for anyone in the crowd and I was taking part in it!

The whole band: men, women and children marched into the arena, carrying everything required to erect an overnight camp on the prairie. To my continued amazement I discovered this construction task was women's work: erecting long poles, covering them with canvas and skins in order to create tepees. The men folk remained separate from what they saw as only a domestic chore. I tried to look busy without getting in anyone's way. Fortunately, it took just a few minutes to erect a whole camp and I blended in as best I could with my new family group. Then we stood by watching as the men took centre stage. They demonstrated a fierce war dance accompanied by a tom-tom and strange chanting from fellow warriors.

My jaw dropped, and I stared in disbelief at what happened next. Fearsome braves dragged a yelling cowboy prisoner into the middle of the encampment where one of the warriors waited with a huge sharp knife to perform a scalping. Women in the audience screamed in fright. Would my gawping expression be spotted and attract the unwanted attention of a certain someone in the crowd?

'Only pretend!' my sister whispered in my ear. The 'scalped' victim was in reality as bald as the eagles that flew over the Rockies and the 'bloodthirsty savage' waved only a toupee in the direction of the disbelieving populace of Hull.

Even faster than it was erected the camp was dismantled and the whole band disappeared behind the scenes to give way once more to Buffalo Bill astride Old Charlie ready to give his solo performance of sharp shooting on horseback.

It wasn't until I was safely out of public view I realised I'd been so engrossed with what happened under the lights I'd forgotten to seek out familiar faces in the audience. Sal was there with others from the orphanage. Did she notice the latest addition to the Lakota? Would she even know to look out for me? What had happened to George? But Jolly Rodgers hadn't leapt out of the audience to grab me... I breathed freely again. Maybe it was the presence my new allies that daunted someone who I came to recognise as a coward and a bully.

Laughing Waters and I weren't able to return to our previous vantage point until after the end of Buffalo Bill's display of marksmanship. This episode was far from the last of his involvement in the show. Buffalo Bill Cody *was* the show.

Even before the applause for his act could subside the crowd gasped in amazement again. Right in front of them burst a herd of wild bison running loose in the arena. The sight of a domesticated cow was a novelty for many of these town dwellers. Seconds later Bill returned with a group of braves. They galloped after the bison, firing blank cartridges as part of a simulated buffalo hunt.

The hunters singled out one animal and steered it away from the herd. Frank Richmond announced to the audience that at this point in a real hunt the animal would be shot dead. The great herds of hundreds of thousands of bison had almost disappeared from the North American prairies thanks to overhunting which had left only a handful of much smaller groups in inexistence. These luckier bison would live to see another day. The performers herded the steaming animals out of the arena and back to the safety of their corrals.

The final act of the show was yet another confrontation between the old and new inhabitants of the West. An attack on a lone scout by a marauding band of tribesmen was broken up by the intervention of a group of stalwart rescuers led, of course, by Buffalo Bill Cody. After the successful completion of the rescue the cowboy band struck up once again. All the 'dead' warriors came back to life and ran away from the scene, ready to fight again in future performances.

'Grand finale, Sammy!' Laughing Waters tugged my sleeve again.

'What?' I didn't have a clue as to what a *finale* was – grand or otherwise.

'It is the end. We all go to take a bow. The crowd applauds us.' She sounded insistent.

The rest of the cast lined up ready to go back into the arena for one last time, each in order to receive their deserved adulation, but I felt I didn't deserve anything. I was just as much a spectator as anyone sitting in the audience. I wanted to be out there cheering and clapping along with the rest of the locals and especially my friends. I wanted to tell them that everything I had bored them with for years was all true.

I froze. Fear made me resist joining them. Had George by now returned to the orphanage and been forced to tell where I was? That couldn't have happened, I told myself. There wasn't enough time for him to get back. He would probably have lost his way without me but what if he'd met the party from the orphanage on its way to the show? George wouldn't have told on me, I knew he wouldn't but...

'Come! You are one of us now!' I swear she could read my thoughts.

Should I stay and become part of this wonderful world or go back to face Jolly Rodgers and the leering Snelgrave? They would never believe I had been part of the show. Should I join with these people who welcomed me so readily as one of their own or go back to being an unwanted alien in the orphanage?

The decision was mine. It was time to become a man and leave little Sammy Smyle behind in Hull. I followed Laughing Waters and joined the rest of my new band. We marched into the arena and into the blinding glare of arc lamps. A would-be Lakota warrior stood proud as part of the parade and took the applause of the people of Hull rather than the usual uncomprehending stares they gave every time they set eyes on me. There wasn't a single recognisable face – the audience was a pink blur. I kept praying no one could identify me. Mind, I placed myself in the middle of the group, hidden among those taller than myself. The safest place to hide is in the middle of a crowd.

The whole cast came to halt in the centre of the arena and each one removed hat, sombrero or war bonnet before placing hand on heart. The familiar strains of *God Save the Queen* drifted into the evening sky and the entire audience: every man, woman and child rose to its feet as one. The final notes sounded from the band and the company bowed towards the adoring crowd, which remained standing to give a seemingly unending ovation of stamping, cheering and clapping.

The atmosphere was electric. This was a new word to most people back then, but *electric* is the only word I can use to describe how it felt that first time. It still does with every performance. This magical feeling made me realise I'd made the right choice. My stage fright departed. Now I was stage struck.

The lights dimmed, and the performers slipped away from the football field fantasy. The crowd dispersed into the night, to return to the dull reality of a northern English town and away from the unforgettable experience that is the Wild West.

Chapter 9

Later I was to learn that it was the Wild West Show's custom to make its camp alongside the site where the performance took place, but this was not the case on that first visit to Hull. For one thing there wasn't enough space around the football ground but mainly it was because the stay was all too brief. Some of the performers like Buffalo Bill himself stayed the night before in hotels in the town. The cowboys and *my people* (this is how I came to think of them) lodged in the Emigrant Shed beside the dock.

We waited after the show, by the dying embers of our fires outside the stadium, until the multitude had cleared away. As I noticed earlier the skins of the so-called *Red Indians* weren't that colour at all but a shade of brown much like my own. However, in the glow of a campfire every face took on a bronze hue. The braves removed their war paint, not wanting to frighten any townspeople when we made our way through the streets to the Alexandra Dock and the ship returning the whole troupe to the United States. Although removing the paint made them look the same as other men, it didn't take away the pride they held in both themselves and their people.

Open flat bottom wagons appeared, and we clambered aboard them. Perhaps these were the 'fifty rullies wanted' mentioned in the newspaper advertisement George had noticed. It would take that many to transport the whole entourage of the show. I squeezed in between Laughing Waters and Yellow Flower. Two smaller girls spread themselves across our legs, letting their coal black braids dangle around my ankles like tentacles.

'Your new sisters.' Laughing Waters gave a resigned smile.

It was difficult to avoid yawning. It didn't come from disinterest; I was tired. Dog tired as the cowboys would say. I'd really done nothing, but I was still exhausted. There were such tales I wanted to tell George back in our double bed – but I wasn't going to be sleeping with him there that night or ever again.

My hiding place aboard the wagon couldn't have been better if I'd made it deliberately but this wasn't why my new family created it for me. They snuggled together both in affection for one another and to keep warm. Fierce warriors jogging alongside the wagons on their war ponies made me feel even more secure. Only a short time before, I saw them as captors, as sworn enemies but now they were my family and my protectors.

The wagons rattled over the wooden sets in the street floor, clunking and jolting each time they traversed a set of metal tramlines but I was oblivious to everything and fell into a deep sleep. I missed my last chance to see the streets of Hull but I didn't care. Even the masses of locals standing on the pavement cheering us on our way could not disturb me.

***

'Wake up!' Laughing Waters shook me back to consciousness. 'Wake up! We have to go onto the ship.'

I was confused. Native Americans didn't have ships. They used birch bark canoes. I didn't have a clue as to what birch bark might be but my precious novel said this and so it had to be true. The fathers of my fellow orphans had sailed in ships, not very safe ones – that's how all we children became orphans. My real father had a ship but he had lost it or it had lost him. I was still half asleep and confused.

'What ship?' I forced myself up on one elbow.

She smiled again. No one could be better named. I thought of Sal who seldom smiled and was so serious. So different but I came to love them both.

'It is called the *Persian Monarch*. It is taking us home.'

'Home?' What did this word mean? I'd lived in a *home* but it wasn't my home, not anyone's real home. I shook my head trying to drive out sleep from bleary eyes.

'Yes, back to the land the white man calls the United States of America. We will go back to the Dakotas. That is our real home.'

A throng of people jostled around our wagon, all carrying their belongings from out of the huge brick cavern that was the Emigrant

Shed and across the quayside. Everything took on a yellow hue in the gaslights apart from the greasy greyness of the wet dockside cobblestones.

I didn't quite understand why this place should be called the Emigrant Shed as it was normally reserved for people coming into Hull from all over Europe. Maybe it was because the usual migrants who used it were not going to remain in Hull or even in England for very long. Most weren't given the opportunity to stay. They soon continued on their way to the New World, usually to escape from their old homelands and the persecution they endured there because they were different. I knew how it felt to be different. Often it was because their religions or races were not acceptable in the countries they'd been forced to leave. Jews, Mormons and a whole range of other sects came through here on the way to a new and better life. I was on that same quest.

'I'm hungry.' My stomach suddenly rumbled. I'd not eaten anything since attacking the mountain of food John Nelson organised for George and me in the show's marquee.

'Food later. Come with me.' Laughing Waters offered a firm hand to haul me up. She was much stronger than she looked. Lakota women had to be.

She led me into the shed. I felt aware of being followed. I turned abruptly to see two miniature versions of Laughing Waters scurrying into hiding like two frightened mice behind a large wooden barrel. My sister barked an order and the pair re-emerged, pouting with chins dropping onto their chests and avoiding eye contact with us.

'These are our sisters. Moon That Shines and Star Petal.' The little ones giggled but still did not dare to raise their eyes and look directly at the face of a strange new family member.

'They want to watch their new brother to see what a boy does.' Laughing Waters sighed and shook her head.

'As long as they don't see everything a boy does!' I smiled and walked towards them. I stretched out my hands towards their heads. I wanted to stroke their thick black hair, but they ran off as though scalded.

'They will come back.' Their big sister sighed again. 'They always do.'

'Do they speak English?' I was desperate to find someone else in my new family with whom I could converse in my own tongue. It would have been unfair to depend on Laughing Waters all the time.

'They know a few words. They were at the mission school like me before we joined Pahaska. That is what we call Colonel Cody... Pahaska. It means *long hair*.'

'Does our father know any English?' I had a new father but had not yet met him or so I thought.

'Yes, you spoke with him.'

So, Dog That Stands was the inquisitive one, but would I recognise him without his war paint? Red Shirt displayed his wisdom in placing me with a family where I could converse with some of its members. So much wisdom and as John Nelson said, 'And we calls 'em savages.'

***

We trooped from the Emigrant Shed and across the quayside's slippery cobblestones. A large bundle of blankets and clothing made mainly from animal skins had been heaped into my arms. All I could see over the top of this bulk was the steaming funnel of a ship that grew larger and larger as we approached. I followed Laughing Waters across a swaying gangplank bridging the gap between quayside and ship, walking above murky water several feet below.

A sailor's son, who had lived in the Sailors' Children's Orphanage and I'd never been on board a real ship before. Surely someone would stop me and ask me to identify myself, to give a legitimate reason for being there but to my relief no such challenge came. I followed my new sister down the narrow stairways taking us below deck. My load felt heavier and heavier the further we walked. Eventually we ended up in a large cabin deep in the bowels of the ship. For a moment I forgot my hunger and flopped onto one of bunks fastened to the cabin wall ready to go back to sleep. My next surprise was seeing my fellow passengers ignoring the bunks altogether and making up their beds on the cabin floor.

The passage of time had become meaningless on this magic day. The performance in the football ground took little more than an hour but the enchantment of the occasion proved too great for me to realise it at the time. I didn't know how long I'd slept in the wagon. The only thing I'd felt for certain on waking was my hunger had returned. It hadn't taken long to realise that. It never did. No problem now in scaling another mountain of beans and sausages or even devouring a whole roasted bison.

Laughing Waters led me out the cabin and back into the strange world of the *Persian Monarch*. The journey to the dining room took us along many identical corridors. Tiredness didn't help my disorientation. I could still have been dreaming. Everything seemed like a dream, for once in my life a very good one.

As a member of the Lakota I would be expected to eat like one of them. Something else among many things I'd have to learn and quickly to avoid attracting attention. Most of the Lakota preferred to take their food out of the dining room and up onto the open deck where they would squat together talking and eating. Only those who had attended mission schools or who wished to be assimilated into the white man's ways remained seated at the tables. They ate with a knife and fork, but it was only a few who did so. Fortunately for me the family of Dog That Stands fell into this category. I could easily have forgotten any of the table manners I'd had drummed into me were it not for them. However, it was not only the usual way of Lakota dining I would have to get used to seeing. It was also what they ate. Each brave seemed to eat enough beef at one sitting to feed an entire orphanage and I don't think any of them had ever heard of greens or potatoes. George would have fitted in very well with them at meal times although a red-haired Lakota would have been spotted very easily on board the *Persian Monarch*.

It proved a wise decision to eat what they ate. I'd become used to a diet of meat, two vegetables and a slab of bread at the orphanage, but if I'd selected this familiar combination or one of the delicious looking puddings on offer it would have attracted attention.

We approached the bearded men in their white jackets serving the food, but before we got to them Laughing Waters turned towards me and put a finger to her lips.

'Say nothing!' she whispered. For someone deemed to be a savage and also a girl, she was smart. A Lakota child speaking English with a Hull accent would have been very noticeable. The accent was something else that needed to change.

During the meal I restricted myself to grunting and nodding in reply to any whispered words from her. My two smaller sisters giggled all the way through the repast and my new family's two older females admonished them frequently. Dog That Stands didn't stay to eat with us but ate with the other warriors up on deck.

While my meal felt unusual, it was filling. I'd never eaten two such enormous meals in one day, not even when Mrs G. produced the opportunity of seconds. Why had George run off? There was so much food, and he was missing out.

We returned to the cabin. The prospect of my bunk felt even more inviting after all the food. I wanted to wrap myself in a blanket and go back to sleep but there would be no rest for a while yet.

'We all go on deck soon. There will be roll call.' Laughing Waters nodded firmly. 'Wrap your blanket around your head. It is cold. Do not worry.'

I was naïve and unaware of the efficiency of the company's organisation. Everyone who should be travelling back to the United States was on a list. Any stowaways discovered on board when the ship arrived at its destination would result in the American authorities fining the captain.

Worry. Why did she say, 'Do not worry'? I began to worry.

My mind filled with visions of being forced to walk the plank like an unwanted passenger in a pirate story. Worse still a large Hull constable might come aboard and accompany me back to the orphanage in handcuffs.

'Do not worry!' She smiled a reassuring smile from beneath the grey woollen blanket wrapped around her head and shoulders like one of the shawls worn by Hull's poor women. She clasped my hand to lead me back up onto the deck but before we left the cabin she stopped and pointed at my feet.

'Take off your boots! Lakota do not wear boots.'

I pulled off the offending footwear to reveal a pair of heavily darned black socks.

'And the socks!'

The deck felt cold and hard on my bare feet.

'We will have to get you moccasins.' Her words made me wonder as to who might still be wearing this footwear. 'But for now, come like that. It is cold. Pull your blanket around you.'

Once I ran barefoot in the streets of Hull, but my feet had become much softer from more than two years of wearing the polished leather orphanage boots. It felt awkward walking up the flights of wooden stairs. Needless to say, the two little ones followed close on our heels. The giggling made me feel even more self-conscious.

When we emerged into the yellow light of deck lanterns Laughing Waters became serious. 'Keep the blanket over your head! They will not see your short hair.' The ribbon band around my head would not stand up to close scrutiny.

I did as I was told and followed her into the midst of the other Lakota on the deck. All stood wrapped in grey blankets like mine. She was right. It was cold. The wind whistled off the river straight into the Alexandra Dock and around my bare feet. The season was supposed to be spring but such seasonal niceties never bothered the elements in the Humber Estuary.

On the quayside I could see groups of local people waiting to get a last glimpse of their exotic visitors. Some yelled imitation war whoops when they saw us congregating on deck. Under the wool blankets we looked anything but warlike.

A crewman carried a yapping dog down the gangplank. Once the sailor reached the quayside the canine stowaway was thrown to the ground and its behind received a swift kick. Some of the onlookers laughed. One or two tried to give the stray an extra kick as it ran away yelping into the night. Would this fate befall me if I were discovered?

At the end of the deck John Nelson stood beside another member of the show's company who held a ledger and a pencil. Alongside them keeping an eye on the proceedings stood one of the ship's officers dressed in a smart navy-blue uniform and peaked cap.

'Are they all on deck?' the scribe asked Nelson who in turn barked out some words in Lakota.

Red Shirt replied from the front of the assembled mass. I guessed he must have said that everyone on board was present.

The bookkeeper waved his pencil in the air and I could see him silently mouthing numbers and counting heads to double check the chief's assertion.

'We're four missing!' the enumerator concluded. His words took me by surprise.

'Better count again, sir.' The heavily bearded ship's officer spoke for the first time.

The crewman repeated the process but the resulting number remained the same. John Nelson spoke to Red Shirt again before returning to the bookkeeper.

'The chief says Black Elk and three other braves have got lost but maybe they'll turn up before we sets sail,' Nelson said.

'They'd better be quick then!' The ship's officer spoke again. 'We sail when the tide's right and we'll not be waiting for any of these filthy natives who have got themselves lost!' He turned and marched down the deck towards the ship's bridge.

John Nelson shouted out some words in Lakota and the assembly turned to return to the warmth below deck.

'I said *do not worry*.' She smiled again.

Something made me pause. Tucked away, almost hidden in a dark corner stood a large object lashed to the deck. It was the Deadwood Stage. Without its team of mighty sweating chargers, it looked sad and forlorn, as though its lifeblood had drained away. I drifted away from the others to get a closer look at this legendary vehicle but the closer I came to it the more depressing it looked. The tied back curtains looked ragged and torn, as was the leatherwork. The rails on the roof were broken and only held together by knotted string. A wire held the cabin door to the frame with the loose hinge left flapping. Everywhere patches of paint failed to hide emergency repairs made to the bodywork. All the romance I'd associated with the vehicle disappeared. An animal in such poor condition would have been put out of its misery.

A hand tugged at my sleeve. Laughing Water jerked her head towards the open hatch through which all the others were disappearing below deck. She wasn't smiling now. When we got back into the throng she spoke.

'Do not draw attention. We have all seen the stagecoach many times before.'

There were so many novelties to see and to understand, so many things I'd read and dreamed about. I wanted to see them all, experience them all, but I would have to learn to be patient.

At last, I could lie on my bunk. All the others – I guess there must have been a dozen more in our cabin – snuggled in their blankets on the floor. They'd probably dream of the homeland to which they would be returning, at long last. Although tired I daren't sleep now. I was certain I'd wake up and find myself in the double bed beside George. It would all have been a wonderful dream.

Sleep defeated me but it didn't last for long. Vibration from below the floor disturbed me. Grey light coming through the small porthole above my bunk began to flicker.

I raised myself to look outside. The dockside seemed to be drifting away from us until I realised it was the ship that was moving. Hull disappeared from my life. It would be a long time before I saw my hometown again.

Chapter 10

A shaft of daylight broke through the darkness in the cabin like a beam from one of the show's arc lamps. In my slumbering mind I was back in my orphanage bed but where were George's cold feet? What lay hidden inside those rippling mounds wrapped in blankets on the floor? One sniff of dank air reminded me where I was. It hadn't been a dream. I scrambled up on my bed keeping the warm bunk blanket wrapped around my shoulders and looked out through the porthole. Beyond a narrow stretch of flat grey water were green fields swathed in bright sunshine. Surely not arrived at America already!

Laughing Waters clambered up from the floor, intrigued to see what was of so much interest to me.

'Are we there yet?' I wanted to be there.

She laughed loudly. 'You have lived too long with white men! They have made you stupid!'

The little ones joined in the laughter. They didn't have a clue as to what amused their big sister, but I soon discovered that to them anything involving me was instantly hysterical.

'It will be many days before we see America. There will be much sea before we reach land again.' Laughing Waters smiled. This son of a merchant seaman knew less about the ocean than a daughter of the Great Plains.

'And you will have the great sickness. All will have the great sickness.' For once her expression looked serious.

'The great sickness?' I was puzzled to hear of this unexpected revelation.

'Yes, everyone had the great sickness when we came to England. Even Pahaska!' She nodded to reinforce this fact.

'Did anyone die?' I felt apprehensive about the prospect of a deadly plague on board ship.

'No... we only want to die! Then the sea was still again, and the great sickness went away.'

'You mean sea sickness!' I laughed but my bravado was based on ignorance. Later I discovered being a sailor's son granted me no immunity from this problem. Even the greatest sailor in British history, Lord Nelson suffered from this malady. This may have been why Black Elk and others chose not to come back to America with us on what he called the 'big fire boat'.

'He said everyone on the ship would get a great sickness and die!' Laughing Waters still did not seem persuaded by what I thought was a simple explanation. The ocean was far from the natural habitat of the Lakota.

'But no one did. Did they?' I wanted further reassurance that my diagnosis was correct. However, at the time her serious manner amused me. I had yet to learn of the great importance of superstition and prophecy in Lakota life.

For a moment the normal sparkle disappeared from her eyes.

'It's a good job they jumped ship then.' My use of this colloquialism puzzled her. I explained further. 'Otherwise there would have been one too many at the roll call.'

She nodded in agreement but remained serious.

'I'm ready to eat.' I tried to change the subject attempting to break the sad spell she'd fallen under. 'We'd better build up our strength – just in case.'

I picked up my boots and sat back on the bunk edge to pull them on. Laughing Waters frowned and shook her head. Fortunately, Yellow Flower came to the rescue holding out a pair of moccasins. I never learned the exact origin of these replacements for my old footwear. Maybe the Lakota equivalent of goblins lay hidden away somewhere deep in the bowels of the ship, endlessly busy with needle and thread. I doubted this as the tough shoes had been worn before. Not a perfect fit – a little too large – but they became more comfortable with thick socks. I was allowed that concession. Some of my new brothers and sisters had weakened and wore them too. She also equipped me with a battered Stetson hat to keep my short hair hidden from sight.

Laughing Waters took me by the hand or maybe I took hers. We did it automatically whenever we ventured out of our cabin. During these early days I seldom dared to move anywhere without her. Anyone who saw us together must have thought we were twins. We looked about the same size and age. Since Mother died I'd not shared such a level of intimacy with anyone - not even with George or Sal.

We wandered down the wood panelled corridors to the dining room. By 'we', I mean all four of us, of course. My twin and I couldn't move an inch without the little ones trailing close behind us like two pet dogs. It wasn't until later that I discovered how great a boon my arrival had proved to Yellow Flower. She felt her daughters were safe in my company, when all the time I thought it was they who were taking care of me. *Hakatakus* was the word she used to describe me. Laughing Waters found this description highly amusing. It wasn't until some time later that I discovered it meant I was a chaperone as well as a guardian.

Learning to appreciate the Christian white man's food was one of the benefits of a mission school education. Not only did it not look strange for Sioux children to have a bowl of porridge for breakfast but also – treat of treats – the Americans didn't flavour their thick oatmeal mash with salt. I was certain Jolly Rodgers deliberately inflicted this heathen Scottish practice on us as a punishment. The Americans liked their porridge topped with maple syrup. They also liked to eat pancakes in the morning, again smothered with this delicious sweetness.

I continued playing my dumb routine, avoiding speaking to anyone and responding to any question with no more than a nod or shake of the head. If a head movement proved to be an insufficient reply for anyone I tried to look stupid and grinned. Whenever the insult 'dumb injun' came my way I felt pleased with the success of my act.

Afterwards we squatted together cross-legged on the bare wooden planks of the cargo deck. Years of feeling hungry all the time made me greedy. Soon I learned the lesson for indulging in this deadly sin the hard way. The slightest swell would make me disgorge everything but today sitting on the deck in the sunshine with a gentle breeze blowing from a calm sea felt like heaven.

Most of the braves and cowboys were on deck already. No bright costumes or war bonnets today. They were meant for the show. Thick cotton shirts, denim jeans and Stetsons were the order of the day and not only for the cowboys. The main pastimes on deck were playing cards and smoking cigarettes. The Native Americans showed a greater appetite for these white sticks than even the cowboys. I discovered whenever the *noble savage* came into contact with European ways, he always received the worst of the exchange.

Despite much friendly banter between these two groups of so-called deadly enemies, they did not play cards together. Later I learned this was the result of neither enmity nor prejudice on the part of the cowboys but because of the Native American's inscrutable expression. The term 'poker face' could have been invented for him. Too many cowboy dollars had been lost to a red man's ability to bluff.

Up on the promenade deck, resting on a lounging chair, sat William Frederick Cody himself. I didn't recognise the group of people surrounding him. From their dress and the sound of their accents most must have also been members of the company, but others mingled within the group, clearly English outsiders dressed in long dark overcoats and sporting what the Americans called derby hats. Each held a notebook and pencil in hand; poised at the ready to note anything they felt worthy of recording. Not wishing to draw attention to myself, I decided to stay as far away from these men as possible.

The day was Sunday – this I knew – but as to the time of day I had no idea and it didn't matter. Gone was the regimentation of my life by the orphanage clock and the call of the hand bell. My old friends might be attending church now, sitting in pews already, or perhaps about to go. It no longer mattered to me – I was free and I intended to remain so. How I wished George and Sal could share the joy of liberty with me.

Being so close to Buffalo Bill was still a novelty and I was startled when my continued view of him was blocked. Laughing Waters stood in the way, hands firmly on her hips.

'We have all seen Pahaska many times. His eyes are keen. He is a great hunter. He will see you looking at him.' As ever her words were wise, just like Sal's.

That my hero could be an enemy didn't enter my thoughts but, as far as the authorities in the United States would be concerned, I was just as much a stowaway as the yelping mutt kicked off the ship back in the Alexandra Dock. Buffalo Bill Cody was the centre of authority for everyone in his company. Surely, he'd put me ashore and back into the orphanage if I were discovered.

'If he find you when we are far from land it will not matter.' Her words reassured me and we got back to the business of being children.

***

Dog That Stands was unflinching in his loyalty to his people and to Ogila-sa, which was the true Lakota name of Red Shirt, but he was also insightful and could see there were great changes coming for all the aboriginal people of America. He wanted to find out about the white man and his ways. This explained why he sent his daughters to the mission school and why he readily accepted me as his new son. However, this wasn't the impression he gave me during my first days with my new family.

After another enormous meal we four relaxed together sitting on my bunk back in the safety of the cabin. The little ones rocked back and forth, their heels tapping on the bed's wooden side. I decided to raise the subject of his attitude towards me with Laughing Waters.

'Why does our father shun me?' It didn't feel comfortable saying *father* and it wouldn't do so for some time to come. 'He does no more than nod at me. Does he not want me?'

'No! No!' Laughing Waters was true to her name once again. The other two joined in the giggling. 'He wants to say much to you... and to hear even more!'

Her reply came as a great surprise. A grown man wanting to listen to me – little Sammy Smyle! Most adults I'd come into contact with expected me to speak only when spoken to and then to say little, usually only 'Yes, sir' or 'No, sir.' Anything beyond this was deemed to be impertinence and deserving of summary punishment.

'He wants to know all about the white man's world, but he is cautious. He would have to use the white man's words to speak with you. The cowboys would think it strange to hear a Lakota man and his son talking together in their language. This is what our mother tells me.' She nodded. The two little ones copied the movement of their sister's head, although I doubted they knew with what they were in agreement.

Thereafter I made a point of smiling when Dog That Stands nodded to acknowledge me and I swear I saw a paternal twinkle in his eye.

Visions play an important role in Lakota life as they do in all Native American cultures. Dog That Stands' vision quest was different from that of other warriors. He could foresee a future that many of our brothers did not desire. I came to realise quickly that my new father was no ignorant savage but a man of great foresight and wisdom.

***

That night I lay on my bunk with emotions in turmoil: simultaneously happy and sad. I was free and living with a proud people who accepted me as an equal, but I missed George and Sal terribly. How could I feel homesick for the orphanage? I drifted off to sleep but it didn't last. The rhythm of the ship's engines changed and I woke again. I'd have gone back to sleep, but I could hear men's voices, sailors' voices calling out in the darkness. After a while the shriek of the ship's steam whistle split the night. It kept repeating its blast at regular intervals.

I scrambled up to the porthole to attempt to discover what was happening, but I couldn't see anything. Was the steam on the thick glass due to condensation coming from the breath of all the sleeping bodies in the cabin? A rub with my sleeve made no difference. Laughing Waters, half asleep, climbed up beside me. Two smaller persons joined us but they'd need years of extra growth to reach the porthole.

'Fog,' I said, realising the cause of all the commotion outside.

'Much fog in London. Much smoke there. Many campfires,' Laughing Waters said.

My new family had been with the show for many months, visiting not only London but Birmingham and Manchester and other places too. I'd never left the town where I was born, except in my imagination.

'Are there many ships making smoke?' She squinted trying to focus through the thick sea mist.

'I hope not!' I refrained from saying more. Living in a town with thousands of smoking chimneys by the River Humber, fog had been part of my life. Many of my orphanage companions told stories about their fathers' ships being lost in collisions or crashing onto rocks in dense fog.

'Nothing to worry about,' I lied. 'Let's get back to sleep.'

We went back to the warmth of our beds but sleep would not return to me. Despite what I'd said, I was worried. My fertile imagination was working overtime. The throb of the engines died away and I felt the ship's movement come to a halt. There was a loud rattling from the ship's anchor chain dropping into the sea. I heard an authoritative voice calling for two lifeboats to be swung out and my fears were aroused even more. The clinking of lifeboat chains being loosened made me shiver. The steam whistle continued blowing at regular intervals but, eventually, tiredness overcame me once more.

When I awoke it was daylight, but only just. The fog was thinning at last. Sailors' voices from the open deck high above our cabin cut through the eerie silence. A grinding noise came from the anchor being weighed and then the sound from down deep in the bowels of the ship changed once more. Everything vibrated. The steam engines throbbed and took us forward. However, the captain wasn't taking any chances. The steam whistle continued to blast without reply from any other vessels. We were alone in this part of the ocean or so I hoped. The unexpected company of other vessels sailing too close could spell danger.

Fog at sea can return as quickly as it can disappear, and it did. The *Persian Monarch* slowed to a halt again.

I needed to escape the cabin's claustrophobia, not to mention the smell of enclosed bodies. I was not used to it. It must have been breakfast time. I wrapped my blanket around myself and nodded to Laughing Waters to follow me.

'Let's go on deck before we eat and see what's going on,' I suggested.

I sensed something was wrong. My troupe obediently followed me.

I was first on the deck, eager to see what was happening. The two lifeboats were still swung out from the ship's side ready to drop into the sea. I felt puzzled. They would not hold all the ship's passengers and crew. Sailors stood positioned around the deck, some even up in the rigging, all keeping a lookout for the sudden appearance of other vessels or any other hidden dangers. Out in the open air the steam whistle became even more shrill and deafening than down below. The Deadwood Stage took on an abandoned ghostly appearance in the swirling mist. While most animals were housed on the lower decks, some of the show's livestock were kept penned on the open deck. In my wild imagination some horses broke free and took hold of the coach, galloping out into the thick mist with a phantom driver at the reins.

For the first time, I felt alone. I was my own. Laughing Waters remained frozen on the stairway down below the open hatch, afraid to follow me up onto the deck. For once there was no sign of the little ones. I wanted to shout to tell her to follow me up on deck, but the forbidden English words choked in my throat and I returned to her

'Wakan Tanka is here!' she said in a hoarse whisper. A terrible fear blazed in her eyes and all colour drained from her cheeks.

'Who?' I thought it was the name of another member of the band I had yet to meet. Was he a bully like Snelgrave?

'Wakan Tanka. The greatest of the sacred ones.'

I could hear the Master's voice, ranting on about 'false gods' and 'graven images.' None of us in the orphanage had any clue as to what 'graven images' might be. All we knew was that they were the work of the Devil.

'This is as Black Elk foretold!' She remained frozen clinging to the handrail.

'Don't be daft!' I hissed back but she wouldn't move from the security of the stairwell. 'I thought you were a Christian!'

'I am – but I am also Lakota!'

This great dichotomy was something I had to learn to live with. The power of the spirit world was to be a major part of my new life and not only for Sundays, like so much of the religion I'd become used to.

I took hold of her shaking hand once more. It was ice cold. I led her back down the stairs and onwards to the dining room, but I was the only one with any appetite.

A couple of hours after the ship had stopped moving the fog disappeared again, only to return worse than ever at around midday, making it feel more like midnight. Late in the afternoon the mist finally evaporated but, although brilliant sunshine bathed the decks, all the Native Americans remained dubious about going outside.

Below decks the temperature became unbearable and beads of perspiration rolled down my face and neck. After much persuasion my sister agreed to venture aloft again but she wasn't happy about doing so. Perhaps she feared the fog would sweep down again without warning and spirit her away. For the first time in my life I really felt like a big brother. Her hand was no longer cold. It was clammy with sweat now. I gripped it tight and hauled her up into the sunshine. No fog spirits would be allowed to take her away – not if I had anything to do with it.

The two of us were on our own. The little ones preferred to keep to the safety of the cabin and their mother. Together we looked silently across calm water toward the high cliffs on the shore of England. This scenery looked radically different from the bland, hill-free land on the Humber's muddy banks where I grew up. The estuary's pancake flatness was how I believed all England to be and why should I believe otherwise? No one told me otherwise. Most people in Hull knew no more than I did unless they were sailors. I wanted to ask someone on deck where we were. What was this large mass of white cliff jutting out into the sea? I heard a seaman telling one of the cowboys it was called the Isle of Wight, but this place name meant nothing to me. It could have been another foreign country on the way to America.

I was distracted from the conversation by the sight of a large steam ship sailing in our direction. Its passengers lined the deck rails; each person curious to see what they could of our vessel's exotic complement. They must have known the *Persian Monarch* carried the world-famous Buffalo Bill and his Wild West Show. As the ship sailed past I made out the name *Santiago* on her bow. The crowd on her decks waved to us and I could hear the sound of their cheers in the distance carried on the breeze. Many of the cowboys had come back on deck smoking and playing cards again. Cowboy hats were waved in response to yet another appreciative audience. Only Laughing Waters and I were present on behalf of the whole Lakota nation and I was there under false pretences.

We returned below deck. Well, it was time for another meal. This was my third day with the Wild West Show and I was certain my stomach had doubled in size to accommodate all the wonderful mountains of food.

Laughing Waters was able to confirm to all the others that Wakan Tanka had gone back to heaven or this was what I supposed she told them. What she said must have worked because most dared to go back up on deck again.

A balmy evening breeze fluttered across the ship's decks as the cowboy band entertained us. None of their merry tunes sounded familiar. I'd been forced to spend more than two years listening to nothing but hymns. If those sacred dirges had been as bright and catchy as the ditties floating around the decks then I might have been a lot more enthusiastic about singing them. Some of the cowboys and girls danced together around the cargo deck. The Native Americans looked on incredulously. This cavorting was not what they considered to be dancing.

Life felt good again. Life was feeling very good.

***

A booming noise echoed from below us, somewhere down deep in the bowels of the ship. Something was being repaired with a heavy hammer. The cabin felt too warm and I couldn't sleep. I took a look through what had become my personal window on the outside world: the porthole above my bunk. The lights of a town twinkled like pale stars on the shimmering mirror of narrow water between ship and land.

I was desperate to get away from the over-ripe smell of enclosed humanity inside our cabin and breathe in some fresh sea air. I'd not washed since escaping the orphanage and I sensed many of my new companions hadn't bathed for several days either. I made a mental promise to seek out some soap and water as soon as possible. The orphanage had successfully drummed into me the close proximity of cleanliness to godliness.

Everyone else still slept. Laughing Waters looked angelic, if a Lakota girl could be an angel. Why not? She was better qualified than many of the girls I had met, and she professed to be a Christian. I didn't want to disturb her, but I needed to get out of the cabin and onto the open deck to breathe. As my "dumb injun" act had served me well so far, I felt brave enough to venture out alone. With my Stetson pulled down on my head I crept out of the cabin and into the shadows of the dimly lit corridor.

At the top of the stairs I poked my head gingerly through the hatch and looked around. The slightest of breezes stroked the deck of the ship. I took a deep breath. The sea air tasted fresh and sweet.

To my surprise there was a lot of activity on deck. Under the yellow night-lights I saw a small flock of sheep tethered in a corner; that is if only six creatures count as a flock. Probably be on the cook's menu in a short time. They weren't there earlier as far as I could recollect. Piles of fresh cargo lay around the deck waiting to be stowed away down below through hatches. Crewmen were busy with this task already.

There was the sound of voices coming from the water beside the ship. I tiptoed to the side rail and peered over. A large open boat bobbed gently alongside, crewed by men in waterproof leggings and those knitted woollen jumpers sailors call Guernsey's. I didn't recognise any of this boat's sailors. They didn't look like members of our ship's crew. Could they be pirates? They made no attempt to board our vessel and there was no sign of menacing cutlasses being brandished.

Squeezed into another corner of the cargo deck were four bedraggled looking young men. I call them *men*, but they couldn't have been more than a few years older than me. They weren't crewmen and didn't look like members of the show either. One of the ship's officers and two burly looking sailors stood guard over them. I crept nearer; crawling between piles of cargo to get a better look, hoping to overhear what was going on. A loose tarpaulin pulled over a closed hatch cover provided me with a hiding place.

'Are you sure there are no more of them, Mr Bates?' the officer in charge of the guard detail asked a colleague emerging from a forward hatchway accompanied by another pair of crewmen.

'We've searched everywhere, sir. Even looked among them buffaloes but no one would want to hide there… or with them Indians! They'd be safer with the buffaloes. Animals don't scalp 'em!'

The sailors all laughed but the four young men looked beyond humour with heads remaining bowed.

'Let's get these lads into the boat. The constables in Portland can deal with them,' the senior officer ordered.

With the encouragement of prodding by the crewmen the captives shuffled across the deck to the side of the ship.

Another officer joined the deck party. 'Everything in order, gentlemen?' he asked.

The newcomer's manner indicated his importance. The gold braid on his peak cap and adorning the cuffs and shoulders of a long, navy blue jacket reinforced my belief.

'Aye, Captain Bristow, sir.' Mr Bates confirmed my assumption as to the new man's status. 'We've searched from top to bottom, sir, and then back up to the top again. There are no more to be found, sir.'

'Well done, gentlemen. There'd be merry hell to pay with immigration in New York if we'd got stowaways on board.'

The ship's captain sported the finest grey beard I'd seen in many a day, but his words made me feel uneasy.

He turned to speak to the stowaways. 'If you lads want to get to the New World then there are two ways of doing it… either save money earned by honest toil and pay your fare or get yourselves a position in a ship's crew and work your passage across to America. Think yourselves lucky we found you before we left English waters – otherwise you'd have been thrown to the fishes out in the Atlantic!'

His words made me shiver with fear. I pictured myself walking the plank looking down at sharks waiting eagerly below for their next meal.

With his sermon over the captain turned and mounted the stairway up to the promenade deck. Here Buffalo Bill talked with the group of note takers who still remained in close attendance. Even under dim deck lights William Cody with his flowing hair stood out as a very special person.

The stowaways disappeared down a rope ladder and into the boat alongside. So the sailors in the boat alongside weren't pirates after all and the prisoners weren't expected to swim for shore. The party on the promenade deck moved to get a better view of the unwanted passengers' departure.

Everything went dark.

I was being dragged by my feet – under the tarpaulin and across the hatch cover from one side to the other. I tried to grab hold of something but there was nothing to hang on to and my hands went to keep my Stetson on my head. A strong hand put a painful squeeze on my left ankle and it yanked me from out of my hideaway. I yelled out loudly but thankfully only managing to make pained noises. Good sense told me to hold back any intelligible words.

I dropped from the hatch cover and onto the deck with a thump. I rolled onto my back as best I could with my ankle still gripped in a vice. My Stetson slipped loose but I managed to tug it back on.

'What've we got 'ere?' a rough voice exclaimed.

Frying pan sized hands grasped my leg. They belonged to an enormous sailor whose weather-beaten face glowed crimson even in the yellow deck lights. His visage was redder than any so-called Red Indian.

'It's one o' them redskin papooses.' Another huge sailor joined him.

'No! That's what they calls their babies!' My captor corrected the other sailor's suggestion before giving me a close inspection.

Was my game up so soon? Would I be climbing down the ladder to join the other four stowaways?

'Well, my lad. It's time you was in yer bed. You shouldn't be up here this time o' night.'

'Bet he don't understand a bloody word you're sayin', mate.' The second sailor laughed and his companion joined in.

'Let's get you back to your wigwam or wherever it is you sleep.' My captor spoke in a gruff but paternal way.

My ankle was now free and the sailor hoisted me to my feet by my shoulders. His arm stayed tight around me and he led me back to the same hatch from which I'd emerged only minutes earlier. He left me there to find my own way back to the cabin.

Once my skin would have singled me out as being different but now I blended in with the cast of the best show the world had ever seen and probably the finest people too. I began to feel I really belonged.

Chapter 11

It took only three days for timidity to turn into brutality. Well, that's how it felt when two small persons jumped up and down on my bunk while I was still trying to sleep. If I hadn't been so exhausted I might have even enjoyed the experience.

'Ger off!' I yelled.

They didn't know the words, but they clearly understood their meaning. Two frightened rabbits leapt off the bunk and scurried across the cabin to hide behind the bare chest of their father. He sat on his bedding on the floor, smoking a cigarette. This rapid flight to his protection made him laugh heartily at their antics. My precious novel – like many I have read since – did not say anything about the good humour of the Lakota people nor did it describe their family lives. More doting parents are not to be found anywhere on this earth, if my experience of the Lakota is anything to go by.

This was the first time I'd seen Dog That Stands unclothed: or any grown man come to that. *Nakedness is sinfulness*. This had been drummed into me in the orphanage – except at our communal bath time, of course. My new father looked truly magnificent: a natural athlete like so many of his brethren with not an ounce of fat on his muscular frame. However, the torso carried many scars earned in achieving Lakota manhood. Some came from the slash of blade or claw but there were also corkscrew twists left by the impact of bullets. I'm certain a lesser man would have died from these wounds. Cut deep into either side of his chest were two vicious scars. They looked old. I thought then that they must have come from an animal's horns, maybe a bison. Later I learned through personal experience that they came from the Sun Dance ceremony during which a Lakota boy becomes a man, or a man gives thanks for a blessing. At that moment I felt proud this man wanted me as his son and allowed me to call him *father*.

Laughing Waters climbed onto the bunk. She took more care in positioning herself on it than our sisters had.

'I am glad you have joined our family.' She smiled. 'Before you came they jumped on me!'

I remained unresponsive.

'Are you sick, my brother?' Her cool hand went to my forehead. I could see concern in her dark eyes.

'No,' I mumbled. 'Just tired.' I raised myself onto my elbows and told her about what I'd seen on deck in the early hours of the morning.

'It is good that the white men think you are one of us.' She nodded in agreement with herself. 'You can move around more freely.'

'As long as I say nowt!'

Her smile returned, although I'm not sure she understood the meaning of the Yorkshire word 'nowt.'

***

Dog That Stands decided it was time for my holiday to come to an end. Only a couple of days, but it was the longest one I had ever had in my short life. However, I had to earn my keep, like any other member of the Lakota. Life on the prairie had no room for idle passengers. Everyone had to participate. My new working life began with making the acquaintance of some very important members of the band: the ponies. They were penned on the open deck as these animals were not used to being kept inside stables or any kind of indoors, for that matter. There had been problems trying to get them down below decks on the outward voyage. Laughing Waters said she found the *Persian Monarch* to be a much more comfortable vessel for both people and animals than *The State of Nebraska*, the ship that brought them to England. When I considered the cabin we shared, it made me shudder to think about the living conditions on their previous journey.

When I discovered the nature of my work I gave thanks for being out in the open. And it was open – wide open with no sign of land in any direction. My sisters thought it hilarious to see me scampering from one side of the ship to the other trying to spot a shoreline somewhere. I'd no comprehension of how big an ocean could be or that we would remain out of sight of land for several days to come.

Our main task was cleaning up after the ponies. Fortunately, Laughing Waters advised me on the correct way to approach a pony. This helped me to avoid the bruises and broken bones that can come from the hoofs of a surprised animal. I learned another skill quickly: how to throw a bucket of manure over the side of a ship and not have it blow back in my face. What a waste. I thought of all the rhubarb it could have fertilised. For a moment my thoughts returned to Mrs G's wonderful pies. It was hard, smelly work but it was also great fun doing it with my sister. George would have loved every moment, especially rubbing down the ponies with a rag.

It had been in my mind that I needed a wash even before working with the animals. This smelly task made it a certainty. Laughing Waters felt the same need. She led me down many flights of stairs and along a gangway into a cargo hold. Here we found running water. It came through thick flexible pipe attached to a brass tap on the cabin wall. Later, in America, I learned to call a tap a *faucet*.

She took hold of the pipe, saying: 'At home we find a stream to clean ourselves daily, but here we have to use this.' Spurts of water came from the pipe as she lowered it.

Her words made me think. What was a stream? I'd heard of them in stories and poems but never actually seen one. I'd seen the River Humber and the River Hull, but they were too wide to be called streams and too dirty to look inviting for anyone to wash in. Hull also had open drains flowing through the town from the surrounding country. Local lads swam in them. I wouldn't have fancied doing that or washing in their green slime covered waters either.

She dropped the pipe onto the floor and pulled her buckskin dress over her head. She stood completely naked. It was the first time I'd ever seen a naked female body. I don't think a baby sister being washed in a bucket bath counted. I'd never even seen myself naked in a mirror, although I had seen other boys naked on bath nights. Laughing Waters' body was much darker than my sister's. My skin was much darker than Mary's, but I did not think anything about it at the time.

How different a girl's body looked compared to that of a boy, I thought. The female shape was a complete mystery to me, as it was to the other boys in the orphanage. Girls' bodies were always wrapped up like bulky parcels, hidden inside several layers of clothing. The fact she looked beautiful didn't enter my mind. I was still a young boy and a very innocent one at that. She was innocent too even though she was on the verge of womanhood.

'Come on! Take off your clothes. We can wash each other!' There was no hint of shyness in her voice. She picked up the pipe again before loosening the tap head on the wall.

I stared, still intrigued by her gently rounding figure. A jet of cold water shot in my direction. I jumped to one side, my static posture shattered by the feel of cold water.

'Come on!' she repeated her encouragement but without paying me further attention. She was too busy letting water from the pipe gush into her hair and flow down her body.

I pulled off my jerkin and kicked my moccasins into a corner but remained reticent about going further. The sharp sideways glance that came in my direction proved a more powerful encouragement than any of Jolly Rodgers' cajoling. One deep breath and I forgot more than two years of solid religious indoctrination. My leggings dropped to the floor and I moved closer towards her catching the lukewarm spray bouncing off her body.

She picked up a bar of soap from a shelf near the tap and rubbed it into her hair. That familiar carbolic smell took me back to the orphanage.

'You can wash my back.' She thrust the hard pink bar into my hand and thoughts of Hull and the orphanage disappeared, a million miles away. 'Then I will do yours.'

Dutifully I applied the soap to her skin and broke yet another English taboo. I decided that becoming a member of the Lakota meant forgetting old behaviours as much as learning new ones. Her back felt soft and smooth. I had no recent experience of the feel of another human, except for that endured during physical conflicts in the orphanage yard and George's cold feet in bed, of course. She didn't allow me to dwell on this strange sensation. As far as she was concerned it was only another task to be performed like rubbing down the ponies.

'Let me wash you now.' The tone of her voice remained matter of fact. Why should it have been otherwise? She grabbed the soap from me with one hand and sprayed me with the water pipe held in the other. She inflicted a far more vigorous scrubbing to my back than the one I'd given her. I should have felt shame that I was enjoying it.

When we finished our bathing she turned off the tap. The remaining water ran away down through a grating in the floor and out into the Atlantic. She threw me a towel pulled from off a shelf in the corner. It landed on my face, much to her amusement. Drying our bodies was as much a mutual activity as getting wet, as far as she was concerned. She could have been rubbing a pony but it brought back memories of my mother's touch.

'You look sad.' Her head turned gently to one side and long, black hair swirled over a naked shoulder. Large dark eyes enquired into my soul.

'No.' I shook my head. 'Just remembering times when I was happy.'

'Are you not happy now?'

'Yes. I'm very happy.'

She threw the towel around my face again and giggled. Bathing with her was a very different experience from doing it under Jolly Rodgers' sadistic glare. I never knew it could be fun.

The next day after breakfast I suggested to my sister that we could bathe again after our work with the ponies, but she shook her head. She had told our mother about our innocent experience but Yellow Flower was not pleased with what had happened. A lecture on Lakota womanhood had been delivered to Laughing Waters in no uncertain terms. During the rest of this voyage bathing was to be a solitary experience for the first time in my life.

***

As the *Persian Monarch* sailed further out into the Atlantic I sensed an increasing wariness in my Native American companions about going onto the open deck. When any dared to venture out there, they scanned the horizon carefully. Whenever dark clouds were spotted heading towards us, their voices became low and I sensed foreboding in the sound of the words, although I didn't understand what they said. The ocean swell strengthened but it did not yet prove to be a repetition of the rough sea they'd experienced in their crossing from America to Britain. It pleased me that we were still not *enjoying* the great sickness foretold by the absentee Black Elk. However, I had no immunity from the occasional involuntary need to hang over the ship's side in order to set loose the contents of my stomach. After the first experience of what I heard the sailors call *mal de mere*, my appetite at meal times moderated considerably as did my choice of which foods to eat.

Swell or no swell the ponies still needed our care and I discovered the animals, like men, can also suffer from seasickness. I became blasé about going up on the deck alone to tend to their needs. Laughing Waters reassured me that the captain was unlikely to turn the ship around at this point should another stowaway be discovered on board and she was certain Colonel Cody wouldn't allow him to throw me overboard.

I stood alone on deck rubbing the coat of an appreciative black and white piebald mare with a large cotton rag. My mind drifted miles away. I thought about George. My thoughts always went to him whenever I worked with the ponies. And whenever I thought of him I also thought of dear Sal.

A woman's voice interrupted my reverie. I took her words to be in Lakota and I turned with a smile expecting to see one of the squaws.

My expression changed instantly when I saw the origin of these words. A young white woman wearing a red and white gingham shirt tucked into the belt of blue denim jeans stood no more than two yards from me with hands firmly on her hips. Long dark hair was tied back, and her inquisitive eyes sparkled bright blue. I'd seen her before albeit from a distance, but I did not know who she was. Close up something in her face looked familiar. She reminded me of someone else I knew but that moment was not the time to speculate.

She spoke again. I tried playing my dumb act, but it failed me this time. I looked around, desperately seeking Laughing Waters or Dog That Stands or any other Lakota who might recognise my predicament but I could see no one nearby who might help me out.

'Y'all deaf, child?' she broke into English in an American accent as broad as the prairie.

I nodded in agreement, but this proved my undoing.

'You understand English, but you don't understand Sioux!' Her exasperation changed to perplexity. 'What tribe you from, boy?'

The conversation attracted a pair of cowboys from their work tending their animals further along the deck. They strolled across to see what was happening. One stood as tall as a redwood tree with a face dominated by a drooping walrus moustache. I recognised him as the performer the show's Orator announced as Buck Taylor. He performed miraculous tricks on horseback. I had not encountered the enormity of him so close up before. He walked with a severe limp, which I learned later was the result of an accident a few months earlier in London.

'What's goin' on, Miss Arta?' Buck drawled, towering over us all with hands placed casually on his hips. I was pleased to note he did not wear a gun belt.

'This young Sioux buck don't seem to understand his own language.' Miss Arta's full lips pouted slightly.

'Maybe he's one of them Arapaho.' The puzzled Buck scratched his forehead, making his hat slide onto the back of his head.

Buck tried some halting words in another language that sounded equally unintelligible to me. Arapaho Indians also formed part of the company but at that time, I couldn't tell the difference between any of the other tribes or their languages. So much for my great expertise on the subject of the Native American peoples.

'The boy's a breed. Ain't no Arapaho got blue eyes!' the other cowboy said. Like most of the American riders he was moustachioed and tall but nowhere near Buck's impressive stature.

I shrank back into what I hoped was the safety of the shuffling ponies. Possible rescue appeared in the shape of Laughing Waters but alas her arrival came too late to save me. She tried to explain to Miss Arta and the cowboys that I was her stupid brother.

'The boy ain't so stupid... he understands English!' Miss Arta countered my sister's arguments. Her attention turned back to me. 'And he's got blue eyes! Ain't no other blue eyed Indians in this show! Can you speak child?'

I mumbled a reply.

'Speak up, young fellow.' Although Buck's words were demanding, they remained friendly. He was intrigued.

'Yes, sir.' I decided to say as little as possible.

Buck leaned across and pulled off my Stetson. He could reach across tremendous distances by just bending forward.

'I think this brave's been scalped!' he laughed heartily.

The sight of my close, orphanage haircut made the other cowboy laugh. Others around the deck began to gather to see what was happening. It was a welcome break from the voyage's monotony for people who were naturally active.

'What's your name?' Miss Arta looked even more curious.

Laughing Waters interjected with words in Lakota. As yet I still didn't have a Lakota name. There would have to be a ceremony to re-baptise me, but it needed to be postponed to avoid attracting attention on board ship from those aware of Lakota customs.

'That means Lost Boy.' Buck's companion interpreted my sister's words. She must have decided to pre-empt anyone else having any say in my renaming including myself but the name felt kind of right.

The discussion on deck had attracted the attention of quite a crowd now. Any unusual event became a source of immediate interest to everyone. One of the newcomers was John Nelson and I wanted to shrink down into the narrow gap between the boards on deck.

'I seen this kid before!' The words emerged through a whiskery mass without giving any hint of lips moving inside. 'Just before that last show in England!'

My game was finally up.

'I thought he'd run off. He's an orphan... or said he was. Red Shirt wanted to adopt him and his amigo. A long 'n' gangly red-haired kid. Anybody seen him?'

The entire assembled group shook their heads.

'He ran away!' I blurted out. Laughing Waters nodded in agreement.

'We'd better tell Captain Bristow.' Nelson nodded, I think. I always found it difficult to tell what was happening beneath the great mass of beard and his huge sombrero.

'No!' I hugged Laughing Waters and trembled. I remembered the captain's words to the stowaways. Despite her earlier reassurances to the contrary, I fully anticipated becoming mid-Atlantic fish food.

A more senior advocate on my behalf appeared in the shape of Red Shirt. He was wrapped in a grey blanket with a single white eagle feather in his hair replacing his glorious show time war bonnet. He had come on deck together with Dog That Stands and other warriors. I was too busy hiding behind my sister and the ponies to fully understand what was happening.

However, words I did understand came from more than one mouth. 'We'd better tell Bill first.'

***

'Well, cat my dogs!' This was William Cody's favourite expression when taken by surprise. Finding an unexpected new member in his troupe out in the middle of the Atlantic was certainly that. These were the first words I'd been near enough to hear him speak. It was a fine masculine baritone voice as I had always imagined it would be.

At last, here we stood – face to face – but not under the circumstances I'd always imagined it would happen. Our first meeting was going to be an exciting occasion, probably out on the prairie fighting pesky redskins. But here I stood, right in front of him, pretending to be one of the 'pesky redskins.'

Close up he looked even taller than I'd imagined him to be or was it that in my dreams we had always stood shoulder to shoulder? The famous long hair was light brown, as in my novel, although close up I saw traces of silver. The moustache and goatee beard were full, though carefully trimmed. As always he wore a suit tailored from smooth buckskin. It was far better quality than my rough second-hand clothing.

A court of enquiry had been convened in his saloon. Although the cabin was more spacious than any other on board, the interested parties in attendance filled it to capacity. Counsel for the defence consisted of Red Shirt and Dog That Stands. Laughing Waters attended too but only for translation purposes. The Lakota deemed decisions at such a tribunal to be men's work. John Nelson was also present to translate and, although well regarded by the Lakota as he'd married into the band, he was still a white man. The accuracy of Laughing Waters' language skills could be depended upon by them.

The Miss Arta who found me out attended the meeting too. I discovered why she looked so familiar. She was Miss Arta Cody, the daughter of William Cody himself. The white Americans, I learned later, took a more emancipated view of their womenfolk than did the English at that time. I guessed she was present as part of what I supposed to be the prosecution team. There was also a face among this group I didn't recognise. In reply to my puzzled stare my sister whispered the man was Colonel Cody's business partner, Nate Salsbury. He was dressed in a smart dark blue business suit and like Bill wore a well-trimmed beard although it was dark brown and much fuller than that of the man I prayed would remain as my hero. This dapper man only just made it up to the height of his partner's broad shoulders.

I felt unsure as to the nature of Bill Cody's role in proceedings: judge, jury, executioner? He sat cross-legged on a chair covered in animal skins. He'd shot every one of the original owners of these hides. Hunting trophies festooned the whole room. Bill stroked his beard thoughtfully, listening to each side's presentation without comment.

Nate, ever the businessman, saw the legal implications of my presence among the show people: the probability of a fine for Captain Bristow when we landed in New York and even the possibility of criminal proceedings against Red Shirt, the Sioux nation, the Wild West Show and even Bill himself for the kidnap of a British subject… and not to mention all the bad publicity for the show that would go along with such a case. It could become an international incident.

Red Shirt and Dog That Stands looked on stoically, listening to my sister's rapid translation. When it came to the chief's turn, his words spoke not of laws written down by men in books but of the natural laws governing how human beings should behave towards one another. He said it was unnatural for children to be placed in prisons when they had committed no crime. I'd been isolated from my native people, forced to live with strangers who refused to accept me as one of their own. These white people did not want me, but the Lakota readily accepted me. The family of Dog That Stands wanted me as their son. Laughing Waters nodded vigorously in agreement translating this last statement. Until that moment I was unaware that the chief had taken so much interest in me. I felt greatly touched. A tear moistened my eye but I held it back. I wanted to be worthy of my new people.

'Well, that's given me a big, old bone to chew on,' Bill deliberated, patting his lips with the fingers of his right hand. 'There ain't no rush to reach a decision. We don't get to New York for a few days yet.' He looked thoughtful for a few moments before speaking directly to me for the first time.

'Well, young man what do you want to do?' His clear blue eyes were piercing. 'Do you want to go back to England?'

I shook my head vigorously, although I've got to admit thoughts of George and Sal crossed my mind for a moment. They were the only good things I associated with my homeland apart from Mrs G, of course.

'Do you want to live out on the prairie with the Lakota?' The eyes remained fixed on me but they were kind eyes. That's how I remember them and I'm sure that's how they were.

For a moment his words reminded me of the many sermons delivered by the Master asking us rhetorically whether we wanted to go to Heaven or Hell. I made my choice. I knew the most likely place where I would find a heaven on earth.

'I want to stay with my new family, sir.' The one thing I'd never wanted to occur in front of my hero did happen. Tears rolled down my cheeks. I was still a long way from being a Lakota brave.

'The poor lamb!' Miss Arta spoke for the first time in the debate. She rushed across to me, pulling an unexpected lace handkerchief from the cuff of her gingham shirt. In my imagination cowgirls did not have such things. I swear I saw a tear in her eye too. 'Papa, let the boy stay.'

'I'll have to ruminate on it.' Bill nodded sagely.

'What are we gonna do with the child?' John Nelson said, opting out of his translating role. 'Get the captain to lock him in the brig?'

'No, let him stay with Dog That Stands and his family while I give it some thought.' Bill nodded again. 'He ain't gonna run off nowhere… but don't let anyone outside this cabin know what's happened. Tell any others that know about the boy to keep quiet. If Captain Bristow finds out then there'll be no choice in the matter!'

Everyone agreed and the meeting concluded. I anticipated Nate Salsbury would have much more to say to Bill on the subject, but Miss Arta Cody seemed to have defected to my side. This was a very different world from the orphanage.

***

I sat on my bunk beside my eldest sister. A funny feeling came over me: one of almost relief. I was only living half a lie. My hero knew about me and about my circumstances, but he had not decided automatically that I would have to return to my old life.

'I have always wanted a brother. I do not want to lose you.' Clearly Laughing Waters did not share what she considered to be my unfounded confidence. 'My father and my family do not want you to go. Even the little ones are crying!'

'Don't worry,' I said. She leant on my shoulder and I stroked her hair. The brother she baptised 'Lost Boy' didn't feel so lost anymore. 'Colonel Cody's a good man. He'll make the right decision.'

***

During the afternoon an impromptu entertainment took place on the cargo deck. To be precise the audience sat on the cargo deck while the end of the promenade deck, some eight feet higher up, provided a stage for the performers. More infectious toe-tapping music came from the cowboy band who took the opportunity to practise but the show's star attraction came as a complete surprise to me.

Nate Salsbury proved to be much more than simply an astute entrepreneur. To my amazement his talents included those of an accomplished performer too: comic songs, humorous recitations and displays of hilarious skills in face pulling, mime and mimicry. In my short life I had never seen a performance like this before nor could I have imagined any of this coming from him. His stage persona couldn't have been further from the smartly suited, sober businessman I had encountered in Colonel Cody's saloon. A lifetime of experience on the vaudeville stage had enabled him to see the business potential in Buffalo Bill's Wild West Show. Quite what the Native Americans and the Mexicans in the company made of his antics I'm not sure, but they all laughed rip-roariously at his performance, though not necessarily at the points where they were expected to do so.

Everyone felt buoyed up by the entertainment; everyone that is except Laughing Waters. She held my hand tighter than ever and wouldn't let it go, not even when we went to collect our evening meal. That night she climbed up onto my bunk bed, determined to stand guard over me. Anyone attempting to take me away would have to confront her first.

The next morning she was still there perched precariously on the edge of my bunk. She left me no room to move in the night. Although my sister was smaller and softer than my old orphanage bed mate, I felt stiff from enduring the tight squeeze. She must have done so too. Instead of our usual routine of going straight to breakfast, we went up on deck to walk about and rid some of the stiffness from our limbs.

Yesterday afternoon's laughing faces had disappeared. Everyone looked serious. Something was wrong. Had knowledge of my misdemeanour become public? But no one paid me any heed. I nearly forgot my supposed lack of a tongue and felt tempted to ask one of the concerned looking cowboys what was happening.

Fortunately, an overheard snatch of conversation between two performers solved the puzzle, enabling me to maintain my vow of silence.

'Old Charlie's bad! Bill's with him,' the first cowboy muttered in a low tone, shaking his head.

'What's wrong with the old boy?'

'Got trouble breathin'.' The cowboy's expression said he clearly feared the worst.

My earlier feeling of euphoria quickly evaporated. I gripped Laughing Waters' hand even more tightly than she grasped mine. If Buffalo Bill's horse were ill – the one that had carried him for the best part of twenty years, the one he had ridden during his real adventures on the wild frontier – then my situation would be the last thing on his mind.

For the next two days, like everyone else on board, the only thing I thought about was the fate of this beautiful silver white steed. I felt guilty because my concern was more than a simple desire for the horse's well-being. Bill never left the animal's side in its stall below decks. No further entertainment took place; no one felt in the mood for frivolity. The life of an integral member of the great family of the Wild West Show hung in the balance and this fact reflected in the expression on every face, be it white or red.

Old Charlie was one of the stars of the show and the thought of Buffalo Bill appearing without him was beyond anyone's imagination. He was much more than just a horse; he was a friend and not only to Bill. Everyone had either given him a lump of sugar or ridden on his back. All my sisters had done this, led around by Bill himself. Once he'd even carried a Russian grand duke according to what I overheard one of the cowboys say.

On Thursday morning the news everyone feared arrived. I didn't need to be told what it was. Tears filled the eyes of even the hardest bitten rider of the range. The Native Americans weren't given to obvious sentimentality but even they looked sad. Old Charlie died at two o'clock in the morning with his master holding his head and stroking his coat.

Later in the morning members of the show brought the body up on deck wrapped in a dark canvas shroud. He lay in state covered by the Stars and Stripes of the United States' flag. All day a constant procession of people paid their last respects to their late friend. My people – led by Red Shirt – said their farewell by performing a tribal chant over the body. I stood with them, but I didn't know what I was supposed to do. Once again, I took my lead from Laughing Waters and the others.

After tending the ponies Laughing Waters and I remained on deck. Needless to say, we had company. Although the little ones didn't really understand what was happening, they knew it was something important and also very sad. We sat in silence on a closed hatch cover waiting for events to unfold. I daydreamed about Buffalo Bill's great western adventures mounted on his best friend and regretted I'd never get to know this magnificent creature. For once I felt glad George wasn't with me. The scene would have broken his heart. Even Sal would have shed a tear; I knew she had a good heart.

I listened as two of the ship's crewmen, checking the security of the hatch covers, talked about the situation.

'They say Buffalo Bill wants to take him back to America an' bury him.' The first sailor gave a gasp as a slack rope got a hefty tug.

'What an' have the horse going rotten on the deck for three days or more?' His older companion grimaced looking up from his task.

'That's what the cap'n said. Not healthy, that's what he said. God knows what the horse died of. Some sort of chest infection their doctor reckons.'

'That could kill off all the other horses 'n' animals. Maybe people an' all!' The wrinkled old tar looked concerned.

'Cap'n said he would have to be buried at sea and pronto!' The younger sailor nodded firmly.

'Bloody think so, too!' The older man looked relieved.

Later that day the funeral took place. Everyone stood on deck dressed in sombre finery to show their final respects to an old friend. My people were hardly recognisable under the special dark paint they reserved for such sad occasions. The cowboy band played sombre music, which reminded me of the dirges we were forced to sing during morning orphanage assemblies and in church on Sundays. Old Charlie's body had been moved to the edge of the deck with heavy weights added to him. He lay ready to be despatched into the deep through a temporary open space created by removing some of the ship's side rails.

Bill appeared from his saloon looking pale and drained. Miss Arta held his arm. Her eyes and cheeks were red from tears. She too had lost a very special member of her family. Nate Salsbury looked even more sober than usual, no longer recognisable as the man who clowned around on this same deck little more than forty-eight hours earlier. When they reached Old Charlie's body the band stopped playing and a hush fell over the crowd. The lapping of the ocean and the rattling of ship's rigging in the breeze were the only sounds intruding into the silence.

After a few moments of reflection Bill cleared his throat. His words were formed with difficulty.

'Old fellow, your journeys are over. Here in the ocean you must rest. Would that I could take you back and lay you down beneath the billows of that prairie you and I have loved so well and roamed so freely, but it cannot be…'

There was a catch in his throat when he said those last words. Perhaps he was remembering the time when, for a wager of five hundred dollars, Old Charlie carried him for more than one hundred miles across the prairie in nine hours and forty-five minutes. Bill won the bet with fifteen minutes to spare. How meaningless such a contest must have felt at this moment.

Bill continued his eulogy. 'How often at break of day, the glorious sun on the horizon has found us far from human habitation! Yet, obedient to my call, gladly you bore your burden on, little heeding what the day might bring, so that you and I but shared its sorrows. You have never failed me. Ah, Charlie, old fellow, I have had many friends, but few of whom I could say that.'

He paused again for a moment, clearly reflecting on his prepared words. Miss Arta's hand gripped his elbow to steady him. It looked as though he couldn't continue, but a few deep breaths of Atlantic air gave him the strength to continue his eulogy.

'Rest entombed in the deep bosom of the ocean. I'll never forget you. I loved you as you loved me, my dear old Charlie.' A note of anger appeared in his voice. 'Men tell me that you have no soul, but if there be a heaven and scouts can enter there, I'll wait at the gate for you, old friend.'

There may have been further prepared words, but Bill couldn't bring himself to utter them. He looked down on the lifeless mound hidden beneath Old Glory. Was it really his best friend lying there? For a moment a look of incomprehension filled his eyes, until reality intervened and he nodded towards the two pairs of cowboys standing on each side of the corpse.

The cowboy band struck up the chords of Auld Lang Syne and the burial party lifted up the board placed beneath the body allowing it to slide almost soundlessly into the ocean waves below.

Bill turned in the direction of his saloon. He leant heavily on his daughter's arm. They walked back slowly. Everyone else on deck maintained a respectful silence.

I felt a tear rolling down my cheek, but who was it for?

Chapter 12

The black cloud hanging over everyone on the ship with the death of Old Charlie turned into something all too real and it arrived with ferocity far beyond my imagination or that of any of my fellow show people. Storms could be fierce on the prairie, said Laughing Waters, but they did not make the solid ground heave simultaneously beneath Lakota feet. The *Persian Monarch* was the biggest ship in the world as far as I knew – 360 feet long and 43 feet wide – but the Atlantic Ocean's rage tossed her around like a cork from a wine bottle. Black Elk's ominous prophecy of a great sickness followed by our inevitable doom looked to be turning into reality.

The ship rolled, side to side, up and down, again and again and then again. Buckets filled with vomit slopped their acrid contents onto our cabin floor. I lay prostrate on my bunk wanting the absent warrior's prophecy to reach its predicted conclusion as soon as possible. Surely death – the quicker the better – was preferable to this torment. My perception of the world around me altered by the second. Sensations of up and down interchanged continuously. My stomach stayed up when my body went down, that is until they passed each other travelling in opposite directions over and over again. At first the women and little ones in the cabin wailed when their bouts of heaving sickness allowed but now they could do no more than whimper pathetically.

A firm hand denied me the luxury of death by grabbing my arm.

'Come.' Dog That Stands pulled me up. 'Ponies need you.'

He dragged me across the slippery floor. The bones in my legs were jelly. Laughing Waters slid along the cabin floor too, hauled by our father's other hand. In the gangway spluttering oil lamps turned everything an eerie flickering yellow colour, adding to my disorientation. We regained our feet but we both still required our father's firm encouragement to keep moving. Dog That Stands' strength of mind must have overcome the effects of the elements. I would have been full of admiration, if I weren't inwardly cursing him for dragging me away from my deathbed.

A constantly moving mountain needed climbing to get up onto the deck. The rocking steps in the stairwell must have doubled in number. The ship rolled again and I stumbled into the stair treads. A sharp pain hammered into one of my shins, but I was beyond caring as to which one it was.

I thought I could see a sky as black as coal through the open hatchway, until the thin line of the horizon dropped down into view and I realised it was the ocean I'd seen. The only indication of any division between sea and sky was that the heavens were only a slight shade lighter. It was mid-afternoon but darkness engulfed everything until a flash of lightning clearly defined this hell upon earth: but there was no earth. The following clap of thunder deafened me and any sight of the horizon disappeared. My stomach descended once more making me wretch. Although nothing remained inside me, twisting stomach muscles tried hard to find something to evacuate forcibly and painfully.

Hell is a very hot, very dry place or so I'd been led to believe. If I ever saw the Master again I would let him know how completely wrong his description was.

The brass rail on the stairway wall gave support to our continued upward struggle. Outside lay a world of constant movement lashed by stinging rain and spray, occasionally illuminated by flashes of lightning. Sailors and cowboys – all dressed in yellow oilskins – slid across the deck. My red brothers relied as ever on clothing and footwear made from animal skins. This was an alien environment for natives of the Great Plains but they'd been raised exposed to the ferocity of the elements. It was only another test of spirit and courage created for them by Wakan Tanka.

All differences were forgotten in the face of the storm. Warriors from rival tribes mixed together caressing the necks of terrified animals, stroking their heads and whispering comforting words in their ears. I needed someone to comfort me, but this was part of the price I'd have to pay for aspiring to Lakota manhood.

Dog That Stands pushed us in the direction of some young colts. They needed the attention of their mothers. Unfortunately, the terrified mares needed a calming influence just as much as their babies. I stroked the head of a tiny brown and white piebald infant fastened to the deck by a halter around its neck. It couldn't have been more than a few weeks old. This pony, like me, had never seen the prairies of North America. At that moment, I did not think either of us ever would.

I tried to utter words of comfort but what do you say to a frightened animal when you're as terrified as it is, and you don't know a word of Lakota? The Lord's Prayer was the only thing I could think to use to try to calm the creature. I tried whispering into the pony's ear, but finished up shouting out English words, fighting to rise above the howl and crash of the storm. Were these words more for my benefit anyway? In my terror I forgot I was not supposed to draw attention to myself. But no one could hear me. The ominous voice of the Master echoed in my brain. Perhaps he was right. The end of the world must surely have been nigh.

The deck rose and fell beneath my feet. My moccasins were intended for the solid earth of the Dakotas, not for a slippery wooden deck in an Atlantic storm. I continued focusing on the infant pony and repeated all the psalms and hymns I could recall. Words that had been drilled into me. I never thought they'd ever be of any use to me, other than to avoid Jolly Rodgers' wrath if I'd failed to learn them by heart but they were all I could bring to mind at that moment.

Feelings of false security soon vanished. An enormous wave swept across the ship. I held on to the tiny pony with all my strength, glad it was tied to the deck but wishing I was too. The power of the storm threw me across its body. The water flattened both of us onto deck timbers that suddenly jerked up to a forty-five-degree angle. The colt's heart pounded beneath me. I held on but felt the powerful drag of the water flushing me towards the open sea. It swirled beneath my body eager to devour me.

The angle of the deck changed to near horizontal again. Where was Laughing Waters? The colt she tended was alone, slithering back to its feet. She was gone.

'Laughing Waters!' The howling wind smothered my scream. Lashing salt spray filled my mouth and stung eyes.

Where was she? My eyes flitted everywhere. There was no trace of her. I forced myself back up onto my feet, lifting my charge. My heart sank deeper than my stomach. She couldn't be gone. She could not.

I saw a hand; a small, brown hand clutching the bottom rail at the deck's edge.

My moccasined feet slithered and skated. Again, the sodden deck dropped sharply ahead of me, throwing me onto my back. I felt a numbing pain in the back of my head. This new steep angle kept me sliding in the direction of the hand which miraculously still held onto the rail. I hit the side rail and felt a sharp pain in my side.

I threw out a hand and grasped brown fingers that were losing their grip. My other hand swung across and grabbed the wrist. I struggled to my knees pulling with all my strength. A terrified girl's face appeared above the edge of the deck. Her other arm came up and her hand grabbed the rail. I held on to her, praying not to let go. I could not lose someone else I loved. Not so soon.

Stronger arms intervened and took her weight away from me. Dog That Stands knelt beside me, hauling his daughter to safety and pulling me back too.

I hurt. My hand went to the pain in my side and I saw a trickle of blood. Everything went black.

***

'You're a brave, brave boy.' Miss Arta's voice whispered in my ear. A cool hand stroked my hot forehead. 'Papa told me to keep a close eye on you.'

The flickering light from an oil lamp above my head made me blink. My head twitched to one side to escape this irritation. I lay on a bench in a cabin somewhere deep inside the ship. Arta Cody sat beside me. Behind her on another bench I could see Laughing Waters' motionless figure.

'Laughing…'

Miss Arta placed a finger on my lips to stop my hoarse rasp.

'She's all right. Ain't she, Doc?' My new protector asked the question for me.

'Just sleeping.' All I could make out the man's face was a pink blur decorated with florid grey mutton chop whiskers. 'You'd better tell that young brave he needs to get some rest, too.'

Miss Arta spoke to me in what I guessed to be Lakota. For all I knew she could have been reciting the Twenty-Third Psalm or Humpty Dumpty sat on a wall.

'Ain't broke no bones has he, doc?' She stroked my sweating forehead again.

'No, like I said. Only cuts and bruises. He's a lucky young whippersnapper.' I saw the doctor's face more clearly now. He looked perplexed. Was he repeating information he'd already given her? Was she keeping up the subterfuge about my identity? Worry lines knitted together on a pink brow that continued into the doctor's liver spotted baldhead.

More incomprehensible words came from my guardian. Hickory Dickory Dock this time?

The storm must have abated. The ship's violent motion had calmed to a gentle roll from side to side.

I winced with pain trying to snuggle beneath the blanket. Any movement made my left side hurt like fury. I held back the desire to curse out loud and made do with a loud moan.

'Take it easy, young fellow!' The doctor moved towards me.

'I'll take care of him, Doc,' Arta said. 'I'll keep an eye on the girl too. There'll be other folk needin' your help.'

The doctor nodded in reply before picking up his black leather bag and leaving us alone in the cabin.

'They'll be singin' songs 'bout you round them Sioux campfires for years to come.' A warm smile made her blue eyes twinkle.

'Suppose I'd better learn the language, or they might get the story wrong,' I whispered, trying to force a pained smile. 'Only hope I'll be out there to hear 'em.'

She smiled and stroked my hair. Did she know something?

'How's Laughing Waters?' I coughed, and the pain increased.

'She's fine. A bit shaken up. Got a sprained wrist and a few bruises but she'll pull through.' The cool hand stroked my forehead again. 'You get yourself rested up.'

I closed my eyes and dreamed about sitting around warm campfires out on the prairie with my new family. George and Sal were there too.

***

My Stetson hat was long gone, floating somewhere out on the ocean but there was no point trying to hide beneath it anymore. There was no hiding place for me now, although only a few knew my true identity. Everybody – cowboys, sailors, Native Americans – wanted to ruffle my hair or pat me on the back. I preferred the hair ruffling; it didn't hurt. Miss Arta explained away my shorn head as the result of a cure for head lice. Sudden fame had its price.

Although I wasn't hiding any more, Arta still kept guard over me. She – along with Laughing Waters – maintained the pretence of my false identity and translated admiring words into Lakota although I understood the original English version anyway. My sister said she felt much better and wanted to give me a hug of thanks but I kept her at arm's length. The pain would have outweighed the pleasure. I let the little ones throw their arms around me. They could only reach the tops of my legs.

Luckily no one was lost in the storm, but one of the ponies had broken a leg and needed to be put down. The only other serious casualty was the Deadwood Stage, which had taken a heavy battering standing unprotected on the open deck. A hive of activity surrounded it. The ship's carpenter and members of the backstage staff administered rapid first aid to this integral part of the show.

We watched the emergency repair work from the safety of the ponies. Laughing Waters' sprained wrist and my aching side meant we could only make token efforts in grooming the colts. The little one I had comforted was to be given to me as a reward for rescuing my sister but I did not know this at the time.

'We'll need to have the stagecoach ready for when we get to New York,' Arta said.

I threw my new guardian an inquisitive look.

'We've got a season to do on Staten Island and then a tour of Philadelphia, Washington and some other places,' Arta said as she stroked a colt's head.

The place names meant nothing to me. I'd expected on docking everyone would be going directly to the American west. Anyway, all of the United States was the west, wasn't it? For all I knew the names she mentioned could be lawless towns out on the wild frontier.

***

I feared the worst. All my bright optimism evaporated. Heavy feet climbed the wooden steps up to my hero's saloon; as before I was accompanied by Red Shirt, Dog That Stands and Laughing Waters in support of my cause. When we entered the cabin, my spirits rose immediately. No Nate Salsbury this time and Miss Arta smiled at me. I'm sure she winked. I was now certain she had totally defected to my cause. John Nelson was there too, as inscrutable as ever within his thick bush of whiskers.

Bill perched on the edge of his desk, silhouetted in sunlight shining through the glass panes in the doors leading out onto his balcony – mere portholes would not suffice in his accommodation. He turned to face us. His world-weary demeanour made my confidence start to fail but a glance at his daughter confirmed her continued happy countenance. The mixed messages on the Cody family's faces confused me.

'Well, boy. I've been doin' a lot of thinkin' in the last couple of days... and your brave action yesterday sure helped.' Bill remained solemn. 'Been thinkin' about just how important families is to us all. Old Charlie didn't have any family until he was sold to me. He'd lost his momma when he was only a colt. When I bought him I thought he was just another horse. A fine animal... but only a horse. Must've been about the time Arta was born.' For a second his eyes flitted across the room to his daughter.

She caught her breath and a handkerchief came from the cuff of her shirt to wipe moist eyes.

'Well, Charlie became part of our family... and he became my best friend as well.' He paused for a moment.

John Nelson continued translating for my companions. My sister's affirmative nods verified his version of Bill's words.

'Nate don't agree with me but I've decided you can stay and make a new life with my good friends the Lakota. That's if you're wantin' to?' A smile glimmered in tired eyes.

Laughing Waters, forgetting her injuries (and mine), threw her arms around me and shrieked with joy. I shrieked too but it was more from the pain in my side than the great happiness I felt.

Her joy made John Nelson pause in his translation. He didn't need to continue but he did. Even the stoical Red Shirt managed a slight smile at the sight of my sister hugging me. She became my sister officially now. Colonel William Cody had confirmed my adoption.

Later my new sister told me Red Shirt said that Bill had once again proved he deserved the title of *wicasa itacan*. This Lakota title meant he was a leader of men and I was to learn throughout my new life how true this was.

***

Despite receiving Buffalo Bill's seal of approval little really changed in my life on board ship, except perhaps for the constant presence of Miss Arta Cody. She always seemed to be visible whenever I left the quarters set aside for the Lakota. She stood ready to intervene whenever anyone outside the circle of those 'in the know' threatened to come into contact with me.

'How come you were in an orphanage in Hull, of all places?' Miss Arta asked during one of the few moments we were alone and able to speak freely. I was back on deck with Laughing Waters tending the ponies.

'Hull's where I was born, Miss Arta.' I shrugged and shovelled more steaming horse droppings into a bucket. Funny, but I didn't mind this task anymore. I'd hated doing it when Jolly Rodgers sent me out into the Hull streets to gather it for the orphanage garden.

'How come?' She still looked puzzled.

'My father met my mother there when he came from Africa.'

'Africa! Ain't no Indians in Africa.'

'Father came from there. Cape Town he said… wherever that is. He was an orphan too! Brought up by Dutch missionaries, so he said.'

I stopped shovelling for a moment and leaned on the spade.

'Well, lordy!' She scratched her head in disbelief.

I told her about his shipwreck and how he must have swum ashore. I'd still not given up hope. We'd survived the worst storm in the world, why couldn't he?

'Well, the United States is a mighty big place to try an' find somebody.' She bit her lip and paused for a moment. She had no wish to ruin my happy mood. 'Maybe he'll come to see one of our shows. Reckon everybody in the union will come sooner or later.'

I nodded in agreement, not realising she was only trying to be pleasant. The discovery of the sheer enormity of everything in the United States still awaited me.

A loud squawking above our heads distracted us. From out of the clouds a flock of seagulls wheeled down and attacked waste food thrown over the side by one of the ship's cooks. These were the first seabirds we'd seen since leaving the coast of England.

'Must be gettin' near to land.' Arta took a deep breath and gave a look of relief that turned into a smile. 'Soon be home.'

Home. What did the word mean? I'd been in a home but not in a real home since mother died. Maybe I'd rediscover the meaning of this word with the help of my new family. Why weren't George and Sal with me? They deserved to have a real home just as much as I did.

***

During the next twenty-four hours expectation filled the air. For my new people it was more a sense of relief than anything else. The only topic of conversation above and below decks was the nearness of our destination. How anyone could try to calculate this was beyond me. One great relief was that it seemed Black Elk's powers of prophecy would be found wanting again unless something totally unexpected happened in the next few hours. The relieved mood of everyone around me suggested that this was now very unlikely.

Laughing Waters and I hung onto the rail at the ship's bow; needless to say, we were not alone. We strained our eyes, desperate to be the first to see land and leave the endless ocean but the first sight of America wasn't the mountains or green fields I'd expected. It was fog. We'd left England in mist only to find the shores of my new homeland engulfed in the same thick pea soup. Would it hide rocks and other dangers? No wonder so many sailors lost their lives so close to land if all voyages began and ended in this treacherous wet darkness.

In the far distance a pale green shape appeared through a break in the mist. It was a large figure rising from out the sea and it got bigger and bigger the closer we came to it. Had the lookout up in the crow's nest not spotted it? Even sailors on deck must have spotted it. There were no cries of warning of an impending source of danger.

'What is it?' I whispered in my oldest sister's ear. She must know… or so I thought.

'Do not know.' She shook her head. The figure grew even bigger and more ominous. A look of fear came into her eyes. 'Maybe it is Wakan Tanka... come to punish us for leaving our land!'

The figure was enormous now and it held up an arm. Was it trying to warn us off? 'Do not come any nearer!' it seemed to command. There was what looked like a giant club in its hand.

I wanted to ask one of the sailors nearby what it was. Still I dare not risk discovery, not with safety so close, but were we safe? What was this strange monster standing out in the open sea? It looked female and wore a crown. Was it a siren? It did not wail.

Laughing Waters froze, gripping the rail and staring ahead. The little ones craned their necks trying to see what caused so much concern in taller people.

'Ask someone what it is!' I shook my sister's shoulder. She could ask the question I dare not mouth.

'Land ahoy!' a sailor cried belatedly from up in the rigging. Others in the ship's complement ran forward to see. Everyone wanted confirmation that, at last, our journey was coming to an end.

'Go on... ask!' I demanded in a hoarse whisper. None of the crew or any of the cowboys seemed to be at all apprehensive at the strange sight ahead of us. We got nearer and its size kept increasing but it did not make any menacing movement. All the white men looked pleased with what they saw but there was nervous muttering among the Native Americans.

'What is that?' Laughing Waters said, able to form words again. She pointed forward and looked at a heavily bearded sailor standing beside us in a waterproof jerkin and blue bell-bottom trousers.

'That be the Statue of Liberty. Miss Liberty some calls her.' The seaman drawled his words in a heavy accent, which I couldn't place but would come to know years later as English West Country.

'A present from the people of France to the citizens of the United States of America. Built on Bedloe's Island in New York harbour while we've been in England.' A new but familiar voice added this information.

We turned to see our leader, standing on deck with us and, like us; he was trying to get a first glimpse of home. He had not left his saloon since the funeral of Old Charlie.

'Nate says he's got plans for us to take the show to France one day. I'll be sure to thank those French folks for this mighty fine statue. Mighty fine!' At long last, he could breathe air that bore the tang of his homeland. I swear some of the sparkle seemed to be coming back into weary eyes.

His reassuring words made Laughing Waters relax and her smile returned once more. The little ones still didn't know what all the fuss was about until she explained the monument to the other puzzled Lakota on deck.

Statues stood all around the centre of Hull. Mostly they were worthies from the town's history. The most impressive one looked to be made of solid gold. Everyone called it 'King Billy.' It was a man mounted on a golden horse but riding without stirrups like Native Americans do. Folk in Hull said the sculptor went insane and was unable to finish his work, which explained why he left the feet hanging free. This statue awaiting us on the shore of America was of a different order. 'King Billy' stood, at most, twenty feet off the ground but when we drew close to her 'Miss Liberty' towered above us, taller than any building I had ever seen. Behind her a city emerged from out of the mist but she dwarfed its buildings, although they stood taller than any I'd seen back in Hull.

A whole new world of surprises awaited me and I left behind little Sammy Smyle and his life in the orphanage.

Part 2:

Prologue

June 1904: Hull, Yorkshire
The two-storey building looked just as forbidding as the first time I set eyes on it but today was different. I could walk away. I was free. Years of soot and grime had changed its brick colour from cardinal red to dirty brown. I caught my breath. Once again, I could smell my salty tears soaking into the dank folds of Grandmother's heavy woollen skirt.

Up those six stone steps again. My hand paused an inch from the polished brass doorknob. I'd come so far to be here, so full of expectation but what if? Lots of questions but maybe the answers would not be ones I wanted to hear. Bad things happen. Something I knew only too well.

In this new century I lived a very different life. Little Sammy Smyle lived here long ago. It was all in the past. Few nostalgic memories for me in this place. Such thoughts were reserved for a small number - a very small number – of people with whom I'd shared rare pleasant experiences. Would my return here lead to finding them again? I was desperate to know how my old friends had fared. I hoped they had done well. There were so many things I wanted to tell them about my life since leaving: happier, exciting childhood days. I'd escaped without any genuine understanding of where I was going and what I would do. To be honest I possessed little real knowledge of anything in the world back then.

George and Sal must have left the orphanage years ago. What about Mrs G? Was she still alive? Somehow, I thought she would go on forever. She looked old to me back then, yet she always seemed ageless. Like it or not, my search had to begin in this place of many unhappy memories.

I turned the doorknob and pushed. The door's stiff hinges still creaked. The strong carbolic smell remained though the entrance lobby looked to have shrunk in size. A painful ache returned.

Had the small arched window slipped lower down the wall inside? Nearly six feet tall, I was no longer a little boy stretching on tiptoe, craning his neck trying to peep through. The only problem with the Master's office window now was that I had to stoop to look through it. It reminded me of a railway station ticket office. This thought had never occurred to me when I was in the orphanage but I had never been on a train until I reached the United States. What some might call 'reception' had felt like the end of the line to a newly arrived orphan.

Behind the familiar oak desk at the rear end of the office sat a man I didn't recognise. He was engrossed in paperwork. I tapped on the glass. He looked up. I remembered this room so well but it wasn't Old Stoney I saw walking towards me.

The stiff glass panel jerked open.

'May I help you?' The man was clean shaven except for his trim brown moustache. Although he looked only little older than me he still wore the same dark funereal attire as Mr Mason did all those years ago. His hair was short and slicked back. Beards and long hair were going out of fashion with younger men in England.

What did he make of me? A brown face and a red and white check shirt so bright it must have lit up the gloomy lobby – not to mention a fringed buckskin jacket, reaching down to thighs that were clad in blue denim.

'I used to be one of the boys here,' I said. 'I am trying to find my sister and my friends. We were all here many years ago.' I assumed

Mary must have followed me into the orphanage. Grandmother surely died long ago.

'When were these children here? What were their names? Come to that, what is your name?' His eyebrows rose. He had every right to be suspicious of his strange looking visitor.

'I'm Sammy Smyle.'

Would this notorious name be remembered only for the circumstances of my sudden departure? Would the orphanage have preferred to forget about me?

'I'm trying to find my sister, Mary... and my friend, George Smith... and his sister Selina.'

'You're not English, are you?' He stated the obvious. Before him stood a dark-skinned man with an American accent, long black hair in a braid.

'I used to be... once. Maybe I still am but I've been away a long time.'

'Smile, you say?'

'Smyle with a Y. Old Stoney... I mean Mr Mason... the Master always called me Samuel.' It felt strange using a forename that was never my real name and one not used by anyone else in sixteen years. 'I came here in '86 and left in '88.'

His head twitched uncomfortably inside a starched white collar and for a moment he looked lost in thought.

'This was well before my time here.' He pondered, pursing his lips as though sucking a sour pear drop. 'I will need to examine the record books. Give me the details of the children you mentioned, and I will search. Perhaps you could return tomorrow... at say, four o'clock?'

I nodded in agreement, trying to persuade myself that after all this time one more day wouldn't make much difference. I gave him all the information I could recall before going out into the sunlight to examine the changes that had taken place in my absence.

***

Hull still felt small like a town, despite being decreed a city by 'Grand Mother England,' as Chief Red Shirt called Queen Victoria. Perhaps I'd become blasé; too accustomed to things on a larger scale. Everything seemed so small and cramped.

Spring Bank is one of the main roads into the centre of the city. I'd walked along it many times as a boy but today it felt neither as wide nor did any of the buildings seem as high as they used to be. It had become a more modern thoroughfare. New electric trams with their maroon and cream livery shining in the sunlight, clattered along metal tracks only separated from each other by a line of trees growing in the middle of the road. Circular metal cages protected each tree trunk from the passing traffic or were the trees being held prisoner inside them, just as I had been in the orphanage? That's how it felt looking back. Brave tram passengers sat on the open top decks with nothing to defend them from angry swishing branches full of early summer leaves. Was this Mother Nature's revenge for the false imprisonment of her children?

Locals, bemused to see such a strange visitor in their midst, told me the electric trams were introduced only a couple of years earlier, replacing the old horse-drawn ones I could never afford to use. What had happened to all the horses? George would have been concerned about their fate.

Often Jolly Rodgers sent me out to collect droppings from the tram horses as well as the many others that hauled carts around Hull. I'm sure this obnoxious task fell to me more than anyone else. No wonder the orphanage had enjoyed such bountiful crops of rhubarb in its large rear garden. Their strange pink stalks flavoured with sugar provided a delicious filling for many of Mrs G's pies and jam pots. Those steaming fibrous lumps littering the streets appalled me when my tormentor forced me to shovel them up. In my new life cleaning after our animals was an accepted part of the everyday and carried no stigma.

Electric trams weren't any novelty for me. I'd travelled on them in cities on both sides of the Atlantic, so I decided to walk. It was a warm summer day and I wanted to take time to see every new thing in my old hometown before leaving it again. Hull was of no size compared with many of the places I'd visited. Was it still small enough for me to bump into the people I was looking for without the help of the new Master? Would I recognise them now? Everyone changes as they get older. Would they recognise me? I bore no resemblance to Jolly Rodger's little 'pickaninny.'

I promenaded towards the town centre; a strange flamboyant figure strolling among the sombrely clothed townspeople. People stared, but I hoped they were only looks of amazement. Nobody would recognise this son of their city returning home after a long absence. Hull still maintained its status as one of England's major ports but although it traded with the world, its population was not cosmopolitan. Every face I saw was pink for want of a better description. More accurately many of my Native American friends would call them *pale faces*, for most displayed the unhealthy pallor that resulted from lives spent in a northern industrial town. Even though it was summer now few looked as though they'd spent much time in the open air. The town's smoky atmosphere wouldn't entice me to stay outside any longer than necessary.

A new city centre was under construction, sweeping away some of the old rotten properties I used to know. A large modern Hull Co-operative store stood at a major road junction where newly constructed streets met to form the beating heart of a growing metropolis. I wandered past this fine emporium and strolled along Jameson Street, a street still only half completed. Behind me flat-capped roadmen, faces red with exertion, swung pickaxes and lump hammers constructing the missing section of the road. I continued walking and came upon the statue of someone called Andrew Marvell. I had no idea as to who he was or why the town thought he was worth commemorating but with his long flowing hair the figure reminded me of my mentor. Mind, the stern fixed expression staring down at everyone from his high plinth failed to mirror the warmth and excitement of my good friend's personality. The frozen gaze on the statue's face suggested a longing to be somewhere else. I knew the feeling.

These new streets were wide enough to allow trams to glide majestically through the city centre. Teetering cyclists – lots of them – weaved among trams, horse drawn carts and wagons of all sizes.

How did George and Sal fit into this world? These new streets with their tall brick buildings were canyons of prosperity. If my sister and my friends still lived in Hull then surely they must have done well for themselves.

When my Lakota family left Colonel Cody's employment we went to live on the reservation set aside for us by the United States government. This was where I grew to be a man but my early happiness obscured my view of its reality. When I look back I can see we were trapped there just as much as I had been in the orphanage.

The Lakota were denied the freedom to live their natural nomadic life out on the prairie where they followed the great herds of bison that once sustained their every need. Instead we lived on handouts doled out grudgingly by the white man's government and often these were meagre.

Our time with the Wild West Show left us with a false impression of how the majority of the American population saw us. They did not view the Native American as the *noble savage* as some white men fancifully portrayed us. At best, most considered us to be a hindrance to progress. Others said we were vermin in need of extermination. Some friends broke free from the reservation, but the old ways were gone just like the great herds. More white intruders on the Great Plains had continued the work begun by my hero, leaving bison slaughtered by the million. This time the hunters sought only hides, leaving discarded carcasses to rot in the sun. The once mighty bison was on the edge of extinction and the way of the red man was over.

The reservation was also the place where I suffered the greatest sadness of my life, even greater than the loss of my Hull family. Again, my rescue came in the shape of William Cody and the Wild West Show, offering me hope and a new future.

Chapter 13

I couldn't relax. An enforced twenty-four hour wait only increased my anxiety, the feeling of emptiness. It was wrong to be back in this town without my old friends. They were Hull to me: all that mattered about this place apart from finding my lost sister Mary. I needed to see them again and for them to see me. Would they believe that little Sammy could have grown so tall? Would I be as tall as George now? What did they look like? Sal must have grown into a really beautiful lady. So many questions.

Impatience overcame me and I made an early return to the orphanage. Answers I needed to know should be in there or, at least, the beginning of the trail leading me to finding them. No need to be dragged up those steps now. A single bound took me to the outer door. They would not forbid me. Inside the porch my knuckles tapped urgently on the 'booking office' window distracting the new Master from yet more paperwork. He looked in my direction and then glanced up towards the wall where I remembered a large clock ticked loudly.

He stood brushing the front of his dark jacket before crossing the room.

The window slid open.

'Good day, Mr Smyle.' His greeting lacked any warmth. There was more to this than my premature arrival. He must have checked up on me too. What had he discovered? Nothing complimentary in the orphanage records, of that I could be very certain.

I nodded politely in reply. Perhaps I should have apologised for arriving earlier than requested.

'I can tell you something about your sister and your friends. However, I am afraid the information about the Smith children is rather old.' He sniffed. 'They left us a long time ago: in 1890, in fact.

Selina Smith went into service with a family named Johnson in Westbourne Avenue and George Smith was apprenticed to a Mr Wilson, a blacksmith, on Hessle Road. I have written the addresses on a piece of paper.'

My informant paused for a moment. He gave me an enquiring look before opening a heavy black ledger to remove a loose slip of paper from between its leaves.

'You are able to read, aren't you?'

'Yes… and write, as well. I managed to learn to do them both during my time here.' I smiled. I had learned a great deal more since leaving though. 'Now I do them all the time… and calculations as well.'

He handed over the paper.

'I am sorry, but your records…' He looked down and fumbled with the ledger. 'They are rather brief.'

Clearly the information recorded about me by his predecessors did not equate with what the person standing in front of him was telling him. Winners – not losers – record history and here, I had been seen a loser.

'Records entered by Mr Rodgers, I expect.' I shook my head and smiled to myself. 'Is he still with you?'

'No, he left here about ten years ago before I came. He went back to Scotland, so I believe.'

'Good.' I felt relieved. This was one reunion I had no desire to make. Scotland was not far enough away, as far as I was concerned. I wished his final destination would be somewhere much hotter than up there.

'What about my sister, Mary?' I needed to know more.

'She was with us for four years and left in 1896 to become a pupil teacher at Tweed Street Board School.' The new Master's pride was obvious. He was speaking of an ex-inmate doing well. 'Again before my time here… but the staff who remember her say she was a model pupil.'

'Unlike her brother.' I smiled. 'The boy who ran away.'

I felt proud too. Not for myself but for the girl I could only remember as a tiny baby. Yet what did I have to be ashamed of?

'Yes, this is what our records state. "Absconded," it says… and that is the final entry. Nothing beyond that.' His eyes rose from the handwritten pages.

Good old George and Sal! They didn't tell where I went. They gave me the precious time to run away and begin my new life. I owed them so much. I really needed to make it up to them in some way; to thank them.

'Yes. I escaped, and turned my dreams into reality.'

***

Sal was the first for me to check on. The new Master said Westbourne Avenue was not far from the orphanage. Only a short walk up Spring Bank then a right turn at the railway station into Princes Avenue. I'd soon be there, he said. Funny how some things were coming back to me after all those years. Which street was Westbourne Avenue? Was it new?

'Nearly opposite the gates of Pearson Park,' he said. I sensed that he was glad to see me gone.

Now I did feel nostalgic. With the mere mention of the park's name, memories flooded back: sunny days together, playing cowboys and Indians on our imaginary prairie inside it. These childhood games turned out to be a better preparation for my adult life than any of the obedient behaviour drilled into me inside the orphanage. For once I allowed nostalgia to well up inside me because those were events I really wanted to remember: happy times with my best friends.

Where had all the open fields gone? The last time we came to play in the park there were hardly any houses on Princes Avenue. Now it was built up and there were side streets running off it I'd never seen before. Both sides of the main road near to the Botanic railway station were filled with businesses – butchers, bakers, grocers and hardware shops – all with their wares on display out on the pavement. A smart burgundy and cream electric tram rattled past heading north. The eyes of mystified passengers stayed fixed on me even though their bodies continued to be transported up the road. Mouths hung open, amazement registered on their faces. They could never have seen such a strange apparition in their midst before. Sadly, this was the Hull I remembered.

Where were all these people going? When I left in 1888 there was nothing beyond the park, only farmers' fields. Princes Avenue was on the town's outskirts then, but now it lay well inside the new city. Both Hull and I had grown a lot since we parted.

A horseless carriage steamed past, belching out smoke and fumes. An elderly man teetering on a bone-shaking bicycle waved an angry fist and cursed the driver of the automobile chugging beside him. *Too close*, the old man must have shouted, or words to that effect but the driver couldn't hear the livid remonstrations above the engine's explosive cacophony. His goggled eyes were more interested in the approval of the young lady squealing with delight by his side. Both her hands gripped her head, fighting to stop her straw bonnet flying away.

Such vehicles were commonplace in the towns and cities I had visited across North America. I'd even seen them on the crowded streets of London. The expressions on people's faces here told me the sight of a motorcar was still a novelty in the north of England. For a moment it distracted people from looking at me. They stared, wide eyed at a modern miracle that coughed acrid smoke and fumes into their faces. I preferred my transport driven by real horsepower.

The idea of revisiting Pearson Park tempted, but I couldn't face going back inside it alone. It was always a shared experience. George and Sal had to be with me. Entering on my own would be sacrilege and far too painful.

As the new Master said, Westbourne Avenue was opposite the park gates. Most vehicles in Hull used real horsepower and the brown fibrous reminders they'd left behind littered the road; I needed to cross carefully. The volume of uncollected droppings were definite proof Jolly Rodgers was long gone. If my tormentor were still around, some other poor wretch would have taken over from me. I recalled the rhubarb; the jam, the pies and Mrs G's kindness. She'd retired to live in almshouses in Northumberland Avenue, according to the new Master. Another street I did not know. She was someone else I had to see before it was too late.

As well as new housing along the streets off Princes Avenue, saplings sprouted up in the grassy, narrow verges in between pavements and wide roadways. In time, these saplings would grow tall and shade the houses. In my life as a Lakota I came to love trees, though few grew on the open prairie. They told us where there was a source of water, places where we could camp and take care of our horses. Man was part of nature but my life as a town child had denied me this essential bond. The presence of these young trees in this unnatural urban world struck me as strange. Did the sun ever shine long enough in Hull for anyone to require shade, even in the height of summer? Perhaps they were intended to act as windbreaks against the incessant breeze blowing through the city. This made more sense. A sudden cold blast came as a reminder and I raised my jacket collar for protection.

The Westbourne Avenue houses were large. Their imposing solidity told me their owners must be people of both financial substance and some importance in this new city. I soon found the address I sought. So far only a few houses had been built in the avenue, although the clattering of builders at work was a sign of more under construction on both sides of the road ahead. A short path and two stone steps took me to the house's solid, part-glazed front door.

I knocked firmly. Too firmly. My anxiety overcame me.

The sound of heels clipping along a tiled floor echoed in the hallway inside. The heavy door opened slowly to reveal a girl in a white lace cap and a starched white pinafore that almost hid her long dark dress. I sensed her recoiling in surprise at the strange sight waiting on her doorstep.

'What d'you want?' She pushed the door forward again so it stood only slightly ajar. She was half hidden behind its protection.

'I'm looking for Sal… I mean, Selina Smith.' I took a half pace back to reduce my level of "threat." 'I was told she'd come to work here.'

'Ain't got no Selina Smith 'ere!'

The door almost closed on me.

'Maybe I could speak to your mother?' My leather boot slipped into the gap between the door and its frame. I wasn't going to give up so easily.

'Ain't got no "mother" 'ere!'

The girl's hands held onto the door, her fingers curling around the edge. She pushed it further forward, her fingers slipping back inside.

I realised my mistake. It had not occurred to me the girl was not a child of the house, but only a servant, working in service just as Sal must have done. Probably an orphan - just like the rest of us; living in someone else's house with dreams that one day she'd have a home and family of her own.

'Sorry.' I felt her pain and the old hurt returned. 'Let me speak to your master, please.' I removed my foot to allow her to close the door.

'I'll get the missus,' she mumbled and the door clicked shut.

I heard the sound of a key turning in the lock. A strange looking man needed keeping at bay.

What felt like an eternity passed by. Was the maid really speaking to her mistress? Would 'the missus' dare to come to the door and confront the dangerous caller? Did the girl risk being severely chastised if her mistress was forced to confront me?

My attention drifted to the floral patterns in the parallel leaded glass panels in the upper half of the door, but they didn't hold me for long. I turned back to the street to take in my surroundings. Curtains in nearby windows fluttered simultaneously, like a startled flock of birds taking flight. The neighbours were fully aware of the peculiar and menacing visitor to their community.

My patience wore thin and I lifted my hand to knock again but the door opened to reveal a slight but well-scrubbed lady in a sombre black dress. A widow? A spinster? The girl called her 'the missus' but she would probably have called her by this title regardless of her marital status. Maybe she was in mourning for a life that could have been. The pallid complexion stretched taut across bony features told me this was someone who would definitely benefit from a more comfortable climate.

'Are you Mrs Johnson?' I stepped back, sensing that she felt threatened by me.

'No! They left here five years ago.' She had the look of a deer startled by a clumsy hunter. I knew that look too well but my hunting skills had improved. Otherwise my family would not have had much meat.

'What do you want?' She spoke through the narrow gap left by a door almost closed against me again, her long skirt trapped in her haste to escape me.

'I'm trying to find Selina Smith who worked for them.' I wanted to ask my question before the door slammed shut in my face.

'Don't know her. Can't help you!'

'Thank you,' I said but the door was closed already. I could hear harsh words being poured onto the maid.

Knocking at other doors in the street achieved nothing. People inside the houses must have been watching, and would have decided not to answer the door to the forbidding stranger. Did they think I was some sort of peddler of unwanted trinkets? That would have been giving them the benefit of the doubt.

I may have come *home* but the place felt less welcoming now than it did in the days when I was a child. I was only regarded as a harmless novelty back then.

***

It was too late in the day to visit Tweed Street School – the teachers and their pupils would have all gone home. This left me only with the address I'd been given for George's first employer. As I recalled Hessle Road was not a long walk from Princes Avenue but an electric tram ride would get me there quicker; or to be precise two tram journeys: one taking me into the city centre and another back out again into the western part of the town.

Other passengers displayed the reactions I'd come to expect from people in northern England. Some ignored me, pretending I didn't exist. Other expressions verged on disgust to see someone so different, someone they didn't want invading their scheme of things; but I sensed some other new responses too. I felt an element of fear in some. I'm sure that had been missing when I was young. Back then many people only saw me as cute: *a brown pickaninny*, to use Jolly Rodgers' taunt. Now, I stood tall and looked strong. Did they assume I was a threat? Why?

I noticed something else that was different, and it came from some of the young ladies on the trams and in the street. I caught their glances before they looked away bashfully. The eyes betrayed unladylike thoughts. Perhaps things weren't all bad.

The electric tram rattled out of the city centre. I'd climbed up onto the open top deck, preferring to stand rather than sit on the hard wooden seats. I wanted to see as much of my old hometown as possible. I visited these forgotten places during my night-time dreams. Perhaps this was something I could work out of my system at last.

The tram lumbered away from the civic splendour of the new Queen Victoria Square with its dominant statue of the great lady. It juddered past shops and hotels hugging the sides of Carr Lane, a main street, before joining narrower roads leading out of the centre. Maybe Hull had become a city after all. On either side of the tram's route squatted a tight maze of streets and courts, all alive with humanity on the move. Out on the prairie I'd once peered inside a broken anthill and this overpopulated area of Hull looked just like that. Despite a breeze the pungent smell of burnt coal remained heavy in the air. The sights, sounds and smells all around evoked memories long hidden deep inside. Instinctively I knew this had to be the area where I used to live in the days before grandmother abandoned me.

Nostalgia – the feeling I'd managed to keep suppressed – broke free. It can be a difficult emotion to control once it has been released. Maybe it wasn't nostalgia. Perhaps it was a kind of homesickness. Was I homesick for somewhere that didn't exist anymore except in my dreams? Maybe it was somewhere that had never really existed.

'Medley Street!' a voice called from the deck below. The tram conductor's words brought me back to my senses. This was the stop I wanted, although the name was actually Madeley Street. The local pronunciation of the name took time to register. Gradually, I was starting to get used to the Hull accent again, although I'd managed to lose my own long ago. Lakota with a Hull accent provided much merriment for my family and friends for several years, until it finally disappeared.

The tram juddered to a halt and I threaded my way down the tight rear spiral stairway. My boot slipped on one of the narrow metal treads but the conductor's arm arrested my tumbling descent, saving me from the indignity of falling off the vehicle and into the gutter.

'Thanks,' I muttered, regaining my composure. A mother sitting on the lower deck chastised two small children for giggling at the strange man's clumsiness.

'I don't think them boots was meant for goin' up an' down stairs.' There was a twinkle in the blue uniformed conductor's eyes, although I couldn't see whether there was a smile on his lips. A large walrus moustache hid all but a fleeting glimpse of tobacco stained teeth.

'There's not a lot of stairs where I come from,' as I returned what I assumed to be his smile.

'Not from round 'ere then.' He stated the patently obvious.

'Not anymore.'

My reply puzzled the conductor.

I stumbled again – this time down the high final step from the tram onto the pavement. A bell rang and the tram moved off along Hessle Road.

The show had taken me across much of the eastern side of the United States and into many towns and cities up and down Great Britain but here was my first real look at ordinary English people living everyday lives. My usual contact with such folk was when they became our audience: dressed in their smartest Sunday best clothes, faces washed and eyes filled with expectation, waiting to become engulfed by a great fantasy, even if only for a couple of hours. Facing me here on Hull's Hessle Road was reality.

A tide of drooping heads moved as one away from the town centre: a swarm of tired worker bees returning to the nest. Heavy legs trudged along pavements too narrow to accommodate everyone. (I had trouble getting used to the word *pavement* again instead of *sidewalk*.) Most pedestrians were men, shoulders bent with years of exhaustion. All looked grubbily identical. Flat cloth caps flopped over faces decorated with dangling moustaches. Droopy, hand rolled cigarettes hung from nearly every mouth. My lack of facial hair made me feel naked in their company. The men had left a full day's work behind them: long hours of hard physical toil. I was no stranger to long hours: from before dawn until after dusk when necessary, but I didn't envy them having to do it every day, in jobs they hated, and which probably paid them a pittance. I was lucky; I loved my work but in one respect I still envied them. They were making their way to places where they could enjoy the warmth of real homes and families. Twice I'd been part of a family and twice fate had robbed me of its security and happiness.

Ragged offspring were pulled along by mothers looking old beyond their years with heads hidden in the cowls of dark woollen shawls. Children continually spilled off the pavement's edge and needed yanking back from out of the gutter. What caused their rush? Were the women desperate to arrive home before the head of household returned, expecting a hot meal to be waiting on the table after a day's work?

I became one of those children again, looking up into my mother's radiant face. She hadn't been allowed to become old before her time. Mary wriggled in her arms, anxious to suckle again on a warm milky breast. I remembered hopping in and out of the gutter without a care in the world.

The air was filled with the clatter of the wheels of flat-bottomed rullies, drawn by emaciated ponies, tired heads hanging permanently down toward the road ahead. Men on bicycles weaved in and out of slower moving traffic. I didn't envy them their ride and winced in sympathy, feeling every bump of the unyielding road surface made up of hard wooden sets.

The strong smell of chlorine hit me even before I turned left into Madeley Street. A warm gush wafting out of the municipal bathhouse carried the chemical smell on the air. Here I met a scrum of workingmen jostling outside the bathhouse door, copper coins clutched in dirty hands ready to pay to get inside. Some would be going for a swim, trying to exercise away the aches and problems of the day. Others would make do with a hot soak in a slipper bath. These men were volunteering to do what always required compulsion for orphanage boys.

I prayed that the coals in the blacksmith's forge would still be glowing. I didn't want to lose another day. The street wasn't very long and half way down I heard the familiar echoing clang of metal beating heavily onto metal. This must be the blacksmith's shop. Tall gates hung open exposing the smith still at work bent over his anvil in an open workshop, hammering on a glowing but resistant iron rod. He did not hear me walking into the yard, treading across slippery wet cobbles. The sight of my arrival startled him. He jerked backwards almost dropping the livid crimson bar.

'What d'you want?' His fierce reaction took me by surprise. The words came through broken and twisted yellow teeth, almost hidden within a mass of grey beard, which hung down almost onto his thick leather jerkin. Despite advancing years, the rippling, greasy muscles and bull neck on his squat figure indicated he remained a man of great physical strength.

'Are you, Mr Wilson?'

The blacksmith nodded in reply, still eyeing me suspiciously from beneath a brimless leather cap.

'I'm looking for my friend, George Smith. He was apprenticed here... from the sailors' orphanage.' I felt cautious despite towering head and shoulders above the blacksmith. He was intimidating, with both a heavy hammer and a piece of red hot metal pointed in my direction.

He lowered the hammer to a more pacific angle and the crimson rod plunged back into sparking hot coals. For the first time in the day I felt warm. The intense heat thrusting out of the forge felt stronger than any cold breeze I'd been confronted by.

'You're a bit late. 'E's gone.' There was the suspicion of a wry smile hidden deep within the whiskery bush.

'Gone home?' My heart leapt at the prospect of George still working in the smithy.

'No. Gone for good!' the old man laughed, letting his free hand tip back his cap before scratching a bald head. 'Went to join the army. Not seen 'im since. Fightin' the Boers, last I 'eard. Why d'you want 'im? You don't look like somebody from round 'ere.'

My heart sank. What had happened to my friend? Was he still alive? People get killed in wars; I knew this only too well from personal experience. I took a deep breath and commenced my story. The smith listened attentively, leaning on the end of his hammer's long shaft.

''E was a good lad, was George. 'Ard worker - but 'e'd rather ride an 'orse than shoe it.' The sweaty head got another scratch. 'Maybe you should go an' ask 'is sister. Bonnie lass. Ginger like 'im. She might know what's 'appened to 'im. Lives further up Hessle Road somewhere, last I 'eard.'

'D'you know where?' My heart leapt. Maybe I wasn't completely out of luck. Sal couldn't be far away, if what he said was correct.

'Somewhere near the fish dock, I think.' Now he scratched at a chin hidden somewhere beneath grey foliage. 'The missus'll know.'

The hammer shaft flopped onto the ground with a clunk and the smith waddled rather than walked across the yard to a house door covered in flaking red paint. He pushed it open with the flat of his hand and shouted inside.

A few moments later, a woman – as lean as her husband was broad – appeared from inside the house. She dried dripping wet hands on a stained calico apron. As with everyone else my appearance produced a look of surprise on her wrinkled face. Her husband recounted what I'd told him.

'You're Sammy! The one what ran away with that Buffalo Bill and them Red Indians?' I gave a sigh of relief at her words. Someone else knew of me. My best friend hadn't forgotten me. 'George said you was nowt but a little lad!'

'Well, I grew!' I extended both arms out to indicate my adult expansion.

'Lad wants to know where 'e is. I said 'is sister might know,' the husband interrupted.

'Aye. Good little lass that Sal. She'll know – if anybody does.' The old woman echoed her husband's opinion.

'D'you know where she lives?'

I prayed she could give me a more precise address.

'Down West Dock Avenue, last I 'eard. Married to a fisherman. House opposite the school. Don't know what number though.' A gnarled hand scratched at her scalp through thinning crinkly grey hair.

At last, it seemed the trail to my friends was warming up. Sal was married. I hoped she was happy and prospering. I'd never imagined her as a *yes, ma'am; no, ma'am* skivvy in domestic service. She had too much fire in her to kowtow to any domineering madam especially like the one I'd come across earlier in the day.

'Thanks. When Number One – I mean our Advance Booking Office comes into to town in a couple of days, go and tell 'em I sent you. They'll give you a couple of complimentary tickets for the show. Just say Sammy Smyle sent you.' I was far more thankful than a couple of free tickets.

***

West Dock Avenue was less than a mile away, so I walked. Something inside me said there were things I needed to experience at the level of the street. Things still looked and felt familiar. The images and smells all around me tried to spark memories but the sparks did not light a flame. My instincts told me this was home but I didn't recognise anything or anyone. It was all too long ago. Much had happened to me since the time when I considered myself to be a native here.

Hessle Road's narrow canyon of tall buildings widened the further west I walked from Madeley Street. The evening sun broke through the shadows. The streets on either side of the main road looked different. Again, these were new streets, built since I ran away. They looked wider than the older ones closer to the city centre but, judging by the number of returning workers and the women standing waiting for them on the doorsteps, they were just as densely populated as those others I used to know. Hordes of ragged children milled around, playing in the streets.

I noticed something else: a foul reek. Fish. Raw fish, cooking fish, rotting fish. The stench was everywhere and getting stronger. The wind coming from the nearby Humber did nothing to take it away. In fact, the sour river smell mingled with it. It not only fouled the air; it was in the fabric of the buildings and even in the clothes and skins of the people themselves. Hull had really flourished as a fishing port in my absence. It was the reason for building all these new houses and for all the people who had come to live in them. The stink was part of the price paid for the city's new prosperity. Give me the smell of livestock any time. Better still let me inhale the perfume of the open prairie's sage bush and the pine forests of the north Dakotas and Canada.

The imposing Star and Garter Hotel with its plate glass windows standing bold on a street corner told me I'd reached West Dock Avenue. Once again, a steady stream of workmen came from this street, apart from those who lingered to enter the public house. The smell of fish became even stronger as they brushed past me. Heavy boots thundered along the pavement. Protective metal strips nailed onto soles and heels grated and sometimes sparked on the flagstones and kerbs.

More rullies rattled out of the side street and onto Hessle Road, flat decks laden with wet wooden boxes. From the strong aroma there could be no mistaking what was packed inside them. The young drivers displayed the casual manner of strutting youths out to impress. Reins hung loose and legs dangled nonchalantly over the cart sides. Despite their youth, they also sported the drooping walrus moustaches, which seemed to be the symbol of manhood in England (and also North America if truth be told).

Maybe at last I would find one of my friends in this street and discover what had happened to her brother.

Chapter 14

Tall Board School buildings took up nearly half of one side of the street. They rested in darkness empty until the next morning's invasion by hundreds of children. The flickering yellow glow of gas lamps lit up lots of houses but in which one in the street 'opposite the school' did Sal live? If indeed she still lived in any one of them.

The recent experience in Westbourne Avenue made my heart sink when I looked at the number of doors I would have to knock upon. Fortunately, many in the long continuous terraces facing the school were either shops or other business premises. One emporium caught my attention: *Henry Tiplady, fisherman's outfitter*. It occupied three of the houses, so there must have been a great demand for Mr Tiplady's goods. The shop was closed for the night, but I could see wares on display through large window panes: knitted grey marl jumpers and bright yellow leggings, jerkins and sou'westers. There were lots of other items on show but my time in the Hull Sailors' Children's Orphanage provided me with little help in guessing what use a fisherman might have for any of them.

Facing the school house, number forty was the first door to be knocked on but the building also contained a business. Painted in large black letters across the grey wooden double doors of its adjoining archway were the words: *John Capes – Needle Maker*. Images of someone creating fine tools for local seamstresses came to mind but later I discovered these needles were well over six inches long and made of wood, not steel. The wives and mothers of the area used them to make and mend fishermen's nets: definitely not for creating delicate embroidery. Local women had neither the time nor money to indulge themselves in such dainty relaxations or any other idle pastime. Leisure was an expensive luxury few could afford around here.

According to the smith's wife, Sal married a fisherman, not a needle maker, so I began my search by knocking on the next door. Number forty-two looked like it could be occupied by ordinary working people. The front door was set back from the pavement although its carved wooden frame stood proud from the wall. My triple knock echoed in an empty passageway. No other sound was heard inside. I tried again but still without response.

I sighed and turned to move on to other doors but as I walked on, something caught my attention. Two small eyes stared at me through the sash window from inside the front room of number forty-two. The sight made me pause. I tried to make eye contact with the child. There was a terrified squeal and a mop of dark hair disappeared into the darkness. A pain stabbed me through the heart. Suppressed memories of two other pairs of small dark eyes in heads with long black hair returned. I'd come too far to stop now.

'What d'you want, mister?' a faint voice floated out of nowhere.

A woman appeared out of the gloom in the covered passageway that divided number forty-two from the neighbouring house at ground floor level. A dark shawl covered her head and shoulders merging into a shapeless long dress that hung low enough to sweep the pavement floor.

'I'm looking for somebody,' I stammered, startled by the unexpected appearance.

'You're not from round here are you?' The tone of her voice was accusational. Why did everyone here seem compelled to state the obvious? Were strangers such a rarity?

'Used to be. Long time ago,' I replied almost mechanically.

'Sammy?' The weak voice sounded familiar. 'Is it you, Sammy?'

The cowl slipped back slightly to reveal a few loose strands of hair. Even in the darkness I could see they were red. A movement in the folds of her skirt distracted me. Two dark eyes stared up again.

'Sal. Is it you?' I looked up again to look more closely at her.

Before the woman could answer the child tugged at the long skirt and began to mewl loudly.

'Give over, bai'n!' The woman bent to lift the child. The shawl slipped back further, falling onto her shoulders. The long red tresses flowed onto her shoulders just as they did that first time outside the orphanage kitchen when she pulled off her cloth cap. Nearly twenty years fell away too.

'It's your Uncle Sammy come to see us.' The child rested in her arms now. Sal's blue eyes looked right into me.

'How you doing, Sal?'

Obviously, she was not doing well. Even in the darkness I could tell her clothes were old and worn. She looked exhausted. Not what I'd expected, not what I'd hoped to see.

'Not as well as you, Sammy. Not by the looks of you.' Words seemed to choke in her throat and she swayed unsteadily towards the wall.

My hand went to her shoulder to steady her. I feared she'd collapse and drop the child. Seeing her again aroused unanticipated feelings. I wanted to throw my arms around her and hug her like I used to hug Morning Star, or my sister Laughing Waters when we were still children, but she looked so frail I feared hurting her. Any sudden movement might have frightened the child hanging precariously onto her mother's neck.

'You look as though you could do with sitting down, Sal.'

'Reckon I could, Sammy.' Her weary body leant into the solidity of my arm. 'D'you want a cup of tea?'

'Not had a decent cup of tea in nearly twenty years.'

She turned and led me into the dark passageway burrowed beneath the first-floor level of the two terraced houses. A few yards down the passage was the gate to number forty-two's walled backyard. In the corner, a water tap dripped into a sink beneath a dirty window. At the far end two ragged wooden doors fronted an outhouse. The facilities looked much better than those shared between several houses from my pre-orphanage days, but the house did not amount to what my idea of gracious town living should be. Mind, I'd become more used to a nomadic outdoor life.

Sal led me through the back door into the scullery. On the bare brick floor stood a rough wooden table and a corrugated metal tub. I remembered that this was known locally as a dolly tub. This was where a family's dirty laundry was put into hot soapy water and churned by something called a dolly stick. This was a wooden contraption that looked like a milking stool with a long handle fixed into the centre of its seat. It all came back to me. In the corner of the room was a brick fireplace where water could be boiled. No heat came from that direction. Long dead flakes of grey ash sat in the cold hearth.

A single stone step in an inner doorway led up into a larger room. Pale moonlight from the backyard strained through a dirty window, making the jaundice yellow distempered walls look even sicklier. Sparse furniture stood on bare floorboards: two rough wooden chairs alongside an even rougher table. A torn oilcloth with a faded china blue and white pattern failed to cover the whole of the tabletop. The coal fire in the black metal range was about to give up on life. I knew this provided not only the main source of heat in the house but also the sole means of cooking.

'I'll give it a rake.' Sal sat the child on a pile of rags in the room corner before picking up a bent black poker lying on the hearth. She tried to prod life into embers which were only managing a terminal glow.

'Looks as though it could do with some fresh coal.' I regretted suggesting the obvious. Did she possess any more of the fuel?

'Aye, I'll get some.' She looked as though she didn't have the strength to lift an empty shovel, let alone one filled with coal.

'You sit down, Sal. Which door in the yard is the coalhouse?' I paused. 'How did you know it was me, Sal?'

She smiled. 'I'd know them blue eyes anywhere, Sammy.'

Sal's look said pride wanted her to turn down my offer to collect more coal but she didn't possess the strength. This was not the Sal I remembered.

'First on right.' Her voice faltered behind me.

I walked through the bare scullery back into the yard, empty coal shovel in hand. The large coalhouse was dark and almost empty. It could have held half a dozen sacks of coal but all I found was a small heap made up of mainly gritty dust. Raking through it with the shovel I found a few hidden lumps. I took the coals back and carefully placed them by hand on the dying embers. I put my face close to the grate and blew into the grey cinders trying to encourage a glow of life back into them.

'Is your husband out of work?' I tried to be polite. Was he drunkard, boozing away all his wages in the Star and Garter pub at the end of the street? Was he in the workhouse? Had he deserted them altogether? I didn't know him, hadn't met him but I hated him for the state in which I had found one of my best friends and her child.

'Wish he was!' She gave a sardonic laugh. 'Dead. Lost at sea, nearly six months ago.'

My head jerked back from the grate and I turned to look at her. I should have expressed regrets for someone I did not know but I was more concerned with Sal's current condition. Bitter recent experience told me that words were not enough.

'So how have you been getting by, Sal?'

A faint glow of life appeared in the fire. I stood up and looked at the sad wretch Sal had become. I owed her so much. It hurt to see her in such a poor state.

'You call this gettin' by.' Her laugh became a world-weary sigh. 'The last of Stan's wages ran out weeks ago. Mainly depending on handouts now. George helps when he can but he's got Annie and their bai'ns to look after.'

I hardly noticed the mention of my best friend's name. I was too concerned with Sal's weak condition.

'It's either go on the parish or go on the streets!' She took a deep breath. Her head dropped and tears streamed down her face. 'Not that I'd get much selling meself on the streets – the state I'm in!'

'Don't worry, Sal. You won't need to do that!' It was my turn to take a deep breath. 'I'm here. I'll help.'

'What for? You don't owe us owt!' A note of weak defiance returned to her voice.

'Sal, I owe you and George more than you can ever know!'

A hissing cinder spat out of the fire and landed on the floor as if to emphasise my words.

A grocer's shop further down the street was still open. I was able to leave Sal and Martha with full bellies and enough food to give them a good breakfast the next morning. I wanted to remain but she was concerned about what neighbours might think about a strange man staying in her house overnight. I didn't give a damn about their petty opinions but I wasn't the one who lived there.

I felt guilty returning to the comfort of the White Horse Hotel in the city centre. Not as grand as either the Royal Station or the Imperial, the hotels that Bill and the others used back in 1888, but compared to Sal's mean abode it felt like a palace.

Although I was not rich, I vowed to make a difference to the lives of Sal and her baby. It was also much more than about repaying an old debt. Debt doesn't come into consideration where real friendship and love are concerned.

***

West Dock Avenue's morning traffic was moving in the direction of St Andrew's Dock or the 'Fish Dock' as everyone called it. Metal horseshoes and steel wheel rims clattered on hard wood sets. Why anyone had named this street *avenue*, I don't know. There wasn't a single tree on its entire length. Every building faced directly onto the pavement, except for those down narrow terraces that ran off at right angles on the school side of the street.

A well-trained carthorse waited obediently in the shafts of a coalman's cart parked at the Hessle Road end of the street. Its master was making deliveries, humping large black sacks of dusty coal on his bent back.

'How much for a bag?' I shouted across the street to the coalman.

The man was about to heave another dark sack onto his back. He paused and two white eyes broke through a charcoal visage, looking for the origin of the unexpected request. His was the first non-white face I'd seen in Hull and this only because it was covered in coal dust.

'None for sale mate. They're all spoken fer.'

'I'll pay you double for one of your sacks today… and I'll have some more tomorrow.'

The man leaned back onto the sack as it perched on the edge of his cart. He considered my offer for a moment before being distracted by his solid dray horse. It snorted loudly and struck a hoof on the road as if to tell its master my offer was too good to refuse.

'O'right. You've twisted me arm. Where d'you want it tekin'?' The coal merchant nodded agreement with his horse.

'Number forty-two. Down the passage alongside. I'll pay you when you deliver.'

I turned in the direction of Sal's house and moved off before he had the opportunity to tell me I was '*not from round 'ere.*'

Today I was supposed to be distributing more posters around Hull to advertise the arrival of the Wild West Show and I felt guilty about abdicating this responsibility. Major John Burke, the man responsible for all the publicity, would not be pleased, but I would have felt even guiltier not doing something about Sal and little Martha. Colonel Cody would understand. Bill agreed to let me come to Hull – well in advance of the show – because he knew how important it was to find these special people from my childhood.

Hull's ordinary folk used the back entrances of their houses rather than the front ones, even though it meant walking further. Front doors, and front parlours if they had them, were kept spotless for special occasions: *for best,* as they liked to say. So, I went down the side passageway again, into the backyard and knocked on the rear door.

There was no reply, but I could hear raised voices coming from inside. They were angry voices. The child was bawling loudly. Little Martha hardly made a murmur the previous night. She didn't possess the strength then or so it seemed, but she certainly had it now.

I pushed the door open. I didn't wait to be invited in.

'My offer's still goin', Sal!' said a man's voice.

'You know what you can do with yer offer!' The pitch of Sal's words was almost a scream. Martha howled even louder.

'You're sittin' on a fortune, Sal,' the man said sarcastically.

'An' I'm stayin' sat on it!'

I reached the living room and could see Sal's antagonist. He looked a similar age to myself and was dressed in a smart brown suit with a black derby – sorry, bowler-hat – perched at a rakish angle. Something lurking behind a dark brown walrus moustache felt uncomfortably familiar. The facial hair failed to conceal scars left by childhood acne.

'What's going on?' I interrupted the argument.

'I'm here for the rent. Not that it's got owt to do with you!' the visitor leered at me. Instinctively I hated him. I wanted to hit him.

'Doesn't sound like collecting rent to me.' I wanted the man to feel the heat of my breath.

'Wants it in kind!' Sal shrugged angrily. 'Knows I ain't got no money!'

'How much do you want?' I thrust my hand into a jacket pocket and pulled out a handful of coins.

'More than you can afford, brown boy!' the *rent collector* sneered. Those words. Instantly I knew his identity. Years had gone by and I believed I'd finally managed to push him out of my memory but here he was once again dogging my footsteps.

'Snelgrave!' The old anger erupted in me again and the coins dropped to the floor. My hands were around his throat before he could move.

'Stop, Sammy! He's not worth it!' Sal grabbed my arm.

The child shrieked again. Sal let me go in order to pick her up.

My hands left his throat. One slipped around the back of his neck to grab his shirt collar. The other hand grabbed the thick leather belt under his jacket and I lifted him up off the ground. His feet kicked back at me but flayed uselessly in the air, failing to make contact.

'Sammy? Not the little pickaninny?' I saw the same terror in his eyes as on that day I thrashed him in the orphanage yard. 'Thought you were dead!'

'Not so little anymore... and certainly not dead!' I lifted him further off the ground to frog marched him through the scullery and out into the yard. I threw him into the dirty passageway. I thrust the sole of my boot into his back projecting him towards the street.

'Get out and stay out! If I catch you interfering with Sal again, you'll be very sorry!'

'You're the one who'll be sorry, nigger boy!'

He was safely out of my reach now, scurrying out into the street only narrowly avoiding collision with a surprised coalman heaving a sack off his cart.

***

'There, there bai'n. It's o'right now. The bad man's gone away.' Sal paced up and down the bare living room, cuddling her sobbing child.

'Sorry, Sal. I shouldn't have done that.' My heart was still banging loudly in my chest. I tried to calm down.

'Don't matter, Sammy.' She kissed the child's tear stained cheek. 'He deserves a good hidin'!'

'What was it all about? Sounded up to no good to me!' I put two large lumps of coal on a fire that was nearly dead again. 'Some people never change, do they?'

'You've changed, Sammy.' The child slept now, her head slumped on Sal's shoulder.

'I hope it's for the better.' A smile was forced through my anger.

'Aye, you're a man now. You was just a little lad when you left.'

'Yeh, I've been through a lot. Seen a lot of people… A lot of places.' I tried to shrug off all the things I'd been through – especially the painful ones. I'd survived them to fight another day which was more than I felt Sal and her child were managing to do.

'Tell me about 'em, Sammy… an' tell me about you. Last night all I did was tell you about our woes.' She sat down, still hugging the child who now snored loudly. 'Did you ever find yer father?'

I sighed and slumped back on to a hard chair.

'No. I asked every Indian I met for years and most of the white folks as well. Searched the faces in the crowd of every show but few of them were brown. In the end I accepted he must've drowned and I really am an orphan… like you and George. It was easier to accept than dreaming about a father who probably didn't want me, if he was still alive. Maybe I've grown up.' I tried to smile. 'Mind, I've kept company with two fine men who proved to be just as good as any real father.' I felt an ache as I said these words. One of those was lost to me too.

'I'm happy for you, Sammy.' Sal sat on the other chair. She gave a weak smile continuing to rock her sleeping baby.

'You still haven't told me what our friend, Smelly, was after.' I wanted to change the subject and pressed her for an explanation of what I'd heard. 'Sounded like he wanted to have his way with you.'

'He was wantin' more than that, Sammy.' She looked lovingly at the child and kissed her forehead.

Her answer puzzled me.

'He's got a knockin' shop… an' he's wantin' me to work in it!' I got a glimpse of the old defiant Sal.

'Knocking shop?' I remained puzzled. Not an expression I was used to.

'A brothel, Sammy. Wants me to be one of his whores!' The blue eyes flashed. It was like the old days. She was beautiful when she was angry. Why had it taken me so long to notice? I could feel something stirring inside me. Maybe I really *was* a man now.

I thumped the rough table, regretting not doing Edward Snelgrave more permanent damage when I had the opportunity. 'Sittin' on a fortune,' he'd said. I knew whose fortune he intended it to be.

'I wouldn't be the first lass who's lost her husband an' got behind with the rent in one of his houses… an' then finished up havin' to degrade herself! With profits from there he buys more houses to rent out an' so it goes on.' She looked weary again and her head drooped. It would need more than a bag of coal to keep her warm in this cold world.

'So that's where he gets his money from?'

'That an' tekin' bets… he's a bookie… not legal, of course, but the police turn a blind eye… an' he's got a club in the next street where the fishermen can go an' get a drink when pubs is shut. Owt where he can make money out of the folk round here.'

'Sooner you're out of here, the better, Sal!' My mouth worked faster than my brain.

'Where'd we go, Sammy?' Her head shook gently with disbelief. She looked at her child. 'It'd be the orphanage for Martha and the workhouse for me.'

'I'll sort something out, Sal. Don't you worry!' I knew I must, but how I was going to achieve it was something I still needed to work out.

Chapter 15

'Well, I never! Sammy! It can't be!' George looked up from his dinner plate in amazement and jumped up from his chair. Loose black braces dangled down to the knees of his thick trousers. Nothing had changed. In my memories George and food were never far apart.

'It is him, George!' I think it was the first time I'd heard Sal laugh. She jogged Martha gently in her arms. 'Just look at 'im now.'

'It's me, George. The black sheep's come home again!' I held out my arms. The long tassels on my sleeves hung loose. My arms must have looked like an angel's wings but any resemblance to a heavenly body ended there.

He threw his arms around me and squeezed me in a bear hug. I stood slightly taller than him now and while his short-cropped hair was still the same bright red, the freckles had faded.

Two tiny boys scurried from their play in front of the open fire to hide behind their mother's long skirt. They'd never seen anything like me before. They must have thought their father was wrestling me. Two small heads – one red-haired, the other brown – peeped slowly from their safety behind skirt folds to watch what the strange intruder was doing.

The living room looked as sparsely furnished as Sal's but I felt something different here. It felt like a home. The warmth in the room came from more than the glow in the fire grate.

'We'll have to have a party!' George shouted over my shoulder. 'Get blind drunk!'

'No you won't!' his wife laughed, stroking the boys' heads. Now two more pairs of large eyes stared up at me.

'Us Red Indians are not allowed firewater, didn't you know that!' I looked over his shoulder and gave the two women a wink. He continued holding on to me. Was he frightened to let go in case he let me disappear from his life again?

'There's lots to talk about,' Sal said. 'Sammy's got lots to tell us.'

'I expect George has a few tales to tell as well,' I said. 'Especially about South Africa. That's one place Bill's show hasn't been yet.'

'Bore you to death, he will.' George's wife shook her head in mock dismay. It was the first time I'd taken more than a glance at her. She looked familiar.

Finally, he let go of me and I could breathe again.

'Don't I know you?' I took a closer look at George's wife.

'Course you do, Sammy!' Sal interrupted. 'My best friend – Annie Phelps, as was!'

Time had been kinder to Annie than Sal, although the thin mousy brown hair and large teeth were just the same as all those years ago. I hoped for George's sake she still possessed her old easygoing disposition.

'I think I'll tek the afternoon off work!' My oldest friend stood back to take a long look at me.

'I think you won't!' Annie's hands thrust onto her hips. 'Jobs are hard come by. Took you long enough to get this one.'

'She's right, our George!' Once again it was the old Sal telling her brother what to do.

'I'll still be around when you've finished work. Don't worry.' I was in no hurry to run away this time.

***

I had jobs to do for the show in the city centre: visits to be made to the offices of the local newspapers: the *Hull Daily Mail* and the *Hull News*. I had to arrange for advertisements and to deliver letters, written by Major Burke himself, to the editor of each publication. The Major loved the personal touch: 'Make people think you care; make 'em think they're special.' Visits had to be made to every suitable local store, the ones located in prominent places, in order to persuade them to accept window posters. It would be in exchange for complimentary tickets to the show, of course. The Major asked me to pay a courtesy visit to *Holders' Piano Warehouse* in Whitefriargate. This was an important call on my itinerary because it was where the show's advance tickets – the expensive ones – were sold. He said a visit from a *real* Red Indian might inspire them to fill more seats. Really, he only wanted me to find out how advance sales were going.

Sal came with me after Annie volunteered to take care of Martha.

'Not been in town for ages.' She gazed out the window of our tram as it rattled along Hessle Road. 'No reason to go. Can't even afford to go window-shoppin'... You don't dare do that unless you think one day things will get better.'

We made an unusual sight – the threadbare, red-haired fishwife and a tall brown man dressed in buckskin. I felt conscious of people staring at us. Something to give them to gossip about. Despite our age and experience we were both innocents at large. I should have known better. At any moment we could have been subjected to a torrent of bigoted abuse because the sight of a white woman accompanied by a "darkie" might have offended someone. Fortunately, all we got were strange looks and whispers behind our backs. I'd spent a lifetime becoming used to them.

In the city centre Sal behaved like a stranger to her own town. She gazed into shop windows and at the other people in the streets, all dressed in their *best,* as she described their clothes. I felt guilty bringing her among all these people in her worn dress and tattered shawl. I saw her gazing longingly into the window of a lady's outfitter in Prospect Street. This was a street where the more affluent of the city came to shop. The window glass reflected the grey stone face of the city's main hospital, the Hull Royal Infirmary. The dresses on display looked like ones I anticipated seeing again soon but they would be worn by ladies seated in the most expensive seats in the show. I saw Sal's eyes moisten and her face became sad. Window-shopping is an expensive business for someone with nothing in her purse and no prospect of this ever changing.

'Fancy a new dress, Sal?' I regretted my words. Did they sound like an insult? I didn't mean them to be.

She sighed. Her eyes left the display of expensive silk. I thought how beautiful she would look wearing one of them, flowing down a wide staircase beneath glittering crystal chandeliers. Cascades of red curls would tumble over bare shoulders. Every eye would admire this grand entry into the ballroom. A Cinderella to end all Cinderellas, deserving a prince to take care of her.

'Aye, but not from here. Too good for the likes of me.' She sighed again and turned to face me.

'Nothing's too good for you, Sal.' I wasn't going to let her demean herself. She was special. The feeling that suddenly overwhelmed me the previous night returned. It was a good feeling. It was much more than a simple determination to make her life better.

'Don't you go bein' daft, Sammy!' She slipped her arm into mine and her head came to rest on my shoulder. I wondered if she had the same feeling as me. 'You sound like Stan when he was home from sea... an' drunk!'

'I'm serious, Sal. Would you like a new dress? I want to treat you.' I wasn't going to take 'No' for an answer.

'Aye, silly hapeth!' She looked up and smiled. I'd never seen Sal smile this way before. The first person who'd ever smiled at me like this before had been Laughing Waters. It made me feel very happy but at the same time very sad.

'What's up, Sammy? Are you cryin'?' Her hand reached up and touched my cheek. The skin on her fingers may have been rough but the touch felt like magic.

'Nowt!' I slipped back into my old dialect without thinking and forced a smile.

'Let's go down the market. A posh frock's not much good for donkey stoning the front step.' She gave my arm a tug.

***

There remained one person I needed to find. I decided it was best if I found Mary on my own, so I put Sal on a Hessle Road bound tram with her bundle of shopping and instructions to put on her new dress immediately. There was to be no waiting until Sunday.

I caught another tram: the Anlaby Road service.

My timing was right. Hordes of children teemed out of the Tweed Street Board School like the raging torrent of a river in full flood, which then divided into a hundred tributaries. A thousand small eyes stared at the strange sight in the street, cutting through their throng like a ship fighting against the tide to head upstream.

I entered the school through the open green painted doors of a porch. On one side of the corridor the lower sections of the walls were coated in polished white tiles. A single run of brown tiles indicated the end of the sterile whiteness and the beginning of yellow distempered walls. My boots echoed on the scrubbed flagstone floor as I walked past rows of empty hooked metal coat pegs on the other side.

The matronly shape of a middle-aged woman in the doorway at the end of the corridor blocked my further progress into the school beyond.

'May I help you?' Her manner was formal. Bright light shone from behind her and I could make out neither her features nor her expression. From the tone of her voice I knew neither of these welcomed me.

'Good afternoon, ma'am.' I reckoned the schoolmistress would tolerate nothing other than polite behaviour from me. No, she would demand it. 'I am looking for Miss Smyle. I was led to believe that she is a teacher here.'

'What business might you have with Miss Smyle?' Her head moved slightly to one side. My obstacle wore large round spectacles with hair tied back in a tight bun. At least her reply seemed to confirm Mary still worked here.

'I have a message to give her from a relative.' I wanted to reveal as little as possible before seeing my sister. I wanted to be the first to tell her who I was.

'I believe Miss Smyle is an orphan and doesn't have any family!' Contact would not be allowed without a struggle.

'It's from a very distant relative.' I decided sixteen years and a gap of more than four thousand miles made me *very distant*.

'Wait here!' she said before disappearing into the large hall. Her heavy shoes clip-clopped on the polished wooden floor.

I edged further forward to get a better look into my sister's world. I guessed this large bare space must be the room where morning assembly took place. It must have been twenty feet high with windows sited more than halfway up the white painted brick walls. The sun shining through them created pools of light on the polished floor. It brought back memories of a time and place I'd rather have forgotten: all those mornings suffering the Master's droning voice leading us into endless religious dirges and long unanswered prayers. During those times my mind could be guaranteed to drift away into my own version of heaven, which always involved my lost family and my hero. In reality, if anyone brought me salvation, it was William Cody and the people who the rest of the world believed to be only heathen savages.

The echo of more footsteps disturbed my reverie.

A slender young woman walked towards me across the school hall.

My stomach turned a somersault. Her size, her shape, her sway. It was my mother walking towards me. Every movement I saw triggered so much pain. She drew closer and I could see she wasn't the person in my imagination. The face looked identical: the eyes were the same deep blue, but the skin was darker. The tied-back hair was not blonde but dark brown with thin streaks of a lighter colour running through.

The older woman reappeared at the far end of the hall. She maintained her distance but kept a watchful eye on events.

'Can I help you?' The same voice. Twenty years had passed and it was as though only a moment had gone by. It hurt.

'Are you Mary? Mary Smyle.' I stumbled over words catching in my throat.

'Yes, can I help you?' I could sense impatience in her voice.

I was a total stranger to her. There was no obvious recognition. Why should there be? She was only a baby the last time...

'You told the headmistress, Miss Conway that you have a message from a distant relative.'

'I'm Sammy.' She must know me.

'Yes, but what is your message?' She looked at me as though I was an idiot.

The agitated Miss Conway took a couple of paces forward.

'I'm Sammy... Sammy Smyle. Your brother!'

She recoiled. Horror overwhelmed the beautiful face.

'No! No! He's dead! Ran away! Drowned!' Her hands rose and she pushed her palms forward to ward me off. 'How dare you! Go away! Go away!'

She ran back down the hall towards the headmistress. Miss Conway marched in the opposite direction. My direction.

'Get out, young man!' she shouted. 'Get out before I send for a policeman!' She steamed towards me like a battleship about to launch a salvo.

I turned and rushed back down the corridor like a naughty schoolboy trying to escape a thrashing. Out into the yard, through the gates and into the street, with tears streaming down my face. Why did every close contact with a woman seem to end in so much pain for me? Every woman – except for Sal.

Chapter 16

'You look sad, Sammy.' Sal's arms were wrapped around my shoulders in a reassuring hug. She stood beside me as I sat slumped at her living room table. An untouched cup of tea sat on the table by my elbow. The cheering glow from hot coals in the hearth did nothing to improve my spirits.

'She didn't want to know me, Sal!' I fought back tears welling up inside me.

'Must've been a big surprise for her. Thinkin' you was long dead an' all.' She pressed her cheek onto mine. I could feel her cheekbones through thin skin. 'Then a big bloke like you turns up... out of the blue like and says *Hello love, I'm yer long lost brother.* You was a shock for me an' I guessed who you was! Well, you ain't changed all that much. You'll never change them blue eyes, Sammy.'

I forced a smile.

Her cheek still clung onto mine. I could taste sweet tea on her breath. I turned my head and our lips met. It felt the natural thing to do. She did not resist.

'Well now, that's a surprise!' She gasped, looking startled rather than shocked.

'Nice surprise, I hope?'

Please let it be a nice one, I prayed.

'You're full of nice surprises, Sammy Smyle.' She straightened herself.

'I love you, Sal! Always have!' My heart leapt.

'Steady on!' She took half a step back, but her hands didn't leave my shoulders.

'I loved you when we were children. Thought of you as my big sister then, but now...'

'That didn't feel like no brotherly kiss. George only gives me a peck on the cheek.' She trembled. Fear? Excitement? Both?

'But we're grown up now. I'm a man and… you're a beautiful lady, Sal.'

'Don't feel beautiful, Sammy.' The sad face reappeared.

'With your new frock on there'll not be a better-looking woman on the whole of Hessle Road. No! In all Hull! The whole world, Sal!' I was up and on my feet now. Earlier events forgotten for a moment. 'But you don't need posh frocks, Sal. You're beautiful all the way through.'

'Where did you learn such talk, Sammy Smyle? Them Red Indians don't talk like that, do they?' She raised her right arm, the palm of her hand held towards me. Was she rejecting me too?

'No, but their emotions are honest. I learned more from them about life and what really matters than I could have learned in a million years in that orphanage.'

I inched closer. Her hand touched my chest but her feigned resistance lacked any strength and her arms slipped around my back. I pulled her close; wanting to kiss her again but she jerked back her head.

'Have you got one o' them squaws back there? You know… in America?' Her eyes were fierce as only her eyes could be. 'Don't think you can…'

'I had a wife, Sal. Never thought I'd ever love anybody again… not until I saw you yesterday.'

'What happened to her?' I tried to hold her close, as the memories hit me, but she still held back.

'Measles. One of the white man's gifts to the Indian nation! She died along with the baby she carried. Our baby. All her family as well …and all my family. All gone, Sal!' Any need to kiss Sal evaporated and my head drooped.

'Poor bai'n! I know how you feel, Sammy.'

Sal's head nestled beneath my chin and I could smell her hair. It had just been washed but no rich perfume lingered in the long red tresses, only the honest smell of soap. It was Morning Star's head beside me again. Guilt hurt. How could I love someone else?

Her arms wrapped around me again and her hug tightened. Her head sank deeper into my chest. She began sobbing. The trembling vibrated through my body.

'What's up, Sal?' I half whispered.

'I'm roarin'!' she muttered through the sobs. 'Bawlin' me head off!'

'There's no need to cry for me. It was all a long time ago...' I lied about my hurt; all the time in the world could never heal the pain.

'Not just cryin' for you, you daft 'apeth!'

Her head slumped back onto my chest and I felt her tears seeping through my shirt. This was not a good day for dealing with women or so it felt to me. Two women and I wanted to love them both; I wanted them both to love me but just how to manage it lay well beyond my understanding.

I lifted her. She felt as light as a feather. I sat down by the table again and gently slipped her onto my lap. She continued sobbing for what felt like hours. My mind drifted away until I almost fell asleep.

A hand stroked my cheek.

'People called me a hard-faced bitch, Sammy. I hear 'em behind me back.'

Her hand stroked the back of my head. I could feel moist breath warming my neck and chin.

'*You need to* have *a roar. Let it out an' you'll feel better*, they told me. But not hard-faced Sal. She was goin' to be strong.'

'You are strong, Sal. Always have been ... but you're not hard faced.'

I lowered my head to kiss her again. Gently. First on the forehead, then on lips hot and salty from her tears.

'Are you one o' them witch doctors, Sammy? Are you castin' a spell on me?' Large eyes begged an answer.

'No! You're the one with the magic, Sal.' I laughed. 'And we – the Lakota – have what you'd call medicine men... not witch doctors!'

She raised her head and kissed me. I wasn't going to question what was happening now. We were two people who needed each other and at that moment it was all that mattered.

***

'We'd better go an' get Martha.' Sal's words brought me back to reality. My head rolled back onto the feather pillow and I looked up at the bedroom's whitewashed ceiling. We didn't care what the neighbours might think.

'What are we goin' to tell George an' Annie?' Sal looked perplexed again.

'Tell 'em you're going away to live with me in a tepee out on the prairie! Scrub clothes in a stream!'

My hand stroked the taut bare skin of her flat stomach. It would get a lot plumper, if we had anything to do with it.

'You what!' She propped herself up on her elbow in a flash. 'You live in a tent? In a field?'

Her incredulous look made me laugh.

'Haven't lived in one for years.'

She punched my shoulders playfully. I grabbed her fists: one in each hand. She tried to break free. Long red hair, allowed to fall loose, fell into my face. As we struggled playfully I noticed how thin she'd become. I could see her ribs through creamy pale skin. My wife Morning Star's skin had been almost bronze.

'Maybe Annie could look after Martha for a bit longer?' My arms wrapped around her and I pulled Sal back onto me. Our mouths met again.

For an instant my mind tripped back in time. This was little Sammy with Sal – the good girl who helped in the kitchen. What would Mrs G think of her two favourites now? My thoughts returned to the present. I wanted her but that wasn't all I felt. I needed her. The way she touched me said she needed me too but there was much more to how we felt about each other.

I'd been without the touch of a woman for too long. Sal was worth the wait.

***

'I was beginnin' to get worried,' Annie said rubbing flour from her hands onto a grey pinafore.

'Has she been a good girl?' Sal looked at Martha playing with her two cousins in front of a crackling fire.

'Good as gold.' Annie smiled at the children.

'Just like her mother,' I whispered in Sal's ear. A sharp elbow in the ribs was all I received for my pains.

'We've been bakin'… ain't we bai'ns?'

The children looked up briefly, nodded in agreement and then went back to their play.

'Gave 'em some bits of raw pastry to play with... to make some shapes to put in the oven. Wouldn't fancy eatin' 'em though!' Annie pulled a sour face at the thought. 'What you two been up to?'

'Been shoppin'!' Sal said proudly, pulling off her new navy-blue shawl. She twirled around displaying a matching blue skirt and a crisp white blouse, all bought in the market. 'Sammy got 'em for me. A bit on the big side but he says I might grow into 'em.' She looked at me and giggled.

Annie gave me what I can only describe as an old-fashioned look before turning back to her sister-in-law. 'All dressed up and nowhere to go!'

'But she has,' I said. 'If she's willing to come with me.'

'This is all a bit sudden!' Annie must have seen the little smile Sal gave me.

'Sooner the better!' I gave Sal's hand a squeeze. 'Get her as far as possible away from the clutches of our old friend Smelly Snelgrave. The show's only got another couple of months in England and then we're off back to America.'

Sal's worried look returned. 'I hadn't thought about that.'

The same feeling gripped me as the one I felt all those years ago when George ran off and left me with the Lakota. I couldn't lose her now.

'Let's have a cup o' tea.' Annie picked up a large fire blackened kettle and put it on the lip of the fire grate. The drinking of cups of tea, I discovered, was the Hull equivalent of smoking a pipe back in the lodges of the Lakota.

***

'Well, who'd have believed it?' George looked astonished but he didn't seem too unhappy to hear our news. 'A bit sudden, ain't it Sammy?'

'We've known each other for years!' I said.

'But we was only bai'ns back then.' He leaned back against the front wall of his house in the street. We'd left the women inside with the children.

'I always thought Sal was something special. She looked after us back then and now I want to look after her.' I leant with one elbow against the wall.

'You're goin' to tek her away?' I could see the concern in his eyes. 'To America?'

'Yes, to the real Wild West. But it's not all that wild anymore!' I laughed and rolled back, leaning on both elbows. 'The air's so clean you can get drunk on it. What's Sal and little Martha got to look forward to here? Walking the streets for Snelgrave's profit... and Martha put in the orphanage like we were.'

'You're right.' George sighed, breathing out through his nose making his sparse ginger moustache ruffle. He gazed upwards to look over the grey slate rooftops into the last of the evening sun or what could be seen of it through smoke from ten thousand chimney pots. 'It's just that... well, Sal's always been there lookin' out for me. Even when I was born Sal was there... waitin' for me.'

'And what have you got to keep you here, George?'

He turned and gave me a quizzical look.

'Looking after other people's horses. Tired old nags that pull smelly carts off the fish dock. You could be out there with us. Have your own horses... and your own land to graze them on. See your lads grow up in the sunshine.' I took a deep breath, letting my mind cross a wide ocean. I could see acres of long grass swaying in the sunshine, but these were not like the visions of my childhood imaginings in Pearson Park. This was real. I had been there.

'Sounds too good to be true to me, Sammy.' George straightened up and turned to go back into the house. 'An' how am I gonna pay for us to get there? It's a struggle to find enough money to keep us fed and a roof over our heads!'

'I'll get you a job with the show. If you're half as good with horses as I think you are, Bill will find you a job and all of you can go back to America with us. He pays a good wage to a good man for a good day's work.' My hand went onto his shoulder. I didn't want to let this fish wriggle off my hook again.

'I'll have to talk to Annie about this.' He turned away from me. I could some sense his reluctance but not a lot.

'Just think of it. The three of us together again... and Annie and the bai'ns. I dreamed the dream, George... and it came true! It can for you, as well.'

***

The night was as black as pitch when we left the Smith's house. What little of the moon there was lay hidden behind dark clouds.

'Watch your step!' Annie warned. 'Streets are full o' dog mess.'

'Don't worry. Us Indians can see in the dark!' I loved kidding her along. She still had a serious nature.

West Dock Avenue was only a couple of streets away so we didn't need to take care where we trod for long. We talked quietly not to disturb Martha who became a little bundle, fast asleep on my shoulder. I could feel her heart beating gently and her warm breath trickling down into my collar.

'You've got a way with women.' Sal smiled at the paternal way I held her baby.

'Some women, maybe.' I still wondered what my next step would be with Mary. There had to be something I could do.

'I think Annie liked what you was sayin' about us all goin' to America.' She slipped her arm into mine, letting her head come to rest on my shoulder.

'Maybe those pale ales helped persuade her. Did they work on you, Sal?'

'I'm comin' round to the idea.' She hiccupped.

'You've had too much to drink!'

'Me! Never! Not *sensible Sal*!' She hiccupped again.

'George didn't seem too keen, though.'

'Don't worry... I'll work on him. He's just like he was when he was a lad. A bit like one of them old hosses he looks after. Once you've got him pointed in the right direction, he's o'right!' She giggled and hiccupped simultaneously.

'You *are* drunk!'

We were back in West Dock Avenue and into the darkest part of our return. Not a single light shone from the shops and businesses, all closed for the night. Black school buildings on the other side of the street looked ominous in the dark. Only the flickering gas flames of the street lamps lit our journey.

'I don't think I should leave you in your condition,' I said. We were near number forty-two.

'Just a bit tipsy. That sounds like an excuse to me, Sammy!' Sal giggled and kissed my cheek.

'Maybe.' I shrugged. 'Do I need an excuse?'

Before she could reply figures emerged from the dark passageway between her house and number forty-four.

'Ain't this pretty! You might need to charge less, Sal, if your customers know you've been with a black man!'

Even though I couldn't see his face in the dark I knew it was Snelgrave and I could sense him sneering even without clear sight of his acne ravaged face. Like George he hadn't changed in all the years I'd been away, except for the worse. Two men accompanied him. Both were considerably larger than him. Nothing had changed.

'I thought I'd told you to leave Sal alone!' The old hatred seethed hotter than ever, but this time it wasn't only me who he threatened.

'And I told you, you'd be sorry.' He laughed without a hint of mirth.

The two larger bodies moved in our direction. Sal grabbed the slumbering Martha from me and ducked into the shelter of her home's doorway.

From the lumbering way the two men came towards me I guessed they relied on brute force rather than guile in doing Snelgrave's dirty work. Wrestling steers to the ground ready for branding would stand me in good stead, I hoped. The first bully lunged at me. I swayed to one side like a matador and swung a solid kick into the side of his knee. This was no time for fighting fairly.

The second bully was immediately upon me. Another sway took me out the way of his would-be haymaker. I felt the breeze as it passed my cheek. A swift punch to his kidneys made him gasp but his partner was back at me. The sore knee only angered him and he grabbed me by the throat.

'Want to get rough d'you?' I shouted. My elbow jabbed backwards catching him below the ribs.

It made the thug pause long enough for me to pull his hands from around my neck and to swing him to the ground. His head cracked on the flagstone like a coconut falling from its perch in a fairground shy. He was either thick skulled or didn't have the sense to know when he was injured. He came straight back up again, cursing loudly.

I felt a sharp stabbing pain in my back. My other attacker landed a hard blow, only inches above my pelvis with something harder than a human fist. He held a block of wood and I felt it land again but across my shoulders this time. Luckily he missed the back of my skull.

Sal screamed. I staggered drunkenly. Martha cried in terror.

'Finish him off!' Snelgrave demanded.

Both his henchmen were on me now.

'Get him on the ground and give him a good kicking! Quick! I'll shut this silly tart up.'

'You bastard, Snelgrave!' Sal screamed.

I lay flat on the pavement now. A blow from the wooden club across my ear stopped an attempt to get back up again. The taste of dirty flagstone mixed with blood in my mouth.

'Do it! Go on! Do it!' Snelgrave sounded sexually excited.

I felt the first kick into my ribs, but another body fell on top of me and it caught the second boot.

It was Snelgrave.

'Stop! Stop! It's me! Stop!' he screamed.

Another body fell on the pavement. One of my attackers' heads thumped on the stone floor beside me, thunking like another fcoconut.

I scrambled onto my feet. A new man had joined in the melee, but he was on my side. He threw the last of my assailants into the front wall of number forty-two. I heard the back of his head crack on the bricks before he slid down the wall to finish up slumped unconscious on the pavement.

'You o'right?' It was George's voice.

'All the better for seeing you, son!'

I grabbed the assailant who was lying alongside his master. I yanked him off the ground and threw him towards the house wall. 'Grab your mate and push off!'

The defeated bully did as he was told, dragging his slumped confederate back to his feet. They scurried down the street in the direction of Hessle Road.

Snelgrave remained on the ground curled in a foetal ball, screaming at his fleeing men to come back to help him. He screwed himself up tighter, expecting to receive the kicking he deserved.

'Shut up, Smelly!' I said. 'I've got something better in mind and more permanent than putting my boot into you.'

'What you doin' 'ere, our George?' Sal's voice still quaked although she was calming down. Martha continued to wail loudly.

'Annie told me to come. Said to tell you we want to go to America with you!' Strong as an ox but it was still someone who told him what to do. Nothing had changed.

Lights had turned on in houses close by and heads peeped out of doorways to see the cause of the commotion in their street.

'Is it far to the Fish Dock?' I asked George.

'Couple of hundred yards or so.'

I grabbed Snelgrave by his arm and hauled him to his feet.

'Come on! I've had more than enough of you!'

Snelgrave's protests against being dragged towards the dock soon ceased. A hard slap across his mouth with the back of my hand was sufficient persuasion.

Chapter 17

We dragooned a very unwilling Snelgrave along slippery pavements; down into the subway road beneath railway lines linking Hull's docks to the rest of the country. The possibility of further swift pain kept the coward quiet. The railway tracks formed a physical barrier between the Fish Dock and the warren of streets where the families of fishermen and dockworkers lived. The lingering reek of pungent spillage from ten thousand fish carts hung in static air trapped below ground level. Yellow gaslights high in the iron roof reflected in greasy puddles below like shimmering stars in a dirty heaven.

'What we goin' to do with him?' George's voice echoed off subterranean wall tiles green with ancient algae.

'See the last of him! The world'll be better off without the likes of our old friend here!' I gave his arm a sharp yank. Our captive struggled again. A swift punch to his ribs dissuaded any further complaints.

'Steady on, Sammy! This ain't the Wild West!' The subway's echo turned George's words into a yell.

'A lot wilder… if you ask me.' Even my coarse whisper reverberated eerily around the wide underground passageway.

Snelgrave dragged his feet across the uneven paving stones, the toes of his shoes clip clopping on the edges. It was the only resistance he dared to make. Maybe I'd have done the same in his position but his arm still got an extra yank. I'd had more than enough of him for one lifetime.

'I've got a better idea,' George tried to whisper. 'An' it won't get us hung!'

'All right.' I wondered what he had in mind. George wasn't a schemer. He'd always left such things to Sal and me – well, mainly me – to dream up but I was prepared to listen to him now. I'd no wish to risk a severe penalty even if I believed it was for justifiable retribution. I had something worth living for now.

Our frog march took us back upwards toward the subway exit and the entrance to the pier. The air smelled fresher up here but not by much. At least the breeze coming off the river made it move. The iron railings flanking the pavement ended at the gate to St. Andrew's Dock. George swung his arm around our captive's shoulders and we staggered drunkenly towards the entrance looking like three very unwise monkeys.

'Let me do the talkin'. Keep your hand across Smelly's gob.' George took command of the situation. This was something I'd never seen before. Maybe he had changed.

'Where are you lads goin'?' an unseen gatekeeper's voice demanded from inside the darkness of his wooden sentry box at the gate.

'To our boat!' George replied. 'We're off on the next tide.'

'What's up wi' yer mate?' Our interrogator wanted to know more. He moved forward but became no more than a vague shape still inside the gloom of his sentry box.

'Had a skin full, mate! Can't take his drink. Two sniffs o' the barmaid's apron an' he's under the table! He'll be all right by time we get to the mouth of the Humber! Spew it all up by then!' George continued speaking on our behalf. My new accent would have been a giveaway. I doubted if there were any American fishermen sailing out of Hull or even brown ones for that matter. Luckily the darkness concealed my skin.

Snelgrave's mouth stayed shut too. I made sure of it.

'You lads never learn!' the dock guardian laughed. 'What boat you on?'

'The *St. Marcus*,' George replied.

I hoped such a trawler really existed, but the gatekeeper seemed satisfied with the ship's name.

"Ave a good trip, lads.' The guardian went back inside to what he had been doing before, probably snoozing.

We staggered on towards the blurred shapes of buildings and a smell of fish so strong that even the sharpening breeze couldn't dilute it. I kept my head low. A brown face and a dangling braid of hair would soon have attracted unwanted attention, if there was anyone else around to see them. When we had walked a few yards further, weak moonlight began breaking through the moving clouds. It flickered on the water's greasy surface although it was only visible in the centre of the pool. Tight rows of small steam trawlers crammed the wooden pier on both sides; all waiting to embark on their next trips out into the North Sea to search for haddock, cod and anything else that would turn a penny for their owners on the fish market.

'Let's get Smelly onto the *St. Marcus*,' George said. So, it did exist.

He led us to a fishing boat moored along the quay. Its side was raised up about three feet higher than the quayside. We scrambled up it and dropped onto the deck. Needless to say, Snelgrave required extra cajoling as well as lifting aboard.

'Is this it?' I was still a poor climber, especially when it also involved keeping a tight grip on a reluctant companion.

'No – it's the one at the end.' George pointed across the queue of gently bobbing fishing boats ahead of us. My heart sank. There would be more vessels to cross before I discovered finally what he had in mind for our unwilling captive.

A swift and very blunt word of advice went in Snelgrave's ear. I made clear my continued willingness to use a more permanent solution. It proved sufficient persuasion to prevent any further trouble especially when I jerked his head in the direction of the stinking oily water in the narrow gap between two trawlers bobbing up and down.

A docile Snelgrave was necessary for the remainder of our journey as well. I thought the dock's waters would be calm but the trawlers moved up and down randomly against each other. A small difference in height could rapidly become a drop or even a climb of four feet or more to the deck of a neighbouring steam trawler as they both rocked gently on the faint swell. Although the fishermen lashed their vessels together with heavy ropes, a gap could appear between them without warning. On Coney Island in New York a fairground attraction called the Cakewalk had a similar motion, but it had nothing on this. The Cakewalk doesn't offer the possibility of being crushed to death, if you fall down in-between the sides of two boats.

While Edward Snelgrave showed good sense in avoiding being deliberately awkward, he wasn't the easiest package to shift from one bobbing fishing boat to another. Even in weak light I could see his complexion turning sickly green.

The further out we went the more unpredictable the motion of the ships became. I call the vessels 'ships' but all the locals called the steam trawlers *boats* and I found this diminutive description unsurprising. I'd have been wary of sailing as far as the dock's lock gates, standing between their mooring and the River Humber, in anything so small as one of them, let alone out to where the fishermen took them to find and harvest their quarry: into the North Sea and sometimes far beyond. A ship the size of the old *Persian Monarch* is the smallest vessel I'd willingly sail aboard and it was many times bigger than any of these craft.

'Let's chuck him in the dock,' I whispered my original intention in George's ear. We'd struggled to get from the third to a fourth trawler and I'd become exasperated with our companion's unwillingness to move.

'No! We're nearly there!' George's expression told me my words put the fear of God into him. The look on Snelgrave's face said he feared wherever we were heading even more than meeting his maker.

George's idea of *nearly* still looked a long way off to me.

The drop onto the next vessel became much steeper in the brief instant between jumping from its neighbour and hitting the deck. We landed with a loud thump and fell in a heap.

'What's goin' on?' an aged voice croaked from deep in the bowels of the vessel.

'It's all right, mate!' George replied. 'Just goin' on board *St. Marcus*, ready for the tide.'

A dark shape staggered uncertainly from the boat's bridge. In the faint moonlight I could just about see the figure of an old man in a flat cap and thick overcoat. Glazed eyes examined us as closely as they were able through smoke rising from a clay pipe. He tugged the pipe out of his mouth and looked away briefly to hawk up phlegm from deep inside his lungs and spit it into the water.

'What's up wi' yer mate?' He nodded towards Snelgrave, pipe back in mouth.

'Drunk!' George replied. 'Needs Dutch courage to go back to sea. Be all right once we get out into the open water.'

'Aye, I knew lads like that when I was at sea.' The old man's laugh made his lungs rattle like a bag of loose nuts and bolts. 'Make sure 'e pukes up over the side an' not on board!' He rasped another cough and spat into the greasy water again.

'We'll take good care of him!' George and I laughed but Snelgrave felt nothing amusing in the exchange. I don't suppose having an arm twisted behind his back improved his humour. The old man went back to the comfort of the bridge.

'Only the watchman,' George whispered.

Much to my relief our final crossing was easier.

'Now what?' I still wondered what he planned.

'Let's find some rope.' George glanced around the deck of the trawler.

The *St. Marcus* looked like all the others along the quay. It was all open deck, apart from the stern end where sat a funnel together with the small hut that served as the trawler's bridge. The open work area could not have been much more than ninety feet in length and less than twenty wide. This vessel, and many others like it, provided the basis for the livelihood of thousands of Hull people. Too often they also provided the coffins for the men who put to sea in them and never returned home.

George found what he wanted and nodded to me to drag our prisoner towards the stern. He pulled open a hatch door on the deck and looked into the space below.

'Good! She's been coaled.' I sensed relief in his voice. 'Don't want tons of coal droppin' on him.' He turned to look at Snelgrave. 'Let's ger him tied up.'

George displayed his expertise in tying knots. My hand remained tight across our captive's mouth until an unsavoury gag of overly aromatic torn sacking completed Snelgrave's bondage.

'In you go, Smelly!' George pushed our trussed nemesis onto the mound of black rocks down in the hold. 'They'll not find him until they're out at sea.' He replaced the cover and my friend's smile lit up the darkness.

'Won't they bring him back? Once they find him,' I asked.

'Eventually.' George smiled again. 'I know the skipper o' this boat. He's a strict Methodist. He'll make Smelly work out there – out o' spite! Won't take no bribes to bring him back. When they've left the Fish Dock the skipper won't turn back until they've caught all the fish they can. Lost time means lost money.'

'How long will that be?'

'At least a month – maybe two!' George appeared to be about to have one of his giggling fits. We were back in our orphanage bed once again.

'Shh!' My hand went across his mouth just as it did in the old days. 'Let's get away from here!'

Without the burden of erstwhile captive our return journey across the continually bobbing vessels was a lot easier to accomplish. The old watchman's loud snoring told us he wouldn't query why we'd jumped ship so soon. We didn't dare risk the gate bobby again and decided to cross the open railway lines instead. We clambered through the broken fence all the time looking furtively for any sign of trains moving on the tracks. It looked safe although trains were being marshalled only a few hundred yards away. We heard the clattering and clanging of the railwaymen's preparation of freight wagons to carry fresh fish coming into the city on the next tide to all parts of the kingdom. Once safely across we climbed back into the street through a gap in the rough wooden fence. This route was probably one used by thieves wanting to avoid using the official entrance to carry off stolen fish.

Back in the safety of West Dock Avenue George burst into laughter as we walked down the street.

'What's so funny?' I couldn't see any reason for the laughter. The relief in knowing Snelgrave was out of the way and probably wouldn't return until we were safely aboard ship bound for the United States felt sufficiently satisfying to me but it was hardly hilarious.

'It's Smelly...' He couldn't get the words out for laughing.

'After you left...' More giggles. 'After you left... we started doing sailing lessons. Had to row a boat across Humber Dock. Smelly got seasick every time!' George howled with laughter. This was why he was turning green as we hauled him across the moving vessels.

Above us a sash window slid open with a thud.

'Shut up! Don't y'know it's gone midnight!' an angry voice yelled at us in the darkness.

***

'Ouch!' I winced, now lying safely on Sal's bed upstairs in number forty-two. She applied a cold flannel to the lower part of my ribs. A large purple bruise would appear soon.

'You men are such babies!' The old scornful Sal had returned, and I realised how much I'd been missing her all these years. So different from Morning Star and my Lakota sisters, yet I loved them all.

'Perhaps mummy could kiss it better?' My flesh felt very weak but the spirit remained willing.

'We'll have none of that, my lad! It must be one o'clock in the mornin'' and from the look of you, you'd do yerself a mischief if you tried owt!'

'Can I stay though? It's a long walk to the White Horse… and it'll be locked up for the night.' I knew there was a night porter but I was prepared to do some serious begging to stay.

'As long as you promise to be a good lad!' She smiled and tweaked my nose playfully but then her expression changed. I sensed she regretted showing me encouragement the previous night.

What would people say? Were we back into that?

'I'll be as good as gold as long as I can sleep in mummy's bed.' I tried my little boy hurt look. 'I might have bad dreams!'

'But stay on your side!' She leaned across me and gave me a little peck on the forehead before crossing the room to turn off the light from the gas mantle on the wall above an empty fireplace.

I stood up in the dark and removed the rest of my clothes, letting them drop in a heap on the floor. I turned and saw Sal caught in a shaft of moonlight about to slip under the thin blanket. Wearing only her long cotton slip she looked so thin; nothing like the energetic girl I'd known all those years ago, but I would take care of her. She had become a woman and I knew she was the one I wanted, I needed. I hoped she needed me enough to not have second thoughts about coming on a great adventure.

I climbed under the bed clothes feeling every ache and pain inflicted by Snelgrave's henchmen. Tonight was for resting. There would be other times; there would be better times – for all of us. I'd make sure of that.

***

The next morning we breakfasted on bread and fresh strawberry jam and hot cups of tea.

'I have to go back to join the show,' I said. 'I've done all the advance jobs.'

'But yer comin' back, aren't you?' Sal looked shocked.

'Course I am!' My hand slipped across the table onto hers, narrowly missing an open jam sandwich. 'The show will be here on the first of July... on the fairground. If I can, I'll try to be back before then.'

'I'll miss you, Sammy Smyle.' Sadness reappeared in her eyes for the first time since her tearful outburst the previous day. 'Promise you'll come back.'

Martha looked up inquisitively from the floor where she sat sucking on a sticky, thick bread doorstep.

'I'll soon be back and the next time I go away you and the bai'n will be with me... and George and all his tribe. That's it – we'll form our own tribe! The Smyling Smith tribe!'

Sal forced a smiled, although I could see a tear glistening in an eye corner.

'Couldn't stand it if I lost you again, Sammy. Think I'd do meself in!' She'd been living her life on a knife-edge for too long. Her hand gripped mine tightly, her nails digging into flesh below the knuckle.

'Don't talk daft. This isn't the Selina Smith I know.' I paused for a moment. 'You're not Smith now, though. What is your last name?'

I'd been skirting around the subject of her late husband ever since she'd told me she was a widow. Was it fear of causing her pain or was I too embarrassed to ask? From experience I knew there's relatively little words can do for grief. Too much experience.

'Vicars... Selina Vicars. You remember Stan, don't you?' Her head cocked to one side to give me an inquiring look.

'Stan Vicars... of course I do. Big, gangly lad... he couldn't do his tables or add up to save his life.' I wanted the floor to open up and swallow me for speaking ill of the dead. 'Nice lad, though.' I tried to recover ground. 'I always got on with him. He'd let you have his last ha'penny... mind, he never had a farthing to his name.'

'That was my Stan. Too easily put upon but I took care of him when he was ashore.' This description bore all the hallmarks of her relationship with her brother. It made me wonder about the nature of her marriage to the poor lost Stan.

'Well, Sal. It's time somebody looked after you... and little Martha too.'

She relaxed her tight grip.

'Old Smelly's out of the way for a few weeks… all being well. If he'd still been around I'd have stayed.' My turn to squeeze her hand. 'I'll make sure you've got more than enough to make ends meet while I'm away. It'll only be for a few days.'

'What about your Mary?'

'Not sure what to do about her.' I let go of her hand and scratched my head. 'And there's Mrs G. I'd like to see her as well.'

'Aye, she'd know what to do.' It was the positive Sal again. 'Ain't seen her in a long time.'

'Let's go and see her. We've got to do that before I go. She's in the almshouses on Northumberland Avenue. That's what the new Master at the orphanage told me.'

***

Sal looked beautiful in her new clothes, but I was biased. Martha wore a pink flowery dress that she'd really outgrown. Most of the time she wore cast offs from the Smith boys. Often it was only her long dark hair and pretty face that told anyone she was a girl.

Travelling by tram proved a novel experience for a small child. Big staring eyes took in everything they saw. Everything that is except for the sneers from some of the locals. She was far too young to comprehend their behaviour; as if anyone is ever old enough to understand bigotry.

What sort of woman would have anything to do with a brown man? That's what their expressions told me. *A wonderful woman!* would have been my reply, if any one of them dared to ask this question out loud.

We changed trams in the city centre, getting off our Service D from Dairycoates to the city centre in St. John Street and took the short walk around the corner into Savile Street to catch a Service B tram bound for Beverley Road.

Our claret and white rattled along, first up Bond Street taking us past the statue of Andrew Marvell, the longhaired man who had once reminded me of Colonel Cody. I pointed it out to Sal, who told me he had been a poet in Hull long ago, although she couldn't recite any of his verses. To me, Hull and poetry didn't seem to go together. We drew near to something more to my taste than rhyming couplets: the Hull Brewery Company. The aroma of fermenting beer was far more appealing than the Hessle Road stench of fish, but when we turned into Albion Street the alluring yeasty smell drifted away behind us. There were fine buildings here: the Royal Institution, the Church Institute, the Albion Congregational Church and more. There was even a smart new Public Library building. Perhaps Hull really had become a city after all.

The tram lurched around the next turn, taking us into Prospect Street, past the grey stonework of the Hull Royal Infirmary. From this point on we began to leave the city centre behind and rumbled past the new shops springing up on its edge. Soon we reached Beverley Road, a more spacious highway than Hessle Road. Its tall buildings stood well back, flaunting its residents' greater affluence towards anyone travelling past… and blessedly not a hint of fish.

This final leg of our tram journey was short. We were back on foot needing to cross the main road towards the Sculcoates Union Workhouse on the corner of Fountain Road. We'd have to walk down this to find Mrs G's new home in Northumberland Avenue.

'Is this where you'd have finished up, Sal?' I looked across at the workhouse. The red brick building had a similar appearance to our old orphanage. Why was it that such establishments seem to have had far more thought and money spent on their exteriors than on the care needed by the poor wretches doomed to inhabit them?

'No, it would've been the one on Anlaby Road.' Sal gave me a big hug, squashing Martha between us like the meat in a sandwich. She still needed reassurance. 'You will…'

I stopped her in mid-sentence. 'Of course, I'll be back. Nothing can stop me coming back for you! Both of you!' My arm slipped around her slender waist to tow them both across the main road, safely past the threatening workhouse and towards Mrs G.

The narrow, terraced streets off either side of Fountain Road were alive. A multitude of very young children ran about, playing games that told us we were back in a densely populated area of the city.

'What a crowd!' Sal commented.

Their older brothers and sisters could be heard chanting times tables through the open windows of the Fountain Road Board School. Not as large as its West Dock Avenue counterpart but with identical red brick architecture. Teachers' voices droning inside classrooms brought back memories, ones I'd rather forget. At least they didn't sound Scottish today.

As far as we knew it wasn't a long walk to Mrs G's new home, but the warmth of the day soon made Sal flag. Her strength needed building up. She had gone without proper nourishment for too long. I put my arm around her waist and lifted Martha from her, up onto my shoulder. The little girl seemed to have accepted me quickly. Maybe I did have a natural paternal instinct. Sal's assessments were usually correct.

I was tempted to carry both of them the rest of the way but we'd attracted enough stares from the locals already. Sal would be the subject of attention whenever she accompanied me in public. I hoped she'd learn to cope with it. The sooner we left these overpopulated urban and so-called *civilised* areas the better.

We'd paused to lean on the wall of a bridge over a stream of water. Sal needed the rest. I held up Martha to let her look down into the water beneath us. 'What river is this one? Is it the River Hull?'

'Don't be daft!' Enough of Sal's strength returned to be able to rebuke me. 'This is just a drain. River Hull's not up to much but it's wider 'an this!'

'Wondered why there were no boats on it,' I shrugged. 'Are we nearly there yet?' I assumed Sal must know.

'I think the homes are not much further on, Sammy.' She took a deep breath. 'I'm parched. Could do with a cup o' tea.'

'Maybe Mrs G will rustle one up for us.' I hoped she was still resident in the alms-houses. I wondered what our friend would be like after all this time. In my memory she looked old the first time I saw her nearly twenty years earlier, but to a ten-year-old anyone over thirty was considered decrepit.

We continued our trek and soon came to yet another bridge over a waterway, but this stream seemed even narrower than even the first we'd crossed. The sluggish water below was green with algae.

'Not the River Hull either!' I spoke before Sal could correct me. A resigned smile came in reply.

Alongside this open drain was yet another school building. It looked just like the one we'd passed only a few hundred yards back along Fountain Road. The familiar sound of chanting voices masquerading as education drifted through open classroom windows.

'That's the second school down this street. Must be lots of children around here,' I observed. 'Not surprising, I suppose. All these houses.'

'Town's grown a lot since you left, Sammy.'

'Don't like towns, Sal. Give me wide-open spaces any time. Somewhere where you stretch out your arms and breathe.' I wanted to throw my arms wide but what they held onto was far too precious to risk dropping.

'Tell me it really exists, Sammy. Not just in stories… like ones you told us when you was a little lad.'

'They do, Sal. You can ride out for a whole day and not see another living soul… Then you can stand up in the stirrups of your horse and look in any direction and still not see anyone for another day's ride or more. Mind, sometimes I don't have stirrups!' I couldn't wait to take her and Martha away from here, to see and breathe this paradise.

'Here it is!' Sal pointed, interrupting my rambling. 'Northumberland Avenue. Thought we'd never get here.'

The avenue criss-crossed Fountain Road. The only large building around was at the end of its section branching off to our left. This place had to be the alms-houses. From a distance it displayed the all too familiar visage of a residential home: the look I'd come to loathe. Maybe the powers-that-be wanted ordinary folk to be fearful of losing their freedom. However, when we came closer it didn't look quite so forbidding. The outside walls seemed to contain more windows than brickwork. It looked less like a prison. In the centre of the building was an archway, high enough and wide enough for the Deadwood Stage itself to pass through. A tower rose high above this with a large clock facing us ticking time away.

We walked into the archway and from warm sunshine into cool shade. Martha shouted out wordlessly. Her voice echoed back at us. She stood up in my arms with eyes almost popping out of her head. She called out again and giggled.

'Eh! You'll get us thrown out before we've had chance to see Mrs G!' Sal wagged a finger to remonstrate playfully with her child but we soon left the echoing archway and walked into a large grassed quadrangle.

'Ain't this nice!' Sal smiled, taking in the view of the tidy buildings across the neat lawn.

A continuous square terrace of buildings formed around the grassy area, but this didn't look like the endless boring terraces in the streets surrounding this refuge. These were buildings of character set in bays while on the far side stood a chapel.

I put Martha down on the grass. She raced away from us, squealing loudly, exhilarated by space and freedom. I took off after her but our play was soon halted by a woman's voice coming from inside a doorway behind us.

'What do you want?' Her tone sounded aggressive. The words came from a large, middle-aged woman in a black dress and white pinafore. Her grey hair was topped with a little white bonnet not unlike that of a nurse.

'We've come to see Mrs G... I mean Mrs Grainger.' Sal was almost apologetic.

'Oh, Mrs G!' The voice softened immediately. 'Are you from the orphanage?'

'Used to be,' I said, finally getting Martha back under control and swinging her up onto my shoulder.

'She gets more visitors than the rest of all our folk put together.' Our interrogator even managed to smile. 'I'll tek you to see 'er.'

I gave a sigh of relief. So did Sal.

Chapter 18

It wasn't flour that made her hair white now. This was the only evidence that betrayed her advancing years. Otherwise Mrs G looked just the same as she did when George first took me to her kitchen door. But there was one other difference. She was seated. I don't think I'd ever seen her sitting down before. She was always on her feet; far too busy organising the satisfaction of children's insatiable hunger.

'I don't need to guess who you are. Oh my, Sammy Smyle! How you've grown! I was hopin' you'd come an' see me.'

How did she know I'd returned to Hull? How did she even know I was still alive? The orphanage records said nothing.

She continued speaking without pausing to take a breath. 'An' you, Selina Smith... with that red hair. Sit down. Sit down. You're makin' the place look untidy!' The voice was the same, but it lacked the old strength from the days when it kept a full dining room of unruly youngsters in order.

'An' who's this lovely little bai'n?' She held out her arms. 'Come to your Aunty Alice.'

Aunty Alice? It never crossed my mind that Mrs G had a Christian name. *Alice Grainger? She was just Mrs G.*

Martha tried to hide in the folds of her mother's skirt but Sal mouthed the words 'Go on' and the child waddled tentatively towards *"Aunty Alice."* She stopped half way across the room and looked to her mother ready to scamper back.

'I think I might have a sticky bun for somebody.' Mrs G swivelled slowly in her chair toward the table by her side. The frilly white starched cloth covering the tabletop hung over the sides. In the centre a faded portrait of the late Queen Victoria frowned at the world from the lid of a large flat tin. Mrs G opened the tin and took out of it one of her special treats: a pastry glistening with sugar coating.

'Would somebody like this?' She dangled the delicious temptation in front of the child.

It soon found its way to Martha's mouth. I remembered a young boy who couldn't resist exactly the same temptation nearly a score of years earlier.

'Martha Vicars! What do you say?' Sal frowned at her daughter.

'Fankoo,' the child mumbled through a mouth full of pastry, allowing crumbs fall onto the floor. This was the first time I'd heard the child say anything resembling a word.

'Let's all sit down an' have a nice cup o' tea!' Mrs G commenced the ritual by lifting a steaming kettle from the edge of the crackling fire in the black leaded range.

I looked around the room. As well as the table and four dining chairs it also contained a polished brass bed in the corner covered by a red flowered quilt. This wasn't what I'd expected when I heard she lived in an almshouse. I'd anticipated something altogether more Spartan and communal, but this institution wasn't meant to be a place of either punishment or correction; it was meant to be a proper home for those who deserved it. She, more than anyone else, deserved the best in her retirement.

'I'm not supposed to have this many chairs in me room but I get so many visitors they got fed up o' me borrowin' them from t'other rooms. Matron said it was makin' t'other old uns jealous… Y'know, with me sayin' I'd got visitors again.' Mrs G smiled contentedly.

I'd never thought of her as an *old un*, not in the sense of being aged. She always seemed old but also somehow simultaneously timeless.

'Got me own pantry an' a coalhouse. Better off here than at the orphanage!' She laughed. 'I'm always bakin'. Can't break the habit of a lifetime! T'others here don't mind when I've got owt goin' spare!'

Martha sat on her new aunty's knee, tucking into a jam tart now. Mrs G always knew the quickest route into a child's heart.

'You said you hoped I'd come and see you.' I interrupted her flow. It pleased me to hear she was happy but I remained intrigued by what she'd said earlier. 'How did you know I was back in Hull?'

Her expression became serious. 'Another old girl from the orphanage came to see me last night. Told me about this strange lookin' brown man who turned up an' said he was her brother.' Mrs G brushed crumbs from her dark skirt. She kept the child balanced with her other hand.

'What did you tell her, Mrs G?' I asked.

Sal's sideways glance over the rim of her teacup told me I was pushing too hard.

'Sorry Mrs G, but when I saw Mary... Well, she wasn't very happy to see me. Not happy at all. Said she thought I was dead.'

'That was your grandmother's doin'!' For the first time in my life I heard Mrs G sound genuinely angry. 'I don't like speakin' ill o' the dead... She was your grandmother an' all but she was a bad lot! An evil... wicked... spiteful woman, she was.'

'Did you know her?' I was more intrigued by how Mrs G came to this conclusion about my grandmother rather than taking any offence at Mrs G's description of her. I'd guessed she must be dead by now but this was the first I'd heard anything of her since the day she'd dumped me at the orphanage. It didn't have any effect on me. Why should it?

'I met her after you ran off.' She gave a weary sigh. 'The Master an' Mr Rodgers didn't seem too bothered that you'd gone. Reported it to the police eventually but that's all. Just went through the motions, they did.'

Why did her words not surprise me?

'I went out lookin' for you. Went to see your grandmother in case you'd gone there... but she'd even less interest in what'd happened to you than them in the orphanage. "Good riddance to bad rubbish" she said an' then she told me a lot more. Her tongue was loose 'cos she was on the gin.'

Martha shuffled restlessly and looked about to fall off Mrs G's knee. Sal took her back from her new aunty.

'Mean... spiteful things she said. Don't know if they was true. Don't even know if I should be repeating 'em to you!' She looked and sounded both angry and sad at the same time. 'But she said 'em all to Mary while she had the poor lass in her clutches... That's afore we got her. Surprising she turned out to be such a good un... but that was no thanks to your grandmother!'

'What did she say about me?' Life had prepared me for any abuse that might have come from my grandmother.

'About you... about your father... about your mother!' She shook her head. 'Wicked spiteful things!'

'You can tell me.' I knew so very little about my past and my natural family. It was time I learned something, be it fair or foul.

'Not sure it's right I should be tellin' you in front o' Sal.'

Sal stood up holding Martha to her breast. I held out my hand to prevent her leaving.

'We've not had chance to tell you but Sal and me are going to get married.' I hadn't actually proposed to Sal yet. 'Aren't we, Sal?'

Sal relaxed back onto her wooden seat and smiled. Maybe this got both proposal and acceptance out of the way.

'There shouldn't be any secrets between us.' I glanced at my newly intended before returning my attention to our hostess. 'What did she say?'

'For a start you an' Mary are not proper brother an' sister. Well, she said you're only half-brother an' half-sister. Same mother... different fathers. Didn't you notice Mary's not as brown as you?'

I hadn't given it a thought until then, but it was true.

'The old witch called your Mam a whore who liked to sleep with brown men! Said Mary's father was probably a Spanish or Portuguese seaman off one o' the big boats. Said she was carryin' on with one of them while your father was at sea. Said your mother couldn't resist... if there was a bit o' brown around. Mary's father could 'ave been any one of a dozen men, according to her but I think that was the gin talkin'.'

My mother was an angel. Blue eyes... blonde hair. I could see her face. It glowed, just like in the pictures of angels in churches. I trembled. One of the foundations of my life had been shattered. Sal took a tight hold of my hand. Now I was the one who needed her strength.

'Called your father a stupid, brown fool!' Mrs G continued. 'Your mother told him that Mary was his, but she'd come out a bit paler 'an you did. Said he was nowt but a romantic dreamer.'

The description of father was the only thing I could recognise. Perhaps the only thing I wanted to recognise.

'What does Mary think about all this?' I said.

'She'd got used to the idea of bein' illegitimate an' bein' half Spanish or whatever. Then you appears an' turns things upside down for her. Black as the ace of spades, she said you were.' Mrs G looked old now.

Old and very sad. 'You frightened her. She was never sure whether your grandmother's words were just lies. You arrived out of the blue like a nightmare!'

'So she was content with only being a half Spanish bastard, if you'll forgive my language.' I shook my head. 'Better than being half Indian. Having a touch of the tar brush.'

I knew all the expressions used to describe what others considered to be my place in the world, the white man's world. Oh, how I wanted to get back to the company of my friends in the Wild West Show, to where the people accepted me for who I am, not what I am.

I slumped back in my chair and felt Sal squeeze my hand.

'I don't think that half o' what she said was true, but Mary had it drummed into her afore she came to us. She turned out a good lass an' she's a fine teacher. You can be proud of her.' This sounded like the Mrs G of old. The Mrs G who didn't have a bad word to say about anyone.

'But she's not willing to accept me... even as a half-brother.' I felt an old deep sadness I'd not felt since Mother died: as though my only remaining blood relative had passed away. I didn't have a sister anymore.

'This is Hull, Sammy. She's got to live here. And you'll be gone.' Mrs G told the truth.

'I will be,' I mumbled and went deep into thought.

'I could do with another cup o' tea, don't know about you two.' Mrs G changed the subject. 'An' I think I know somebody who'd like another cake!'

'I'll make the tea.' Sal stood up, letting go of my hand.

Martha waddled back to her Aunty Alice. Sweet temptation again overcame childish reticence.

'You've not told me what you two have been up to all these years. An' that brother o' yours. George?' This *was* the real Mrs G, taking an interest in those who through no fault of their own had been rejected by society. She'd been mother to over a thousand children and now in her old age she deservedly reaped all the happiness for which she'd sown the seeds in generations of us.

'There's lots to tell.' Sal put the soot black kettle back on the grate. 'Sammy has such tales. You wouldn't believe 'em.'

'Let's start with the day you ran off from the orphanage. What happened?' Our guardian angel sat back in her chair ready to listen to my story.

Telling her about my adventures made me feel much happier. Stories full of wonderful people for whom I cared and who cared about me. They included uplifting experiences in strange and exotic places. As I unfolded my life story I knew I was only a visitor now. When Buffalo Bill's Wild West Show and Congress of Rough Riders of the World rolled out of the city after the performances I would be taking its best with me. It was unlikely I would return.

***

There was more life in Paragon Railway Station than in the heart of beehive. Departing travellers, unable or unwilling to afford the services of station porters, struggled with their luggage, fighting their way onto the platforms to board the trains before they left without them. Others newly arrived in Hull attempted to exit the station and enter the city centre. Meanwhile, other lost souls hung around the concourse, gazing aimlessly, drawn like moths to a flame by the magnetism of the exciting hubbub of the mainline terminus. More than twenty years earlier a little street urchin marvelled at the sights, sounds and smells of the largest covered space in the town. Often as not the porters chased me off. Occasionally, in later days, George came here with me during our free time. We tried to guess the destinations of the different trains but no guard ever called out to inform travellers that one was leaving Hull Paragon bound for the Wild West of America.

Locomotives built up steam pressure like huge metal dragons champing at the bit waiting to escape from an enormous cavern. Clouds of smoke and excess steam rose from a dozen engines and hung heavy in the air. Although the station's canopied roof lay more than thirty feet above everything, these emissions managed to fill every inch of space available.

Whoosh!

Travellers jumped several inches in the air to escape the horizontal gush of steam from a locomotive relieving itself of excess pressure. Martha screamed, leaping into Sal's arms. The incident on the platform deflected any curiosity there might have been from the strange looking couple carrying a child towards the Sheffield bound train.

We reached the door of my third class carriage. Colonel Cody would have gladly paid for a first class ticket but it was only a short journey back to the show's latest encampment. I wasn't going all the way to Sheffield, only to a place called Rotherham to rejoin them. I felt more comfortable travelling with ordinary folk. Maybe I wasn't one of them, but I'd have felt even more out of place among first class passengers.

'You will come back, won't you?' Sal's free hand gripped mine like a vice. Her nails dug into my palm. She looked more frightened than sad.

'Back! Back!' Martha had a new word. It made Sal smile, although it didn't stop a tear rolling down her cheek too.

'It's Tuesday today. The show will roll into Hull in the early hours of Saturday morning... and I'll be rolling in with it! The posters are all over town!' Her hand got a return squeeze. 'When it leaves next Monday for York you'll be with me, both of you... and George and Annie and their lads.'

'I love you, Sammy.'

'Uv you, unka!' a little voice echoed.

'I've always loved you, Sal.' The train guard's sharp whistle nearly drowned out my words. This indication to the driver warned us there was only enough time for a quick kiss through an open carriage window before the train began moving. I'd then be on my way back to the exciting fantasy that was my reality.

Sal was tall but I still needed to hang low through the window to kiss her. I leaned forward, allowing my hair to fall over my shoulder. When our lips met Martha's hand swung to grab my braid but she couldn't reach.

'Martha Vicars!' Sal scolded her.

I held out my arms to give the child a goodbye kiss. Without hesitation Sal handed her over. She trusted me with her most valuable possession. She must have loved me. I felt very happy. It was a wet raspberry kiss on Martha's cheek before I handed her back giggling to her mother.

'Saturday!' I shouted trying to be heard above all the station noise. I still had their platform tickets. I thrust them into Sal's hand. 'Come to Walton Street Fairground! Early! The best breakfast you've ever had!'

The train moved off. Sal walked quickly along the platform, trying to keep up with it. She'd become so much stronger in only a few days. In less than a minute there was no platform left to walk along and she came to a halt at its end, standing in the sunshine beyond the station roof. Little Martha waved. Soon the two precious figures waving me off became dots in the distance. I slid the window shut and saw the forbidding rear end of the Hull Union Workhouse standing beside the track.

Well, that's two you won't be getting your hands on! The thought gave me the greatest of pleasure.

***

'Well, cat my dogs!' My mentor's face beamed. 'You don't let the grass grow under your feet, young man! Not been gone a week and you've found yourself a wife and a readymade family! You move faster than a prairie jackrabbit.'

Bill gave the end of his moustache a twirl. Booted legs stretched out under the camp table on which his Stetson rested.

'Is it all right?' I felt like a nervous schoolboy in the headmaster's study, although it was only a tent in a field outside Rotherham in Yorkshire. Not just any old tent but the Pahaska Tepee, or 'Longhair's Lodge'. Outside I could hear the noise of hammering and shouting coming from the Wild West Show's smooth machine gearing up for the next episode in its British adventure.

'Couldn't be happier for you, my boy. Are you sure you're making the right move?' He gave me a quizzical look. In matters of matrimony Bill was cautious. His own marriage – to a wife who always remained in the United States – was known by everyone in the show to be an extremely bumpy affair. 'How well do you know this lady?'

'I know Sal better than any other woman on the face of the earth… and there's none better on it!' I was ready to use any superlative I could dream up to describe her.

'Well, I can see you're as determined as a buzzard round fresh killed meat. If I know you as well as I think I know you, Sammy, this marriage won't fail 'cos of you.' The old blue eyes twinkled. 'I wish you well and I can't wait to meet this angel of yours.'

'What about my friend, George? Do you think…?'

'You say he was in the British cavalry fighting in South Africa?' Bill became more thoughtful. He flicked long greying golden locks out of his jacket collar.

'He's great with horses. Don't know anyone better with them.' I didn't know this to be a fact but I did know George. No one could love horses more than him. This kind of equine devotion provided the basis of every great horseman I knew – whether they were riders or wranglers. It was certainly true of Bill.

'I've known you now for many years, Sammy and I've never known you say a wrong word or commit a foul deed. Your opinion's good enough for me. I'll leave it to you to go and see W.W. to sort out work for your friend.'

With Bill's say-so Mr W. W. Reedy, the Superintendent of Bronco Stock, would not dare object to taking on George but I reckoned I'd have persuaded Will anyway. He was another good friend of mine.

'And you'd better go see John Porter to sort out accommodation for all these new folk. We'll have to give some consideration to what jobs the ladies can do.'

Our tightly knit community had no room for passengers. Every man, woman and child had to earn their keep.

'I'll leave these matters to you to sort out. We've got a problem in the show I need to attend to.'

'What's happened?' I'd only just arrived on site and was unaware of recent events.

'Carter had an accident yesterday. He didn't land right and hit an arc lamp! Knocked himself out! Right in the middle of the show!' Bill shook his head ruefully before smiling. 'The crowd loved it... thought it was part of the act!'

I didn't know *Carter* – or George Davis to give him his real name – very well. His act was new. He was dubbed the 'Cowboy Cyclist', although I didn't think he'd ever been west of the Mississippi. He descended eighty-five feet down a ramp on his bicycle before shooting across a gap over forty feet wide, propelled by his own momentum, to land on another ramp. The nearest thing to a man flying ever seen by anyone.

'Is he all right?' I asked.

'His head's covered in bandages but he's keen as mustard to do his act again today.'

'Just like falling off a horse, I suppose. Get straight back on again,' I suggested.

'I guess it is, but I reckon his steed might need some repairs doing on it.' A brief smile crossed Bill's lips. 'Then Frank Small tells me there's been some reporters round asking if there's been any trouble between the Cossacks and the Japanese boys on account of this war going on out east between Russia and Japan. Don't think any of the boys knew there was a war going on... Not until these newspapermen turned up!'

One of William Cody's rules was to keep politics and religion well outside the show's camp. With so many different races, creeds and religions among us all, such things could only lead to disharmony. However, I knew he held strong opinions. He was a staunch advocate of the rights of my brothers. Some said he was the best of enemies. I say he was a best friend. He believed in women's rights too which made him many female friends in Britain.

'Who'd run a Wild West Show, boy?' With a hearty laugh Bill slapped me on the back.

'Nobody better than you, boss!'

'Hey, thought I said I'd never heard you tell a lie!' Bill gave one of his hearty guffaws. It was good to see him cheerful. We all knew this long tour of Britain was taking its toll of him. 'Go sort things out, boy.'

Colonel William Cody was the best boss and friend any man could ever wish to have. Every member of our community loved him but none could have loved him more than I. If Mrs G was my fairy godmother, he was my godfather.

Chapter 19

That night I dreamed of Morning Star.

We stood together on a hilltop holding hands and looking down on a herd of bison. They swarmed over the prairie far beyond the horizon. I tried to speak to her, but only mumbled words came out of my mouth. She smiled at me as though she understood what I tried to say. A Lakota hunting party galloped towards the bison. At its head was Dog That Stands. He was the greatest hunter I have ever known and one of the greatest men. Then I stood alone. The herd, the hunting party and Morning Star all disappeared. The lush prairie grass turned into dust. Alone except for the sound of someone sniggering behind me. I turned around. It was Edward Snelgrave.

Our train jerked to a halt. I woke soaked in sweat. A chink of moonlight crept into the carriage through a gap in a window blind. We'd arrived at our latest destination and soon the process of setting up the show's camp would start all over again. The previous night we'd dismantled everything and loaded it all onto our trains. It took less than two hours to do this after Bill and the entire troupe had taken a final triumphant bow before yet another excited audience. By midnight I was deep in sleep aboard one of the three trains heading towards Lincolnshire.

The field we left on Sheffield Road, Ickles outside Rotherham stood deserted except for hundreds of spent cartridge cases that would be collected up by youngsters as souvenirs, and animal droppings I hoped would fertilize many gardens.

I was not alone in the long carriage. Nearly fifty men shared it with me. Most of them still slept, lying in bunks four tiers high on either side of the central gangway. Spartan conditions maybe, but we spent little time on board the trains. There was always too much to do:

setting up camp, the arena, and doing the show before knocking everything down again – usually all done in less than twenty-four hours before moving on. The Wild West Show was a well drilled, well-oiled machine.

What did my dream mean? Maybe Morning Star was saying goodbye to me, something she was denied in life. Fever even stole this moment from us. Was she saying it was all right for me to be with Sal? But why was that devil dog Snelgrave there? He was someone I really wanted to say goodbye to. Had I seen the last of him? I prayed George's scheme worked and Smelly was somewhere out on the North Sea catching haddock and cod, either that or thrown overboard as a stowaway. As long as he was out of our lives. That was all that mattered.

Trying to make sense of the dream kept me awake. I shuffled uneasily on a flock mattress stretched across the wooden slats of my bunk, trying to find a comfortable position, but further sleep escaped me. Somewhere along the carriage a cowboy snored loudly or maybe it was a Russian Cossack or a Bedouin Arab or any one of dozen and more nationalities that now formed our special congregation. The harmonious way we worked together gave me hope for the world in this new twentieth century. Surely if we could achieve this then the rest of the world could too.

The hiss of a match bursting into flame told me someone else was awake and lighting up a cigarette, or maybe a pipe. The strong rush of burning sulphur filled the air. A welcome smell in our confined carriage. Dozens of men shared the space and each one of them ate, at least, one healthy portion of American navy beans every day.

Soon our work would begin again and, for one day only, Highfield Farm, Gainsborough would be the Wild West of America. Twenty-four hours later, "Hard Backsides" Custer, as the Lakota called him (although this is a polite translation) would be making his Last Stand again – twice in one day – in Grant-Thorold Park, Grimsby. Then I'd be back on the train bound for Hull and Sal and the rest of our family.

***

It was the morning after our Grimsby performances and Lincolnshire lay behind us. A dark night sky over Yorkshire was lightening to grey. Our train was the first to roll into the sidings near to Albert Dock. I knew I was back in the city long before the locomotive clunked onto the buffers at the track's end. Although we'd passed the Fish Dock the air was still filled with the noxious cocktail of strong ammonia from rotting fish mixed with the bonfire smell of smoke houses. For once – only once – it aroused a pleasant feeling inside me.

'No wonder you ran away from here, Sammy!' a cowboy yelled from his bunk somewhere up above me.

'Lord, this place stinks!' another shouted. 'And I thought Grimsby was bad!'

In dawn's half-light, the strangest procession seen in Hull for many a year made its way across the sleeping streets. Gaslights and oil lamps flickered on as slumber was disturbed. People peered out of their windows to discover the cause of the commotion. Why were so many horses' hooves and metal wheel rims clattering over the road's wooden sets? Why so early in the morning? Sleepy-eyed children wandered outside, when they should have been fast asleep, building up energy for the coming school day. What they saw would have been worth all the whacks of the cane received later as punishment for dozing off in class. Our clattering parade would be something to tell their children and grandchildren: about the day the Wild West came to Hull.

Thankfully the strong winds that afflicted us on the other side of the River Humber had subsided and a fine morning lay in prospect to help us to set up our nine-acre camp on the Walton Street Fairground. Our army of roustabouts was a well-practised mechanism. Working in groups of ten, their sledgehammers would drive over twelve hundred stakes into the ground. All done within an hour. A large tented village would rise up from the ground like an impatient armada of hot air balloons eager to take flight.

By seven o'clock the camp's first hungry customers were eating hot breakfasts in the marquees. A visiting group of dishevelled reporters from local newspapers looked on, awestruck at the hectic scene. Tired faces beneath derby hats told us they weren't accustomed to being up at such an early hour, let alone ready to devour a huge meal. A choice of beefsteak, stewed tripe, or liver was available, all served up with bacon and potatoes, to be followed by strawberries and cream. And the food was downed with lashings of good hot American coffee. Funny how I'd come to love the hot brown liquid I'd hated so much on my first acquaintance. I wondered how George would cope with it now.

Where was Sal? Maybe she didn't think I'd intended her to arrive quite so early in the morning when I'd shouted 'come early' through the train's carriage window. I left my work with the horses and went to find her.

The fairground was a triangular shape: its longest side backed onto a railway line while its shortest edge on the south ran along the railings of a large public park called West Park. The third side and the only open one faced Walton Street. Here the formidable figures of police constables in dark uniforms and helmets stood in position to hold back our eager public until the time we were ready for their custom. Already a bustling crowd of several hundred onlookers needed to be kept in order by these officers of the law. Each member of the local constabulary stood more than six feet tall and seemed almost as wide. Every one was what my grandmother would have described as 'a fine figure of a man.' From my childhood recollections the whole system of justice in Hull usually began and ended with one of these local Bobbies. Detection of criminal behaviour and physical punishment for misdeeds were usually simultaneous, especially for any young offenders and for many adult ones too come to that. The administration of justice was usually swift and took place well outside the local courts of law.

My eyes scoured the faces in the milling crowd on the pavement behind the officers. All I could see was a rippling tide of walrus moustaches and flat caps together with shawls but no sign of flowing red hair.

'There's one o' them Red Indians!' someone shouted. Elsewhere from deep in the throng another voice squawked an imitation war whoop. A genuine Lakota war cry would have made the entire crowd turn on its heels and scatter in all directions. I found it amusing that these citizens of Hull couldn't recognise one of their own, but then again…

'Sammy!' a thin female voice called out from deep within the crowd. Someone did recognise me.

A flash of red hair poked out between the shoulders on the front row. A woman tried to force her way to the front but an absence of male gallantry kept her back.

I slipped between two policemen to reach into the crowd.

For a moment all voices were stilled when the people in the crowd saw me pull a red-haired woman from in their midst

'Watch out! 'E'll scalp you!' a local wag called out.

'What's goin' on?' I felt both the strong hand of the law on my shoulder and its hot breath warming my neck.

'It's all right, officer.' I turned to look into the beetroot red face of a moustachioed constable. He looked surprised to hear a wild savage speaking English. 'She's with the show, constable. Got lost on the way here.'

'Aye, sir. Got lost!' Sal nodded vigorously. The policeman must have failed to notice her local accent because he let her pass unhindered.

I wanted to hold her close. Three days apart felt like a lifetime. I controlled my feelings until we were in the privacy behind the tents and out of sight of an audience almost as big as the one for the show itself. The only person I wanted to see her was Bill. I needed him to see the truth of everything I'd said about her.

Her eyes and cheeks were red from tears.

'What's wrong?' I forgot everything else. 'I told you I'd come back!'

'Smelly's back!' She threw her arms around me and sobbed heavily into my chest. 'His bullies gave George a good hidin'. Only reason they didn't do him in was 'cos George had stopped you from killin' him!'

'What about you and Martha? Annie and the lads?'

'We managed to keep out of 'is way.' Her voice quaked and her body throbbed onto mine.

'How's George?' I tried to contain my rage.

'Black an' blue but no bones broken. Thank God!' Her tears eased.

'Thank God!' I repeated. 'George should've let me throw Smelly in the dock... when we had the chance!' I exhaled heavily and tried to think what to do next.

'But you're not a murderer.' She paused and looked up into my eyes. 'Are you, Sammy?'

'I shoot three or four men every night!' I tried to smile. 'But only in the show! With blanks! How did he get back so soon?'

'The skipper had to send him back!' Sal's words were scornful. 'He thought Smelly was gonna die! He was seasick all the time an' I heard there weren't even a swell on the sea! Sent him back to Hull on one of the cutters with some of the fish they'd caught.'

'Pity he didn't let him die!'

Her head sank into my chest again. 'What are we gonna do, Sammy?'

'We'll go and see Bill. He'll know what to do!'

***

'Well, cat my dogs.' Bill leant back in his chair, pausing to consider the situation. 'Never a dull minute when you're around, Sammy!'

I didn't allow him the time to work his charm and pass on compliments to Sal, much as I thought she deserved them. The old twinkle was back in his eyes. It was ever present whenever he shared the company of an attractive woman. I gave him the full story at breakneck speed, not even allowing him the opportunity to offer seats to us.

'Out west we'd tar 'n' feather this Snelgrave hombre and ride him out of town on a rusty rail but I don't think the aldermen and constables of Hull would take too kindly to us doing that!'

He sucked his teeth and the silver blond moustache wriggled on his lip like two long hairy caterpillars. He was silent for a few moments but the way he stroked his beard told me the matter was receiving serious thought.

'Best thing to do is take a wagon down to your friends and bring 'em back here. They'll be safe with us. Take a couple of the boys… Jake and Harry. There'll be no trouble if you have those two tough hombres along with you.'

Jake and Harry were the largest of all the roustabouts in our camp. Others may have worked in teams but this pair worked as a team all on their own. They could do the work of ten; they were almost the size of ten men put together. The cowboys called them mountain men, but I was never sure if they said this because the two had been trappers up in the Rocky Mountains or simply because of their sheer size. Probably both. The two of them were very taciturn in discussion of their pasts as were a lot of men in the show's camp.

Within minutes our wagon passed through the throng of spectators still waiting in excited anticipation along the fairground's edge and all the way down Walton Street. Sal sat up front beside me. I took the reins of two of the strongest horses in camp. These were no show horses but solid hard workers like every man and beast toiling behind the scenes to make performances tick as smoothly as the finest Swiss timepiece.

'Makes me feel important. Sittin' up here with all these people lookin' at us.' She gave a wave to a group of truanting schoolboys trotting beside us. 'I feel like Lady Muck!'

'You are important, Sal!' I tried to sing her praises but all I got in response was an elbow in the ribs, almost knocking me from my seat. Sal hadn't changed, and I was glad.

Jake and Harry saw and heard none of this. They lay in the back of the wagon snoring loudly. The ability to catch a few minutes sleep at any time of day was an important attribute of everyone working for William Cody. He paid well, but every cent had to be earned. You took rest at any legitimate opportunity that came to you.

Less than fifteen minutes after leaving the fairground we passed large houses belonging to local merchants in a wide tree lined avenue named The Boulevard: except Sal told me all the locals called it *Bullyvard*. This was the second time I'd driven past these houses in only a few hours. The first time I hadn't paid them any attention. Some must have stood here back when I was a child. Although I'd lived less than a mile away I'd been totally ignorant of their existence. This affluent reality would have been as alien to me in my childhood days as any of my American frontier fantasies, if not more so.

'Used to work in there.' Sal pointed at a large house to our left. Its bay window protruded out into a pocket handkerchief front garden that was protected from the world by waist high iron railings. 'Master of the house liked to tek liberties with 'is servant lasses, but I wasn't havin' none of it. Good job Stan came along. Would've been me last job in service. No references likely to come from there!'

For a moment I turned my head away from the road to give her a quizzical glance.

'I'd have got none 'cos I didn't let him do what he wanted with me. Would've had to go an' work in a fish house instead, if it weren't for Stanley. Maybe worse!'

The main road came into sight, but I'd lapsed deep into thought. Her words made me ponder the nature of her relationship with the late Stanley Vicars and how it had begun. I hoped she'd loved him and he'd loved her. Maybe in time she would tell me more. When she felt ready.

'Where to now, Sal? You said in Eton Street.'

'Turn right here.' She pointed. 'They're all at Ma Conroy's.'

'Ma Conroy?' Nothing registered in my memory.

'Annie's aunty.' Sal's expression told me I should have remembered this woman, but my face remained blank. 'She came to see her sometimes. Always brought a tribe of bai'ns in with her.'

'Oh!' I vaguely remembered someone, although I always kept well clear of visitors whenever they were allowed into the orphanage. I never expected any. This information prompted a question. 'If she had an aunty, why didn't she live with her?'

'She had twelve bai'ns of her own! Those that lived. God knows how many didn't!'

We turned the corner out of the Boulevard's opulence on to the main road. The wagon clattered over the tramlines into the overpopulated reality of the rest of the Hessle Road area.

'Next left!'

Sal pointed at a large building on a street corner. It was faced with bronze hued brick and had gold lettering curving around the arch above its double doors. The letters announced proudly that here was the *Yorkshire Penny Bank*. Its customers must have come from the Boulevard. Most of the people in the other Hessle Road streets didn't have the two ha'pennies to rub together for a single penny deposit.

Eton Street was a street of courts, like the most of the ones I had known as a child. Parallel rows of terraced houses branched off at right angles: Gertrude's Terrace, Alma Terrace, Towler's Terrace – rows of two up, two down houses confronting each other across narrow courtyards. The houses on the street itself were terraced rows, all tightly packed and facing directly onto a narrow pavement swarming with young children. No neat gardens behind railings here. A housewife knelt at her doorstep scrubbing it with a donkey stone, changing the step's colour from its natural grey to a deep shade of yellow. In front of other houses, the wives and mothers of fishermen worked busily on large nets interwoven in a wide warp and weft pattern strung across the house walls. They were using long wooden things to weave the string.

'It's called net braidin'.' Sal could see me puzzling over what they did. 'Mendin' or mekin' nets for fishermen to tek back to sea. Them wooden things in their hands are called needles. Mister Capes next door to us in West Dock Ave makes 'em.'

Before I could ask if she could braid nets too she spoke again.

'We're 'ere!'

I tugged back on the reins and applied the handbrake. The jolt woke our two passengers.

'What now, Sammy?' Jake asked through his black bush of mountain man beard. He was the most talkative of the pair but only just. Both wore stained denim jeans and leather waistcoats over brown and white checked shirts. Stetson hats were left behind. They'd have made our place of origin too obvious. The sheer size of this pair would attract enough attention anyway but hopefully it would also act as a deterrent to any undesired interruption to our mission.

'Stay 'ere and keep an eye on things while I go and get our folks out,' Sal said.

I looked up and down the street anticipating the sight of that slug Snelgrave and his henchmen sliding out from hiding beneath stones at any moment.

Sal ran ahead of me and knocked on a door halfway down one of the courts. A grey face appeared and admitted Sal. I guessed this must be Ma Conroy. I did not recognise her. She looked ancient but everyone I'd ever known in Hull was much older now.

I remained outside, standing at the terrace end to keep watch. The houses in this court were still relatively new but already panes of glass in large sash windows were cracked and paintwork was peeling. Beneath a leaking gutter a long green stain trailed down one house front.

A sorry sight appeared through the open doorway of Ma Conroy's house. A patchwork of cuts and bruises covered a freckled face with one blackened eye.

'I can't leave you for a couple of days without you getting into mischief!' I held out my hand to George. 'It's all sorted, son. There's jobs for all of you and passage across to America, if you want it!'

'Don't care where it's a passage to!' He winced and a gnarled hand went to his ribs. Even speaking hurt him. 'As long as it's as far from here as possible!'

'Get all your stuff together and we'll get back to camp.'

Sal reappeared carrying her whole world: Martha and a large bundle wrapped in a white bed sheet. The Smith boys followed with smaller bundles dangling over their shoulders like burglar swag bags. Annie struggled out with two larger ones.

'Take one of these bundles, George!' Injuries were no excuse as far as Annie was concerned.

The grey face returned, supported by a small, thin body wrapped in a dark shawl.

'You take care, our Annie,' a croaky old voice said. Skeletal hands held on to Annie's arm. 'Look after them bai'ns. Write me a letter from wherever it is you're goin' to.'

'I will, aunty.' Annie hugged the old woman with her free arm and gave her a kiss on the cheek.

I grabbed Sal's bundle and we marched back to our transport.

'Anything happened?' I asked but our two bodyguards shook their heads. They didn't regard the appearance of more curious figures on doorsteps or women taking a break from their net braiding as something of consequence.

Sal viewed the scene. 'Tongues are wagging. This'll be all the way down Hessle Road in half an hour. Don't you worry!'

'Them's lovely animals.' George's attention had diverted from more pressing matters and he went to admire the coal-black mares that brought us from the fairground.

'George!' Sal and Annie said in unison.

'You can rub 'em down when we get back,' I promised, almost adding 'to the fairground' but I swallowed the words. I was wary as to who might be listening.

George pushed his bundle into the back of the wagon and was about to climb in with the others.

'You can ride shotgun with me!' I tugged my head to one side to indicate he should sit up front. The old partnership was together again.

'You've got a shotgun?' George looked amazed at this imagined prospect.

'No, it's only an expression. It means sit up here.'

He tried to drag himself up onto the seat beside me. I could see him wince with pain. He didn't have to struggle for long: Jake's strong arm hoisted him up gently.

I wished I did have a shotgun. I knew who my target would be.

***

'He's real! He's really real!' George couldn't believe it.

Bill stood waiting for us when the wagon rolled back into the camp. The fantasy figure in tan leather jacket and breeches I'd described to George so many times when we were children greeted us. The young George had seen him in a grand parade years before but never as close as this. Bill waved his white Stetson hat, letting his long silver blond hair flow in the breeze.

'Welcome, pilgrims,' Bill called out and we drew to a halt. 'You'll be George.' He held out a hand to my oldest friend.

'He called me George!' my friend muttered loudly under his breath.

'Daft ha'peth, more like!' Sal as ever had the measure of her brother.

'Sammy, get these folks into the dinner tent. They look like they could do with some good American vittles!' Everyone smiled. It was probably the first time for days they'd all managed a smile in unison, probably longer.

'I was goin' to rub down these hosses,' George muttered, easing himself down from the wagon still holding on to Bill's hand.

'Don't worry, George. We've got more horses for you to rub down than there's bison on the prairie. Go get some good cowboy grub inside you first.' Bill laughed heartily and pointed my party in the direction of food.

I followed my friends, but Bill stopped me. 'Any problems?' he asked quietly.

'No, everything's fine, boss.'

'Good! Then you can sort out some of mine!' He gave a loud guffaw and slapped himself on the thigh before heading back towards his tent.

I caught up with my new extended family. Jake and Harry led them towards food. The two roustabouts carried all the bundles plus two small boys riding pickaback.

'He called me George!' my friend muttered again to Sal and Annie.

***

'No wonder you grew into such a big lad, Sammy!' Annie eased herself back on the bench seat, letting her legs stretch out under the dining table. 'Never seen so much food in me life!'

'Was this specially for us?' George considered a lonely uneaten sausage still waiting for him on his plate. 'Normally it's only Sundays when we have a bit of meat.'

'Shank end – if we're lucky!' Annie scoffed. Her plate still had islands of mashed potato surrounded by a sea of gravy.

'No. This is normal.' I shrugged. 'You'll need meals like this, once Bill gets you working!'

'It's like the meals Mrs G used to do for us.' Sal snuggled beside me on the bench. Martha rested on her lap, poking a fork at remnants on the plate she'd shared with her mother.

'Better than that!' George said. 'You don't need to go for seconds!'

'George Smith… not wanting seconds! Thought I'd never hear the words!' I swung my arm to slap him heartily on the back but held back before impact, remembering his injuries. The slap turned into a gentle stroke of affection.

'I don't think I've ever been so happy.' Sal started to become tearful again.

'Steady on, lass!' George cajoled. 'We ain't seen what we've got to do yet to earn all this grub. This Buffalo Bill sounds like a bit of a slave driver to me.'

'And you haven't tried American coffee yet! There's not much tea drunk around here.' I tried to add a touch of levity. 'Once we've had a drink we'll get your things stowed away. Usually we go straight back to the trains after a show and move on during the night but we're in Hull for two days.'

'That's a pity.' George looked downcast again. 'I'd like to be off as soon as possible.'

'Got a special treat for you! We'll be sleeping in a genuine Lakota tepee tonight. Not quite the prairie but Walton Street Fairground will have to do for now.'

Chapter 20

Of course, this blissful state couldn't last. Life's like that.

First, two performances in one day needed to be taken care of. Seeing the Wild West alive in all its glory was going to be an exciting experience for most of my new family. Sal had seen it years ago with others from the orphanage on the day I escaped. Alas not George, he had missed the spectacle. The show was much bigger and better now. And I was in it!

Although I had been in the performance Sal had seen, she didn't know, at least not until I told them all about what happened to me after George ran off. We laughed when she said the Master and Jolly Rodgers must have been looking straight at me and didn't know it. I suggested all brown people probably looked the same to them.

I'd told them so much about the show and now they would be seeing it for real. Knowing they were in the audience watching me perform provided a special thrill. Perhaps I did show off and overact more than usual However, pride often comes before a fall. Maybe it needs to.

It happened in the dining tent during the afternoon after the first performance. I sat with Sal, little Martha was snoozing contentedly on her knee. Sal had another *feast* in the offing. For the show's crew it was only a normal repast. Performers drifted into the tent, all still in costume, ready to do it all over again at eight o'clock. Earlier I'd noticed George's boys looking very warily at me in my face paint. I remained an exotic stranger to them.

'Which one was you, Sammy?' This was the woman I loved speaking. 'All you Indians looked the same to me! In all them feathers an' that war paint. Really scary!'

All my attempts to look especially brave and fierce in the arena came down to this. Taking the lead in the attack on the immigrant wagon train and trying to wrest control of the Deadwood Stage from its driver at full gallop seemed to count for nothing. Not to mention my demonstration of skill in winning the horse race against all the cowboy riders. Well, maybe I did show off. After all, I'd fallen in love again, and the woman I adored was watching me or so I thought.

'Buffalo Bill was good though. Shootin' down all them glass balls from up in the air an' sittin' on his horse at the same time.' She nodded firmly.

At least she appreciated one of the best parts of the show.

'Mind, Martha didn't like all that shootin'. Bawled her head off every time a gun banged! She'll get used to it, I suppose. Have to.' Sal stroked the sleeping child's head, but this brief moment of calm couldn't last.

'Wonderful! Wonderful!' George entered leading his family into the dining tent.

'What a mob out there!' said Annie tugging two very excited little boys behind her. It would take a long time for the magic to wear off, if it ever did. It still hadn't with me after all those years.

They'd managed to free themselves from the horde, twelve thousand strong, that had come to see the first of our four performances. Now, the audience had to return to reality, taking the magical illusion away with them, fixed in their hearts and in their memories... and hopefully, telling all their friends and neighbours how good it all was. Perhaps they would come back themselves, if they could get tickets.

'Maybe I should've run away with you, when I had chance!' George looked rueful.

What he said made me wonder how things might have turned out if he had remained after Red Shirt offered both of us a new life. Would the two of us blended in with the Lakota people on board as well as I'd been able on my own? I doubted it. There are very few, if any, red-haired Lakota. Would we have been despatched back to England at Portland Bill together with those other poor stowaways on board the ship? Would we have even made it out of the Hull dock?

'Then you wouldn't have married Annie and had the boys.' I tried to put his history in a positive light. George smiled looking at his children gazing starry eyed at the cast and crew surrounding them. 'Things have a way of working themselves out, George.' Maybe I was trying to persuade myself.

'Aye!' Sal slipped her arm into mine and laid her head on my shoulder.

'You're right smitten, lass!' Annie plonked herself onto the bench opposite us. 'Who'd have thought it?'

'Who?' I smiled but maybe what really amused me was the strange sight we must have presented to the world: a Lakota warrior in full war paint and feathers with a beautiful red-haired, pale woman resting on his shoulder. Not even one of Ned Buntline's dime novels could have explained this away easily.

***

'I've just seen Bill… and we think you'll enjoy your first job in the show!' I hoped my smile would confirm this. 'But you'll have to wait until the first performance tomorrow.'

My friends looked up inquisitively. An hour had passed since eating and they remained in the dining tent, still digesting their second enormous meal of the day… if not the week or even the year. It would take some time, especially for George, to realise that while a mountain of food was available at each mealtime, he didn't have to attempt its conquest every time. Living well above the breadline was a new experience for them and would continue to be so for some time to come.

'Don't be so mysterious, Sammy!' Sal begged.

'He wants us shovellin' up after the hosses!' For once George became the scornful one.

'Oh, you'll have to do that anyway!' I gave George a wink. 'No… tomorrow you'll be part of the wagon train attacked by the Lakota.'

'Sal, you'd better watch out for that big Indian up front. He'll have more than your scalp!' Annie giggled.

'Annie Smith! Don't know where you get such ideas from!' Sal blushed; her face glowed nearly as bright as her hair. 'Don't you listen to your Aunty Annie!' I heard Sal whisper to Martha who lay tucked in her arms.

'Then later, you'll be riding in the Deadwood Stage!' I knew they'd like this.

'Can't we do it tonight?' George forgot his aches and pains. His boys became interested and looked up from playing around his feet on the tent floor. Everyone wanted to ride in the Deadwood Stage. The nearest I'd ever got to this was leaping aboard as an unwelcome new passenger.

'The Lord Mayor and his aldermen are riding in it tonight. Wherever we perform the local knobs get to ride the stage. Usually the audience want the Indians to win!' I laughed. 'They always want to see 'em getting scalped!'

'Have you ever? Y'know?' George gave me an uncertain look.

'Scalped anybody?' I tried to sound serious. 'All the time! We don't have a barber in the company.' I pulled a large, gleaming Bowie knife from its sheath and waved it in the air, trying to look menacing.

'Give over, Sammy. You're scarin' the bai'ns!' Sal demanded. 'Put that thing away!'

How I'd missed her all these years. The jagged blade went back into the safety of its sheath. Under the paint I smiled.

***

'Sammy, you've got a visitor,' a voice whispered loudly in my ear. My friend Henry Thunder Eagle, one of the Lakota braves, shook the sleep out of me. He could speak better English than most white folks. He'd been to the mission school along with Laughing Waters.

'What? Who?' I tried to blink the tiredness out of my eyes and looked around the tepee. So, my dream wasn't just a dream. Sal was still there, asleep only inches away from me on our soft pillow of brown bison mane. Between us I could see the head of a little girl, still asleep. I wasn't supposed to be there. I should have been sleeping with the other single braves: Sal and I were not yet married. Bill had turned a blind eye to me sharing the tent with my new family. He allowed this on the strict condition I tied the knot with Sal as soon as practicable. Technically, I was keeping guard.

'An old white lady, Sammy! Says it's urgent!'

Everyone else in the tepee remained asleep. George snored away like a hive of overexcited bees. I'd forgotten about that. I slid from beneath our blanket, careful not to disturb anyone. Henry held back the tepee's entry flap for me to follow him out into the daylight.

I wondered who this old white lady might be and why she might want to see me so early in the morning but I should have guessed her identity. Only one old white lady in the whole city knew me, and she sat on a camp chair resting beside a smouldering open fire wrapped tightly in a dark blue woollen shawl, even though the day was already warming up. A matching blue bonnet was shackled in place by long hatpins.

'Mrs G! What are you doing here?'

'It's Mary, Sammy! That Edward Snelgrave's got her!' She trembled. I'd never heard her voice sound like this before. The rock everyone could lean on looked in need of strong support itself. A frightened old woman sat in front of me – not our Mrs G.

'What d'you mean, Mrs G?' My fists rubbed eyes still half closed.

'Says he'll not let her go until you go an' see him!' Old grey hands wrung anxiously becoming nets of blue veins.

'Don't suppose it's just for a cup of tea either!'

Once again Smelly proved true to type, misusing the only two people in Hull outside our encampment for whom I cared. But what did I owe Mary? She didn't even want to know me.

'He was always a bad lad, that one,' she muttered looking back toward the smouldering fire.

'Have you told the police?' I didn't know whether I wanted to become involved in Snelgrave's game.

'Fat lot of good that'd do! Big pals... his family an' the Chief Constable... an' with the Council an' all!' She snorted. 'If a bobby went round he'd just say he was only entertainin' her. Then like as not, the School Board would hear she was with him an' give her the sack! Call her a scarlet woman, they would! Bad moral influence on the school bai'ns, they'd say!'

'I thought Hull had become a city... but it's still just a big village!' I cursed. I knew I'd have to do something about Mary, even if only for Mrs G.

'Aye... an' all the same folk are still in charge!' She looked old and dispirited. 'An' always will be, Sammy!'

'What's goin' on?' Sal came out of the tepee, wrapped in her shawl and running fingers sleepily through her long hair. 'Mrs G!'

I recounted what Mrs G had said.

'You don't owe her nowt!' Sal was adamant. The old fire returned with a vengeance. 'She didn't want to know you... the little madam! Will he hurt her? What did he say?'

'In this town the likes of Edward Snelgrave can do what they like! She might be a schoolteacher but she's still an 'alf-caste! He'd make sure everyone knew about her brother – the fake Red Indian! He said so.' Mrs G sounded world-weary, her voice trailing away. 'Who'd believe the likes of Mary against a *fine* family like the Snelgraves? Pillars of society! Even when it's the black sheep o' the family, but he's the one who greases all the right palms in the town.'

'I've got to do something, Sal. Maybe she rejected me, but she's still the only kin I've got left in the world. I didn't want you finishing up on the streets and I don't want her having to do that either!'

Sal slipped her arm around my shoulder and kissed me on the cheek.

'You've spent too long in this show, Sammy. Good winning over evil... twice a day! In the real world, it's evil that usually wins... especially where poor folk like us are concerned!'

'Maybe it's time I evened things up a bit!' I needed a plan of action.

***

Even though he'd not been involved in a real campaign since the Ghost Dance Rebellion back in the winter of 1890, William Frederick Cody remained a master strategist. Unfortunately, he had not been involved in that Native American tragedy until it was too late to prevent the murder of his old friend, Chief Sitting Bull, or to stop the bloody massacre of hundreds of my people at Wounded Knee.

Today he was back in business. The old sparkle returned to his eyes. He thought out loud during our council of war in the Pahaska Tepee. Hanging on his every word with a sleepy-eyed George were Sal, Mrs G and trusted friend Henry Thunder Eagle.

'If you go down there by yourself, Sammy, he could say you'd come to rob him and this sister of yours was in cahoots with you. The police would believe him... if, as this fine lady says, he's got 'em eating out of his hand. You'd finish up in prison... that is if he ain't done you by then.' The moustache twitched and the beard got its usual pensive stroke which showed he was giving matters serious thought.

'We need to get in without being noticed... Grab the girl and get away. Then again there's another way.' The eyes twinkled brightly and a broad smile crossed his face. A plan was forming in his mind. 'What we need to do… is to create a diversion. A Lakota war party swooping down the streets of Hull would attract attention…that is, unless we want it to attract attention!' Bill's thoughts raced way ahead of the rest of us.

***

For the first time in decades the Deadwood Stage would be involved in a real life drama. Sal insisted on being a passenger on this journey and, much as I tried to dissuade her, I couldn't deny she'd be a useful addition on our mission. She knew the layout of the house where Smelly held Mary. She'd been in service in an identical adjoining property.

Even though Sal demanded a part in our plan, she still had misgivings. 'How d'you know she's really a prisoner? She might've gone there willingly! Might be Smelly's floozy for all you know! You know nowt about her, Sammy!'

I didn't want to admit she might be telling the truth. My mind returned to the school hall and the woman walking towards me but it wasn't my sister I'd imagined then. Grandmother's story about my mother that Mrs G had repeated to us came back to me. Maybe Mary was no better than this too. I felt confused. The possibility of learning even more unpleasant truths about my family hurt.

'I'm comin'!' Sal said. 'If she's playin' you false, she'll get more than a piece o' my mind.'

An unbelievable transformation had taken place in this woman in a little over a week. Her appearance changed even more drastically when we prepared ourselves for action. The Lakota women in the camp had plaited Sal's hair into two tight braids which she had tied up into a bun ready for action. She sat on our bedroll, struggling to pull on a pair of borrowed blue denim jeans.

'Never worn men's trousers afore. Though some said it was me who wore 'em in forty-two West Dock Avenue!'

The real owner of the jeans wore the leg bottoms rolled up and Sal needed to let them down again. Until she put them on, I'd been unaware of how long her legs were, always hidden inside a skirt that touched the floor. They looked shapely from the brief glimpse I was allowed to see. Maybe a little thin but time and a few good cowboy meals would sort that out.

'If you're going to be running around, that skirt of yours will get in the way.' I'd said. 'Anyway I've got to wear a costume too!'

For once I dressed in cowboy gear: the jeans, a red cotton shirt and my hair tucked inside a Stetson. 'I'll be the brownest cowboy Hull has seen!'

'They're a bit big 'round the waist.' She ran a hand down into the wide gap between the front of the trousers and her stomach. 'I need a bit o' string to tie 'em up with.'

'You'll need to wear jeans all the time... once we get out into the real west. When we've got a spread of our own.'

Sal's arms wrapped around me like an excited octopus and the slack jeans slipped down until the waist hung around her knees. 'Tell me it's true, Sammy!' Salty tears ran down her cheeks and onto my lips.

'Bill's got a town named after him... out in Wyoming, near the bend in the Shoshone River. He says we can have some land out there.' I tried to paint a picture of a rural idyll far from the fish dock's evil reek.

'There's a town called Buffalo Bill?' The tears subsided and Sal became inquisitive again.

'No! It's called Cody!' We both laughed and I hugged her.

Before I could chivvy her along further, Annie and George burst into the tepee. My shirt was unbuttoned and Sal's jeans still hung around her knees.

'Steady on, old lad!' George chortled. 'Time for all that when you've done your rescuing and got wed!'

Annie giggled too. 'Sammy was tellin' me about...'

Sal gave up trying to explain and pulled the jeans back up. 'Oh! Go away you two!'

A loud raspberry blown by a practising cowboy trombonist reminded us the game was afoot. Swiftly we sorted out our clothing and left the tent to join a special parade waiting to move out of the fairground.

Some of the players from the Cowboy Band had piled into the front wagon. They were dressed in their full show uniforms of wide brimmed hats, long sleeved shirts and hairy chaps. Each man's belt held a studded holster, although this was purely for effect as musicians were never required to fire a revolver or even to pull one out during the show. Few of them, if any, had ever punched cattle, let alone shot a bad guy. It was all part of the great illusion.

This particular selection of players was designed to create a loud noise rather than produce melodic harmonies: trumpets to herald our arrival and a big bass drum to emphasise the point. Leading them, cornet in hand, was Bill Sweeney who had directed the band since 1883. There was no way he was going to miss out on this. Even the narrator's megaphone had been loaded on board in order to help announce our arrival.

I followed Sal into the stagecoach cabin and checked each of the two Colt Navy revolvers sitting in holsters tied to my hips. The weapons looked almost antique but these were the guns that won the West or so the stories said and they were the ones people expected to see. I'd loaded the right-hand weapon with blanks; the other carried live ammunition, just in case.

'Only pull that one out if you really need to use it! Remember where we are.' Bill's words of caution rang in my brain. He knew I'd be tempted but he trusted me and his was a trust I could never betray. My gun belt held only blank cartridges.

'Everyone ready to roll?' Bill called from the saddle of a golden palomino prancing nervously alongside our column.

Riders and wagon drivers indicated their readiness to move off.

'Wagons! Ho!' Bill yelled and waved his hand forward in the tradition of a wagon master about to lead a band of settlers off to new lives in a magical promised land.

The band struck up a chorus of 'Yankee Doodle.' Their wagon led the rest of us out into Walton Street, turning left in the direction of Anlaby Road. As well as the Cowboy Band and the Deadwood Stage, Lakota warriors followed in full paint with war bonnets of eagle feathers flowing in the breeze. Leading them was Henry Thunder Eagle; behind them rode U.S. cavalrymen in dark blue uniforms with jingling sabres glistening in the sunshine.

'I ain't never been in a fine coach like this afore.' Sal looked out onto the pavement at the gangs of pedestrians who had been standing in wait, hoping to see anything going on inside the camp. Some cheered our column and Bill took off his Stetson to acknowledge their adulation.

'Now I know what old Queen Victoria must've felt like!' Sal waved to onlookers through the narrow open window.

I resisted the opportunity to pay her a compliment. The last time I'd done this while riding beside her, an elbow in the ribs had been my only reward.

We followed the same route as the day before but our destination this time did not lay as far away from camp as Ma Conroy's house. At the end of Walton Street we turned left onto the main road but were forced to a halt after only a few yards. The railway level crossing gates had shut to allow a train to pass as it travelled on towards its destination at Hull's Paragon Station. The noise of the Cowboy Bandsmen managed to surpass even the rumble and hiss of the steam locomotive. Our unusual assembly drew the train passengers' attention. Carriage windows rolled down to get a better view of this unexpected free entertainment welcoming them into the city.

The train had passed through and the white gates swung open, clattering to a halt parallel to the road. Road traffic could move again, and more bemused travellers rattled past us sitting aboard a tram going in the opposite direction. Ever the showman, Bill rewarded them a cheery wave of his hat.

Beyond the railway crossing we travelled only a few more yards before turning right into the Boulevard. Little more than twenty-four hours earlier I'd been unaware of the street's existence and now I was about to travel it again. Traffic heading in the opposite direction remained in the slow-moving queue that had built up waiting for the level crossing to re-open. Now we had to wait for them. More Hull people took the unique opportunity to see some of the entertainers who would be performing in their city later in the day. Maybe this sight would persuade some to return to enter our world of make believe. What they didn't know was this time some of us were only pretending to make believe. Today I played for real.

None of the travellers on Anlaby Road could have expected to see such a sight on this or any day. They'd never see the like of it again on the streets of Hull.

Eventually, the line of opposing traffic moved on. I dare say it would have cleared a lot faster if it weren't dawdling to get a good look at us. At last, we could turn off the main road and enter the Boulevard. Now battle could really commence.

Chapter 21

'Almost there,' Sal muttered under her breath, then thrust her head through the open coach window to shout the same information to our leader. Bill turned and nodded to her before lifting a white-gloved hand in the air to halt our procession. He trotted his horse back to us for further directions.

'The house is just down there... opposite the fountain!' Her forefinger stabbed vigorously, pointing fifty yards further down the street.

Time for Bill's master plan to go into action and like every performance it began with an overture. In the bandwagon Bill Sweeney, cornet in hand, took to his feet. The instrument went to his lips. As the first note blew the others joined in unison. A trumpeter and trombonist had exchanged their usual instruments for fifes. The familiar chords of the tune 'Gary Owen' cut through the morning air as they did at every performance.

Today it was not announcing the arrival of the doomed General George Armstrong Custer's Seventh Cavalry on the banks of the river known to the Lakota as the Greasy Grass. Only the white man calls it Little Big Horn. Despite all the musicians' energies the vigorous sound echoing back from the street's buildings was much thinner than the one to which we were accustomed but it had the desired effect. They played on with gusto as the bandwagon rolled ahead. Meanwhile the rest of our street theatre cast waited in the wings ready to play different parts.

Attracting attention was our aim and we looked to be succeeding. Intrigued bricklayers working on unfinished buildings downed tools and leaned on high scaffolding. They could enjoy a grandstand view on the strange events unfolding down at ground level. Householders together with their children and servants came outside to see what was disturbing their normally quiet Saturday morning. All stood by looking on agog: men, enjoying the good fortune of not having to work on the sixth day of the week, came from their breakfast tables, still in shirtsleeves with watch chains dangling across waistcoats; maids with white starched pinafores and tiny bonnets perched on tied back hair; and excited small boys in knickerbockers jumping up and down. So this was the affluent face of Hull; a face I didn't recognise.

A fountain stood in the centre of the road, like an island, at the Boulevard's junction with two side streets. Here was to be the stage on which our diversionary play would be enacted. Summer heat had turned the fountain's flow into a limp trickle into the bowl at its base. A place where only stray dogs and small boys would dare risk refreshing themselves.

The music ceased and the bandwagon came to rest beside the fountain. Our orator, Mr J. J. McCarthy, in his formal attire of long black frock coat and top hat rose to his feet. He took up his usual position behind the large metal megaphone. Here he could declaim with verve that would match that of any stage actor. Well, I'd seen a theatre play when we were in London. I think it was called *Romeo and Juliet*. I couldn't tell exactly what went on because the actors spoke in a strange language, but I knew the ending was sad because everyone cried.

'Ladies and gentlemen of Hull... Buffalo Bill with his Wild West Show and Congress of Rough Riders of the World are appearing today on the fairground in Walton Street. We proudly bring you a taste of our show and hope you will all grace us with your presence later in the day!'

The band struck up again. A short but rousing chorus of 'The Stars and Stripes Forever' blasted out before our orator recommenced.

'Let us present to you that most legendary of all vehicles: the Deadwood Stage. It is about to receive the unwanted attention of a band of Native American aboriginals led by Chief Thunder Cloud.'

Was Henry aware of his sudden promotion to the position of war chief? Something I intended to tease him about later.

With a crack of his whip the driver put our team of horses into a brisk canter, rapidly increasing it to a gallop. I held onto my borrowed Stetson and hung out the window to check everything was going to plan. The war band allowed the stage enough time to get up speed before charging after us, letting out a wild cacophony of war whoops.

I pulled the Colt from the right holster and turned to face my erstwhile colleagues who now were in hot pursuit. It felt strange to be on the opposing side for once. I pointed the revolver in their direction and loosed a blank shot. Screams came from females and small children in their front gardens. I let loose another blank round. It brought the same response. I thought I could get used to being the hero instead of my usual role of a villain.

The bandwagon moved on a few yards further before coming to rest in front of a short terrace of villas overlooking the fountain. The choice of the wagon's position was no accident. The familiar sound of 'Gary Owen' struck up again. The bass drum joined in but more in fervour than in time with the music.

The stagecoach slowed to circle the fountain. Somehow the pursuing band of merciless braves never quite managed to catch up.

A couple of rotations and the war band made a brief diversion into Gordon Street, which was to the right of the fountain. Lady spectators shrieked, fearing for their lives – if not worse. These wild men in their flowing war bonnets and livid war paint sent the crowd scattering in all directions. No male dared to stand his ground to protect against a possible threat to a lady's honour. They were too concerned with holding onto their scalps.

This was a diversion within a diversion. Our coach took the opportunity to jerk to a halt beside the bandwagon and the next stage of Bill's plan could commence. Sal and I jumped out followed by our secret weapons, Jake and Harry. When they leapt to the ground the coach rose up several inches on its suspension. I could imagine it giving a gasp of relief. The four of us clung behind the shelter of the bandwagon leaving a much lighter stagecoach to continue its circling of the fountain. Its Lakota pursuers could now resume a chase of their quarry allowing the Hull folk scattered in the side streets to feel safe again.

'Number hundred and forty-nine's the one at the end!' An intense Sal nodded vigorously at the row of houses standing behind the bandsmen, who still played with great energy, even if not up to their usual standard of musicianship.

We sidled around the wagon. I glanced over the heads of the musicians and towards our target. The net curtains in the house's upstairs' windows were pulled aside to allow the occupants a better view of the free show below them. There were a lot of faces looking down into the street. Only male faces. No sign of Mary.

I threw my Stetson into the bandwagon and led my group around its rear. The driver had been well briefed as to where to stop and his wagon provided perfect cover for us. It hid us from the peering eyes of Snelgrave's companions just in case any eyes should stray from the spectacle in the street.

We hung low creeping away from our cover and into the narrow open side garden of number one-four-nine, slinking towards the tall wooden gate at the rear of the house. I clicked the gate sneck and pushed. Nothing happened. It was bolted on the inside.

Jake brushed me aside. With one lunge of his shoulder the bolt and hinges ceased to resist. I grabbed the door handle to stop the gate collapsing to the ground and making the loud crash that could give us away.

The rear garden took me by surprise. It didn't belong in the Hull I knew, any more than I did. Luxuriant green shrubs edged a long neat lawn but the garden's flora held no interest for me. All my attention focused on the single storey extension at the rear of the house. Sal said we'd find the back door there.

We edged along the extension's wall towards a solid looking door.

'The scullery,' Sal whispered.

The locked door proved no match for Harry who took his turn at battering an entrance open. A single charge from a granite shoulder was enough. I prayed those inside would mistake the noise for another of the loud gunshots still cracking out in the street.

The polished red tiled floor reflected the glowing coals in a black leaded grate. A large black kettle stood close by ready to boil water while a row of shiny steel pans hung from a wall rack. A lingering smell of recently fried bacon made me lick my lips but the taste turned sour in my mouth. I remembered the damp grey poverty of Sal's kitchen in West Dock Avenue only a half mile away. Both properties belonged to Mr Edward Snelgrave. One paid for the other.

I could hear raucous voices yelling from the front of the house. Was everyone here still distracted by the free show? No one could fail to be excited by the sight of the chase taking place only yards away outside in the street. Loud voices but they were all male. Where was Mary? If she were really in the house she was not with the men. I imagined her gagged and bound to a chair in a darkened locked room.

We crept from the scullery into a large room furnished with a long oak table and matching upholstered chairs. A tall Welsh dresser laden with rows of blue and white patterned dining plates stood by the wall. I'd never lived in a house anything like this but I took this to be the dining room. I'd not lived in a house of any kind in over twenty years. This was Sal's domain. She deserved a good home. She would have as much to teach me in our new family life as I would her.

'Nice bit of Wedgwood,' Sal whispered but her words meant nothing to me. All I could think about was how Snelgrave earned the money to pay for this house and all of its expensive contents. Despite the reassuring presence of Jake and Harry, I remained uneasy about having Sal with us but she knew the layout of the house. She knew the territory.

Real adventure is different from the make believe we performed twice a day. After our performances both friend and foe could share a meal and a joke together. Everything we did now had been planned but without the benefit of our normal careful rehearsal. If anyone got hurt during our show's performances it was an accident. Here any injury would most likely be deliberate and there was someone I wanted to hurt very much, if the opportunity arose.

'There's a middle room.' Sal pointed to the far end of the dining room and an open door leading into a hallway.

I held up my hand to halt the others at this door. I slid through it alone and into the hall to find the next room. Dappled sunlight filtered through colourful stained glass panels in the front door, creating a fluid mosaic that floated just above the hall's tiled floor. Without needing an extra step, I reached the intended door and turned the handle. It swung open in silence and I glanced inside but, apart from even more expensive furnishings, the room stood empty.

I returned to my confederates and shook my head.

'Upstairs?' Sal whispered and urged us on with a nod.

I signalled to the others to follow. This would be more dangerous. This was where most of the men in the house were. We could hear them hollering, presumably out a window at the show.

We tiptoed across the black and white chessboard of the hall's tiled floor and up the staircase but such caution wasn't really required. Thick carpeting in the centre of the staircase deadened our footsteps and so much noise came from the outside the house, a herd of bison stampeding would have gone unnoticed. My Lakota friends whooped fiercely; loud shots fired into the air echoed around the street and all the while the band played on. Shouting and cheering continued in the front rooms – both up and down stairs – but it was still only male voices. The volume told me we were outnumbered.

We were halfway up the staircase. Cold sweat trickled down the back of my shirt collar and onto my shoulders. I felt Sal breathing heavily behind me. If we were discovered now we would be trapped.

The staircase turned a right angle before reaching the top landing. At this point a closed door faced us. Like the front door its top half was also glazed with a coloured pattern in the shape of a red, blue and yellow peacock.

Sal gave a firm nod towards the door. I turned the brass doorknob and pushed but again our way was barred. Was the door locked to keep visitors out or to keep someone in? The melee outside went quiet and we paused waiting for the resumption of noisy action.

'Ladies and gentlemen!' J. J. again addressed the local populace. He could have been delivering his oration inside the house such was its volume. 'In the nick of time, the Deadwood Stage and its passengers are saved by the grand hero of the Great Plains, Colonel William F Cody together with the United States Cavalry. Ladies and gentlemen… Buffalo Bill!'

A loud cheer came from outside in the street and also from the occupants in the front of the house. They didn't know they were the great man's true adversaries and the real attack was on this house. A bugle blast told everyone rescue was at hand, even if a certain person might be unaware that she needed saving. We heard the sound of more gunfire outside. Bill and the cavalry had commenced their part of the action.

I indicated to Jake. A solid boot applied directly to the lock provided the key to entry. It surrendered and the door swung open.

A startled young woman in a long black dress turned to see a strange band of unexpected visitors standing outside the door. 'What do you want?' Did Mary think we were uninvited skivvies come to bring her morning tea?

'It's you we want! Silly cow!' Sal wasn't going to stand any nonsense. Hardly what I'd expected at the first meeting between my sister and my future wife, but my family, such as it was, wasn't like other families.

'I'm Mr Snelgrave's house guest and...'

'Grab her!' Sal gave the orders now. 'An' stick some't in her gob afore she starts to scream the 'ouse down!'

Jake shot across the room faster than anyone would have believed possible for such a bulky frame. A hand larger than a grizzly bear's paw smothered not only Mary's mouth but the rest of her face too. His other hand lifted her like a sack of feathers into the air several inches from the ground.

'Out!' I tried not to shout but my excitement made it difficult.

We raced down the stairs with Harry in the lead.

'Front door!' I whispered although perhaps stealth no longer mattered.

'What the hell!' A man appeared in the hall coming from the front room. Why wasn't the entertainment outside still enthralling him? A round moustachioed face beneath dark greased hair turned puce.

Harry was a man of few words, usually none at all. He thrust both hands deep into the man's chest. Our discoverer's feet lifted off the ground and he flew backwards into the front room. He landed out of our sight with the sound of the crash of breaking glass.

Harry's huge frame created a barrier between the front room and us. He stood his ground and we slipped behind him to take the shortest escape route, which was via the front door. Mary continued to struggle but she provided no contest for Jake.

Yet another door was locked. I freed the top bolt and Sal took care of the bottom one, but our exit route remained locked. There was no sign of a key anywhere.

Two more of Snelgrave's confederates rushed out from the front room. Harry grabbed both their heads – one beneath each arm. They cracked together with a hollow clunk. Their owners dropped onto the floor in a single crumpled heap.

Above us floorboards creaked. At the top of the stairs faces looked over the banister. Edward Snelgrave's was among them.

'The dresser!' Sal leapt towards a tall wall stand. She pulled open a drawer below a large fitted mirror and rustled through its contents. She searched frantically but there was no key. She cursed loudly.

'Looking for this?' Snelgrave leered. He stood half way down the stairs, waving a large brass key in the air. True to character he taunted us from a safe place, tucked behind two more large henchmen.

Sal looked in a second drawer. She turned smartly and glared back at him. She also waved something in the air.

'Snap!' she yelled. She also held a shiny brass key.

His changed expression told everyone he wasn't enjoying the experience of being upstaged.

'Get them! Quick!' Snelgrave urged his underlings.

Sal had the key in the lock already. Jake stood beside her. Momentarily he let his hand slip from Mary's mouth and she tried to call out. His hand went back in place and silenced her again. I stood shoulder to shoulder with Harry to block Snelgrave's progress. Well, shoulder to elbow.

The man who'd practised involuntary flight only a few moments earlier re-emerged from the front room. He looked battered. He also looked angry. A broken bottle waved in his hand. One of the men coming down the stairs pulled a jagged sheath knife from his belt.

Instinctively a Navy Colt went in my right hand and I fired a blank shot in the air.

All motion in the room became a photographic image as though time stood still.

'Stay back or one of you gets the next bullet!'

The pistol moved downwards by ninety degrees and I pointed it towards Snelgrave. Unfortunately, it wasn't the one containing live ammunition. I wished it had been but, as always, Bill was right. I edged back towards the front door with Harry sidling along beside me.

The front door swung open. A gush of fresh air... and a blast of music. Surely now our escape was assured. I kept the revolver levelled and pointing at Smelly.

Fate took a hand. Jake also backed out, still holding Mary in a bear hug but he was unaware of the thick hall doormat in front of the door. A loud crash and he fell to the floor still clasping my sister.

'Help!' Mary screamed and broke free leaving Jake in a heap.

It distracted me and I turned my head. Only for a second but it was too long.

Snelgrave's cronies made their move.

I turned back and pulled the trigger.

Click! Click!

All my blanks were spent. My left hand went down to a full holster.

'No!' Harry's right arm swung back and he pushed me towards the door. He knew about the live ammunition in the other revolver.

I collided with Mary, now free and trying to rejoin Snelgrave. I grabbed her arm.

'Get off! Leave me alone!' she screamed.

I wanted to punch her, to shut her up but someone beat me to it. A slender but very strong female arm grabbed her around the throat. Sal yanked Mary off her feet and dragged her back in the direction of the street. A large body brushed past me almost knocking me over. Jake was back on his feet and going shoulder to shoulder with his partner.

'We'll take care of these outlaws, Sammy,' Jake said. Both my allies laughed. I helped Sal haul my unwilling half-sister out into the street.

Outside the man in buckskin with flowing silver hair held everyone's attention. No one noticed a cowboy and a flame-haired woman dragging another female around the rear of the bandwagon. Well, no one that is except for our orator who had been given the additional task of keeping a careful watch on the house. He shook the lead musician by the shoulder and shouted into his ear. The umpteenth repetition of 'Gary Owen' ended abruptly to be replaced by 'Yankee Doodle.' This was the signal for the next act in the street theatre to commence.

The Redskin war band broke off its attack on the stagecoach and allowed itself to be chased around the fountain by Bill at the head of the blue uniformed cavalrymen. Polished sabres glistened in the sunlight. The coach diverted from the action and came to a halt by the bandwagon again.

We heaved Mary into the gap between the two wagons and bundled her on board the stagecoach.

'Grab her!' I shouted to the remaining occupants, two more roustabouts. 'She don't seem to want to be rescued!'

Sal followed her up and into the coach.

My foot was on the step ready to board. A hand gripped my shoulder and yanked me backwards. A fist caught the side of my chin and I reeled more in surprise than pain. The back of my head hit the side of the coach.

'Got you at last, brown boy!' It was Snelgrave. How did he get past Jake and Harry? He must have slipped out the back door.

Another lucky punch knocked the wind out of me. I slid down the side of the stagecoach unable to breathe. As I lost consciousness I saw a foot at the end of a blue denim leg lash out from inside the coach. It landed under Snelgrave's chin and lifted him into the air. I remained aware long enough to see his head hit the iron rim of a bandwagon wheel.

I wandered somewhere between this world and the next but I could hear Sal's voice. Her face became visible though there might have been two of her. One was enough; one was plenty. I could feel myself being lifted from the ground.

'Sal – you're beautiful.' I mumbled; I was rambling. Sal's face changed to Jake's face.

We were moving. The band kept playing. People cheered. Everything went dark.

Chapter 22

I heard a voice.

'Sammy. Sammy.' It got closer.

A wet flannel cooled my forehead. I opened my eyes. A drop of water trickled into one of them.

I blinked. It really was Sal's face now, not one belonging to a very large roustabout. She looked relieved. I blinked again. Above her head I could see a patch of blue sky through the vent in the top of the tepee.

How did I get back here? I had no recollection of anything after the rescue.

'Don't go doin' that again, Sammy Smyle! You had me worried!' Sal smiled but I could sense her insecurity. She remained dressed in what she called 'men's clothes.'

'Lucky punch!' I croaked trying to appear blasé, but words felt painful. A *lucky punch* that made both my stomach muscles and the back of my head ache, but the pain didn't prevent me trying to lever myself up by my elbows.

'Steady on! You've been a hero once already today.' Soft hands took hold of my shoulders and eased me slowly back onto a soft and hairy pillow. 'That's enough, my lad. No need for you to prove it again!'

'What happened?' I winced with pain. I tried to recollect what happened after Smelly caught me unawares. The last I remembered seeing was a foot flying in the direction of his ugly face.

'We got away. Obviously! An' now we're here.' Sal gave me a sour look. Did she think the punch had turned me into a simpleton?

'Mary? Snelgrave?' Brief words. Speaking hurt. My tongue tried to examine my teeth expecting to find loose ones, if not worse. My mouth still felt numb.

'That stupid half-sister of yours got a piece of me mind! A big piece! Now Mrs G's havin' a go at her!' Her shrug told me she thought Mary a hopeless case. A big *cat got the cream* smile came over her face. 'Last we saw of Smelly, he was staggerin' off down Cholmley Street like a drunken sailor.'

'Was it your foot, Sal?'

'You bet it was! Got him right under the chin.' She lifted her leg to let me admire the offensive weapon at its end. 'Wanted to do that for years! Wished I'd kicked somewhere else an' all!'

'You look good in jeans.' Even trying a smile hurt but I still tried.

'Don't you go sweet talkin' me, Sammy! Just 'cos we're alone!' She pressed her index finger on my dry lips. 'Time for all that once we're wed.'

'So you've accepted my proposal then?' I forced a smile. It was worth the pain.

'Reckon so; though I'm none too keen on me new sister-in-law.' Her expression became pained.

'Well, your brother and his family will make up for her.' Smiling inwardly wasn't painful.

The tent flap flew open. Bill entered with his usual flourish, still dressed in the clothes he wore for our assault on the Boulevard house: his show time clothes of buckskin suit and white Stetson.

'How's our wounded hero?' he asked.

'Comin' the old soldier, if you ask me, sir!' Sal could be very unsympathetic at times. A lifetime spent with her twin brother George made her wary of male malingering.

'A bit sore but I'll be all right.' Reality returned to me. 'What time is it?'

How long had I been unconscious? There was a show to do at two o'clock.

Bill pulled a gold pocket watch from his jacket pocket. 'It's twelve-thirty. Don't you be worrying about time, my boy.'

I'd been unconscious for only minutes. So many things had happened, and it was still only half past twelve. It was lunchtime. This explained George's absence. Again I tried to get up.

'You stay where you are,' Bill ordered. 'Enjoy it while you can. You've got a good nurse to take care of you.'

There was no need to look at Sal. I could feel the heat coming from her blushes.

'Henry will lead the attacks this afternoon. It's not often I give anyone the chance to rest. Make the most of it, my boy!' Bill gave a hearty guffaw and slapped a leather-clad thigh.

'But Henry might get used to doing it!' It was only mock indignation. Henry deserved a bit of the limelight after all he'd done for me today. I appreciated everything he and everyone else had done, even if my sister didn't.

'You rest a while, my boy,' the boss commanded and I did as I was ordered.

***

With Martha's assistance Sal kept me wide-awake.

'You're not to nod off. Doctor's orders!'

Some hot coffee and a bowl of chicken soup were all I could manage. I enjoyed being cosseted. I could easily have become accustomed to it but I knew Sal and Bill would not allow that to happen.

'Don't think I'll be doin' this all the time. I'll expect you to help 'round the house! That's when we have one.' Sal was one of these new twentieth century women but it was something I could learn to live with, something I wanted to live with. 'It's just that today's been a bit special and you've been a bit special an' all.' Her forefinger drew a gentle line on my cheek.

'And so have you! You took a big risk today for someone you don't even like.'

'I did it for you... an' to get one over on Smelly!' She smiled. This was a new Sal; a happy Sal. 'It was great!'

I took her hand and pulled her down onto the bed beside me. We kissed. I heard the sound of Martha giggling behind us.

Gradually I began to feel normal and got up to walk slowly around the tent. I regretted giving up my moment of glory in the arena. I was still stage struck after all these years but took solace from the fact that Henry had more right to be there. After all he was the genuine article, a real Lakota.

Annie and a well-fed George came to see how I was mending, but it still left one person I wanted to see. There would have been no point to our morning adventure, not to mention my sore head, if Mary still believed she had been Snelgrave's *'house guest.'*

Nearly show time. The cowboy band was back to full strength. Its programme's familiar opening tunes filled the air, urging the audience to take their places. Excited voices could he heard, shouting above the noise of more than a thousand pairs of feet crunching across the fairground shale. My senses responded to these familiar signals: my heart pounded and adrenalin rushed around my system preparing me for a performance I would not be making today.

'It's time you got yourself into one of those prairie schooners.' I nodded towards the entry flap from our seat on soft, furry blankets. 'I'll look after Martha. Go on. It's show time.'

'It's all right.' Sal's head came to rest on my shoulder. 'I'll do it tonight.'

She snuggled closer and lay back watching Martha ferreting around the other bedding in the tepee. The child had new clothes: a buckskin dress; multicoloured beads hung around her neck. Her hair was tied in short bunches, not long enough yet for braids. The Lakota women had taken a real shine to the new child in camp.

'Only been here twenty-four hours and she's a Lakota papoose already. Took me a lot longer to achieve that level of acceptance!' I said. Only about a day longer as I remembered.

'A what?' Sal turned. Her questioning expression returned.

'Papoose. It means baby.'

'Don't think you're gonna turn me into one of them squaws!'

Indignation, indignation… but I loved it.

'There is absolutely no chance of that, Selina Smith,' I said, forgetting her married name. There didn't seem a lot of point in becoming used to it anyway. Her surname was soon going to change again.

A familiar face appeared through the entry flap to interrupt our sweet talk.

'Mrs G!' We spoke simultaneously.

'Are you all right, Sammy? Mrs G queried, standing half in and half out of the tepee.

'Nowt wrong with him now!' Sal replied for me. 'He's just swingin' the lead. Men are all the same!'

'I've brought somebody to see you, Sammy.' Mrs G's attention remained directed towards me.

'Come on in.' I gestured to emphasise the invitation. It hurt.

Slowly, very slowly Mrs G straightened herself. The stooping position required to enter the tepee was not to her liking. A sheepish looking Mary Smyle followed her inside. She looked a very different person from the one we'd thrown into the Deadwood Stage only a few hours earlier.

Sal turned her head away, pretending to concentrate on her child. I could only see the back of her neck but I knew her complexion would be turning red. There would be a scowl on that beautiful face.

'We've had a long talk an' Mary's got some things to say to you, Sammy.' Although it wasn't the strong voice of old, Mrs G's tone held firm.

'Sorry'd be a good place to start!' Sal's head turned brusquely before returning to looking at Martha.

'Steady on, Sal!' I gripped her hand tightly.

'She's right!' My mother's voice spoke the words. Eighteen years since I'd last heard it and it remained imbedded in my brain. 'Sal's right. I am sorry. Sorry for how I've treated you. Sorry for listening to Grandmother's lies, and to that Snelgrave. For being a silly fool.'

'I've been puttin' her right on a few things!' Mrs G remained serious.

'I've been foolish!' Mary looked down, examining her feet.

Sal turned her head again ready to interrupt but her hand got an extra tight squeeze to stop her from speaking out.

'Maybe we can start again?' I suggested, continuing to squeeze. Sal's fingers must have hurt.

'Can we?' Mary's tone of voice suggested impossibility.

'Of course we can! We're family. The same blood,' I said.

Sal relaxed, her body leaning into mine. She understood the meaning of my words. I loosened my grip.

'Sit down both of you. Would you like something to drink?' Sal's demeanour changed in an instant. This was her temperament: quick to fire but equally fast to cool down again. She found it difficult to hold grudges against anyone, apart from the likes of Snelgrave, of course. 'There's only this American coffee stuff, though.'

'That'd be nice. Thank you.' Mary smiled.

I hadn't seen Mary smile before. Again, I saw the face of the woman who held me as a child and rocked me to sleep. It hurt more than all my bruises, but it was a sweet ache.

Sal left the tepee to go to the campfire and make coffee. We could hear the band playing loudly. From their tune I knew exactly what was happening in the arena but the events in those few square feet inside the tepee took on a far greater importance for me.

Mrs G gave our conversation motherly encouragement. She knew all of us as children and could fill in lots of gaps. I wanted to learn everything about Mary and how much she enjoyed being a schoolteacher. She wanted to know about my adventures and about our mother, the woman she had no memories of, except for what our venomous grandmother had told her. She wanted to hear all about the woman who died while she was still a baby. I painted a very different picture from the crude caricature she'd grown up with. It may not have been completely true but it was a better description than the one she had been taught. Mine came from the heart, from love.

The band continued playing. Interspersed with the music were the frequent sounds of gunshots and the thunder of people cheering, stamping and applauding, over and over again. Were they also cheering our family reunion? It felt like it.

I stared at Mary. I tried to stop myself but it was as though mother had returned and not aged a day since I last saw her. Yes, well maybe both the hair and the complexion were darker... but her eyes... her expressions... her voice... her way of moving. Everything was the same.

Gradually Sal joined in the conversation with a shy child taking safe refuge on her mother's knee. Sal and Mary had much in common as orphans who had come through the same children's home. All of us had been lucky to have Mrs G as our guardian angel. Maybe Sal and Mary didn't love each other as sisters when we finished talking but, at least, they were on speaking terms. This made me happy.

I didn't notice that the band had stopped playing, or the noise of cheering had faded as thousands of feet trampled across the fairground after two hours of magic. It was a shock of red hair and an even brighter face bursting into the tepee that brought me back to reality.

'It was great! Fantastic!' George was beside himself with excitement. Annie and the two boys followed behind him looking in a similar state.

'Should've been there, Sal! Great!' They came back down to earth when they noticed our visitors.

'Mrs G!' Both he and Annie spoke simultaneously. Somehow they must have missed seeing Mrs G in the camp.

'And this is my sister, Mary.' There was no way I'd refer to her as a 'half-sister.'

'Have you got things sorted out?' Annie looked awkward.

'Yes. I think everything's sorted now.' Mrs G summed up the state of play.

Her words made me think. A certain Edward Snelgrave still remained in Hull and he would be a lot less happy now than he was a few hours ago. In twenty-four hours we would be on our way out of town and moving on to York but Mary would still be here and vulnerable. Had things really been improved?

***

The charm of Colonel William F Cody knew no bounds as he entertained my entire family during our evening meal. The familiar twinkle returned to his eyes when noticed Mary with us in the dining tent. She was an attractive young lady again, no longer the struggling baggage he'd seen us bundle aboard the Deadwood Stage.

My bruised stomach still ached but I didn't care. I was so happy I thought I'd burst. Two weeks earlier only Bill was the nearest thing I still had to family. Now I enjoyed the company of a sister and a soon to be wife together with a daughter and in-laws, not forgetting a real fairy godmother who once again had waved her magic wand over us all.

After we'd finished dining, Bill took me to one side in the Pahaska Tepee.

'The Chief Constable has been to see me.' A more serious visage replaced Bill's normal smile. 'He wasn't very happy about our unexpected display in the street. Said we should have gotten the permission of himself and the City Council. Took a lot of fine malt whiskey to settle him down, not to mention a passle of free tickets for tonight's show.'

'Thank you, sir. I'm sorry to have caused so much trouble.' I'd never be able to thank him enough for all he'd done today for me and my family during that day.

'Trouble! Trouble!' I thought he was going to burst and he did so – with laughter. 'Ain't had so much fun since I don't know when! Jake and Harry will be telling the tale around campfires for years to come. Yes, even Harry!'

'Do you think we could work it into the show?' I suggested cheekily.

'Somehow I don't think the Wild West of Hull would be such a crowd pleaser.' He stroked his beard in mock thoughtfulness. 'Pleased me though, Sammy.'

'Maybe not one for the show.' I turned to leave the tent but he motioned me to stop.

'There was one unfortunate happening though… after we completed our little show.' He paused, looking serious again. 'A man was run over by a wagon in a street nearby. The Chief Constable reckons a coalman's horse got excited with all the commotion and bolted.' He gave a shrug. 'Said the man was wandering down the middle of the street. Looked like he was drunk.'

'Is he all right?' I felt concerned about causing injury to an innocent bystander, whether he was drunk or not.

'He's dead, the Chief Constable said!'

My heart dropped. I was feeling so happy until that moment but this news ruined everything.

'I feel guilty!' I leaned forward, both hands holding on Bill's table for support. 'I must do something. It's my fault.'

'No, the coalman should have tethered his horse properly. It weren't your fault, my boy.'

Bill's hand came to rest on my shoulder to give it a supportive squeeze, but I felt near to tears. My emotions had been on a roller coaster ride all day.

'Do you know the man's name?' I felt the need to do something to help the poor man's family. There might be a widow and children. More orphans.

'Said he was a Mr Snelgrave.'

I remembered Sal telling me Snelgrave had wandered off dazed after her kick struck his chin. The roller coaster took a ride upwards at great speed. No wife. No orphans to take care of. No Edward Snelgrave. No problem.

'Thank God!' I muttered feeling relieved.

Bill looked surprised by my sudden change of response.

'It was him! He was the one! He kidnapped Mary! The bully in the orphanage! At last, I'm finally rid of him. We're all rid of him!'

***

Bill's arm needed a twist but he let me take part in the show's final Hull performance. Mind, there was no way he would allow me to leap onto the lead horse of the Deadwood Stage this time. Henry retained that honour, but I didn't mind.

At last, Sal joined the wagon train and became a pretend settler heading west to start a new life. Soon this fiction would become reality. Martha sat in the audience in the company of Mrs G and her new Aunt Mary.

After the show I enjoyed the luxury of a second night in one place because the next day was Sunday and for one day there were no shows to perform. My new family marvelled at the speed and efficiency of the whole crew when we struck camp on Sunday morning. George's boys attached themselves as apprentices to Jake and Harry who appeared to be enjoying this new adulation. By noon all the equipment and the whole of the crew were loaded back onto our trains. We were on our way to York where we would do it all over again with afternoon and evening performances on Monday.

Mary and Mrs G left us with promises that we'd all keep in contact by letter. I suggested we might manage a visit back to Hull before we sailed to America, although I knew in all probability we'd not be able to do so. Maybe we'd return to England and to Hull one day with the show. Financial need would persuade Bill to keep performing long after he should have hung up his Stetson and spurs to retire to the town named after him. However, he'd announced previously that this was 'positively the final tour of Great Britain' long before we came to the north of the country.

Our trains rolled out of the dock sidings and the smell of fish disappeared, left behind us for the last time. I took a final look through the carriage window at my hometown before turning my head away.

'Tell us what happens next, Sammy?' George swung his legs, sitting perched on a bunk in the middle row of one of the tiers.

Sal sat beside me on a bottom bunk stroking a sleeping Martha's head. She looked up at her brother. I could tell from her expression she thought he was bound to fall off the bunk like a sack of potatoes.

'Well, we finish our tour in England in October at somewhere called Hanley.' The place name meant nothing to anyone judging by the blank expressions surrounding me. 'Then we sail back to the United States from Liverpool.'

'Then what?' Sal asked. This was all a new world to her.

'When we get back there's that piece of land Bill promised us near the bend in the Shoshone River or...' I paused to keep their attention.

'Or what?' George knew instinctively that once again I had a new scheme brewing inside me. As far as he was concerned I had not changed.

'Well, I've got this idea. Have you seen a bioscope moving picture show?' I tested their knowledge.

'Aye, Stan took me to see one of them at the music hall.' Sal's sad expression told me she recalled a happy time with her late husband. 'There was this train an' I swear I thought it was gonna come right off the stage an' run us over! There was women screamin' an' faintin' all over the place...some men fainted too...but it weren't real!' She became so animated in recounting the event she almost dropped Martha onto the carriage floor.

'Well, a company called British Bioscope has been taking moving pictures of the show and it's got me thinking.' I tried to remain calm.

'I'm not sure I like it when you get to thinkin', Sammy,' George frowned.

'I heard there's people out on the west coast of America in California making bioscope moving pictures with stories... you know, like plays but without any words!' I became excited now. 'There's lots of great stories about the Wild West we don't tell in the show. They could all be told by the bioscope and shown all around the world. We could do it! We could make 'em!' Sal just stared. 'Think about it though.' I gave Sal a hug. 'We could share our dreams with the world.'

'Bioscopes?' George crinkled his forehead, as cautious as ever. 'I don't know. It'll never catch on.'

Historical Notes

In July 1903 Buffalo Bill's Wild West Show and Congress of Rough Riders of the World fired the imaginations of the people of Hull during its final lengthy tour of Great Britain. In Hull alone 20,000 people came to see the show during its second visit to the city. The first was in 1888 when it made a single performance on the 5th of May before sailing back to the USA the next day. This was the end of a tour which began a year earlier as part of the American Exhibition at Earls Court. It enjoyed a six month stay in London which was attended by the Royal Family including Queen Victoria. After this came short seasons in both Manchester and Birmingham before it departed for home from Hull.

William Cody was a genuine Wild West hero. His prowess as a buffalo (bison) hunter earned him his nickname. Almost single-handed he'd supplied the builders of the American railroad with vast quantities of fresh meat. In addition he had been a Pony Express rider and an army scout. It was in this latter role that he earned the rank of Colonel. Shortly after Custer's Last Stand he was involved in a skirmish with the Cheyenne, which culminated in a hand-to-hand duel to the death between himself and Chief Yellow Hand. A restaging of this fight became an essential part of the show for many years although other Native Americans had to substitute for the luckless chief.

Cody's exploits caught the attention of the writer Ned Buntline who made him the hero of many best-selling dime novels. In turn this new reputation led to this larger than life figure becoming a master showman.

The American frontier had been won on horseback. Buffalo Bill's show was a celebration of the horse and all it had done for humankind. In previous visits to Britain the show had concentrated solely on showing the wonders of the American West. In this final tour the show was expanded to bring audiences representatives of native equestrians from around the world including Bedouin Arabs, Argentinean gauchos and Mexican vaqueros.

The show adopted the name *Rough Riders* from the description used by President Theodore "Teddy" Roosevelt in the Spanish-American War. Some of the troopers from the real Battle of San Juan Hill took part in its re-enactment in the show.

Of more contemporary interest was the inclusion of Russian Cossacks and the Japanese Imperial Troupe of horsemen. Their respective countries were at war with each other but the *Hull Times* reported only 'friendly rivalry' between these two groups of entertainers. Tragically only a short while later this war was to impact on the people of Hull when the Russian Baltic Fleet attacked unarmed trawlers in the North Sea in the mistaken belief they were Japanese motor torpedo boats.

The real centre of attraction in the show was the Wild West itself. Genuine cowboys, United States cavalrymen and Native Americans brought examples of frontier life to an enthusiastic Yorkshire audience. A hundred Native Americans – drawn mainly from the Sioux nation – gave displays of war dances and horsemanship. They were then cast in the role of villain in re-enactments of attacks on an emigrant wagon train and the famous Deadwood Stage plus, of course, the Battle of the Little Big Horn in which General George Armstrong Custer and his Seventh Cavalry had their last stand.

Whenever a rescue was required it was led by Buffalo Bill himself, although not even he could re-write history in the case of General Custer. Colonel Cody reminded everyone of his skill as a sharpshooter by shooting down glass balls thrown in the air. The fact that he did it from horseback made it all the more impressive.

Apart from the colour and excitement of the show itself one of the most impressive aspects was its organisation. In the early hours of Friday 1st July four specially constructed trains rolled into sidings at Hull's Albert Dock. Only a matter of hours earlier the troupe had given two performances in Grimsby. By breakfast time a tented city had been erected on Hull's Walton Street Fairground and enormous hot meals were being served. At three o'clock that afternoon the first performance commenced with thousands of people seated in the portable arena. As the company was more than 800 strong together with over 500 horses, it was no mean feat of logistics. It is reputed that while the show was in the city a mock battle took place in the streets as a publicity stunt.

After the last of the four Hull performances on Saturday the company would do the whole thing all over again in York the following Monday and in Scarborough the day after that.

It was perhaps appropriate that this final visit took place at the very beginning of the twentieth century because it was from this time that real horse power – like Buffalo Bill himself – began to disappear into history. It was only a couple of years earlier that the tram system in Hull had gone over to electric rather than equine traction. Meanwhile back in the USA two of Cody's fellow countrymen were able to claim to be the first men to get off the ground and stay in the air. The world would never be the same and we would never again see the like of Buffalo Bill.

At the end of the 19th century there were two orphanages in Hull for the children of lost seamen. Both homes were in the same area of the city as the one in this story but neither of them is the model for the Hull Sailors' Children's Home.

Frank Beill, Summer 2018

Other novels, novellas, historical non-fiction and short story collections available from Stairwell Books

Carol's Christmas	N.E. David
Feria	N.E. David
A Day at the Races	N.E. David
Running With Butterflies	John Walford
Poison Pen	P J Quinn
Wine Dark, Sea Blue	A.L. Michael
Skydive	Andrew Brown
Close Disharmony	P J Quinn
When the Crow Cries	Maxine Ridge
The Geology of Desire	Clint Wastling
Homelands	Shaunna Harper
Homeless	Ed. Ross Raisin
Border 7	Pauline Kirk
Tales from a Prairie Journal	Rita Jerram
Here in the Cull Valley	John Wheatcroft
How to be a Man	Alan Smith
A Multitude of Things	David Clegg
Know Thyself	Lance Clarke
Thinking of You Always	Lewis Hill
Rapeseed	Alwyn Marriage
A Shadow in My Life	Rita Jerram
Tyrants Rex	Clint Wastling
Abernathy	Claire Patel-Campbell
The Go-to Guy	Neal Hardin
The Martyrdoms at Clifford's Tower 1190 and 1537	John Rayne-Davis
Return of the Mantra	Susie Williamson
Poetic Justice	PJ Quinn
Something I Need to Tell You	William Thirsk-Gaskill
On Suicide Bridge	Tom Dixon
Looking for Githa	Patricia Riley
Connecting North	Thelma Laycock
Virginia	Alan Smith
Rocket Boy	John Wheatcroft
Serpent Child	Pat Riley
Margaret Clitherow	John and Wendy Rayne-Davis

For further information please contact rose@stairwellbooks.com
www.stairwellbooks.co.uk
@stairwellbooks